THE COLOR OF SHAME

For information about this title, contact the author:
Hollie Smurthwaite
hollie@holliesmurthwaite.com
https://holliesmurthwaite.com

ISBN: 978-1-7371189-7-8

Cover Design by Sarah Hansen, Okay Creations
Interior Design by Olivier Darbonville
Edited by Joyce Lamb

Printed in the USA
First Edition

THE COLOR

of

SHAME

HOLLIE SMURTHWAITE

For Elke – so beautiful inside and out, and one of the kindest people I've ever known. Even if you used to dribble.

Faith – my first critique partner back when I wrote about white T-shirts in the rain, proofer extraordinaire, and my spice buddy.

Bridget – nobody makes me laugh like you, and I'll never look at a fat moon without thinking of one of the most hilarious nights of my life. Also, we'll always have Paris.

Reputation is an idle and most false imposition, oft got without merit and lost without deserving.

—William Shakespeare, *Othello* (Act II, Scene III)

CHAPTER ONE

Sara

SARA NEVER THOUGHT SHE'D MISS ASS-PINCHING drug dealers, endless strategy sessions, and an inscrutable boss who occasionally tried to read her mind. However, the agonizing drip of time during her hostessing shifts at La Cuisine had her reconsidering. She'd only been there a week.

She pressed the scar on her stomach into the edge of the hostess stand, trying to soothe the itch. The disfigurement was a powerful reminder that there were worse things than boredom. Tracing a manicured fingertip around the swirling woodgrain pattern of the podium, she imagined it opened a portal to a dance club with thumping music and hopping bodies.

Instead of a gateway to fun, Sara's least favorite customer so far burst inside with his ever-present condescension and a blast of February chill as he held the door open for his mother.

"Convery. C-o-n-v-e-r-y," he said as he flicked the lapel of his cashmere coat to shake off a few flakes of snow. "We have a one o'clock reservation for the corner table." He had a cultured voice that had probably been dry aged in a château, which he brought out to complement the clink of sterling silverware on porcelain plates.

She'd met him last week, on her first day, when she'd had to ask him to spell his name twice. A typical Chicagoan, he'd spelled it the first time too quickly, as if he were in a rush. It wasn't her fault letters and numbers sometimes moved around. The second time, he spoke mockingly slowly, as if she were four. It appeared as if that was now his go-to greeting.

"Of course, sir." Sara gave him and his mother her best smile, mostly because she thought it would bother him since he clearly didn't like her. Possibly, it would make him think she was even dumber, but she didn't care. Killing with kindness always baffled jerks.

He was a fifty-year-old trapped in a trim, thirtysomething's body, wearing a textured vest and a pocket hanky with his suit. Attractive in that high society way, which meant he was more interesting than actually handsome, though he had great lips, the bottom with a tempting little dip in the center. He had beautiful hair, too, neither short nor long, ending at his collar. Of course, it wasn't hard to have silky, dark locks when you paid two hundred dollars for a haircut. Not that she had proof of that, but she'd bet the pitiful bit of savings her ex-boyfriend, Jorge, had left her that Convery had a standing appointment with a barber that charged at least a hunny.

"Right this way," Sara said, careful to take small enough steps that her tight skirt wouldn't make a snapping sound as she walked. She could wear anything she wanted in this job as long as it was professional and black, white, charcoal gray, or a combination of the three. Sara liked the challenge of sticking to a color scheme. It was her favorite part of the job.

Today's outfit was all ebony, from her past-the-knee skirt to the tucked-in cashmere sweater and her favorite Manolos. The cinched waist was definitely on the uncomfortable side and cut into her scar, causing her to press her wrist into her stomach to curb the impulse to scratch. But the ensemble had already boosted her tips, so she considered it a fair trade.

Convery certainly wasn't going to tip her, not after she'd accidentally seated someone at their reserved table last week, forcing him and his mother to sit in the middle of the room. *Gasp.* But his lingering displeasure only motivated her to give him even better customer service. She hoped he dreamed about it. Dudes like him hated to be thought of as cheap.

Their regular spot, table number twenty-three, was the best table for two, a quarter-circle bench tucked into the corner of the dining area.

Sara handed a menu to the woman who followed the same old money dress code as her son and had brown eyes the same shade of dark cognac, though she was twice as snobby as her offspring. She wore a power suit in fear-me red and a jade statement necklace. If they'd been friends, Sara would have recommended something less chunky to make Mrs. Convery appear younger. From the waxy smoothness of her forehead, looking youthful was on her agenda.

"I heard a rumor not a half hour ago that the prawn lunch special was running low," Sara said with a wink, handing Convery Jr. his menu. "You've been warned."

"Thank you," Convery Sr. said, a clear dismissal. Her voice mostly stayed in her nose. Rhinoplasty gone wrong or an on-purpose affectation? Sara wasn't sure.

"Beckett, I think not preparing something is a mistake," Mother Convery said to her son, treating Sara as if she'd suddenly disappeared.

Beckett. Perfect name for someone so pretentious. Sara couldn't have been more than six or seven years younger than him, but his poshness made the age gap feel like a century. Beckett had been born dusty. The mother's name was likely Portia or Camilla.

Sara returned to her purgatory podium. The Converys might have been awful, but most of the restaurant's clientele were at least polite. Some were nice. A few were even interesting. But this was the life she'd chosen. Normal and easy and absolutely no guns or criminals she had to seduce.

The Agency had released her from the criminal life, setting up the hostess gig as a parting gift. *Sorry you got shot, but here's a boring but legal job.* Without a legitimate work record, it wasn't as if she had a banquet of options. She couldn't screw up, couldn't snap at dismissive asshats, couldn't slap her creepy supervisor. Chill—that was all she could do if she wanted to make this last until she had her scar reconstruction surgery three months from now.

Sara surveyed the dining room: the elegance of white tablecloths and silver candles, glittering chandeliers, and domed food. The restaurant was tastefully dim, minimalist but with every detail screaming *quality*, from the weight of the silverware to the cut of the crystal glasses. Money. Power. Prestige. And Sara on the outside, watching from the wings.

Did organizations like the Agency ever really let people go? Or did they simply set them aside until they found a new use for them? And Sara had few uses beyond her attractiveness and ability to manipulate people, particularly men. Those attributes had made her an impressive spy, but she was not so talented at anything else. Her femme fatale days were over and would stay that way.

Sara needed to escape, go off-grid as soon as she'd recouped some of her lost cash and had that surgery. No way was she going on the run with her disfigured body, not when the Agency would foot the bill. And they *should* pay, since it was technically a workers' comp injury.

Three tiny months. She had the surgery scheduled in May, and afterward, she'd disappear. Somewhere they wouldn't think to search for her. California, maybe, where beautiful women were more plentiful. Too obvious? She still had time to decide.

All she had to do for now was not call attention to herself. How hard could that be?

CHAPTER TWO

Beckett

ECKETT SIPPED HIS WATER AND TRIED TO organize the argument in his mind first before talking to his mother. Ever since his father had remarried, she'd been particularly brittle and overly involved in Beckett's life. Few things were worth resisting, but this was one of them.

"Mother, if I don't bring up the students we've lost in the psychic enrichment program, Ahmad and the other leaders might think I'm unconcerned. That is the diametrically opposite conclusion I want him to draw." He set his napkin on his lap and moved the knife a centimeter to the left.

"Yes, but then you project the image of someone focused on problems and negatives and not on the solutions."

He blew out a breath. "It would help if I had a strategy. I don't know why or how Dominion is stealing our mentees, and I'm flummoxed as to how to stop them."

"You should track down the deserters and simply ask." Since she always ordered the salmon salad, her perusal of the menu was for show.

"Andrew tried and was met with quite a bit of hostility." His friend and co-founder of the young memory magician program had tracked down all five student mentees they'd lost, and none would talk. "We have no idea why they decided to leave the Moralists, but the goal is to make the situation better, not worse." At least only memory surgeons, the most common type of memory magician, had left. Their ability to experience and remove memories from others was the only magical ability known to the public. Few people outside the magical community knew that some people could tap into short-term memories, basically a form of mind reading, and fewer knew some could do both. Luckily, none of the lost participants were bi-talented.

Beckett didn't like the idea of ranking pupils, as if having an ordinary form of memory magic, like his own short-term memory gift, made them less valuable. However, the Moralists' leadership, the Philotimo, would likely look at them that way. Without the Philotimo's support, there would be no program.

Beckett had a vision, and as a professor, he knew inspired ideas weren't as commonplace as literature would have people believe. This training curriculum would become his mark on the magical world, the testing ground for what he hoped would inform how the Moralists ran their faction of memory magicians. Pairing the exploration of magical gifts with the ethics of how they would be used should lead to not only greater power but protection from a reactionary public.

It could safeguard them all, especially as they were discovering more types of memory magic, and Beckett thought the emergence of new magic a foregone conclusion.

"You don't think you could find a way to lure the lost magicians back?" his mother asked, her tone a challenge—the kind meant to inspire.

If the college students weren't committed to wanting to expand their memory magic ethically, then the program wasn't right for them anyway. Still, losing almost half their pilot participants was devastating.

"It's too late for that," Beckett replied. "I could use Ahmad's guidance, and I think he might like that. I think he's still considering me heir to his position in the Philotimo. If I heed any advice he gives me, he might recognize I'll still value his counsel once his term ends next year."

Beckett turned his attention to lunch. He usually rotated between a few dishes, but damn if that Sara hadn't planted a desire for the prawn special by proclaiming it almost out of reach.

Was there a way to leverage scarcity in his recruitment process? He didn't need to fill all twelve allotted spots, but it would be advantageous to add a student or two as a cushion in case he lost any others.

His mother sighed. "You might be right about the counsel. Men do like to have their opinions sought out, but it's better to ask into your strength and not your weakness."

"If I ask for pointless advice, it's patronizing." He rubbed the back of his neck. "I started the program to get on leadership's radar, but it's evolved. It's power, education, philosophy, and community all rolled together, the whole greater than the sum of its parts. A legacy. I need it to succeed."

She put a hand on his, a rare display of affection. "You are the most brilliant person I know, Beckett. Trust me, you'll figure it out."

* * *

THE CONVERSATION TURNED TO THE MUNDANE, WHICH SUITED BECKETT and his mother better. She talked about her charitable causes and art, and Beckett spoke of changes he'd implemented in his teaching curriculum. The prawns were delicious, and if anyone but Sara had given him the recommendation, he would have sought out that person to thank them. But he detested women like her, beautiful women who succeeded despite their incompetence. She could barely manage to work a simple reservation system, and when she made a mistake, she smiled and simpered and assumed everyone around her would adjust to compensate.

It never occurred to Sara that they might need the corner booth because of his mother's loss of hearing in her left ear. Virginia Convery refused to wear a hearing aid in public, so they came to the same restaurant every week specifically for this accommodation. If they sat in the center of the room, Virginia had a hard time understanding him, and then she would become flustered and insecure, which diminished her as a person. Last week, Sara had carelessly given their table to someone else, figuring one seat was the same as another.

He glanced at the podium, hating how his eyes always sought her out when he wasn't vigilant. She was the most beautiful woman he'd ever seen. Her eyes were a deep blue, like cobalt or lapis lazuli, a color rare in people but common in dolls and cartoon characters. The symmetry of her face and the plumpness of her red lips threatened to enthrall him every time he glanced at her.

A businessman was talking to her on his way out. Her laugh floated through the room, a ridiculous combination of innocence and sin. She seemed genuinely amused. It made him want to know what she found so humorous, even though he knew her lure was simply hormones and a societal conditioning to value beauty. What good was attractiveness when there was nothing in the mind?

His mother pulled back the cuff of her suit jacket. "Beckett, dear, my tennis bracelet is missing."

"Are you sure you put it on today?" he asked, because she'd been mistaken in the past.

"Positive, because it kept snagging on the sleeve. I'm going to check the lavatory. Would you please search the staff, darling?"

By *search the staff*, she meant for him to use his memory magic. He didn't think his mother would fabricate a mislaid item of jewelry to encourage him to practice and hone his gift, but he also wouldn't die of shock if she confessed to that later. Beckett drew clear lines for himself for when it was acceptable to pry into someone's mind. Since there was zero evidence that foul play was involved in the vanished bracelet, he wouldn't typically use his power, but he wanted to ease his mother's concerns.

The situation was one he would present to the students in his program during their Sunday meeting. This ethical conundrum—when was it morally reasonable to use their talents—was one he wanted them to consider in advance. Because, as he was currently experiencing, there was rarely enough time to truly explore all sides before making a decision.

His mother had already lost so much in her life, and while this was just a bracelet, he didn't want her to lose anything else. Nobody would be the wiser if he took quick skims.

Beckett started with the server.

"Jennifer," he said after folding a twenty into his palm. She'd caught his movement, as he'd intended, and readily shook his hand. "My mother seems to have mislaid her diamond tennis bracelet. Could you inquire with the staff about it?"

He engaged his gift, a low buzz sounding through his mind and then . . .

* * *

I wish I had enough money to go handing out twenties every time I misplaced something. Of course I'll have to literally ask everyone now I've taken the cash.

* * *

MICHAEL, THE MANAGER, WHO ALWAYS DRESSED LIKE A DAY TRADER, WAS Beckett's next target. He didn't bother with a financial incentive this time, just extended his hand, adding a clasp at the elbow to prolong the contact. "Any chance there's a lost and found? My mother cannot locate her bracelet."

* * *

Misplaced? Does he think someone here stole it? Michael could think of nobody who . . . Sara. He thought of her pouty lips and tiny waist. With lips like that, she had to give good head. Fucking cock tease. Flirting with everyone but never delivering.

21

She had an eye for shiny things, and her wardrobe spoke of quality. If she had funds at her disposal, why would she be working as a hostess? His suspicion of her had nothing to do with her refusal to go on a date with him. Thieving might be how she financed her clothing addiction. Her shoes alone had to cost hundreds of dollars.

He'd search her locker. Even if she did have some connection to the owner, Kohl wouldn't allow an employee who stole from patrons. Michael couldn't wait to fire her.

* * *

"Let me check in the back, Mr. Convery," Michael said, dashing away.

Beckett swallowed down the bile that had splashed up his throat at Michael's vile thoughts. He might have disliked Sara, but nobody deserved to work with someone like that. Hopefully, she hadn't stolen anything.

Sara stood by the bar, talking to the bartender whose name Beckett didn't know. He came for lunch, which precluded ordering alcohol. Appraising her with a more practiced eye, he had to admit Michael, as weaselly as his musings had been, had a point. Her shoes were either new or extremely well cared for, the sleek and simple black patent leather heels five inches high, clearly designer made, and perfectly suited to her ensemble.

Her tight skirt should have been conservative since it hit well below her knee, but the way it highlighted her hip-to-waist ratio bordered on the obscene, and though her sweater wasn't scandalously fitted, her perfect hourglass figure was unmistakable.

And now he was objectifying her almost as badly as Michael did. He shifted his focus.

Sara wore her ice-blond hair in a complicated pretzel-like twist in the back, with no flyaway strands or visible bobby pins holding it together. How could a restaurant hostess afford such clothing and someone to style her hair?

He'd know for certain shortly. As he approached her, he fished another twenty out of his billfold and folded it into a neat square. "Sara," he said, extending his hand. "My mother is missing her bracelet."

"Mr. Convery," she replied with a smile that was too bright to be genuine. She arched an eyebrow at his extended hand, but took it anyway.

* * *

* * *

NOTHING. HER MIND WAS A BLANK. IT WAS AS IF SHE WERE A STATUE and not a person.

She tucked the twenty into a tiny pocket in her skirt before turning to the bartender, oblivious to Beckett's attempt to read her.

"Hey, Nick, can you check if there are any bracelets in the lost and found?"

"No jewelry," Nick replied, his eyes never leaving Sara. "I go through it every morning, so I know what's in there, and there's been nothing new so far today."

"When did she lose it?" Sara asked Beckett.

Maybe she had an unusually strong resistance to memory reading. Beckett reached out and grabbed one of her hands, unable to stop himself.

* * *

* * *

STILL NOTHING.

Wait.

He sensed a wall but far away. She tugged her hand, but he kept hold. "Please," he said, his mind scrambling. "Please help me search for it?"

"I'll check the bathroom," she said, finally extracting her hand.

Memory reading couldn't be felt, so he didn't need to worry about that, but forcibly holding on to her hands was definitely something she'd noticed.

"I beg your pardon," he said, scuttering to find an excuse for his improper behavior when there could be none. He'd been entirely captivated by the impenetrability of her thoughts.

She smiled, perhaps a bit tighter than usual, probably working up the words to brush off his impertinence.

Luckily, his mother approached them, breaking the moment, her bracelet dangling from pinched fingers. "I found it on the bathroom floor of all places."

Beckett removed his pocket square and held it open to receive the soiled jewelry, pleased to take action. "I'll get it cleaned, Mother, no worries. I'll also have the clasp reinforced."

His mother beamed, but all Beckett could think about was that distant, blank wall. Could there be a way to block memory magic? He'd never heard of it, and he'd read all the available research.

Finally, he had something to discuss with Ahmad that wasn't about his failures and on which he could use the leader's advice.

If Sara truly was capable of what he thought she was, he could be looking at the solution to everything. Not just a way to save his program, but a guaranteed path to becoming an important figure in the Moralists community.

Maybe even an heir.

CHAPTER THREE

Sara

SARA TRIED HARD NOT TO GET HERSELF FIRED. She'd only been there a month, and getting canned that soon would have been embarrassing. Besides, the hostess gig was bringing in decent cash.

But it had been a *very long* month of working at La Cuisine.

She'd already gotten a write-up for talking to other employees too much, though she suspected that had been more about not sleeping with Michael than anything else. That was at least one decision she didn't regret. Michael was a tool.

She tapped a pen on her wooden podium to the tune of "We Will Rock You" and willed herself not to step away. So what if Nick at the bar appeared as bored as she was, or the restaurant was in that lull between lunch and dinner? Sara wasn't a toddler. She had self-control.

She stopped tapping the pen, realizing she was pressing her hand against her stomach again. She dropped her arm, but the impulse tugged, as if her hand were a magnet and her belly iron.

The compulsive tummy touching had grown worse, though the scar no longer itched. Instead, she now compulsively checked to ensure her wound wasn't visible through her thin, rayon wrap dress.

In the four months since she'd been shot, the raised skin had thinned some, but even if the appearance of the scar had improved, the revulsion she felt about it had gotten worse.

She touched it again, then dropped her hand when she heard the swish of the front door opening. She straightened, pulled her shoulders back, and slapped on a smile.

Ugh. She'd forgotten that Tuesday afternoons meant the arrival of Beckett Convery and his mother. They were outfitted as she imagined British aristocracy dressed, him in a camel hair coat he hadn't bought on sale, along with his usual vest and blazer, this time in green and brown. Mrs. Convery wore real fur, mink or fox, regardless of the forty-degree temperature, with a buff-colored dress, matching heels, and a power-red lipstick that suited her complexion. He held the door for her, and she swanned through like a duchess.

"Convery," the older woman said, though they both knew Sara knew who they were by now. The woman must love the sound of her own name, or wanted to remind Sara of when she'd struggled to find their reservation *a month ago.* "C-o-n-v-e-r-y."

"Mrs. Convery, welcome," Sara said. She'd called her *Ms.* Convery once and wouldn't make that mistake again.

She'd googled the Converys and discovered they were as rich and socialitey as she'd first thought. One day, she was totally going to call the woman Virginia and watch her head explode.

Sara grabbed two menus, hoping to stave off what usually happened next. She wasn't fast enough. Every week he became bolder—or more desperate.

"I found this out front," Beckett said, holding out a men's black leather glove.

Another ruse. This third attempt in as many weeks was clever and effective. She couldn't not take it. As she reached for the glove, doing her best to try to grab just a fingertip, he dropped it, and when they both bent to pick it up, he brushed her hand with his.

When memory surgeons attempted to read her thoughts, time always paused for a moment. It took her a while to recognize what that lack of feeling meant, but it had become unmistakable.

She snatched back her hand. Although she would have liked to enjoy Beckett's slight scowl, all she really wanted was for him to stop battering her brain as he tried to pry into her memories. Not only would it be a violation if it worked, but she didn't appreciate being his challenge. She especially didn't appreciate the headache that bloomed behind her right eye, evidence that he must have been pushing a lot harder than usual. Part of her wanted to shout at him to knock it off, she couldn't be read.

But then he'd know she knew, and she refused to give him the satisfaction.

Sara walked the Converys to their regular table, feeling them studying her in an unflattering way, which she was used to from them.

"Enjoy your meal," she said in her huskiest voice. She might have also added an extra swing to her hips as she walked away—nothing tacky, but a bit jaunty.

Michael, the man-douche manager, was waiting for her at the hostess station.

"I'm going to need you to work a double today. Candy just called in." Michael wore a quality, tailored suit that should have been flattering but managed to make him appear spindly. The narrow collar emphasized the thinness of his ferret face, and his fine hair did him no favors. He should have invested some of his wardrobe money on a decent haircut. He ought to ask Beckett for his barber's name, but she wasn't going to suggest that.

"Sure, Michael."

If she'd known she would be working a double, she would have worn her Manolos instead of her Dolce & Gabbana heels, but she'd manage. With the extra pay, she'd find a Groupon for a foot massage.

"Do we have to talk about your clothing again?" Michael stood too close.

"I don't think so," she replied. The wrap dress covered everything, though it did highlight her assets: big tits, slender waist, generous hips. All of which were how the Agency had gotten her hired here in the first place. Her hotness brought in return business, appealing to the male clientele who seemed to think she'd someday agree to date them.

Even if she didn't have a horrendous scar, she was done with men for a very long time. The last man she'd dated had dumped her at the ER, then run away with most of her money. The man she'd slept with before that? He'd shot her in the gut. Fuck men. Or, rather, *don't*.

"You look like a prostitute," Michael hissed. His eyes lingered everywhere but on her face.

"Everything is covered, per your earlier requests." Her headache grew from a sharp pain to a dull throbbing.

"Well, you still look like a whore."

"If anything, I look like a high-end escort." Sara tapped her lips with a gel-polished fingernail in shimmering gold. "Would you like me to wear a burqa next time? Muumuu? Potato sack?"

"Do I have to write you up again?" He would have made a great witch hunter.

She studied him. He'd been bullying her for over a week, the result of her categorically rebuffing his advances. He thought he was in charge and that she was a helpless, hapless victim. The restaurant's owner knew only Michael's suck-up persona.

Sara had tried to let his bullying slide, but obviously, he needed a lesson.

"If this is how you want to play it." She sashayed over to Nick. His eyebrows arched when he saw Michael trailing behind her. He held his smile in check.

"Hey," she said. "Can you take a photo of me with your cell and text it to me?"

Nick shrugged. "Sure."

"What do you think you're doing?" Michael said. He didn't usually treat her shitty in front of other employees, but he must have sensed she had an agenda that threatened his perceived power.

Holding up his cell, Nick asked. "Both of you?"

"God no," Sara said. "Just me."

"What—" Michael's face turned red and splotchy.

"Hey," Sara said, smiling for Nick's photo. "Fire me, but when I talk to the owner, I'm going to show him this pic of what I'm wearing, and I'm also going to share your comments and the fact that I've refused to go out with you several times. I'm sure he'll draw the correct conclusion."

Nick bit down a grin. Nobody liked Michael. "Sent," he said.

"Thanks, honey," she replied, giving Nick a wink before returning to her podium. Michael followed.

"What are you insinuating?" He stood too close again, probably hating she had an inch on him.

At six feet tall, he was used to towering over women, but her four-inch heels erased his advantage. She also had vast experience dealing with truly scary people, so Michael had zero chance of intimidating her.

"In the 1980s, you definitely could have gotten away with firing me because I won't fuck you, but we're living in a different time now."

"Lower your voice." He sneered like a man who'd never failed to get what he wanted. "Nobody's going to believe you over me."

But a man who'd never failed, never learned how to play the big games.

Sara glowered at him with all her hate. "I guess we'll have to see about that. Brush up your résumé, because being fired for sexual harassment isn't an attractive look."

"I've never sexually harassed you."

"You might want to grab a dictionary."

"Sara." Beckett put a hand on hers, presumably to catch her attention. Time paused, and her head thudded once like an earthquake.

She jerked her hand away. "Stop doing that."

"I'm sorry. Doing what?" Beckett said with the lamest attempt at wide-eyed innocence she'd ever seen.

Why did men with power always think they could do whatever they pleased? *Because the world rewards them for it.*

"Touching me. Stop touching me. It won't work."

"Sara, you're fired," Michael said, his voice like a whip. His sneer highlighted his less-than-white teeth. Another place his suit money would have been better spent. "We do not tolerate rudeness to customers."

"Of course not. All this place tolerates is harassment."

"I-I . . ." Beckett's cheekbones burned bright red. "Please. I meant no disrespect."

"I apologize for her behavior. It's unacceptable," Michael said, ignoring Beckett's clear discomfort over her firing. "Of course, we'll comp your meal."

Michael would take the price of that free lunch out of her check.

Beckett grabbed the back of his neck. "No, no. Forgive me, it's all been a misunderstanding. I did . . . touch Sara without permission, though I had no inappropriate intentions."

"Bullshit," Sara hissed. Losing this boring job with its stupid reservation system and tedious hours of standing was a profound relief. Now that she'd snapped at a prized customer, no way would the Agency try to salvage it for her. So, she had no incentive to keep her thoughts to herself. "You," she said, pointing a finger at Beckett. "Quit trying to get inside people's minds." She turned to Michael. "And I'd rather have a screaming case of genital crabs than go on a date with you."

"This is all a mistake," Beckett insisted as Michael gaped at her in stunned silence. "Please, I'm close friends with the owner's brother-in-law, Ahmad Sofer. I'm sure once he hears the particulars, he'll be understanding of the situation."

His superior tone made her want to roll her eyes. Okay, she *did* roll her eyes. Yeah, successful business owners always gave employees ranting about genital crabs a second chance.

"No, I think you both need to find a new plaything. I'm outta here." She smirked at Michael. "Pity about Candy."

Let that asshole work not just a double shift, but double duty.

CHAPTER FOUR

Beckett

HOURS LATER, BECKETT'S SHOCK AT THE DISCOVERY of someone who could not only block a memory reading but could sense it happening had not abated. He attempted to soothe his misfiring neurons by doing laundry, but then his friend Andrew had called to talk about . . . something, and Beckett had blurted most of the story.

Now it was after dinner, his nerves clanging like the bells at railroad crossings, and he regretted allowing Andrew into his house and the sacred space of his laundry lounge. He concentrated on his ironing instead of snapping. The task was usually like meditation for him, but it was not currently providing any zen.

"But are you positive? Her comments aren't conclusive that she knew you were using memory magic," Andrew said, picking at the frayed ends of the hole in the knee of his jeans. He sat on a cream Barcelona chair, legs wide, and watched Beckett iron as if it were a competitive sport in which Beckett would dominate.

He should have chosen an activity that needed more of his attention.

Andrew continued, "I think it's a mistake to claim you found someone who can shield without confirmation from another memory magician."

Part of Beckett wanted to agree. If he was wrong, it would be beyond humiliating. But he couldn't take a leadership position if he wasn't willing to be a leader. "Ahmad was able to schedule a meeting with her for me," he replied, shifting his dress shirt on the vacuum ironing board so he could attend to the collar. Luckily, Ahmad's brother owned La Cuisine and had been the one to hire Sara, so he had been able to contact her. "You'll see. This will change everything."

"Teaching Shakespeare doesn't make it okay to be a drama queen," Andrew said with a laugh. He'd had crooked teeth as a teenager, and kids had teased him about it, but he'd since had them straightened and brightened. His smile had become his best feature.

"And teaching philosophy does not make it acceptable to question every choice I make."

"Dude, that's all philosophy is, questioning choices."

Beckett stared at Andrew, and they both broke into laughter.

They were so different, but those differences only made their friendship richer. Currently, Andrew was on a self-assigned mission to make Beckett relatable and cool to the college students, in spite of Beckett's lack of interest. Beckett would never be the breed of teacher Andrew was, wearing jeans to class with T-shirts that showcased the results of his long hours in the gym, allowing the kids to address him as Andrew or Drew (but never Andy, as Andrew had *some* standards), using the word *dude* unironically. Nor did Beckett want to be.

Part of him envied Andrew's blond, blue-eyed attractiveness and his ease with people, though Beckett believed in keeping a professional distance between teachers and pupils. Without that hierarchy, the youths had less respect. With less respect came less effort.

Beckett maneuvered the shirt so the shoulder yoke lay on the board. "I shouldn't have said anything to you until after I've met with her."

Andrew had a way of making Beckett say far more than he intended.

"Of course you should have. This is exciting. If you've found someone who can block us from reading her memories, that's potentially game-changing, but sensing a memory read, too ..."

"I know." Beckett didn't need to be reminded of the magnitude of this potential discovery. If the Moralists could learn to shield against magical intrusion, they could secure their secrets. Beckett could be a pioneer for the memory magician community on the scale of Jonas Salk and the polio vaccine.

He shook out the shirt then placed it buttons down on the board. "She might only be immune to my type of short-term memory magic, though even that would reveal a plethora of possibilities. Imagine what a relief it would be if we could guard ourselves against a memory breach."

"It would be amazing," Andrew said, bouncing to his feet. "You should let me come along. I can test her resistance to a long-term memory magic probe. I'm better with people than you anyway, and she might not be as friendly to you. You know, considering you got her fired and all." He laughed again and took a sip of whiskey from the Waterford crystal tumbler.

"Yes, but you're a stranger." More important, Beckett wanted to apologize again for his inadvertent role in her lost employment. And he didn't want Andrew there to play Cool Dude.

"Come on, let me come with you." Andrew grinned a little too widely. "I'll be good."

Beckett scowled. He didn't want Andrew's sometimes cavalier attitude toward women to add to Sara's poor perception of Beckett's character. Or for her to find Andrew charming. "Our definitions of what constitutes *good* differ considerably. I think not."

Andrew laughed, sending a spray of whiskey droplets onto the carpeting.

Beckett closed his eyes and counted to ten. *Just a few drops. No big deal.* "I'm going to take care of this meeting myself."

Andrew rubbed his socked foot over the spill, his version of cleaning up the mess. Typical. His habitual ennui made it impossible for him to properly behave. "All right. Let me know how it goes."

* * *

THE MORALISTS WERE ONLY ONE FACTION OF MEMORY MAGICIANS. MOST of the gifted weren't organized at all, and because the groups were secret, many memory magicians had no idea these communities existed. Beckett knew of only a few, though he was certain there were numerous groups and organizations.

Finding more factions didn't appeal to Beckett. He'd found his home base with the Moralists. The Chicago branch was led by the Philotimo, the three men who had started the Moralists with nothing more than their ideals and a network of connections to government, corporations, and memory magicians.

Ahmad had attended Wells College back when Beckett's mother had been Dean of Students, and Virginia had introduced Beckett to Ahmad Sofer, the head of the Philotimo, when Beckett's gifts had manifested for the first time at age twenty-three. Beckett considered Ahmad a mentor, and he'd been one of the first to join Ahmad's newly founded Moralists.

Because of their close past, Ahmad had given Beckett almost carte blanche to do whatever he could to persuade Sara Strausser to work with them.

Initially, Beckett had wanted to set up a meeting room at the Union League Club, but when he'd considered how many students he'd lost to the rival memory magician program, called Dominion, he decided the prominent venue would have garnered too much attention.

Doppio Coffee House on Lincoln was his final decision. It had outdoor seating, it was near his tailor, and he enjoyed its blueberry-lemon scones.

Beckett arrived fifteen minutes early, bought a café mocha and scone, and chose a round table farthest from the entrance with a view down the street. He shifted it a few more feet away from nearby tables until he was satisfied nobody would be able to eavesdrop.

He spotted Sara when she was more than half a block away. She sauntered next to a Black man wearing a black cashmere coat over a bespoke navy suit and a pink and blue tie that was Italian, like his shoes. They walked close enough that their shoulders occasionally brushed.

Beckett straightened his posture and focused on taking a sip of his coffee, allowing them to approach without his scrutiny. Their relationship status was irrelevant. It wouldn't change anything.

When they approached the table, Beckett stood, openly assessing both in a businesslike manner. He extended his hand to Sara's companion. "Beckett Convery."

The man smiled, his teeth white and perfect, the grin relaxed and practiced. "Ryan Caldwell. Nice to meet you."

Sara made a small noise as they shook, but nothing scornful appeared on her lovely face. Instead of the professional restaurant attire he was used to, she wore relaxed-fit jeans with short-heeled black boots and a lightweight trench coat in a pink so pale it was neutral. Her bright pink T-shirt was adorned with gold sparkles that spelled out *Princess*, and she'd styled her hair in a high ponytail, a tiny braid covering the elastic. The only holdover from her hostess persona was on her wrist—a thin, black elastic bracelet with a golden bead and black clasp. A sentimental accessory, perhaps.

"Ms. Strausser," Beckett said with less confidence than he'd like. "Sara. Thank you for agreeing to meet with me."

"Mr. Convery," she replied in his exact tone, adding a head tilt. "Beckett."

"Sit, Sara, and be good. I'll go get us drinks," Ryan said with a mock glare in her direction. "Let's save the antagonism for when we're all caffeinated."

"I'm always good." Her voice oozed innuendo.

Ryan made a scoffing sound, stared at her for a full three seconds, then left them alone at the outdoor table. They sat and said nothing, each of them busying themselves with their phones.

At last, Ryan returned with beverages. His facial hair was sculpted so precisely the man either took an hour to curate it or he had it professionally done. Even his nails were buffed to a high shine, and his dark skin glowed with health.

This man clearly understood business and image, and Beckett relaxed a bit. *Between the two of us, this should be easy.*

"I brought you here today to discuss an employment proposition," Beckett said as soon as everyone was situated.

Sara turned to Caldwell. "You said he wanted to say sorry."

Caldwell grimaced. "No, I said he wanted to make amends."

Beckett spun his coffee cup until the handle was at a ninety-degree angle with his chest. No matter what he said next, it would appear that he'd never intended to express regret. "I do want to apologize for our misunderstanding."

"Which means nothing if you don't also take responsibility for what happened," she said, then muttered, "*Misunderstanding.*"

Beckett stuffed his irritation down into his stomach. "As you may be unaware, your particular manifestation of memory magic is, yet, uncharted, and we'd—"

"Memory magic?" she asked, her face scrunched into a frown, her bottom lip pouting out in a way she probably thought was sexy. "What are you talking about?"

He tried not to think about the plumpness of her lips. She wasn't his type at all, and he could never find someone so vacuous and shallow appealing. Not in the long term.

"There's more out there than memory surgeons, apparently," Caldwell said with a raised eyebrow and a playful nudge of his elbow.

"Okay, but I'm not"—she waved a manicured hand in the air—"magical."

Caldwell chortled. "Sweetness, you are most definitely magic."

She grinned at him, swirling her finger through the whipped cream on her drink and sliding it into her mouth. Ryan shook his head but wore a wide grin. Were they negotiating as a couple?

"*Anyway,*" Beckett said, "as your gift is fresh, we are very motivated to have the opportunity to explore the depths of your talents."

"You want to explore my depths?" She sighed and tilted back her head. "If I had a dime for every time I heard that."

Caldwell coughed into his fist, covering any hint of a smile. "Sara, this is serious. It's not simply a deal for the memory magicians, it's for your benefit too. You know, since you lost your source of income."

"That wasn't my fault." She lifted her cup, pinky extended. "But let's start there, then. What do you want, and what's in it for me?" This she addressed to Beckett, peering at him over the rim as she took a tentative sip, all of her usual perkiness gone.

He'd already figured her hostess personality had been fake, but her open hostility right now gave him pause. He took a deep breath and straightened his spine. "Ms. Strausser, we propose you work for Wells College, specifically as my assistant. It's an entry-level administrative position."

She orbited the bracelet around her wrist. Otherwise, she had no reaction.

Beckett continued, "The tasks are simple, and your skills are sufficient to handle them. It will get you off your feet, too." Considering the shoes she favored, this would be more than a small benefit. Too tall heels led to all sorts of physical maladies. Internal organs could shift. "Your duties would also involve letting me assess the acreage and limits of your magical abilities."

"Uh-huh," she replied, sounding bored.

Beckett plowed forward. He'd get a reaction from the most exciting part of the pitch. "We will pay you one hundred thousand dollars a year." He paused for dramatic effect. "We will also provide housing for you in Arden, our apartment complex. The recruits in the memory magician program are all housed there. It's a few short blocks from the college. I was informed you are accustomed to a two-bedroom situation, and we are able to accommodate that."

"You want me to live in a dorm?" she asked, not excited or upset, only curious.

Frankly, he'd expected some gratitude. This job would be an upgrade from hostessing, and the salary was considerable for such light-duty admin requirements.

"It isn't a traditional dorm. We've converted a four-story apartment building. The ground floor is a common area, including a dining hall. There are separate study spaces on each floor and two conference rooms where we do our training and mentoring." The structure was far superior to any dormitory and had been designed to encourage community among the students, as well as giving them their privacy. "Meals are included, except for Saturdays, though you'll have a full kitchen in your lodging should you choose not to partake. Everyone has their own rooms—singles, unless they request a roommate."

"Okay, so a dorm."

He held back his frown. "You'll live on the girls' floor, but you won't have much in the way of supervisory duties."

"'Not much' implies there are some," she replied, her gaze flicking to Caldwell, who sat in a relaxed pose that would have worked if he'd moved at least a little.

"You only need report any inappropriate behaviors or situations," Beckett said.

"You want me to snitch on a bunch of teenage girls?"

"As you are an adult, I don't believe *snitching* is the appropriate term or attitude."

"Sounds to me like someone has some buried hall-monitor issues."

They fell into a hush as a group of five walked past their table.

Beckett refused to rise to her bait and was glad of the pause. It would actually be better if she had little contact with the students. Her dismissive manner wouldn't inspire anyone to do anything other than slack, but he needed her, and he was determined to fix his mistake. "You are also eligible for discounted classes at the college, should you wish to attend."

She wouldn't, of course, since women like Sara didn't need an education to get what they wanted. It was a shame she would never appreciate this opportunity. Wells College might be a small institution, but it maintained impeccable standards.

"How would I take classes when I'm busy delivering you coffee?"

His frown broke free from its restraint. "We would make arrangements in that case."

Sara let out a dramatic sigh. "And what if I'm perfectly happy with where I am now?"

"Unemployed? You couldn't possibly be."

"Why? Because someone like you wouldn't like it?" Sara moved her head in a way that swished her platinum ponytail. "You think I don't have any choice now that you've gotten me fired. I appreciate the offer, but no, thank you." She focused her attention on Caldwell. "I'm done, Ry. Want to do some window shopping?"

"We are just beginning our negotiations," Beckett said.

Sara stood, Beckett and Caldwell following.

"I'm afraid our discussion is at an end, old chap," she said in a spot-on English accent.

"Sara," Caldwell said, his chin tucked, a warning tone in his voice. "We should—"

"That's all right, I can look on my own," Sara said and walked away, her stride like that of a runway model. She had a magnetic pull. It was a shame she didn't put it to better use.

"I'll speak with her," Caldwell said, sliding his hands in his pants' pockets. "She needs a moment to process, but she'll come around."

Since she hadn't appeared remotely interested, Beckett didn't share Caldwell's optimism.

Beckett hadn't realized how much he'd counted on her accepting his offer. Without her, his plan of impressing Ahmad and the rest of the Philotimo was moot.

CHAPTER FIVE

Sara

"**S**ARA!" RYAN'S VOICE CUT THROUGH THE RUMBLE of Lincoln Avenue traffic and the pedestrians between them who were ambling along and enjoying spring.

Though she wanted to continue walking to punish Ryan, he'd only chase her down. She stopped but didn't turn.

"Sorry," he said. "I know—"

"You didn't give me a heads up," she said, finally facing him. "Not one fucking word. I thought we were friends."

"Of course we're friends." Ryan rocked back on his heels for a moment. "Which is why I didn't tell you. You're better on the fly."

When a family maneuvered around them, they started moving again. Sara hadn't been down this section of Lincoln Avenue before, and her eyes kept trailing to the windows, searching for items of interest and finding plenty.

"Are you listening?" Ryan asked, his voice sharper than she'd heard in a long time.

"Not really."

"That wasn't a job offer and not a request. It's an assignment, Sara. You can't say no."

"What?" She shook her head, feeling as if the words he'd spoken were like words on a page: jumbled, moving, hard to decipher. "No. I quit the Agency. They said I didn't have to work for them any longer. I got—I got . . ." She didn't finish. Ryan already knew what she didn't say. She'd been shot in the line of duty, and she'd earned her goddamn retirement. They couldn't ask her for more.

But, of course, they had.

"I'm so sorry," Ryan said, grabbing her shoulder and drawing her into a hug. "I thought this was something you'd get a kick out of, and so I left it as a surprise. Beckett's not wrong. This will be an easier gig than the restaurant job and have more variety. You can—"

"Manage a schedule?" Her gut twitched and twinged, and she caught herself pressing her wrist into her scar. Again. Nothing about this situation was bearable. "I can't keep my own calendar. And what do you think Mr. Stick Up His Ass is going to say when I continually make mistakes?"

Shit. She'd never told Ryan about her reading troubles. Only their team leader, Stadler, had known, and now he was dead. Nobody knew.

"I had no idea you hated him that much," Ryan said.

"I hate his entitled face." And that he'd won. "*Misunderstanding*. You wouldn't believe how creative he got trying to find a patch of bare skin to touch. Jolene would have been impressed."

Ryan laughed. "I miss her."

"Do you think she hates us?" Sara asked. Jolene was a memory surgeon the Agency had recruited by pretending they were a legit government agency. Sara had thought the ruse fun at first, but as she'd gotten to know Jolene, she'd felt guilty. Not enough to tell her, though. And because of that, Jolene likely would never forgive her.

Ryan slung an arm around her shoulders. "I don't know. She won't return any of my calls, but at least we have each other."

No sense stewing about the past when she had her messed up present to entertain her. She kissed his cheek. "You're stuck with me." It was like old times. Even if it wasn't.

The Agency once again directed her life. The calcifying feeling inside her chest hurt, but she yanked her mind hard in another direction. Although part of her wanted to regret joining the Agency, she couldn't. If Stadler hadn't basically rescued her off the street and given her purpose, she would have ended up in a darker place. It was too late to change anything anyway.

"The job might be fun," Ryan said, though he couldn't hold back a wince.

"Easy for you to say. You don't have to work for Mr. Roboto." Beckett wouldn't mock her outright—he was too classy for that. But he'd treat her as if she were an idiot, using big words he'd assume she wouldn't understand, but she probably would. Or, worse, he'd be right, and she wouldn't.

He'd secretly enjoy how much more superior he thought he was. Get a kick out of watching her struggle to spell easy words, like *proper*, which she couldn't remember if it had one *P* or two, and she'd often write the *P* as a *B* or *D* or *Q* instead.

Ryan tried to stop their forward progress when she tugged him toward Waxman Candles, but Sara barreled them into a space filled with colorful candles and the scents of flowers and spices. He sighed and relented to her will. "You'll have him eating out of your hand within a week."

"True," she said, though she doubted it. Beckett had a preconceived notion of her, and he wasn't the type to examine his assumptions. She grabbed a shopping basket. "So what's the actual assignment?"

"What do you mean? The Agency wants you working for Beckett as an admin and letting him assess your talent, like they do with everyone, so the program can hopefully replicate it."

Sara snorted. "You forget I used to work for them." Still worked for them. "What do they really want? There's got to be something in it for them."

Ryan shrugged. "This gig is legit, above board, nothing sneaky. One of the leaders of the group that's sponsoring Beckett's program has a brother who was an Agency VP before opening La Cuisine. It's like when rich people sponsor other rich people to join a country club. They're supporting college kids with powers, and when they graduate and want jobs down the line, the Agency is going to be one of the first places they consider."

Sara didn't buy it but didn't argue. "And how exactly is Beckett going to test the *acreage and limits* of my abilities? Remember Jolene's stories about the labs and keeping a journal and all that other weird stuff? What if they lock me up?"

Ryan shook his head. "Nothing medical—no blood tests or MRIs. It's like meditation and shit. Non-invasive."

Because she couldn't refuse, not since she had to stick with the Agency until she had her scar surgery, she stopped asking questions.

Ryan strolled to the other side of the store, checking out the wall of tapers. She sidled up to him, elbowing his arm. "Did you check out the zodiac candles?"

He pursed his lips as if he planned to ignore the old debate, but he couldn't stop himself. "Where the stars were positioned when you were born has no effect whatsoever on who you are as a person."

"You are such a Taurus."

Ryan shook his head. "Do you honestly think every single human being born at a certain time of year has identical personalities?"

She didn't. People were more profoundly shaped—nurtured or stifled— by their environment. If she'd grown up with love and support, instead of being forced to run away from home at fifteen, she'd be a completely different person. Still, messing with Ryan was a joy she'd missed. "The science is clear," she said. "These concepts were developed from observation and intense study."

"Science? There's no science involved in astrology."

Sara ignored him and put a bright yellow column candle sporting a circle with horns, the Taurus astrological sign, into her basket. "This is going to be my gift to you."

"I hate candles," Ryan said, his voice overly loud, especially considering they were in a candle store. "They mess with my asthma."

Since Ryan had never suffered from asthma in the seven years she'd known him, she wasn't concerned. "These are scentless."

"Nothing is without scent."

"What about water? I mean, not Chicago water, but I don't know, stream water?" She flashed a grin and wondered if he noticed the strain in it.

Everything was okay. She wasn't trapped. This would be an opportunity to get enough money to run all the faster and farther. All she had to do was last two months. She'd always been valued for her body, and this wouldn't be all that different.

Ryan rolled his eyes. "This candle isn't stream water."

"Well, you'll know for sure tonight."

Ryan was her friend. They were both scrappers and had learned early that to survive they had to look out for themselves first. But they were also family. He was the only family Sara had left.

"I'm not taking it home." He crossed his arms over his broad chest. Because his suit was tailored, the shoulders didn't pull.

She cocked her head. "Don't make me track down where you're living, break into your house and . . ." She tapped a nail to her lips. "On second thought, okay, don't take the candle."

She'd find him and stuff his place with astrology paraphernalia, light the Taurus candle, and hopefully not burn down his apartment. Remind him of how close they'd once been.

Ryan scratched under his chin with all his fingers like Marlon Brando as Don Corleone. "Fine. I'll take the candle."

"And light it tonight."

He had to care about her. More than a little. More than the stupid job.

"Give me the damn thing." Ryan held out his hand, reminding her of her freshman math teacher who'd always wanted kids to spit their gum in his hand instead of into a trash can.

Whatever happened to that guy?

Sara slapped the yellow candle into Ryan's hand. He'd see it in his place and remember her and all the days they'd spent together planning, scheming, laughing. Surviving.

"You're going to light it tonight, right?" she asked. "Send me a photo as proof of life."

* * *

WHEN SHE GOT HOME, SHE SET HER PAPER BAG OF FRAGRANT CANDLES on the floor and started filling the tub with water. Walking hadn't drained her anxiety, so she'd try relaxation. She lit a *Sexy*-scented candle, sweet with a little spice, and undressed. The tumble of water in the background didn't soothe her nerves as she studied herself in the mirror. She spun her hair in a messy bun. Stared. Stared. Swallowed.

The top of her pink scar dominated her reflection. When she rose up on her toes, almost her entire scar was on display. If it had been on anyone else, she might have sung "Anchors Away" or something nautical themed to mock the double-hook-shaped monstrosity and lighten the mood. She removed the silicone tape from the deformity. It was two or three centimeters thick at various points, smaller and flatter than when she'd first seen the aftermath of being shot, four months ago in the hospital. But being less hideous now didn't make it *not* hideous.

Her mind replayed the shooting before she could stop it. Walther, the scariest man she'd ever had to seduce and one she'd thought at the time she'd left far behind, staring at her with those shark eyes. The black gun. Stinging sweat blurring her vision. A punch to the gut. Jorge's scream. Pain. An explosion. Smoke.

Two more months. She could have her reconstructive surgery in two months. The appointment was set—as long as the scar was ready, which, of course, it would be—and then the scar would be thinner, nothing but a red line, like detonation cord. Six months after that, she could tattoo over it.

Nobody would ever know what lay beneath the beautiful body art.

Her phone chirped, and Siri read Ryan's text message to her as she sank into the warm water. Movers would be coming on Saturday. Her new digs would be in the Arden building Beckett had mentioned, in the Bridgeport neighborhood. He ended his epic text with the info that she'd be paid twice a month, her paycheck directly deposited into her account at Liberty Bank.

The Agency knew where she banked? She'd opened a new account after Jorge had taken all but a grand from her former account. Nobody should have had access to her info . . . except La Cuisine. Which was owned by someone who'd worked at the Agency.

She stuffed her big toe into the faucet trickling hot water. The candle flickered what should have been soothing patterns onto the white tile, but they reminded her of ghosts and danger. The scents of vanilla, fruit, and spice filled the room.

Sara decided she couldn't control the Agency, couldn't change the past, so it was pointless to wallow in feelings of betrayal and helplessness.

The present and the future were all that mattered. Getting her body back. Pushing through. Beckett Convery didn't scare her. He intimidated her, yes, but that was manageable.

Ryan sent a photo of the Taurus candle burning behind him, his expression caught in mid-eyeroll. She took a PG-rated photo of herself in the tub giving a thumbs-up, her own candle burning in the background.

No matter how hard she tried, though, she couldn't push up her mood.

Another text arrived, this one from an unknown number. Sara refused to worry or panic. She commanded Siri to play the message.

"Good evening, Ms. Strausser, this is Beckett Convery. I was pleased to hear you have decided to accept our offer. Pursuant to that, I've emailed you an invitation to a faculty party that's on Saturday. I would like you to confirm my attendance and inquire if I should bring anything. Your professional response on my behalf will be an opportunity to put your best foot forward and introduce yourself to the academic environment. Although I appreciate your enthusiasm, I want to be clear that profanity is unacceptable."

"Prick," Sara muttered.

Her phone chimed again.

"Mr. Caldwell was kind enough to share your personal email, but we'll set up your Wells email on Monday. In the meantime, I've sent a few more requests—individually, so as not to confuse you—that you'll need to address by, say, two on Sunday. If you have any questions, you can respond to this number. Texting is for more immediate concerns, but I check my email hourly. Oh, you should do the same. It might help for you to set an alarm as a reminder at first, until it becomes a habit."

Sara gaped at her phone, though it wasn't as if Beckett could see her slack-jawed response. If he'd been anyone else, she would have thought the messages were jokes—hilarious jokes—but she had no doubt Beckett was serious. She lamented not bringing a glass of wine with her into the tub.

Another chime. Sara prompted Siri again, fascinated.

"I've also emailed you an employee handbook with all the college's rules and regulations. Over the weekend, I'll compose an addendum with regards to the . . . club duties, the extra responsibilities . . . You know what I mean. Please examine the handbook and bring any questions or concerns to me."

She wasn't an email person. For one, emails were rarely secure; second, Stadler had always catered to her preference for briefings in person or by phone; and third, who the hell did Beckett Convery think he was?

Another chime.

"Are you fucking kidding me? Hey, Siri, read text."

"To summarize, we'll be meeting in my office promptly at eight in the morning. Ms. Strausser, please acknowledge you have received these messages."

Sara dried her hand on the towel hanging next to the tub. After hitting the microphone button, she said, "Acknowledged," hit *send*, then got out of the bath and into a clubbing dress.

* * *

WHEN SARA STUMBLED INTO HER APARTMENT, SHE WAS STILL SMILING. She'd managed to attach herself to a bachelorette party and had found them a place to do karaoke and pole dancing. A raucous time had been had by all.

Sara plugged in her phone to charge and noticed yet another message from Beckett. Since she didn't want him killing her buzz more than he already had, she decided not to listen.

Instead, she flopped onto her couch, giggling. She'd forgotten for a time what it was like to have fun—real fun. Working for Beckett would likely mean a slow and painful death. She couldn't get out of the job, not with the Agency watching her and holding all the power. But they always underestimated her, like Beckett—like most men. It was time to show them what she could do.

CHAPTER SIX

Beckett

SARA FINALLY RESPONDED TO HIS LAST TEXT AND confirmed his RSVP to the faculty party. When he saw her on Monday, he would make clear his expectations of prompt replies. He reminded himself she was new to administrative work—it wasn't as if hostessing was all that related, and even then, she'd struggled, hadn't she? Perhaps he had unfair mandates. Well, they could discuss that as well, allowing her to witness his fairness as a boss and learn that communication was a two-way street.

Beckett checked his clothing in the mirror for a final time. Alpheus Cohn, head of the English department, had indicated this would be a casual dress party to celebrate spring break. Since it was also a work affair, Beckett couldn't justify wearing jeans, so he'd chosen khaki pants and a crisp, blue chambray shirt and Peter Christian houndstooth vest and jacket. No tie. He tugged his shirt cuffs so they just peeked past his jacket. Perfect afternoon wear.

He didn't believe in affirmations, per se, but he did steel his eyes in his reflection and mined strength and resolve. Under his breath, he mumbled the six social talking points he'd prepared so he wouldn't have to make small talk extemporaneously.

Beckett had been so focused on memory magician recruiting lately that he'd neglected the networking portion of his associate professor position. One day, he would run the English department, on top of the psychic enrichment program for young memory magicians, and the groundwork needed to be set.

Beckett attempted a smile. Grins never looked right on his face. Like his mother, he'd been born to be serious and accomplished, not an affable fool like Sara.

Why was he thinking about her? Maybe because happy-go-lucky people like her baffled him. Well, that was a worry for another day.

* * *

ALPHEUS OPENED HIS DOOR AND GAVE BECKETT THE BIGGEST GRIN HE'D ever seen on the man's craggy face. He wore a thick cable-knit cardigan with frayed elbows in an awful moss color. Casual indeed. "Beckett!" Alpheus clapped Beckett on the shoulder.

They weren't friends, merely friendly, and the vigor of the greeting sent Beckett's talking points tumbling out of his brain.

"Alpheus, thanks for having me." Beckett remained on the stoop, holding a bottle of Montrachet, waiting for Alpheus to step back and let him inside. Apprehension numbed his lips. Beckett couldn't read Alpheus's thoughts through his jacket, and he wished he could. Something was off.

"I've got a surprise for you," Alpheus said with a sly smile.

Beckett hated surprises.

"Hi!" Sara Strausser burst past Alpheus and slung her arms around his neck. "You're surprised, right?"

Beckett couldn't respond, not with her breasts pressing into his chest and the fragrance of her perfume, something exotic, more woody than floral, in his head. She moved back before he managed to push her away. His face burned. Her behavior was shocking in its inappropriateness.

Sara pinched the skin at her throat and turned to Alpheus. "Oh no, I was afraid of that. He's not happy."

With her knee-high boots, she was almost as tall as he was. She wore fitted jeans that were several shades lighter than his shirt and a blazer. He had to wrench his eyes away from her cleavage, though his brain was already intent on discovering if she wore a blouse beneath that blazer. He didn't think so. Like most of her clothing, the blazer was incongruously suggestive, as if everything morphed into something sexy the moment Sara put it on her body.

"I'm so sorry, Becks," she said.

Becks?

She fidgeted with her hands. "I know you weren't sure how to introduce me to everyone, even if we have been dating for *over a month*." She gave him a mock glare. "And I thought . . ."

Dating? For over a month? What the hell was she doing?

She sighed. "I didn't want you to get anxious about it, so I thought it would be better to rip the Band-Aid off, and since you didn't know it was coming, you wouldn't get worried about it. Are you mad? You look kind of mad."

"Oh, that's just his face," Alpheus said with a chuckle.

Sara wrapped her arms around herself, looking dejected and vulnerable in a way that made Beckett want to do something. Put a coat over her shoulders. Tell her everything would be okay.

Except it wouldn't. He shook his head to clear his mind.

Sara reached out and took his hand in hers with an ease that spoke of intimacy, the movement both alien and natural. She squeezed once and then released him. "You want to go somewhere in private and, like, yell at me? Should I go?"

"Nonsense," Alpheus said, putting a hand on Sara's shoulder. His fingers were short and wide, making his hand a mitt.

Beckett supposed that was where *get your mitts off her* had come from.

"I've got that cabernet you like, Beckett, unless you want to open the chardonnay. Come on inside and relax." Alpheus still had his hand on Sara.

Beckett walked between Alpheus and Sara, forcing his coworker to drop his hand from her. "Come on," he said to Sara, glaring at her as he passed, his sense finally returning. He wasn't sure what game she was playing, but this was his life, and he wouldn't let her ruin it.

"We've been arguing," she said, suddenly ebullient and all smiles. "Cadbury Eggs. Yes or no?"

"Cadbury Eggs?" No doubt that topic was her doing. Usually, at the English department gatherings, they talked about books and literature and had ethical debates about Flannery O'Connor's brilliance versus her bigotry. Well, that had happened once. The rest of the time, the others discussed TV shows and which streaming services they preferred.

"Alpheus says no, they're overly sweet to the point of causing diabetes, but I think there's merit in the overindulgence." Sara looped her arm through his and leaned into his shoulder as they headed for the kitchen. Her smile never dimmed, and she didn't try to send him secret communications with her eyes or blink a message in Morse code. Was she delusional? Did she think they were actually dating?

"This will be better, you'll see," Sara said, her breath tickling his ear. The lower tone held a seductive purr that had to be intentional.

"Better than what?" Beckett needed to regain control of the situation, but he was unsure how.

She winked at him and released his arm as they entered the kitchen. "Before you got here, I was helping Pam with the cheese platter, talking about how we met and the sweet way you asked me out."

"You what?" Beckett raised his brows at Alpheus's wife, who was head of the political science department and beamed at him like she was a proud parent. "Pam, nice to see you." Beckett wrapped her in a hug and jumped into her thoughts, desperate. "What did Sara tell you?"

Pam's mind flared, a streak of her persimmon-colored contemplations rising in Beckett's magic.

* * *

Sara grinned. "It's the best meet-cute story ever."

Pam couldn't get past Sara's beauty. She looked like a model or a movie star. And she was so gregarious as she described how she and Beckett met.

"I have to say, I was so hot for teacher," Sara said, giggling. "He's so serious— and quite bossy—but this waiter spilled some butter sauce on my white silk blouse, and everyone was, of course, staring at my breasts, because if butter is going to spill on something, it isn't going to be on a sleeve, you know?

"But Beckett stood up and threw his suit jacket over me like some real, hard-core, knight-in-shining-armor shit. He walked me to the bathroom and told me when I got home, I needed to sprinkle talcum powder or baking soda on the stain, let it soak up the oil, then wash it with some dishwashing liquid, then take it to the dry cleaners."

* * *

"She told all of us how you two got together," Pam said.

* * *

Sara's laugh was contagious. "He didn't ask me out until the next week. He's such a gentleman."

Maybe he was different with Sara than other people. It's not like Beckett was ugly. He was adequately attractive, just stiff and a bit severe. But Sara was shiny and vibrant.

* * *

Beckett stepped back, his brain floating back into the moment as he parsed through Pam's thoughts. Sara had truly told everyone present they were dating, inventing a story involving a ridiculous butter stain. Her rendition of events would never have happened, but it *did* sound plausible.

He decided not to spend any time considering Pam's assessment of his character. He focused on the issue at hand: Sara's claim they were together. Romantically.

If Beckett announced they weren't involved, then Sara would seem unhinged. He definitely couldn't justify keeping an assistant who ran around claiming to be dating her boss. What was she attempting to accomplish?

"Are you almost done helping?" Beckett asked Sara as others from the party came into the kitchen, looking for snacks. "Can I talk to you for a minute?"

"Yes, but you have to give your official opinion on the Great Cadbury Egg Debate."

He wouldn't allow her to make him appear foolish. "Cadbury Eggs are a combination of sugar and chemicals designed specifically to be unhealthily addictive. They're vile."

"I concede the sugar and chemicals part, but raise you a cultural icon and family tradition," Sara said, cutting uneven slices of a cheddar.

"Tradition? Whose?" he asked. Pam and Alpheus had a back garden that would be the best place for their conversation. He could make the interaction brief and send her on her way.

"You didn't get Cadbury Eggs in your Easter basket as a kid?" Sara asked. "They were a staple in my house."

She was acting so strangely and sounding so different, and everyone was watching him watching her. Beckett felt as if he were in a fever dream, and any second now, he'd realize he had to give a lecture only to discover he either had a rip in his trousers or they were missing altogether.

"No, we didn't eat junk food. My parents cared too much about my health and basic nutrition."

Sara's eyes flicked up to him, something he couldn't name in her expression. It sank into him like a barb that threatened to make everything worse if he tried to remove it. "You're better off," she said. "Those things *are* wicked addictive."

"Should we get you some?" Alpheus asked.

Sara tossed back her head and laughed. "God, no, but you are so sweet to offer." Then she winked at Beckett, and her smile softened into something that looked like affection.

Beckett's significant others had never looked at him like that. He wasn't a tender person and didn't attract women with that quality. Sara attempting to make their relationship appear sappy wouldn't fool anyone.

"You said there was wine?" Beckett asked Alpheus, refusing to watch Sara any longer.

Alpheus gestured to the island, where several bottles of alcohol were lined up on the marble top.

"Do you guys have plans for spring break this week?" Pam asked Sara.

"Staycation," Sara said. "What about you?"

Beckett saw the wineglass Alpheus held out to him, but his brain was so fixated on Sara, he almost didn't take it. He needed her to stop talking. "Has Pam shown you the garden, Sara? I know how much you like greenery."

She smiled. "I do! No, I haven't seen it yet." She cocked her head, her long, blond hair falling in loose waves, glowing under the kitchen's canned lighting. He wanted to touch its softness. "Show me?"

He blinked. "Sure."

She met him at the back door, a bounce in her step. "You know what I was thinking?"

He opened the door and gestured her through. "I have no idea."

She stepped outside, talking to him over her shoulder. "Remember how your mom thought—"

When Beckett shut the door, she stopped talking. Good. He grasped her upper arm loosely in his hand and led her down the stone path to the back of the yard. "What do you think you're doing?"

"Yeah, the assistant deal was never going to work for me. This is better."

He dropped her arm and his voice, though nobody was around. "Do you have an undiagnosed mental disorder? I am *not* going to date you."

She rolled her eyes. "No shit. We're *fake* dating. Look it up. It's a thing."

"It is a trashy romance novel convention and not a real thing, and absolutely no one would believe we are together romantically." Beckett's throat filled with fire, and he swallowed twice in an effort to calm himself. Losing control would mean losing the argument.

Sara chuckled. "There's a kitchen full of people who already believe, Professor. Give me a month, and Pam will be offering to go ring shopping with you so you don't fuck it up." Her smile widened. She should have been cold and shivering in the chilly air, but she perused the foliage and the green shoots barely poking out of the ground as if enjoying herself.

He'd never wanted to read a person so badly in his life. What scheme was she hatching? Was she trying to sabotage him, or was she simply rash and foolhardy? "I would never marry someone like you."

Her smile dropped. "I know." She plucked at the shoulders of her blazer, though it didn't need straightening. "Hey, I get you like to be in control and that you have this preconceived notion of how best to move forward, but this plays to both of our strengths, not only yours."

"What is that supposed to mean?"

"It means I'm of better use to you as a girlfriend than as an assistant."

"Use?" As if he thought of her as nothing more than an object. "This arrangement was mutually beneficial and an opportunity for you to be a part of something bigger and more important than yourself. At no point did I treat you like—like . . ."

"Chill, Professor. I'm sure your intentions were admirable and completely reasonable. Unfortunately, the people you work with aren't quite so upstanding."

"Nonsense. We are the Moralists; our values are directly in the title. What specific nefarious acts do you suspect us of implementing?"

"How should I know?"

Apparently, she thought she could make vague accusations to make herself look like a victim and raise doubts about what he was trying to accomplish. "Do you know anything about the memory magician factions?"

"There are factions?" She snorted. "Of course there are. This is what happens when people band into groups. You can't just be special; you also have to be important."

This wasn't the venue for this discussion. "We can address this further at another time—Monday at the office."

She nodded. "Sure. I'd love to see where my lover works."

The word *lover* tore through him like shrapnel, and a combination of mortification and fascination washed over him. Even when Beckett had had a lover, he'd never used that term. It was too . . . intimate. "We are not . . . that."

"To the rest of the world, we are." She shrugged, a dramatic raising and dropping of her shoulders. "Too late now. What's done can't be undone."

Macbeth. Had she inadvertently quoted Shakespeare or was she mocking him? He countered, "This is not a thing without remedy. I can fix it right now."

Her smile was as hard as her eyes. "You think so? What are you going to do? Go in there and say I'm actually your assistant? Do you make a habit of shtupping the help?"

She was right. Somehow, she had exploited the situation, and now he was stuck in a fabricated relationship with her. Any bad behavior on her part would reflect on him.

His reputation was now in the hands of a woman who had no scruples or decorum. Beckett had no idea what she would do next and had several hours of a party left to find out.

CHAPTER SEVEN

Sara

AMATEUR. WORKING WITH BECKETT WAS GOING to suck—no avoiding that—but at least she wouldn't be his employee.

Beckett had obviously grown up in a rose-colored world where good triumphed over evil and all people needed to do to succeed was show a little initiative. *Check your privilege, buddy.*

He walked a few feet then stopped to offer her his arm. Sara didn't trust when actions didn't match emotions. While she didn't think he'd squeeze her hand until tears welled in her eyes or push her into one of the rose bushes with the tight buds and protruding thorns, she'd been fooled before. Beckett was a man used to being on top, and she'd bested him.

She brushed her left hand over her stomach. Damn it, she had to stop doing that.

Sara stood as tall as possible and looped her hand in the crook of his elbow. She'd rather stay out for a few more minutes and enjoy the afternoon sun, but not enough to argue about it.

He didn't rush her back, as if trying to make her stumble. He didn't clamp down on her hand on his arm. He didn't glower at her—or talk, which was fine with her.

As they walked, she gathered together all the cheerful feelings she'd had earlier. The chirp of birds helped elevate her mood. She liked Beckett's coworkers, and she loved being back in the game, especially since it was one of her own making. This would be the best of the job with none of the worst. If he'd been an Agency target, she would have had to bend into the exact woman he wanted, screw him how he wanted, and bury anything she craved for herself deep inside. But with Beckett, not only would she not have to sleep with him, she could rebuff any other men who expressed interest.

She could flirt and have fun with abandon. She'd make herself emotionally indispensable. Kick ass. And not schedule a goddamn thing.

But then what? What would the Agency demand of her next?

She had to last only two months.

Sara leaned into Beckett's shoulder as they approached the back door and caught another whiff of his cologne, the citrus a little stronger than the herbaceous complement. A hint of violets. Lovely. She almost forgot what she'd planned to say.

"They're going to ask us for more specific plans about spring break," she said.

He huffed. "Ms. Strausser, I can assure you they have better topics to discuss than my *staycation* plans."

"Mmhm." She hoped he knew more about Shakespeare than human beings, because he was clueless about the way people worked. How could he not know that his aloofness incited curiosity? For someone who regularly spied on what others were thinking, he hadn't learned a damn thing.

"So, what kinds of things do you have planned for your staycation?" Pam asked them the moment they stepped into the kitchen.

"You tell them, Professor," Sara said, giving Beckett a playful elbow to the ribs.

Beckett paused only a second before saying, "A lot of reading."

Definitely an amateur.

* * *

SARA DRIFTED BETWEEN GROUPS OF PEOPLE, HER PRESENCE CONSISTENTLY opening a space for her. She gushed about Beckett in each conversation, sowing the coupleness of them everywhere. Beckett was the type who wouldn't be into PDAs, but that didn't stop her. Like a rube, he stiffened every time she touched him. If the stakes had been a little less high, she totally would have draped herself over his lap just to fuck with him.

Beckett wasn't friendly enough to make the rounds with the party guests. He tucked himself into a corner of the living room between a tall floor lamp with a flower-shaped glass shade and a large window with a view of the side yard. He stood with perfect posture, the way his body angled away from the room putting his discomfort with social interactions on display.

Beckett liked to lecture, not converse. Sara would have the entire party eating out of her hand in an hour. Word of them as a couple would spread like salmonella through potato salad nine hours into a ninety-degree day. Everyone would love her, and if he treated her badly . . .

Sara checked in on Beckett's whereabouts and spotted a short man with shaggy hair and John Lennon glasses closing in on him. He carried a paper plate with some of the cheddar she'd sliced, rounds of salami, and water crackers. The man was preparing to use memory magic on Beckett.

Sara didn't think. Her body seemed to move on instinct as she skipped across the room and wrapped both hands around Beckett's biceps, spinning into him with the biggest, brightest smile she could conjure. "There you are!"

Beckett grimaced at either her contact or her too loud voice. She didn't allow him to say anything, though.

Sara turned toward the encroaching memory surgeon, digging her nails into Beckett to hold him back while stumbling a bit to make the move appear natural. "Oh, hi, I'm Sara." She giggled and held out her hand for Lennon Glasses to shake. He set his food on a side table so he could whip out a two-handed grip when he took her hand.

As she'd expected, he tried to read her. He pounced into her mind with a power that felt like claws scratching deep. Nobody had ever attacked her with that much force at the get-go. He was either seriously powerful or a first-rate douche.

"Rider," the man said with a slick smile that made her want to throw up on his chest. Then he frowned.

Sara eased her hand away without clenching her jaw. "Nice to meet you." She spun toward Beckett again, grabbing both of his hands. "You promised me a dance, and I'm collecting. No arguments."

"Rider and I—"

"No arguments." She tugged him to the other room firmly enough he'd need to cause a scene not to follow. A few of the younger staff, or maybe their assistants, were dancing in one big group of five as an Ed Sheeran song played from a speaker. Someone must have spilled a beer here, because it smelled like a bar.

Sara led him to the far side of the dance floor and slung her arms casually over his shoulders, her right eye pulsing offbeat to the music. Beckett stood there like a dolt. "Put your hands on my hips," she said through gritted teeth.

He glared at her and barely complied.

She huffed out a breath. "Like an adult, not a kid at his first boy-girl dance."

Beckett jerked her body against his, closer than she'd expected—also closer than he'd expected, if his rigid posture and pinking cheeks were any indication. "I don't appreciate your attempts to humiliate me."

Sara's head ached, so she ignored his ridiculous words. "Okay, but you might appreciate that I just saved your ass from a violent memory assault."

"Rider wouldn't do that."

She reached up and pinched his ear, dragging his face down an inch. "My epic migraine says otherwise."

Beckett took a step forward, and Sara's back hit the wall. He crowded her. She pushed at his chest, but he slid his hand around her throat, and she froze. It was the first time he'd touched her without trying to read her.

The unexpected move spiked her adrenaline, leaving her body trembling, her headache not gone but dismissed. He didn't squeeze, didn't hurt her or even try to intimidate her. He only entranced her. His thumb rubbed up the side of her neck over her pulse, the touch so light it was almost nonexistent. Almost soothing, yet stimulating. Goose bumps broke out everywhere. She couldn't breathe deeply enough, and her lungs strained to get oxygen. Her nipples chafed against her bra. This wasn't possible.

"You're sure?" His voice was low, like a vocal manifestation of his caress.

For a moment, she had no idea what he was talking about. She should push him away, but she needed to maintain their cover—and, honestly, she didn't *want* to put distance between them. He'd never been more fascinating, and a part of her she'd thought was dead had just been resurrected. Not that she wanted to be turned on, certainly not by arrogant, clueless Beckett. But the unexpectedness of her reaction didn't diminish its power.

She arched her back, pressing her breasts against his chest. It was more a reflex than anything else, but it sent delicious shivers through her body. "I'm positive."

His breath hitched, and the thumb that had been teasing the side of her neck stilled. He leaned closer to her, his mouth close to her ear, tickling the tiny hairs there, sending a cascade of want deep into her core. "How do you know? That's a very serious accusation."

Sara, absurdly, wanted to squirm against him. Her hypersensitized skin hummed at every point of contact. "Would you believe me if I told you I could just tell? And then he pretty much slammed into my mind."

"I believe you." His hand slid down to her collarbone as his lips brushed her jaw. "If we run into him again, I want you to let us shake. I'm going to take a look myself."

His take-charge attitude wasn't sexy. She hated alpha men. *Hated* them. But his brand of alpha had a quiet confidence, something encoded into his DNA and not something he'd had to cloak over himself.

Beckett would always lose if he stuck to the rules of fair play, but if he had the stomach to take on anyone plotting against him, she had no doubt he could outsmart them all. Especially if she decided to help him.

"I'll tap your hand twice if I sense him trying to read you."

"So helpful," he crooned into her ear.

It was so unexpected, the heat of his tone. Her knees almost buckled, which she hid by tightening her front to his. "Better give me that dance."

His hand finally released her throat, only to smooth around to the back of her neck. He held her by the hip with his other hand, then slid it to her waist. Their bodies were close, intimate-close, and the numbness she usually felt when she played this role was gone. Her body melded to his, she was nothing but sensation, attuned to his breathing, to the switch of weight from foot to foot as he swayed them in a tight circle.

Although they didn't cover any distance, he clearly led her, and she guessed he was a skilled dancer, probably proficient in waltzing and other ballroom-style dances. Whatever kind debutantes and gentlemen learned as some sort of secret code.

Sara wished, for a moment, the fiction was real. This was a fantasy she hadn't allowed herself since she'd been a teenager. Dancing too slowly to too fast music, uncaring of anything else around her, noticing only the feel of a man's hands on her. He didn't paw at her, try to squeeze her ass, or grab a breast. He didn't jam his tongue down her throat or drag her into a bathroom and onto her knees.

This was like magic, and though she knew it was a lie, Beckett's body was right there, and she closed her eyes to indulge herself. She'd enjoy it until he turned on her, as men always did. It was only a matter of time.

CHAPTER EIGHT

Beckett

BECKETT'S BODY WOULDN'T CALM, AND HE STOPPED trying to rein in his response to Sara. He had always been a think first sort of person, but Sara pushed him into the corporeal and instinct. Feeling instead of thinking. The base part of his brain had usurped his cognitive functions. Nature's witchcraft.

It didn't mean anything, how right she felt in his arms. It was just a chemical reaction.

Beckett wasn't a particularly accomplished dancer, but Sara made him relaxed and somehow bold, the way he'd stroked her throat and held her in his thrall. He was unaccustomed to physical triumphs, beyond fencing, and he quite liked it. He enjoyed her height, an inch below his own, and though he was loath to acknowledge it, her curves were agreeable in his hands. At last, he'd found an upside to the ruse, and perhaps it wouldn't be a bad idea to play along for a while.

Then he saw Rider slipping into the kitchen. He didn't know Rider well, only that he was a memory magician who taught classes on government and politics at UIC, and he was a member of Dominion. They'd had a few debates about the merits of their respective factions, all friendly and respectful, though a thread of tension always ran between them. Beckett strove to consider Rider and the other Dominion people as memory magicians first and Dominion members second.

If Sara was correct, however, then Rider was disregarding the rules of propriety among memory magicians.

Also, why would he be at a Wells College party? Maybe through Pam, since they were both in political science. Or was he there to spy on Beckett and Andrew about the remaining students in their program? Dominion had already taken several of their mentees. How many more did they intend to acquire? Regardless, Beckett decided his need to protect those close to him justified him hunting for information.

"He's in the kitchen," Beckett said in Sara's ear. Her body shivered in his hold, and his answered in kind. "Care for something to drink?"

She smiled at him, a glint in her eye. "Actually, I am quite parched."

He led her into the kitchen, their hands entwined. He wasn't traditionally a fan of any sort of physical displays of affection, but if anyone tried to shake his hand, he would have a few precious seconds to prepare.

Rider approached them immediately, and though Beckett couldn't see anything about the man that spoke of intent to use his gift, Sara tapped his hand twice with her thumb.

"There you are!" Rider extended his hand to Beckett. "Did you have a nice dance?"

Beckett released Sara and concentrated on three memories about his recruits that were common knowledge and should distract the other memory magician. Then he shook Rider's hand.

Rider either had terrible blocking abilities, or he wasn't expecting a counterattack. Beckett's mind flowed directly into Rider's.

* * *

Rider clamped down on his concentration. Come on, you prick, give me something.

He worked hard not to gape at Beckett's piece of ass. How someone as uptight as Beckett could snag a chick as hot as her was a mystery. Well, he had money, so it wasn't all that mysterious.

Damn it. Beckett's memories were muted and packed tightly together. Rider wanted to bust through the barrier, but he'd never used force before, not with another memory magician. If Beckett ever discovered how they'd been stealing his prospects, there could be consequences.

* * *

SARA'S FINGERS STROKED OVER THE BACK OF BECKETT'S NECK, STARTLING him, and Rider's thoughts clicked off like a light switch. The image of his own mind map seared the backs of his eyelids as if he'd taken the flash of a camera full in the face. He'd never read anyone who'd been reading him, and it was disorienting.

Dominion wasn't poaching students organically. They weren't trying to win them over by chance, but by design. He'd suspected, of course, but had assumed they'd used their wits and resources—not magic—to pilfer information from the Moralists. If they could steal fledgling students, they might attempt to lure away higher-ranking members too. Dominion could surreptitiously undermine the Moralists from the inside out.

Sara kissed his cheek. "Do you want another drink?"

He wanted several but would settle for one. "Yes. A glass of port—tawny, not ruby."

"Got it." He wondered if she understood that port was a fortified wine traditionally served in a cordial glass. He wondered what product she used that smelled so enticing. Woodsy and complex.

Sara flounced off, and Rider stepped in closer. "Dude, she is totally hot. How did you manage that?"

Beckett's sense of decorum bristled. The nerve of that miscreant after what he'd attempted. Further, Beckett didn't believe in locker room talk or any discourse that reduced women to bodies and body parts. "Sara isn't simply lovely. She's also vivacious."

"That's why you're dating her? For her vivacity?" Rider raised his hands when Beckett glared at him. "She does seem very nice."

Nice? That wasn't a word Beckett would use, but then, Rider didn't know her. And he never would. "How are things at UIC?" Beckett asked, wanting to try to discover more details in Rider's mind. He wished Andrew were there so he could scope out Rider's long-term memories.

Rider shrugged. "Meh." He grinned. "But it pays the bills."

How much extra was he paid to pilfer Beckett's magicians?

Beckett briefly considered calling him out, but if Rider knew he'd been discovered, avenues of pursuit might end up closed.

Andrew arrived, entering the living area like a playboy prince, and the whole room perked up at his appearance. Beckett intended to make his way directly to Andrew, but Sara returned with his port, in a proper cordial glass, and slipped her hand into his. Her hand was cold, and fine tremors transferred into his palm.

Beckett toasted Rider, who saluted and backed away. His gaze, like everyone else in the kitchen except Sara, had riveted on Andrew. Beckett expected Rider to charge over and try to read Andrew, too, but he exited the other side of the kitchen instead. Rider might assume Andrew more apt than Beckett to access his memories in turn if they had contact.

Too late; we're on to you.

Beckett swallowed his drink, surprised it was the tawny port he'd requested. Perhaps he shouldn't have automatically assumed Sara hadn't known what he was talking about.

Sara rested her temple on his shoulder. Her long, slow exhale tickled his neck.

"Are you well?" he asked.

"Just a headache."

He shifted to examine her face, but she wouldn't meet his eyes. He touched her chin with a single finger, and she raised her face without further prompting. Her eyes were dull and red, and she pressed her lips together.

"Beckett! You're here early." Andrew stopped short, his shock almost comical as he noticed how close Sara and Beckett were. "Oh."

"Hi," Sara said, her face brightening, though she rested her head on Beckett's shoulder again. "I'm Sara."

"*You're* Sara?" Andrew asked, his usual unflappability missing.

"Aw, Becks, you did tell someone we're dating," Sara said.

"You're *dating*?" Andrew's eyes bounced between them. "You did not mention that, Beckett."

If Beckett had truly been courting Sara, he would have told Andrew. As soon as they were alone, he'd explain to Andrew how surprised he'd been himself, and Andrew would have a nice laugh over it.

"It's the fact we don't make sense that makes it work," Sara said with a giggle. "You have to admit, we're absolutely adorable together."

Her acting skills made Beckett almost believe her.

"You are." Andrew laughed and clapped Beckett on the shoulder. "We are definitely talking later." He grinned. "Now, I think I'm going to find some female company of my own." With a wave over his head, Andrew headed into the room where people were dancing.

"Let's get you out of here," Beckett said to Sara.

* * *

Once he was home and alone, Beckett unbuttoned his vest aggressively, Sara's words and actions spinning through his head. Now that he was out of her presence, the absurdity of everything crashed through him.

Beckett had missed most of the party to take Sara home, and though he disliked casual social gatherings, often struggling to connect with others, he didn't appreciate the lost opportunities to network. He'd been so overwhelmed, he forgot to ask Andrew to peek into Rider's memories. Somehow, Sara had sucked him into her spell, forcing sympathetic feelings into him. She'd tricked him, distracted him, but then saved him—in a sense.

Attraction to her would be entirely too pedestrian.

Beckett hated that he couldn't read her, couldn't reach inside her and discern her thoughts. Her agenda would remain a mystery, though what she'd done tonight had illuminated her lack of scruples.

She confused him, and he didn't appreciate the foreign feeling. If she'd been anyone else . . .

But she wasn't, and he would deal with reality and not what he wished were true.

It was barely past seven, so he had hours left to ruminate. He called the one person he fully trusted. "Mother," he said when she answered. "Care for some dinner or drinks?"

"I'd love to, sweetheart, but I'm out the door. I've committed to this art gallery opening. Would you like to meet me there? It's an abstract exhibit from a local artist, mostly monochromatic oils, but a few pastels and a one-off portrait that's gained some press."

"All right. Text me the details." He rebuttoned his vest, examined his shoes and deemed them polished enough.

He brushed his teeth and ventured out to convene with his mother, refusing to entertain the idea that he should have ensured Sara had settled in her new apartment.

* * *

THE GALLERY WAS IN THE GOOSE ISLAND NEIGHBORHOOD OF CHICAGO, to the east of the actual island. Paintings hung on white walls sporting dark smudges that looked like scorch marks, as if a bomb had gone off inside the building. They created a fascinating juxtaposition with the black concrete floors that gleamed diamond-bright.

Immediately upon arriving, Beckett was accosted by the manager of the gallery, a tall, gaunt man who resembled a B-movie funeral director in his black suit, black tie, white shirt ensemble that drooped off his bony frame. He greeted Beckett and breathlessly explained that a grenade had exploded in the space four months ago—"Isn't that astonishing?"—and how the gallery owner had decided to keep that particular scar, the singe marks a testament to survival and overcoming adversity.

"Was anyone hurt?" Beckett asked.

"That's all in the past," the man said in a quiet voice, his breath a touch wine-soured.

If he didn't want to talk about the story, why had he brought it up? He clearly hadn't thought through his approach.

Beckett thanked the man, then found his way to the drink table in the back and had the bartender pour him a glass of pinot noir. He sipped the subpar wine—which explained the manager's breath—as he meandered through the paintings. It was early enough in the evening that only six other people walked the room as the funeral director hovered in the corner, watching them all like a pickpocket choosing a victim.

It wasn't that Beckett didn't appreciate art. He just didn't comprehend the finer points, missing themes and symbolism and often the painter's vision. Books, he got, even the deeper layers and cloaked meanings. Shakespeare had always shone for him.

The other patrons moved at sloth speed and spoke in hushed tones, as if in a library, but Beckett had been to enough art openings to know that this was protocol. He didn't care for the way the muted words made the openness of the space too apparent, his self-awareness too sharp.

His favorite piece was a portrait, though it was listed NFS—not for sale. The woman lay back against a fainting couch, one arm resting over her head, the pose reminiscent of classic paintings, except the smirk on her face was modern. She was pretty. Her long, blond hair had dark roots, the overall color warmer than Sara's by several degrees. Naked from the waist up, she had high and round breasts proportionate to her frame, her body muscled and strong.

Why wouldn't his brain stop comparing the woman to Sara?

He mused about whether Sara would pose nude for an artist. He didn't know her well, but it was easy to picture her shrugging before dropping her clothes, completely unselfconscious in her nudity.

"It's weird if I stand here, right?" a woman asked.

He looked at her and saw the woman from the painting. She wore a sleeveless black dress that displayed her toned arms.

"Uh. . ." He wouldn't be the one to tell her that her clothed presence next to her naked representation would not relax the crowd.

"There you are." A movie-handsome man strode up and slid his arm around the blond. "If you don't want attention, this isn't the best place for you to hang out." He held out a hand to Beckett. "Cass Stuart, the artist. This is my fiancée and model extraordinaire, Jolene."

As a reflex because of the day he'd had, Beckett sank into the cavern of his mind, opening to the connection that would form when their palms met. Though he'd primed himself, he didn't push or pry, shifting his focus at the last moment to guarding his own thoughts. Would that be his reflexive response now? Preparing to invade total strangers' minds?

Thankfully, Beckett's mother showed up then, walking straight past him to Cass, her own hand extended. "Virginia Convery. I'm so pleased to meet you in person, Mr. Stuart."

"Thanks," Cass said, shaking her hand and giving her a charming smile. "Call me Cass. The pleasure is all mine."

Cass was one of those men who were so attractive they carried significant cachet without having to accomplish anything. He had an open, welcoming aspect, and though he likely didn't comprehend how influential Virginia Convery could be to his career, he gave her his full attention.

Beckett's mother looped her arm through Cass's, ensuring he would stay on her right, the side with her functional ear. "I had an early viewing yesterday, and I have some questions about some of these pieces."

Cass shot his fiancée a wide-eyed plea but didn't attempt to extricate himself from Beckett's mother. It was a wise choice, because Virginia Convery was not a woman easily escaped.

Beckett stood near the model for a minute, possibly two, before he excused himself to shadow his mother so they could speak as soon as she was finished talking with the artist. Luckily, he didn't have to wait long.

His mother beckoned him outside. The temperature had cooled down, dipping to freezing or below, but his mother wore her fur coat. She extracted a silver cigarette case from her handbag.

"I thought you'd quit," Beckett said in as neutral a tone as he could manage despite his irritation.

"When your husband leaves you for a child pageant princess, then you can judge my coping mechanisms," she snapped.

"I don't think lung cancer is the resounding comeuppance you think it is."

His mother arched a sculpted eyebrow—or tried. She must have had a recent Botox treatment, because her face barely moved, though she didn't need it to display her displeasure.

"Come on, Mom. You promised me you were taking care of yourself."

"Yes. I take care of myself, so it's not your concern. What is it you wanted to talk to me about?" She lit her cigarette with a gold filigree lighter, took a long drag and blew a plume of smoke into the air with a sigh.

She'd gone more than ten years without a cigarette. Her divorce had ruined that too. They'd focused so much on Beckett's problems lately; he'd neglected to ensure she was managing. She wouldn't appreciate his inquiries now.

"I had a meeting earlier this week with Sara, the hostess at La Cuisine, to bring her into the program working with me in an administrative capacity. She—"

"Administrative? That girl couldn't find a standing reservation with the date and time, and you're going to entrust her with your calendar? Surely, you can simply pay her for her time while you run tests and trials. Why bother with giving her an admin job?"

Beckett decided not to mention his involvement in the fact that Sara no longer worked at La Cuisine. "I'm afraid it's worse than that." He wished he could explain the situation in a way that wouldn't make him sound like such a buffoon. Without twisting facts, it would be unavoidable. He'd stick to the dispassionate details. "She showed up at the faculty party and told everyone we're dating."

Virginia almost dropped her cigarette. "Why would she say something so preposterous? Nobody would ever believe someone like you would be interested in someone like her. I've got shoes smarter than that girl."

Beckett didn't understand the spire of heat in his chest. He'd had similar thoughts, but after spending some time with Sara, he had to concede, though she certainly wasn't a scholar, she was hardly vacuous.

"What happened when they discovered she was telling tales?" His mother's mouth quirked in a way that made him miss the days when she could smile naturally.

"I . . . uh . . . It was so unexpected, and everyone already believed, and . . . I suppose . . ."

"You didn't correct her?" Virginia stopped cold.

"Sara raised some valid points. We can utilize her in more situations with a romantic relationship dynamic, and it isn't as if I truly have to date her. Also . . ." Beckett glanced behind them. Though nobody was within earshot, he lowered his voice. "She has the ability to detect when memory magicians are preparing to use their gift."

Virginia tossed her cigarette to the ground and crushed it with the toe of her stiletto. She encircled her mink coat tighter around her. "Let's take a short walk."

They turned from the business area down a residential street, the lights dimmer here. Tree branches, still stark from winter, dappled the metal halide lamp glow onto the narrowing sidewalk. A dog barked in the distance, and the air smelled clean when Beckett wasn't inhaling the combination of Chanel N°5 and nicotine surrounding his mother.

She squeezed his arm. "If Sara has one gift you didn't know existed, she might have others. Consider that."

"If she had any magic beyond shielding and detection, wouldn't it have appeared before now? I've never heard of a power genesis over the age of twenty-five, and she's twenty-four."

"You need to be open to the possibility that the rules are neither set in stone nor static. If you think things aren't possible, you'll never find the impossible." She patted his hand. "I hate to say this, dear, but I think you're going to have to play along and keep the ruse part a secret."

The two- and three-story flats of the neighborhood were lit from within, some with large bay windows allowing sneaking glances inside people's living rooms. It created an intimacy, an atmosphere for secrets.

"Of course. Only the Philotimo—"

"No, the Philotimo especially have to believe it's real. If you tell them what you've discovered and that the relationship is fake, they might find a use for her elsewhere. You need to take charge of this, Beckett." Her voice tightened like a violin string. "If you and the girl are dating, then you can control who she helps and who she does not. That's a power in itself. This is actually a fortuitous turn of events."

Beckett imagined controlling Sara would be like trying to restrain an avalanche, but he let his mother's thoughts unroll without interruption.

"The stronger and tighter your ties to her, the better—at least to outside eyes. You just be sure to remember who she is and who you are."

"Mom, I think your concern is misguided. She's not my type at all." He dated sophisticated, educated women with staunch manners and impeccable taste.

Sara had none of those qualities, and yet, being in a relationship with her didn't seem as ridiculous as it had earlier. And that was the most dangerous thought he'd had all evening.

CHAPTER NINE

Sara

SARA SHOVED THE LAST OF HER WARDROBE BOXES into the second bedroom. The movers had done a decent job moving her into the Arden building, where only Beckett's memory magic students lived. All the kitchen shit was in the kitchen in boxes labeled *kitchen*. They'd even set up the bed. Sara had never moved like this. The Agency had relocated her clothes everywhere, but they'd always left the furniture behind when she'd headed to the next assignment.

The apartment had been freshly cleaned—no dust—and the wood floors shone and smelled like Murphy Oil Soap. No spots or streaks on the windows. No crumbs on the counter.

Since her headache had finally dissipated, she should unpack the kitchen, find the laundry room to wash her bedding, and organize her makeup in both bathrooms. Instead, she checked out the building's third-floor lounge: black, industrial carpeting with crimson furniture; a plump, L-shaped couch and chairs that looked like eggs split open; a glass dining table with six chairs. No residents to be found.

She knocked on the first three doors on her floor, hunting for company. Either the apartments were empty, people were out, or introverts hid inside, holding their breath, desperate not to be discovered.

Finally, at the last door, a pale face appeared in the crack of the door. "Yes?" she asked.

The girl was short, with brown, curly hair falling into her eyes.

Sara pointed her thumb down the hall toward her own apartment. "I moved in today. I'm Sara."

"You're a student?" The girl's eyes were narrow and mistrustful.

Sara took an immediate liking to her. "Oh, hell no. I'm here as some kind of science project because I can't be memory read. Professor Beckett is keeping me here to study me." She waggled her eyebrows then winked. "Not really. I'm his girlfriend, and now we're taking things to the next level. Hasn't he mentioned me?"

No smile. "Not once."

"That's fine." Sara nodded. "He's a private dude. We should totally become friends. I've got no sugar to lend you, neighbor, but if you need a mud mask, body shimmer, or something like that, come and see me."

The girl squinted and shut the door without saying anything more.

Sara sighed. Jeez, tough crowd. Not allowing one grump to deter her, she hopped down the stairs to the second-floor lounge, which was a green version of the third floor's red, to find someone else.

* * *

THE TWO BOYS THERE WERE GREAT FUN FOR THE FIRST HOUR, WITH their wide eyes and slack jaws. It made Sara wish she'd dressed up so she could have really blown their minds. Their reverence at the idea she was living in their building was hilarious. Beckett owed her big-time for the hero worship in the kids' eyes.

They settled down eventually, going back to their PlayStation and their studying, and Sara drifted back upstairs, bargaining with her distracted half for guilt-free screen time in exchange for a minimum amount of unpacking. Beckett would have an aneurysm if he saw her apartment's unpacked state.

When she reached her door, it wasn't locked. She'd been so caught up in seeking out other people that she'd neglected to ensure her door was secured. She'd lived in plenty of places where a mistake like that meant you could kiss your TV goodbye. Before Stadler had recruited her into the Agency, she'd had to rely on the kind of men who'd take in a homeless girl, and they didn't live in penthouses or buildings with doormen. They lived in rentals with bars on the windows, roaches in the kitchen, and drunk buddies who expected her to be receptive to whatever they had in mind.

The apartment was dark as she walked in. She thought she'd left the kitchen light on. The bedroom lamp too. Her instincts flipped to fully alert, urging her to run, but she grappled with the logical part of her brain that thought she was being ridiculous. She was always forgetful, though she was far more likely to leave too many lights on than to shut them all off.

Sara decided to return to the rec area under the ruse of asking for volunteers to help her unpack.

As her fingers touched the doorknob, her body was jerked back by a hand in her hair. A second, gloved hand clapped over her mouth before she could scream. The scents of leather and cigarettes clung in the fabric.

"I'm here as a warning," a gruff voice said into her ear. His breath was hot and wet, his grip crippling. Parts of her mind shut down like hurricane shutters, determined to protect as much of herself as possible.

Her learned survival mode kicked in, and her body relaxed. No resistance. He might still hurt her, because some people enjoyed delivering pain and terror, but her seeming submission would mitigate some of it. Unless he was here to kill her. Though anyone who wanted to murder someone usually just did it. No discussion needed.

"Good." The man's grip loosened, but he didn't release her. "Let's have ourselves a civilized conversation over on the couch there, all friendly-like."

Sara didn't like the phrase *friendly-like*. She didn't know this man, but she was familiar with his breed. Most of the criminals she'd seduced had been like him. He got off on feeling superior and in control, on her fear and acquiescence. So, she walked toward the buff-colored armchair without protest. He shoved her onto the couch instead so he could plop right next to her and loop an arm across her shoulders as if they were on a date. Part of his game.

He looked rough, like he was five minutes away from being homeless. He had green or gray eyes that gleamed and narrowed, his jaw too square and big in relation to the rest of his face. His stubble looked at least two days old, too thick to be fashionable.

"What do you want?" she asked, breathy with a hint of quaver. It was too early to wobble her chin, but she had the move queued up in case she intuited that level of helplessness would help her cause.

"It isn't about what I want, Princess. It's about what you were ordered to do."

An Agency guy. She should have known.

"What?" she asked, rounding her shoulders as if his touch and tone made her uncomfortable—which they did.

"Nobody gave you permission to change the script."

Fucking Beckett. Figured that entitled prick would run off to the Agency as soon as he could, whining and complaining about what she had done. "Better to play to my strengths," she said, shifting so that her hair fell across her face.

Sara could cry on command, but she didn't think it was time yet.

"Did Caldwell give you the green light on that?"

Ryan. Where was Ryan? She was a terrible friend. "No. I didn't tell anyone. Where is he?"

"Reassigned, Princess. You got me now. This is what happens when little girls are naughty."

And there it was, that threat of sexual violence she'd known was coming. He would definitely hurt her if he thought it'd gain him an edge.

"I've been told you got kinda fucked up on the last job," he sneered. "That true?"

Her PTSD flared. Shark eyes. Black gun. Smoke in her lungs. The hot wetness of her blood.

The room was turning with the tension and the direction of the conversation. He was fishing for her soft spot, and he'd come entirely too close. She'd have to redirect like a motherfucker. Make him think she cared about anything other than her scarred body.

She let the first tear slip down her cheek. "I thought he loved me." She held back the crying long enough that when a sob escaped, it jerked her chest. Clapping hands over her face and angling away from the Agency goon, she let loose. "He—He—He—almost k-k-killed me. I didn't think ... How could he—"

Sob, sob, sob. Fetch something for her running nose—well, try, because she was yanked back onto the couch. She pointed to the stack of napkins from her lunch on the coffee table.

He leaned over and slapped a napkin on her thigh. She snatched it up and blew her nose for as long and as wetly as possible. Plenty of men got off on a woman crying, but almost none wanted any contact with snot.

"Listen, Princess, guys'll say pretty much anything to get some pussy. You're hot and all, but business is business. Try not to take that shit personal-like." He stood, which was the best outcome she'd anticipated. "Now, wipe your face and calm the hell down before I smack you quiet."

Sara could have shut it off like that, but she opted for a slow taper. She blew her nose one last time, rubbing hard to increase the redness. With her chin tilted down, she peered up at him through her lashes, the picture of submission.

"No more going off script," he said, towering over her. He wore all black—leather jacket, mock turtleneck, cargo pants, combat boots. His gun peeked through his open jacket, and he had a knife strapped to his waist. None of that was necessary to deal with her, but he might have other stops to make after this. More likely, he'd aimed for maximum intimidation. Keep her compliant in one shot.

"Where's Ryan?" Maybe she could finagle him back as her liaison.

The man leered, leaning hard into it so she could not miss his contempt. "He's been assigned a new mission somewhere on the West Coast." He reached behind his back, and Sara tensed, waiting for him to whip out a machete or hunting knife. "Take this." He held out a black iPhone identical to the one she already had.

She took it, already dreading having to keep track of two cell phones. Her phone went missing at least one day every week.

The man continued to hold out his hand. "I need the old one."

Sara contemplated trying to trick him into thinking she'd lost it but determined it was futile. He'd hurt her to get it, and she hadn't built up her armor enough yet to withstand an assault. Certainly not over a phone whose only value was her connection to Ryan, who probably also had a new cell with a new number. Replacing Ryan was a punishment, a warning. *This is what happens when you fuck with us. You get this asshole as a handler.* The Agency had never cared about her.

Her new handler allowed her to go into the kitchen, where she opened her purse to find no cell there. Shit. *Today cannot be the day you misplaced your goddamned phone.*

She edged past the man, who made sure it wasn't easy, the bulk of him filling the kitchen doorway. Sara slipped into the bedroom, and he followed so closely he almost stepped on her heels. Luckily, her cell sat on the dresser. She wondered if he'd already known where it was. He struck her as the type to test.

Sara held out the phone as if it meant nothing.

He let his fingers slide over hers as he took it. Deliberate. He eyed the bare mattress and licked his lips.

Sara patiently waited, careful not to move or react.

Finally, he shrugged, his entire demeanor changing to one of efficient business. "We like the new direction. Keep close to Convery and make note of everything he does. Find his weaknesses. I expect reports at least weekly. Put them in the draft folder of your email and I'll get 'em." He stretched his arms over his head, showcasing his gun and knife. "You run into problems, you call me, but don't get into situations you can't handle yourself."

Legit, my ass. The Agency wasn't suddenly a real boy—it was still a puppet. The soul of the organization was black, the cancer spread too far for them to clear the margins. They didn't want her to make the world a better place, but to find a way to leverage whatever she discovered so they could ultimately use the information to make more money or secure more power. But why would they send a thug to manage her? They were usually more sophisticated than that.

"I don't have your number," she said, and immediately realized it was probably in the phone he'd just given her.

"It's already in there." He gestured with his chin. "Under *D* for Daddy. You need anything, Princess, give Daddy a call."

That tone. That word. Her stepfather's cigarette and Budweiser breath. The sick gleam in his bloodshot eyes. The world lurched, and the reptilian part of her brain exploded with activity. If she'd been hooked up to electrodes, the computer would have lit up, numbers and letters scrolling like mad over the screen. Inside her belly, a small creature scrabbled and scrambled in a tight circle, clawing and climbing but getting nowhere.

Two months seemed a whole lot longer now.

CHAPTER TEN

Beckett

A S HE LEFT THE GALLERY, BECKETT'S PHONE alerted him to an email from Sara asking him to meet her in person. Regardless of the late hour, he agreed since he was already on his way home, and he lived next-door. Not that she knew that yet.

She was waiting for him outside the entrance to Arden, which he owned. It was after midnight, and she shouldn't have been standing alone, practically on the street. An attacker could easily have grabbed her before she could swipe her card and get inside.

Beckett opened his mouth to warn her to be more careful, but she cut him off.

"Nobody can know the dating isn't real. *Nobody.*" Sara stepped close to him, as if trying to physically intimidate him. "And I have a new cell number."

"All right, text it to me." He stood his ground. "My mother already knows."

"I can't text you; this is a new phone." Sara tugged on her earlobe and thrust her cell at him, presumably for him to add his number to her contacts. "But nobody else knows, right? Nobody in your club?"

"It isn't a club. We are an organization, a collection of memory magicians that share a philosophy of ethical responsibility. I wanted to explain all this to you at our meeting, but it's late, so this is just the overview. We are a somewhat loose network, but we're led by the Philotimo, three of our most respected magicians."

"Filo dough?"

"F-EYE-lo-TEE-mo." He overenunciated so she wouldn't continue to butcher the name. On her phone, he saw that she had only one contact: Daddy. Strange. Sara didn't strike him as the type to call her father Daddy. She wasn't from the South—or maybe she was. "It's Greek."

"Of course it is."

"The kids all call them the Phi." When he was part of the Philotimo, he would insist everyone use the full name. *The Phi* sounded too much like a fraternity. He handed over her phone, and she tucked it into the back pocket of her jeans. She'd swapped the sexy blazer for a long-sleeved shirt.

"I'll call them the Phi too," Sara replied. She eyed him as if trying to read his mind. "And you want to be one of them someday? Do you get a special ring?"

"Yes to the first, and no to the second." Each leader was currently deciding on an heir to his position, with announcements expected by summer. Beckett had a strong chance to be Ahmad's heir.

"What happens if someone decides their philosophy no longer fits? Can they quit?"

A vein in his forehead throbbed. "It isn't the Mafia. It's a community."

"With powerful leaders."

"And some powerful members."

She sighed. "Sure. I mean, what could go wrong? It's not like your social club could be infiltrated by a criminal organization and twisted to its purpose."

"What are you talking about?" He pressed his fingers into his eye sockets, trying to stave off the burn of being awake for too many hours in a row. "You watch too much television. In real life, the mob isn't taking over everything."

"How do you think I got here?" She rubbed her hands together, though it wasn't terribly cold. How long had she been standing outside? "Don't you know anything about the Agency?"

"Of course. Kohl Shirazi, the owner of La Cuisine, is a retired executive from the Agency. His brother, Ahmad, heads the Philotimo. That's how we were able to contact you and negotiate the deal you proceeded to alter to your own needs." He paused, not wanting to belabor the point or fall into another argument. "Big business doesn't mean criminal. That isn't what we're about."

"You're just about running around being moral."

He held back an aggrieved sigh. "We're about using our powers with intention and considering the welfare of memory magicians as well as the general populace. It's a work in progress, of course, but we want to grow our gifts in a responsible way."

"Sure." She stared at him, her hands still fidgeting. Her slight pout and pinched brow smoothed. "Regardless of the ethics of your moralist Phi-people, we need to keep our personal arrangement to ourselves. Maybe you have the inclination to report this to the leaders of your cult." She held up a hand before he could protest the characterization. "But this needs to stay between us. It's the only way it will work."

"We should consider informing Ahmad, at least."

"No!" Her voice was louder than he'd ever heard it. She grimaced, and her posture loosened. "Sorry. But telling one person is never telling one person. Secrets don't remain secret if you tell anyone."

"As I mentioned, I've already told my mother."

She fisted her hands then spread her fingers wide. "Okay, but she's not a Phi-person, right? Who's she gonna tell? We can't change that, but we can keep it out of the memory surgeon community, right?"

Beckett realized that what she was arguing for was what he'd planned to suggest anyway. Finally, he'd come out on top. "Very well, I agree, as long as there are no more games."

"Of course not." Her innocent smile protested too much.

He sighed. "I'll introduce you to the students tomorrow. We have a meeting every Sunday morning at eight for an hour or two. We eat breakfast, and then we discuss the ethics of our gifts using the Socratic method. I would like you to be there."

"Socrates? I wouldn't miss it." She frowned. "Isn't this spring break?"

Beckett shrugged. "The moral get no rest."

"Morality through sleep deprivation. Interesting." She cocked her head. "I thought it was no rest for the wicked."

He almost smiled. "Which one are you, I wonder?"

"I'll save you the suspense; I am definitely wicked. See you at eight."

* * *

THE NEXT MORNING, ANDREW RANG BECKETT'S DOORBELL AN HOUR before the meeting was supposed to start. Beckett should have expected he would want to pin him down about Sara early. Beckett wouldn't ordinarily keep something like a personal relationship with a memory magician a secret. Certainly not one he'd already vilified and claimed he was going to bring in as his admin.

He opened the door to his church-turned-home and smiled at Andrew, who held two Dunkin' to-go cups, one that was undoubtedly Harmony Green Tea for Beckett and the other filled with coffee for himself.

"What a surprise," Beckett said, taking the cup Andrew proffered and stepping aside.

"You didn't answer any of my texts, so what did you expect?" Andrew countered, walking the length of the living area, which used to be the nave, to the study.

Beckett followed. They sat in their usual seats in the informal sitting room, Beckett in his alligator leather wingback and Andrew in a vintage Gigi Radice Italian armchair Beckett's mother had bought for him.

Andrew had a way of lounging that was part aristocrat and part jungle cat. He crossed one long leg over the other and somehow slouched without breaking his posture. It was an enviable skill.

"Well, you've been busy," Andrew said, taking an indolent sip of his coffee.

It was too early for Andrew's needling sense of humor. Beckett paused for a moment, considering claiming ignorance and making Andrew ask direct questions, but he didn't want to play around. "I like her," he said, surprising himself with the candor and the fact that it was true.

Andrew's grin widened. "Of course you do. Fucking the secretary? I didn't think you had it in you."

Beckett almost choked on his tea. "God, no. She's no longer going to be my admin. That would be inappropriate."

"Yeah, but in a good way. How's the sex? Is it amazing, or is she too obsessed with finding her light?" Andrew let out a groan. "She was all anyone at the party could talk about. You better keep a close eye on her."

The words were too similar to his mother's remarks. He wouldn't discuss his sex life with Andrew, even if he had one to share. "She's already next-door, so I think that's near enough for now."

"So, how is the *experimenting* going, then?" Andrew tamed his amusement, but it didn't disappear entirely. "Surely you've had a gander under the memory magic hood."

"We're going to have our first formal session tomorrow, and I'll have more data then, but, Andrew, I found out how Dominion's been pilfering our students."

Andrew's eyebrows popped. "What?"

"Dominion's been using their gifts to pilfer information from people's memories about our program. Rider tried to read me at the party, and it made me wonder who else has been stealing secrets from me, from you, perhaps from the Philotimo, and even from the mentees. We need to be extra vigilant." Beckett hated they'd been attacked like that, but telling Andrew about it was a convenient distraction from more questions about Sara.

"How do you know?" Andrew asked, not convinced. "That would be such a breach of decorum."

Beckett wasn't ready to tell Andrew about Sara's ability to detect when memory magicians were about to use their powers. He needed to wrap his mind around that before he shared the information with anyone else. "Sara sensed something . . . unsavory, and when we shook hands . . . I read him reading me. He was pursuing details about the program, Andrew."

"Have you told the Phi?"

"Not yet." He sighed. "But I think I have to."

"Ahmad won't care that your incursion was in response to Sara having a bad feeling about the guy."

"I know." As Moralists, they were supposed to uphold their ethics despite what anyone else did. If he were a member of Dominion, he would be praised for his ambition. If he were a Survivalist, he would be censured for a potential security breach. Regardless of the Moralists' philosophy, however, they needed to protect themselves.

"I think we should tell all the students to avoid contact with strangers and be careful ourselves, but I wouldn't tell the Phi," Andrew said.

"Damn it," Beckett groaned, tipping back his head. "This is impossible."

"At least you're finally getting laid."

Nope. He wasn't even getting that.

Sara

S TUDIO A WAS PAST THE KITCHEN DOWN A LONG hallway with blood-red carpet so lush that Sara's heels sank into fibers that screamed, *Oh my God, I am so posh*. It was as vibrant as if it were new. Maybe it was, or possibly elves came in every night and kept it spotless.

Her neck hadn't stopped prickling since the night before, and she hated that her new handler hadn't given her a name beyond Daddy. She'd call him Dickhead in her mind. That name fit well, as one wouldn't forget or underestimate a dickhead's nature.

It was hard to believe the Agency had once meant safety and family. If she'd known they would turn on her, she would have been long gone already. Clearly, it was her destiny that everyone she considered family would betray her.

Beckett had offered to escort her to the gathering, but if she'd allowed that, she would always be considered his arm candy. Garnering respect would be more difficult. If she arrived early, however, their first impression of her wouldn't be tainted by whatever they thought about Beckett or his girlfriends in general.

Time often got away from Sara, and she was as likely to be late as on time, but when it counted, she could be relied upon, and so she headed for the study room fifteen minutes before eight. Sara didn't need much sleep, so 8:00 a.m. on a Sunday wasn't a hardship, even with the extra time to don a full face of makeup and style her hair in a loose side braid, but she couldn't imagine the kids appreciated such an early hour.

What they would appreciate were the Dip and Sip Donuts treats she'd had Grubhubed. The shop had several interesting custom donuts, like the John Lemon Pistachio, Groovy Pebbles, and Elvis's Last Donut. With college boys at the meeting, she doubted there would be any leftovers to go stale, so she'd ordered at least one of each, fourteen all together. The driver had brought everything in an oversized plastic bag, and she carried it looped over her elbow like a heavy handbag.

When she reached the door, she paused. A plaque declared it Studio A, but she was unsure if she should glide inside or wait. She didn't debate long, because she hated waiting and being caught wavering outside the door wouldn't set the image she wanted. Better to risk a rude interruption of some kind than be seen as weak.

Her grand entrance wasn't as epic as it could have been, since there were only two boys there already. One rested his head on the conference table. The other had his head tilted all the way back, exposing his throat so completely that a shudder ran through Sara as she imagined how easy it could be to slit, the carving hand Walther's.

The smell of char seemed to fill the room. A wave of vertigo. Shark eyes. Black gun.

Dead. He was dead.

"I come bearing sustenance," she announced in a voice bright enough to chase away all shadows. This was a new day.

"Coffee?" the one with his head on the table croaked.

"I'm not your waitress, buuuut . . ." Sara slid the bag with all the donut yumminess onto the table. "Voilà."

"Dude, those smell so tasty. I'm starving, but, like, I also think I might spew." The head-on-the-table guy talked to his friend rather than Sara.

She ignored the rudeness. "You have two choices. Go and puke, then come back and eat, or drink a ton of water and eat slowly and see how it goes."

"Who are you?" the tilted-head boy asked. "Are you, like, a nurse?"

"Do I look like a nurse?" Sara gestured to her jeans and her thin, double-layered sweaters. "And before you ask, I'm also not with the kitchen staff, and I'm not a secretary." Thank God for that. "I'm here to help with the program."

They both blinked at her, bleary-eyed. "You're totally fine," head-on-the-table guy said. "Wilson wasn't just high. We really do have a hot girl in the building. We need more chicks like you in the program."

And we need less boys like you in the world.

"Better not let Beckett hear you say that. He might seem mild-mannered, but he's got a serious jealous streak."

That perked the guys up. She pretended not to notice their gawking as she set up the donuts, stretching a tad more than necessary to highlight her height and curves.

The door opened, and two people wearing chef's coats wheeled in carts laden with what smelled like bacon and eggs. Beckett came in behind them. He paused for the briefest moment, eyes sweeping up and down Sara's body. "Ah, Sara. You're, uh, already here."

"I brought donuts," she said, managing to keep her tone light, even if her words were lame. She waited for the nutrition lecture.

"That's considerate of you." He rubbed the back of his neck, then nodded at the kitchen staff as they rolled their now empty carts back out the door. Several covered dishes sat on the table. "I see you've met Jason and Brian. Good morning, boys."

"Good morning, sir," they both parroted.

Sir? They treated her like a servant, but he got a *sir*.

"How's she supposed to help with the program?" Head on the Desk asked.

Was he Brian or . . . What was the other name?

"We'll be discussing that when everyone arrives. Is your belligerent tone a result of over-imbibing, or do you have a particular issue with Ms. Strausser?" Beckett didn't raise or lower his voice. He remained calm and reasonable, and yet, a strain strummed through the room, a primitive warning.

"No disrespect meant to your girlfriend. It was a rough night, sir."

Beckett almost tripped as he moved closer to the table, and Sara had to stifle a giggle.

He recovered quickly enough. "Drink a lot of water, slowly, and that should ease your hangover. Gatorade after that, if you've purged sometime last night or this morning."

"Yes, sir."

Sara smirked—she couldn't stop herself. "You want me to call you sir, too?"

Their eyes locked, and a rush of adrenaline made Sara inhale a sharp sip of air. A different kind of tension wound between them, heady and delicious, because unlike most powerful men, Beckett didn't physically scare her. His power came from privilege, not brute force.

"I don't think that will be necessary, Ms. Strausser."

Why the hell was it sexy when he called her by her last name? He hadn't lowered his voice or growled or raked her body with his eyes. All he'd done was hold eye contact and speak in a normal tone.

"Let me know if you change your mind, Professor Convery."

"I shall."

Sara laughed, their small exchange recharging her mood. He was going to make an awesome fake boyfriend. "I bought a special donut for you."

"That wasn't necessary," he replied, eyeing the donuts as if they might be poisoned.

"It wouldn't be a considerate gesture if it had been," she said with a bigger grin. "Want to guess which is yours, or should I tell you?"

He held his breath for a count of five and exhaled. "Better just tell me."

"Mexican Hot Chocolate." She pointed it out and gave him a saucy wink.

"Very kind. Thank you," Beckett said, plating the chocolate-frosted donut with a dollop of whipped cream and a coffee bean on top. "This looks quite licentious."

"The licentious-est."

Beckett didn't roll his eyes, but he clenched his jaw.

Andrew and three other students piled into the room.

"Donuts!" one of the kids crowed and dove for the box.

"Miller," Beckett snapped. "Sit down. Once we're all seated, we can fill our plates."

Beckett's spot was clearly at the head of the table, where he'd have a view of the door and his back to the wall. He pulled out a seat for Sara, the place to his left. Her back would also be to the wall. "Thank you," she said as she lowered herself into the chair.

By that time, the surly girl who'd shut her door in Sara's face had shown up, along with two other boys, one of whom she'd met in the common area last night—the studier. He gave her a small smile and a little wave. Andrew sat to Beckett's right, slinging an arm over the chair back so he had a view of the open door.

Five minutes after eight, a tall, lanky boy with his boxer waistband clearly visible above his low-slung jeans strolled in. He wore a faded Mellow Yellow T-shirt and a sloppy man-bun. His eyes were almost shut he was so high. PlayStation guy from the night before.

"Yo, man, sorry I'm late," he drawled, sliding bonelessly into a vacant chair. "Hey, Sara."

"Hi," she said.

"Now that everyone is here," Beckett said, "Sara, please help yourself to breakfast."

She wasn't sure if he was being gentlemanly or treating her like a guest of honor, but she liked it. "Thanks." She snagged one of the All You Need Is Bacon donuts, then three whole pieces of bacon and a hunk of veggie omelet.

Everybody gawked at her plate and then her, and she laughed to cover her discomfort. She waited for someone to ask her where she kept it all, as if it was any of their business if she had a fast metabolism, liked a big breakfast, suffered from an eating disorder, or if she hadn't eaten enough the day before. But no one said anything.

"Go ahead," Sara said, nodding toward the food, but none of the students moved.

Beckett helped himself next. He left his Mexican Hot Chocolate donut on a small plate and spooned some omelet onto another plate, along with a small bit of diced potatoes and a smattering of fruit, heavy on the honeydew. Once Andrew had loaded his plate, then the kids all got to fill theirs. They fought good-naturedly over the special donuts, asking Sara to say what each of them were.

The boys saved the pink donut for the girl—typical—but she refused to eat any of the donuts. Sara wondered if she eschewed anything clearly feminine, perhaps thinking it made her somehow less vulnerable to misogyny. She seemed to deliberately avoid acknowledging Sara.

After ten minutes in which they ate and didn't chat, Beckett set his fork and knife at the top of his plate as if making a pitched roof.

"Let me introduce Sara Strausser," he said.

Sara waved to the table, waiting to see what he would say about her. *She's my girlfriend? She's got a special gift? Her memories can't be read? Her presence is a secret?*

The table all gave her a hello.

"Sara is a memory magician," he said.

That surprised her. Having a non-power didn't make her a . . . she was *not* a magical person. Though some might say her personality was magical. Ha.

"She's joining the program?" Brian—maybe?—asked.

"No, she's working with Andrew and me to further study the breadth and depths of our gifts. She'll be staying on the premises, but she isn't a student." Beckett hesitated, clearly having more to say, and everyone waited.

"Jesus," Andrew muttered, breaking into a huge grin. "She's also his girlfriend. That's what he's trying to say."

Sara grinned, glad to have third-party confirmation. All eyes bounced back to her, their collective gaze digging deep. But Sara was used to being gawked at, and it didn't bother her. Beckett's description of her place in the group, though, made her esophagus prickle as if she'd swallowed a stinging nettle stalk. She had to be more than his girlfriend and a nondescript helper. Living there for free and doing nothing? A moocher? They wouldn't respect her. While the admin job would have given her that, it would have eroded her self-esteem in other ways. She had to contribute in some way, to earn her money and their respect.

"Nice," one of the kids mumbled.

Snickers all around.

"I think you'll find Sara will be a great addition to the team," Beckett said in a tight voice. "Why don't we go around the table and introduce ourselves?"

Sara stopped eating, needing to focus if she wanted to remember everyone's name.

"Andrew Brussell," Andrew said, winking at her.

Sara smiled and didn't roll her eyes. He was studly-handsome, in a thick, wool sweater and stylishly worn jeans, his hair tousled in a way that required time, effort, and significant product to stay in place for more than five minutes.

Around the table they went:

Brian—head-on-the-table guy—was blond and neither attractive nor unattractive. Boring Brian.

Jason—head-tilted-back guy—had dark hair and a pronounced Adam's apple and was average in almost every way. Just Jason.

Marlena—surly girl—wore too much eyeliner and hadn't blended enough. She had high cheekbones and a low attitude. Sara didn't need to give her a nickname since she was the only young woman.

Wilson—the PlayStation stoner kid. Sara thought of Wilson, the *Cast*

Away volleyball, surrounded by a smoky haze. Whooooaaaa Wilson.

Kenji was Japanese. He had lovely skin, shaggy hair, and a crooked smile. His clothes were fashionably ratty and the slightest bit too large, giving him a casual air. Kenji the Casual.

Erik was a dark-skinned Black kid with hair shaved close on the sides and shortish twists on top. He wore a button-down with jeans and several hemp bracelets. Sara liked his eclectic ensemble. Aesthetic Erik.

Last was the boy next to her. Brayton, the studier she'd met the day before, was blond and broad in both face and body. He had a toothpaste-commercial smile and likely received weekly facials. His nails were lustrous. Everything about him was polished. Buff Brayton.

Nobody talked about their specific gifts or shared more than where they were from, and most of them were from one of the many rich suburbs of Chicago.

"Where are you from?" Boring Brian asked with an intensity Sara interpreted as suspicion.

"Pretty much every major city in the country," she replied, which was the truth. She'd grown up in the small town of Goshen, Utah, but she wouldn't share that. She didn't need to revisit her past, even as memories intruded anyway. Her mother had worried more about herself than she'd ever worried about Sara. When men had paid Sara attention, her mother had always blamed her. She'd also made her wear clothing that even the Mormon kids had found conservative. Her stepfather, who'd "accidentally" opened the locked bathroom door on more than one occasion, had considered her a skank because when she'd hit puberty, her breasts had grown big and fast, as if breast tissue caused sluttiness.

"I want Sara to sit in on our meeting today to get a feel for what we do," Beckett said, "who we are, and who we aspire to be. But first, I want to issue a warning. As you know, we've lost five members of the program to the Dominion sect. We have reason to believe they're recruiting by using their memory gifts, so everyone be extra careful about who you let touch you."

"Sound advice in general, I think," Sara said, and most of the kids laughed.

Andrew tapped his hands on the table. "Now, ethical question of the day: If you learn something unsavory about someone via your gift that affects a friend, like, say, a cheating girlfriend, do you share the info with your friend?"

"Yes," said Just Jason.

Sara wanted to ask, *How did you get that information? Were you randomly rooting around in that person's head?* Had the group already determined that snooping behavior was okay?

"Please elaborate, Jason," Beckett said.

None of the other kids interjected, though it was clear a few of them longed to jump into the conversation.

"Our gift gives us a moral obligation to do good with it," Jason said. "Uncovering a deception isn't evil-evil, but not protecting a friend? That can't be right."

"What if the friend doesn't know you're a memory magician?" Andrew asked.

Jason chewed on a hangnail. "Maybe I could pretend I witnessed the skankiness?"

"Even though you didn't?" Andrew asked.

"I don't know."

"Reason it out, Jason. Think out loud, if it helps," Beckett said, his deep voice patient.

Andrew and Beckett grilled Jason, albeit nicely, for at least a half hour, exploring every variation of the scenario. Jason faltered several times but had decisive moments too. The other students watched and listened attentively, some with calculation, as if searching for weaknesses, while others seemed to be answering the questions in their own heads.

Sara found herself riveted as well, but Beckett commanded most of her attention. He'd set aside his usual condescension and authority and encouraged Jason to view all sides. He pointed out that what Jason found acceptable or unacceptable wouldn't be the same for everyone, and that was okay. Beckett's reassurance surprised and softened Sara.

Andrew, on the other hand, was more aggressive and colder, making him the antagonist as he tried to herd Jason into a corner. Or maybe he was the bad cop to Beckett's good cop. Strange, as she would have cast them in the opposite roles.

She didn't like Andrew. He was too slick, too attractive, with overly bleached teeth and a jacked-up physique built for the purpose of his ego. She'd known too many Andrews, thanks to the Agency.

Sara felt guilty about potentially hurting Beckett's faction in order to gain her freedom from the Agency. The Moralists might have connections—known or unknown—to a criminal organization, but at least they had the decency to question their choices and philosophies. Sara had never been allowed to question anything.

Explicit orders weren't required for Sara to know the Agency intended harm. It didn't surveil people to lift them up. Every spy gig she'd ever worked had been aimed at taking someone down, though those targets had been criminals and criminal organizations. She couldn't imagine Beckett was knowingly involved in illegal activities, so that meant the Agency wanted to take something from him. The kids, probably. Assets.

She'd joined the Agency at seventeen, when she'd thought she knew so much from living on the streets, but she hadn't known shit. The Agency had given her a purpose and a family. She'd needed both so badly, she hadn't cared about the price. They'd whored her out, and she'd thanked them for it. Even now, part of her missed that life—the people, anyway.

What would they do to kids who weren't yet jaded enough to understand the depth of evil in the world?

CHAPTER TWELVE

Beckett

ECKETT TAPPED HIS FINGERS ON HIS DESK AND glanced again at his watch. 1:44 p.m. When they'd parted yesterday morning, Sara had agreed to meet him for an assessment of her brand of memory magic at 1:30 p.m. He wanted to see if she could block him in a controlled setting, when he was fully concentrating. The halls were mostly quiet with an occasional squeak from sneakers on the engineered hardwood floors.

Was she coming at all?

Everything regarding her now reflected on him: her attitude, their collective progress on defining and cataloging her gift, her interactions with the students, all of it. And so far, he was unimpressed. Yes, Jason had eagerly participated yesterday, no doubt to impress her, and all the boys seemed to view her in a positive light. Marlena, however, had cast Sara disapproving sneers throughout the meeting. He hoped Sara's presence didn't chase Marlena away. He couldn't lose the only woman in his psychic enrichment program.

If Sara ended up deciding not to cooperate, she could damage his reputation and standing with the Moralists—and possibly destroy his opportunity to win the leadership position as Ahmad's heir.

He should be using this time to do something productive, but his ire continued to snap his attention into little chunks that wouldn't bear any sort of concentration. She had usefully identified Rider as a threat, but her lateness now showed a lack of concern for his time. Punctuality was the base level of respect. Perhaps she imagined preening in front of everyone as his *girlfriend* made her exempt from common courtesy.

She stumbled inside, shopping bags slapping into the door frame. "Sorry! So sorry! I completely lost track of time, and I was downtown, and oh my God, there shouldn't have been so much traffic. It's not even two!"

Beckett stood, a reflex from years of learned decorum. He held up a hand to stop the tirade of woes. "Ms. Strausser, I'm not interested in the details of why you behave so disrespectfully. I think—"

"I don't—I mean, I didn't—"

"Let's get to work so we can salvage something from this afternoon. We can discuss your lateness later."

"Okay." She set her bags right at the door. "Are we going to do it here? Why are we in your office during spring break? Should I sit down? Lie down? Stand?"

Beckett held out his hand to indicate the Miro armchair in front of his desk. "Sit. Please."

She slipped into the green wool seat, hands on her thighs, posture perfect. "Yes, sir."

He pursed his lips and ignored her childish innuendo and sat too. "I'll start where I always start. How much do you know about memory magic? I assume little since you typically use the term 'memory surgeon.'"

"If there're more than memory surgeons out there, then it's news to me. You call yourself a magician, though, right? Does that mean what you do is a trick?" Her body tilted forward as if she really wanted the answer to that question.

"It's not a trick." He shrugged. "It's magic. And what is magic but that which we cannot understand."

"Like math." She grinned.

Beckett tapped on the shiny surface of his rosewood desk. "Scientists have done PET scans and MRIs and ultrasounds, taken blood, urine, and stool samples. They've studied our brainwaves and cardiac rhythms, monitored our core temperatures, and charted our sleep patterns. The research into our DNA is ongoing, but so far, they've turned up no anomalies. Science has no answers for us." He held out his hands. "As Sherlock Holmes says, 'When you have eliminated all which is impossible, then whatever remains, however improbable, must be the truth.' Magic."

"So, what do you want with me?" She used one thumb to rub the nail of the other thumb. Her nails were a glossy pink with gold tips, and Beckett imagined the smooth texture of the lacquer. Had he ever noticed anything like that on anyone else before?

"Being magic doesn't mean we can't learn and grow and expand our talents. We'll work together to see what you can do with your gift and how you might be able to do more. What I really hope is for all memory magicians to have the ability to consistently block others and maybe note when someone is using a gift against us."

"I'm not magic, just stubborn."

Like called to like, and he didn't need to assess her to know his inability to read her was a result of memory magic. A kind he had never encountered before. "An unconscious talent isn't less valuable, Sara. Our organization is a secret because we believe if the general population had an idea of how many of us there are and the breadth of the talents we possess, they would be threatened by us. When people are frightened, they are volatile and dangerous. Your gift, your *magic*, could save lives."

She looked into his eyes, seeming to search for something like confirmation he was speaking truth. Beckett held her gaze, opening himself enough for her to see his hopes and the sliver of fear that haunted everyone who had a memory talent. She was a part of the community now, too—not the Moralists, but the society of memory magicians.

He wanted her trust, and he offered to trust her in return. Suddenly, her lateness, her flippancy, her casual attitude, even her beauty didn't matter.

They were two people, sharing a gift. Sharing a moment. Beckett sensed in her a vulnerability, sensed that she used humor to deflect attention. He wouldn't push—that never worked—but he held on to the connection between them. If she recognized his seeing her, that was a start.

"Okay," she finally said. Although her voice was soft, it broke the spell.

She rubbed her hands over her thighs while Beckett knocked a fist on his desk.

"Let's get started, and we can talk more about the memory magician world later." He rolled his chair around the desk as she stood. "Just turn a bit so we're across from each other."

Once they were situated, their knees almost touched. He held out his hand. She paused before taking it.

"Can you sense my presence?" he asked, though he wasn't doing anything. He needed to ensure the placebo effect didn't color her perceptions.

Sara shook her head and licked her lips. The tension in her hand could have been from the intensity of the earlier moment or dread over the exercise.

Beckett shoved everything out of his consciousness except the task at hand. "Tell me when you sense something."

She nodded.

He opened his mind to his gift.

"Now? I don't feel you in my head, but—" She exhaled. "Oh."

"What?"

"Your eyes." They stared at each other, but it wasn't awkward, likely because they were both so intent on seeing something in the other.

"What about my eyes?"

Her own blue eyes were so brilliant they could easily drown him.

"I don't know." A small line creased her brow.

Beckett wanted to fetch his phone and have her film his eyes to try to capture what she was seeing, but he didn't want to break the energy between them. Something was happening, and what if it was something groundbreaking, and he ruined it with his impatience? "Is that what usually happens when you spot a memory magician—you see something in their eyes?"

She frowned. "You know how sometimes you can tell when someone's annoyed with you, even if they don't do or say anything?"

"Yes, but what does that have to do with my eyes?" He squeezed her hand so she would know he wasn't criticizing. "The more specific you can be, the easier it will be to parse this out."

Sara's fingers jerked as if she'd wanted to yank them away. "I honestly don't know why I said anything happened with your eyes."

He swiped a thumb over the back of her hand to reassure her. "It's okay. This is the first time we've tried to break it down, and I'm not expecting a particular outcome. We're only seeing what's there."

"But you're disappointed."

Briefly, he considered denying it. "I'm not disappointed in you. Any idea how long you've had this gift? Is it new?"

She shook her head. "I first noticed . . ." Her hands gripped his tightly for a moment, then relaxed. "About two or three years ago. My boss . . . I knew he was attempting something. And after a few times, I told him to stop. He did. I'm not sure why or how I put it together, but we had a memory surgeon—sorry, memory magician—on our team, and though she never tried to read me, I just knew what he'd been doing. We never talked about it."

Her voice had grown rough, her eyes shiny. Beckett didn't push.

"When I first got my power, I was old, like twenty-three," he said, changing the subject so she could recover.

She laughed, her spirit rebounding as if she'd never been low. "As a twenty-four-year-old, I'm going to take offense at you calling twenty-three old."

Beckett cocked his head in concession. "Old for a talent to emerge, not old for a human being."

Sara smiled, and he felt that connection again. "Were you scared?" she asked.

"No," he replied. He'd thought it made him special, and he'd been beyond proud, even if it was simply genetics or random luck. "What I encounter when my gift is at work is a buzz of energy, sometimes a sense of floating, or I see colored lights, like comets, in my mind's eye, which I've come to discover is how my brain processes the minds of others. If I reach out, I can delve into their thoughts. Did you experience any physical reactions when you're blocking?"

"Before I get a headache, I do feel something. Not floating, but something floaty-ish? Like the moment between an inhale or an exhale, you know?"

Beckett nodded. This was progress. If he could have read her mind, then he might have seen for himself, but her discovering it on her own was better anyway. "Can you examine a little deeper, if we try again?"

At her nod, he opened his power again, ready but not seeking.

She pursed her lips. "Yeah, kind of a . . . pause. You also don't blink very much when you're . . . ramping up? Preparing? Is that what you're doing?"

"I call it priming, but I don't believe it has official nomenclature."

She smiled, amusement making her blue eyes brighter, though that was likely an optical illusion or his subconscious adding attributes because her smile felt so genuine. "Nomenclature? Do they teach you how to use the most alienating language possible in rich-kid school?'

Because they were staring into each other's eyes, he saw the teasing glint in hers, so he wasn't offended by her jab. "They teach us the power of specificity of language. I'd also like to point out you used 'alienating language' in a sentence. Surely you could have used a less expensive phrase."

She laughed. "I have a habit of picking up the speech patterns of people around me." Her face relaxed, thoughts skimming over her face in ways he couldn't articulate. "I'm not dumb, you know."

"I'm aware." He might have made unflattering assumptions about her intelligence when he'd first met her, but she had an insightful cunning he appreciated. He pressed his gift close to her mind, not attempting to penetrate but prospecting for familiar lines of consciousness. Her mindscape suddenly wasn't empty but barricaded, an opaque fortification. A faint blue line pulsed in the distance.

"You're doing something now, right?" she asked, face pinched in concentration.

"I'm sidling up to your mind but not reaching inside. Does that make sense?"

"Like my brainbox is a house, and you're peeping through the windows?"

His lips quirked into a smile, which he quickly dropped. *Focus.* "It's an apt metaphor. All the shades are drawn on your windows. This is evolvement, though, as initially, I didn't see or feel anything."

"Oh, well, that was probably my moat."

"Hm." Beckett considered that. "You're joking, but you might not be far off. What if you don't have a single barrier but a series of them?" He didn't point out she'd let him past the first one, because he didn't want her to take it back. "How does it feel?"

She dragged her bottom lip over her teeth and blinked. "It feels like . . . It doesn't hurt, but there's an unsettling pressure in the back of my head. Is that where memories are stored? In the back of the brain?"

"No, they're stored everywhere—or so scientists believe. But my gift is only for short-term memory—your current thoughts. Sometimes those memories are coded into long-term memory storage, and other times, they're lost forever." He hadn't whispered, but his tone had softened, as if he was sharing a secret. The tone was unprofessional, but it was impossible to wear his professor hat while staring into Sara's eyes. Her interest seemed genuine and open, and he found himself intrigued, not solely with her gift, but with *her.*

"Is that why I always forget someone's name the second after I meet them?"

"Yes." Something grew in the silence between them, something entirely too intimate. "Are you ready to move on?"

"Okay," she said, the word more breath than voice.

With his mind, he pressed deeper into her thoughts. Except her mind felt nothing like anyone else's. The energy was thick, almost pressurized, and the borders of her consciousness were a pearly white, though he could see the faint blue line, he couldn't reach it. Every step he took forward brought him no closer.

She gripped his hand. "How much longer?"

"Does it hurt?"

"Yes. It starts as an ache in the back of my head, but then it gets . . . bigger and sharper, and I really want to toss you out."

Beckett jumped as if he'd been goosed. "You can eject me?"

"I'm pretty sure."

"Do it."

"I don't want to hurt you."

It was a kindness he hadn't expected, and it did something to his chest, caused an alien kind of warmth. "It's okay. We need to test everything."

A light flashed behind Beckett's eyes as if he'd been bashed in the head. Dizziness bubbled up from his abdomen to swamp his thoughts. He released his hold on Sara's hand. She jumped to her feet and put one hand on his shoulder and the other under his chin, raising his face.

Beckett twisted away and covered his eyes. The light was too bright in his office. Sara ran to the door, and suddenly it was dimmer—she must have shut off the overhead lights. The room was still too bright, but then she rushed to the window and closed the blinds.

Blessed dark filled the room, and Beckett bent over, elbows on his knees, face in his hands. Inside his skull, ideas and snippets of images buffeted around like flotsam and jetsam in a storm. Waves and waves of pain crashed and crashed.

Sara gripped his shoulder. "Drink this."

Beckett took the short, fat, gold-glitter-encrusted bottle she handed him and downed the water. The liquid was cool and cleared a small part of the confusion in his mind.

"What did you do?" he asked. "And how did you know it would hurt?"

She took the empty water bottle and dropped it into one of her giant shopping bags. Bloomingdale's mostly, with a Max Mara and Neiman Marcus thrown in the mix. Did she shop every week? Was she already spending money she hadn't earned? Had she bought any lingerie?

"That memory surgeon—memory magician—I told you about, the one on my team, she was on a job, and someone slammed the door on her while she was rooting around. That's how she described it. So, I thought pushing you out might be the same thing, and I was right." She walked behind him and squeezed the muscles of his neck.

He shouldn't allow it, but . . . they were fabricating dating, so he decided it was acceptable. And her hands felt sublime, the touch of her warm fingers counterbalancing the concussive knocking in his head.

"A . . . regular person did that to her? So, anyone could do what you just did? It isn't another gift of yours?"

"That's my guess. He wasn't a memory surgeon, that's for sure, and he didn't know she was in his mind."

"How do you know he was unaware?" He didn't trust Sara's appraisal when it came to memory magic since she knew so little.

"Because if he'd known, he wouldn't have let us leave." She patted his shoulders. "Not everyone is as forgiving as me when you people pry into our thoughts uninvited."

"You did invite me."

"Only today."

"I apologized already for when we first met."

Her fingers combed through his hair from the crown to his neck, making his scalp tingle. He found it easier to talk to her now that she was behind him, and he'd lost control of the tidiness and rigidity of his mind.

"Are you apologizing, or are you sorry?" She didn't stop stroking his hair. "Those are two very different things."

"I'm sorry, Sara. I would never have attempted if I had known it would distress you."

"Is that what you think makes it wrong? That you got caught? Is that what you're teaching all these kids—go for it, just don't get pinched?" She sounded more amused than outraged, which was confusing.

"It's . . . We need to practice, to hone our skills, and if those we interact with are none the wiser, then where is the harm, truly?" Beckett said, the familiar argument bringing him back to himself.

"So, if I break into your house and read your diary, that's okay if you don't know I did it?" Sara moved her hands to his shoulders and started kneading the muscles there. "What if I go through your browser history and make note of all the porn you watch? Contact all your ex-girlfriends and ask them questions about how the sex was?"

"I comprehend your point, Sara, but what else can we do?"

"Why don't you practice on each other?"

"We tried that at first, actually, but using our gifts on one another doesn't replicate natural experiences. We are all too aware of what is transpiring, and it's quite a harrowing experience to know someone is inside your thoughts. There's nothing natural about it."

"You don't say."

Beckett's cognitive functions wouldn't coalesce, and the argument began to slip through his fingers. "What we're doing here, it might change everything. We're going to make the world a better place, Sara."

She patted him on the shoulders two quick raps. "Sure you are."

CHAPTER THIRTEEN

Sara

S ARA WALKED HOME AT A LEISURELY PACE, THE handles on her bags digging into her palms. She'd avoided returning to her new apartment long enough. The setting sun was at blinding-eye level, and the spring air was sharp, and her head preferred it. Her thoughts looped around, analyzing her situation and her "testing" with Beckett.

Had he intentionally let her hurt him to gain her trust? It was the sort of thing she might do, but it wasn't Beckett's style. He had an earnestness to him that could be faked, but she didn't think he did. If he were going to fake a demeanor, he'd act a lot humbler.

At her building, she dropped her bags and started digging through her purse for the keycard that would open the front door. It wasn't in her wallet, which would have been the obvious place to put it. She searched the side zipper pocket to her purse. Rummaged through the contents at the bottom. Nowhere. Had she already lost the keycard?

She dug through her coat pockets. Lipstick, lip balm, lip liner, a few tissues, a random quarter, and a CVS receipt. At last, she checked her back jeans pocket, and there it was.

Sara let loose a joyful cry and did a tiny shimmy dance before tapping the card on the electronic pad. She opened the door and wedged her foot inside as she stretched to wrangle all her bags. There was an elevator, but since Sara didn't like exercise other than yoga, she walked everywhere she could and always took the stairs. Functional exercise.

At her door, she stared at the keypad. Numbers swirled in her brain like ping-pong balls at a bingo game. Sara had chosen the code, so it should be easy to remember. But, of course, it wasn't. She had too many thoughts shaking loose.

With her eyes closed, she took herself back in time to recall her frame of mind when she'd selected the code. She'd been excited about flipping the script on Beckett. So, something cheeky? Yes. She squinted at the keypad. Beckett Is My Bitch. She checked the letters below the numbers: 2-4-5-2.

Nope. 2-4-6-2? That worked.

Inside, she struggled to see everything at once, checking for intruders. Empty. It had a vacant vibe too, which she trusted—to a point. She released the packages and did a quick tour of the rooms. Closets. Behind the shower curtain. Under the bed. Nobody there.

With a grateful sigh, she kicked off her pumps and skipped back to her haul: jeans, jewel-toned tops, a little black dress.

For the next thirty minutes, she cut off tags and tried on all her new clothes. She went through shoe choices and took photographs to remember what she liked.

After, she strolled into the kitchen wearing nothing but a short, silk robe and panties. She opened a cabinet to snag a glass and found boxed food. Her heart screeched and leaped like a cat avoiding water.

Her brain entertained the thought she'd mistaken where she'd decided to put things, but her bones knew otherwise. Dickhead had been in her living space again, moving objects around to torment her. Proving he could get to her. He hadn't forgotten about her. He was the one in control. He expected a report.

* * *

THE NEXT DAY, BECKETT PUSHED BACK THEIR MEETING TO SIX-THIRTY and asked her on a walk since he'd been cooped up in his office most of the day. Sara had spent her day playing with hairstyles in an effort not to think about the Agency and what they might do to Beckett, to the program, and to her if she didn't betray the first two.

Beckett called her to come down, which was disappointing boyfriend behavior, but when she readied to tell him so, he looked a bit wilted with his loosened tie and creased button-down. Besides, her disappointment would probably mean nothing to him.

Only Marlena was there to witness their interaction, but Sara made a big show of hugging him, pressing her breasts into his chest, and landing a smackeroo on his cheek. He brushed a hand down her back and tipped his head to the side. Sara hated how endearing she found that. He'd definitely won that exchange.

After picking up smoothies from Jackalope Coffee and Tea, they walked to the Henry C. Palmisano Nature Park, a wooden-slatted walking path with a small lake, or large pond, and mostly prairie views, the downtown skyscrapers in the distance.

The evening was warm enough Sara needed only a light jacket, and she enjoyed the thinning sun on her face and the slight breeze. She'd worn her hair in a half-up messy top knot so it wouldn't blow in her face too much.

Beckett relayed his plans for their continued exploration of her "magic," including adding Andrew.

Sara swirled her straw in her wildberry smoothie and ignored the pinch of her gut at that news. "What's the deal with you and him?"

They had almost the whole pathway circling the park to themselves. Beckett's hard-soled shoes clicked on the wood as they walked. "This entire program is something we came up with together." He nearly smiled. "The idea was mine, having grown up in a household that valued education. I thought it would behoove the magical community and our skills if we trained like any other, but not in a vacuum and with a focus on how we fit into the fabric of society. If we give no thought to our power, it's easy to use it thoughtlessly. Andrew and I were already professors at Wells, and gifts typically manifest between the ages of fifteen and twenty-one, so this was the perfect place to run a trial program."

"And Andrew came along for the ride?"

"Not exactly. The program is my passion-project, but Andrew has been with me since the beginning. He was the one who suggested the Socratic method for exploring the ethics of our talents. Together, we made a list of topics we thought we could prospect."

"Like gold?"

"Precisely."

He took a tentative sip of his strawberry banana smoothie, lost in his thoughts. "I'm aware I'm a bit . . . staid."

Sara remembered the sure way he'd guided her the day before and couldn't bitch slap his pride. "Nothing wrong with being overly formal."

Beckett did smile then, a weak and pathetic showing that somehow hooked her ribcage and tugged ruthlessly. "For an embarrassingly long time, I thought everyone was like me."

He plucked his thumb over his straw, reminding Sara of how he'd stroked her neck at the faculty party. Her face flushed, and her stomach did an indolent flip, all the more arresting for the slow, deliberate pleasure.

Beckett met her eyes and then moved his gaze to somewhere else—the past maybe, though he was looking toward the city skyline. "Everybody has several personas inside them. We act differently with our friends than our parents, at work versus at home. I knew this, intellectually, but I never had a carefree irreverence or a truant streak."

Sara couldn't stop her smile, picturing a young Beckett every bit as serious as he was now.

This was bad. She couldn't like him, and yet his honesty was injecting warmth under her skin.

Better to focus instead on the early-blooming yellow flowers around her. Daffodils?

He continued, "It wasn't until I was fourteen or fifteen, when I went to a classmate's house while we were on mini-break to work on a project, and I witnessed him interacting with his father. They were so casual with each other. I'd witnessed similar dynamics in movies and such, and I always assumed it was a Hollywood ideal and that most families were like mine. Formal and respectful, with clear roles and a sort of distance. What a shock it was to discover my family was the anomaly." His deep voice had slid into wistfulness.

"I've seen you and your mom together, and maybe it isn't the warmest relationship, but she clearly cares about you. Not everybody has that, you know." Sara hadn't. "Isn't being loved enough, even if it's not in the way you'd prefer?"

"Oh, I was quite comfortable with our dynamic, but . . . I had a difficult time relating to boys my age. It was as if I were a time traveler from a different era, and I could not acclimate to the culture."

"You do have an old-school gentleman vibe," Sara said, grinning at him. Their arms brushed comfortably. "And, I'll admit you occasionally have your own kind of charm."

"You flatter me," he replied, his dry tone making her laugh. "But we've digressed. We were discussing Andrew."

Hopefully, something about Andrew would prove useful. She wouldn't mind spilling his secrets, and maybe that information would distract Dickhead from Beckett.

"He has an effortless way about him the students relate to instinctively. I've never met anyone with better rapport-building skills than he has." He scratched his nose. "Except you."

"Did you just . . . compliment me, Mr. Convery?" Sara widened her eyes and dropped her jaw. After a beat, she elbowed him and added, "You want to take it back now, don't you?"

"Certainly not," he said, that hint of a smile returning.

Sara made it her goal in life to make Beckett smile a real smile and, as a stretch goal, to make him belly laugh. "So, you and Andrew are only coworkers, then?"

He cocked his head. "We've been friends since boarding school, before either of us manifested any gifts. For our undergraduate work, we both chose Stanford because it has top English and philosophy programs, so we could go there together. But then I wanted to focus my studies on Shakespeare, so I earned my PhD at King's College London, and Andrew earned his doctorate at U of C."

"You moved back here after London?" Sara tried to imagine a life where she went to college in London but couldn't. She could barely manage to envision going there as a tourist.

He sipped his smoothie. "UK programs are shorter, so I came to Wells first and Andrew followed. My mother was still dean here at the time, so I was able to use that connection to secure our positions as associate professors."

Sara giggled. "Your mom gave you your job?"

"She did. My great-grandfather founded the school, so we're both legacies of a sort. I leveraged that to get Shakespeare classes added to the curriculum. Now you know my dirty, nepotistic secret."

His family had built a fucking college. All her mother had managed to build was resentment. Beckett's life had been so different from her own. She'd spent much of her life surviving and never truly living. Never seeing the vastness of the world. Never making choices someone hadn't already made for her.

"So, tell me about your group," she said. *Preferably something scandalous.*

"Safety is always the top priority, for everyone," Beckett replied. "If we consider Maslow's hierarchy of needs, it's clear we can't progress in our development until we're safe, that we have clothing, food, shelter, and are free from physical danger.

"This is where other factions and ours diverge. We believe the way we protect ourselves is by weaving ourselves deep into the fabric of society. If we're seen as being part of the whole, the 'us,' then we're secure. Humans naturally protect their own. We need to be authority figures, innovators, pioneers, icons and thought leaders. Above reproach. If we're the best of humanity, then we're safe."

"But not everybody believes that?"

"No. You were there when I warned the students about Dominion. They're a well-organized faction that agrees leadership is the key, but they want to rule the world by any means necessary. Dominion is convinced that once their power reaches a tipping point, when they've secured enough leadership positions, they can control the population. They're naive and, let's face it, somewhat monstrous in their mission."

"How is reading people's thoughts going to lead to world domination?"

"It's a tool. If you know what the job interviewer desires, you can get that job. Any job. You can blackmail people, prey on a person's specific fear, seduce people in power, manipulate almost any situation. They are going to slip their people into every powerful position they can. Then one day, there's going to be positions and privileges only memory magicians can possess."

The ice in her blood crackled through her chest. "Okay, and the power-hungry people are stealing your recruits? That's disturbing." Too bad she wasn't groping for intel on Dominion. Why wasn't the Agency focusing on them? They seemed like a fated-mate pairing. Maybe she'd broach the subject with Dickhead, ascertain if he could be convinced of a new target.

Beckett sighed. "The promise of safety through your own strength is quite a draw, and it seems so much easier, doesn't it? Make the rules rather than abide by the dictates of others? However, they don't explore or admit to the flaws in that philosophy."

A young couple pushing a stroller greeted them as they passed. Sara waited for them to move out of earshot. "How are you going to fight that?"

"By introducing questions and doubt. A person who challenges everything they hear is less likely to be fooled into a false paradigm."

Brayton, as polished as ever, even in running attire, jogged toward them. Sara threaded her fingers through Beckett's. It was surprisingly natural.

She waved at Brayton with her free hand. Brayton grinned at Sara and saluted Beckett as he loped past. Beckett gave a sharp nod in acknowledgment. So stiff, but . . . it was somehow becoming charming.

WTF.

Sara rested her head on his shoulder—for a moment—breathing in his meadow and violet cologne and the spring air, letting herself believe for a bit that he really was her boyfriend. Not working, not hustling, just being.

But she wasn't allowed to just be, not for long. She nudged him with a soft elbow. "So, you guys are like the brainy high school kids, the power-hungry faction is the popular crowd, and you said there's another one? Like the outcasts?"

"Actually, yes. There's a faction whose sole focus is staying under the radar. They're either hiding in plain sight or establishing off-the-grid communes or underground networks. They're not into meetings and conferences, but dark web conversations and computer hacking."

"So, they're, like, conspiracy theorists?"

He didn't pull away from her, and his hand remained entwined with hers. "We call them Survivalists. Being in a group draws attention, so they aren't typically organized in any public way. It's not that they don't recruit, but they're covert about it. That sort of clandestineness appeals to some young people. It can be like joining a secret society."

"I want to join a secret society!" Sara's brain raced through possibilities: handshakes, special pins, hidden lairs, cloaks. Besides, survival was kind of her thing. She swung their joined hands.

"They are the least fun of all the factions. At any rate, it's too late; you're part of mine."

Beckett had claimed her. Or was he playing devoted boyfriend even with nobody to witness it?

Sara shook her head and laughed into a breeze that brought the aroma of greenery and spring. "You guys sure are full of yourselves: Moralists, Dominion, Survivalists. My memory surgeon friend just calls herself a person."

"How prosaic."

He made a good argument. After hearing his descriptions of all the factions, she wanted to join the Moralists and spy on either of the other cults. But she didn't have the power to do that.

If she had to inflict damage on Beckett's program, though, maybe she could offset her betrayal by contributing something worthwhile.

"You know," she said, "teenagers are joining these groups because everyone wants a place to belong. You're giving them that, but you aren't providing them anything shiny."

"Are you proposing we give them you?" He shook his head. "Have you already forgotten you're *my* fictitious girlfriend?"

It was the most playful thing she'd ever heard him say, and it made her giggle, a real laugh that bubbled up her throat. "No, I'm talking about party planning. That's something I'm good at, and the kids you're recruiting will love it. You think this magic of theirs is going to automatically bond them, but people don't work like that." She thought of the way her Agency team had turned into a family, not because of the job but because of how they'd relied on one another. Maybe she could build a little of that here. She bounced on her toes. "We'll have toga parties, paintball outings, movie screenings—"

"Sara—" He released her hand and shoved it in his blazer pocket.

She put her hand on his biceps, which was firmer than she'd anticipated. It took a moment for her thoughts to realign. "We won't do nightly events, but at least once a week. Doesn't that sound like fun?"

Beckett pursed his lips. "I comprehend the need for levity, but I don't want to become known as the party faction. The stakes are high, Sara, potentially life or death. I don't see how playing dress-up fits into that."

He hadn't actually considered her proposal. "You know, not everyone is like you, wanting to be serious every moment of the day. You're building a program suited to you when you should be trying to appeal to a broader audience."

They tossed their empty cups into a garbage can and turned toward Arden, their outing clearly better ended sooner rather than later, as both their tempers frayed. As if they were of one mind, they took the shorter path back. He said nothing.

"Give me a month, okay?" she said. "Surely I can't fuck up everything in that short amount of time." Her plan would accomplish the opposite, bonding the kids to one another, hopefully tightly enough to weather whatever the Agency had in store for them and Beckett. "Just April, then you can pee on the party and cancel the fun."

"Is it your intention to cast me in the roll of fun obliterator?"

"Uh, you cast yourself in that role, honey. What I'm trying to do is to show you how much better your students will do and how much happier they'll be if you let them be college kids for two damn seconds and not Chosen Ones. I've listened to quite a few fantasy audiobooks, and I can tell you with authority that chosen-one people are never happy."

Beckett clutched at the hem of his vest. "I don't know how to address any of that. They're young, Sara, they always manage to find their own entertainment. I seriously doubt they would be interested in—"He dropped his hands and made a brushing gesture, as if erasing her entirely. "It's immaterial. Our focus is on training their talent. More than that dilutes the purpose and the effectiveness. I want them to take responsibility for their gifts. Parties do not further that goal."

He was wrong. "Okay, so then why am I staying at Arden for free? What's *my* purpose? Because I know you don't want those impressionable young men thinking you're using your position to house your girlfriend. Even if that's the sort of entitled shit your family partakes in."

"In which your family partakes."

"What?"

"It's improper to end a sentence with a preposition, so you would say, 'That is the sort of shit *in which* your family partakes,'" he replied. "If you're going to be insulting, you could at least be grammatically correct."

"I'm not your student," she said, her face burning.

"Clearly."

To her horror, the whirlwind in her brain flung out no words to help her smack that condescending jerk into place. Her mother and stepfather had called her stupid a thousand times.

Good thing you're pretty, because you sure ain't smart.

It didn't matter that she had fantastic interpersonal skills and a keen ability to read people. Because she was also forgetful, her reading and writing were awful, her handwriting was embarrassingly illegible, and she couldn't spell. She couldn't remember if the word *embarrassing* had one or two r's and s's, which was, ironically, embarrassing. And, apparently, her grammar sucked. She wasn't dumb, but so few believed that.

"I'll see myself home," she said, stepping away, shoving the heat roiling inside into a tiny ball that scorched her throat, and then she conjured every crystal of ice formed from years of training.

"Sara, can't we have a rational discussion—"

"No." She turned and strode down the boardwalk and onto the sidewalk. The inferno in her melted all the crafted ice, and her hands shook and tingled with the desire to hit something. Stadler hadn't trained her in hand-to-hand combat like he had Ryan and Jolene, but he'd taught her enough that she had no doubt she could make Beckett double over if he kept talking to her.

Men always thought because they were bigger and stronger they could call all the shots. And mostly, they did, never caring about how their actions affected others, never noticing the damage. Because women—women like her, anyway—were just trophies, pieces of ass, cum receptacles—

"I apologize for my behavior." He didn't shout the words, exactly, but he was obviously walking far enough behind her that he couldn't use his regular, cultured voice.

"Apologize tomorrow. Tonight, I need you to shut up." Sara did shout the words.

CHAPTER FOURTEEN

Beckett

BECKETT STOOD TOO LONG OUTSIDE ARDEN. Comprehending others' feelings was not one of his strong suits, but her pain at his remarks had been unmistakable. If she wanted to be taken seriously, she should speak correctly. His intention had been to help her, and she should have appreciated that. Though he realized the timing of the correction, in the midst of a disagreement, hadn't been ideal.

He'd felt defensive and a bit offended by her assessment of his somberness. Yes, he was a serious person, but that didn't make him defective or less-than-ideal to be around. He was an intellectual and proficient in discourse on a variety of topics. Just not toga parties and body shots or whatever bizarre festivity Sara wanted to plan.

He didn't typically feel remorse after arguments, particularly when he was in the right. She'd been the one to resort to name calling. *Entitled.* Yes, his family had supported him, but he'd worked hard and earned his position. She'd been far out of line.

And yet, his chest had not relaxed. He hadn't pointed out her grammar mistake from a solely altruistic place. Beckett had seen more in Sara than he'd expected, and he'd wanted her to feel the same regarding him.

Her expressive face had shuttered because of him and his careless words. Petty, childish, hurtful. And he hadn't taken a full breath since.

* * *

REMEMBERING SARA'S ORDER FROM THE DAY HE'D MET HER AND RYAN AT Doppio almost a week ago, Beckett bought her a caramel sea salt hot chocolate from Ghirardelli as a peace offering. He hoped she wouldn't toss it in his face. In his experience, women liked to refuse to grant forgiveness for an extended time.

Unfortunately, Andrew showed up before she did. They were meeting in Studio B, the smaller of the study rooms, gray to Studio A's beige and furnished with only a table and two chairs for individual sessions. Beckett had already brought in a third chair from Studio A for today's session.

"Hey," Andrew said. "Where's the girlfriend?" He waggled his eyebrows as if his innuendo had been insufficient.

"She was late last time, so—"

"Check me out, on time and everything," Sara said, bursting through the door in a black and gold sweater dress that clung to her. If someone had taken her picture, there would be nothing to photoshop. Her eyes sparkled, as they always did, and Beckett picked up no sign of her earlier ire.

"I . . . uh . . . brought you this," he said, holding out the cup like a beggar asking for change. "It's chocolate caramel . . . hot chocolate . . . caramel hot chocolate. I got the medium size." Beckett fumbled in his pocket for the Ghirardelli milk chocolate caramel square. "They gave me this, too. You can put it in your chocolate or eat it now. Or you could save it for later. If you want."

Both Andrew and Sara bore his inarticulateness with amusement.

"Thanks, Becks," she said, taking the drink and sniffing the hole in the plastic top. "Damn, that smells delicious."

With a graceful turn of her elbow, she swung her purse around and dropped it onto the small table. She reached out and Beckett almost took her hand before remembering the square of chocolate he held. She unwrapped the chocolate and added it to her drink.

"Well, you're looking gorgeous today," Andrew said. "Obviously, I can't wait to be a part of this. We are making history, you know." He clapped his hands together and rubbed. "Drink up. I want you to give me the kind of headache you gave Beckett."

"I live to serve," she said with an eyelash flutter.

Andrew grinned. "As beautiful as you are, I'm sure it's the other way around."

He laughed, and she chuckled with him.

Beckett wondered how that was humorous. He couldn't help but notice that Sara and Andrew would make a far better pair than Beckett and Sara, but she was *his* girlfriend. Even if fictional.

"I think we should save the headaches for the end," Beckett said, ready to start their session. He had a set agenda, after all.

The energy in the room was different with Andrew added to the mix. Sara showered Andrew with attention, but didn't freeze out Beckett. Instead, she smoothed down his tie, bumped him with her hip, and kissed the lobe of his ear. She acted as if their argument the previous night had never happened.

Beckett searched for the relief he undoubtedly should have felt, but he couldn't find it. If anything, his reaction was worse—an uncomfortable sweat over his entire body.

Andrew scooted his chair right next to Sara, instead of across, their knees almost touching as they held hands. They seemed comfortable with the sustained contact.

Beckett couldn't stop staring at their clasped hands. The countdown on his phone was unbearably slow. Sara closed her eyes. Andrew kept his eyes open but unfocused as his shoulder dipped and brushed Sara's. She didn't move away or fidget.

When he could stand it no longer, Beckett clapped with too much force and startled them both. "How did it go?" he asked, busying himself with a leatherbound pad of paper and the gold pen his parents had presented to him when he'd attained his undergrad degree. It had been long enough ago he'd forgotten the brand.

121

Sara kicked off her shoes and took a short turn about the room, stretching in pedestrian ways that appeared lewd with her figure-hugging dress. "I don't have a headache, so that's nice. You get anything, Professor Slick?"

Andrew winked at Sara. "Not a thing, sweetheart. You were a complete blank." He shrugged at Beckett. "Weird, right?"

"Very odd." Beckett's voice was only a bit loud. Was he the only professional in the room? "Sara posits there may be something in the eyes when a magician is priming his or her magic. We should film the both of us using our gifts and then review the footage to see if we captured it. If we can identify the tell, I'm confident we can hone our senses to pick it up in real time, eventually."

"Really?" Andrew said, examining Sara with a more serious expression. "You think it can be taught?"

"He thinks it can be taught," Sara replied. "I'm not here to think at all."

And there it was.

Then Sara grinned. "I'm here to be director, cinematographer, and script writer." She extended her arms, thumbs connected to make a box. "Picture this." She slowly revolved her hand camera in a circle. "In a world of memory magic, two friends embark on a journey of discovery, mystery, and blatant voyeurism." She lowered her hands and jogged over to her purse. "I've got a vision, a decent phone camera, and I am excited about this project."

"We have video equipment," Beckett said. "I want to be able to zoom in considerably and not lose clarity. Andrew, would you get that for us?"

"Sure," Andrew said. "Back in a jiff."

Finally, Beckett and Sara were alone. It would take Andrew ten minutes at most, but Beckett didn't require that much time.

Sara made a clicking sound. "You're not nervous about letting Andrew into your head?"

It took Beckett a moment to recalibrate, her presence scrambling his cognitive functions. "He won't root around—we're friends. But it's pretty instinctive to blockade when you know an intrusion is imminent."

"If you already know how to block, why do you need me?"

"The way we do it only slows someone down. We don't have a moat, and our barriers are more like plywood. Most of what we do to guard ourselves is to try and guide the memory read where we want it. We can't completely protect ourselves against an invasion, but we can choose, somewhat, what the other magician sees."

Sara laughed, a throaty chuckle that was probably practiced, but still . . . Beckett's breath left him for a moment. She grinned at him. "So, it's like a sleight of brain."

"What?"

"You show them something conspicuous so they don't notice what you're trying to hide. Classic misdirection."

"You're unlike anyone I've ever met." She saw the world so much differently than other people, or even he, did. "Would you be opposed to a battery of tests? I'm curious if you're neurodivergent. That might account for your uniqueness. There isn't actually a medical test for that, but there are several written exams we could utilize. If—"

"No. No writing." Her attention remained fixed away from him. "I suppose you could verbally quiz me, if you wanted."

A fresh picture of Sara came together in his mind. She avoided emails and reading. Her texts were all talk-to-text. During their first encounter at La Cuisine, she'd asked him twice to spell his name. She'd gotten rabidly defensive the night before when he'd made his appallingly rude remark about her grammar. Sara likely had a learning disorder, probably dyslexia.

She wasn't unintelligent, just disadvantaged, and she compensated brilliantly.

"Verbal tests are completely acceptable," he said.

"You sexy beast you. I think I'm blushing." She smiled at him with genuine amusement. His dry personality didn't seem to repel her.

They could easily continue the conversation as is, but he felt compelled to express his regret for his behavior. "Sara, about last night . . ."

She waved a hand. "Don't worry about it."

"I was . . . I was thoughtless and condescending."

Sara shrugged. "Lots of people feel the way you do. I'm well aware you think I'm nothing more than a decorative tool with the intelligence of pinking shears. I've made my peace with it."

That was how she imagined he felt about her? "That's not the way I feel. I was . . ." No, if he gave an excuse, then he wasn't taking full responsibility. "I should not have sneered at your grammar or dismissed you so callously." That was all he'd intended to say, but he was struck by a simple clarity. It would cost him nothing to do this one thing for her, even if the idea that parties would create cohesion was ludicrous. "You correctly conjectured that I am resistant to change. You . . . You challenge me in a way I'm unaccustomed to, and your ideas are fresh and insightful. Although you may be quite lovely, there's far more to you than physical beauty. If you truly want to arrange social events for our group, then I support you. I'll send an announcement email to everyone this afternoon."

Her grin made his stomach tighten.

"Good," she said. "We ought to start going on dates. I'll plan the first one, and then you can organize the next, and we'll go back and forth until we find our groove."

"I'm sorry, what?" Her moods were positively mercurial.

Sara clapped her hands. "I have such a fun first date planned!"

"I thought we could simply go through this questionnaire I found online. It's very thorough."

"What questionnaire?"

He refused to avoid her gaze. "'Fifty Questions to Deepen Your Intimacy.'"

"*How do you handle stress?*" she mocked. "Bo-ring. Unless there's favorite sex position stuff in it." She leaned into him and nuzzled his neck. He flinched, shocked by not just her actions but the affection in them. "See? You can't get comfortable by reading a dossier. Besides, we need to be seen going out."

"Fine." He withdrew his small datebook, giving his eyes somewhere practical to focus. He would not blush. "Let's schedule something."

"It's doggie style, right? Your favorite position?" She smirked. "Yeah, mine too."

He was not going to respond to that. "I've got my fencing class on Thursday nights and Sunday afternoons, so we'll have to schedule around that."

She snorted. "Was the polo class full?"

He stared at her for a beat. "Don't be ridiculous. Polo is a summer sport."

She grinned as if she found him delightful. "Friday night?"

He made a notation in his book. "I'm free any time after four."

"How about six-thirty?"

"All right. What will we be doing?"

Sara's smile grew Cheshire-cat wide. "I wouldn't dream of ruining the surprise."

Beckett frowned, hating surprises, but he needed to atone. "Dress code?"

"Semi-casual. Wear dark clothing."

"Why something dark? We aren't committing burglary, are we?"

She shrugged. "I guess you'll find out on Friday."

He had a bad feeling about the entire situation, and maybe that was why the rest of the session with Andrew went as it did. All three of them were left with awful headaches, and no matter how close he viewed the footage of him and Andrew or how much he slowed it down, he couldn't detect any signs of a power being utilized. Andrew agreed with Sara that they blinked less, but nothing definitive.

Eliminating possibilities was still progress, just the painful kind.

CHAPTER FIFTEEN

Sara

ADEQUATELY GRATEFUL BECKETT HAD GIVEN HIS blessing for her to be the social coordinator (the title she'd requested via text), Sara wasn't sure if she wanted to continue with her date plans. She couldn't stay mad at him, not after his sincerity. He couldn't help being a condescending ass at times, and she was particularly sensitive when it came to her intelligence.

In the end, however, her scheme to get back at him for his arrogance was too perfect for any deviation.

Beckett showed up at her apartment door exactly on time. He wasn't dressed casually. Though he wore black jeans, his onyx dress shirt and silk vest conjured elegance. It irritated her that he was getting more attractive by the day. His outfit was smart and conventional, but the double-breastedness of his vest gave him an edge of rebel. It was too much, which made it just right. The vest was also tailored to precisely fit his body, without being too tight, accenting his flat stomach and a decent waist-to-shoulder ratio.

"We'll wait out front for the Uber," Sara said while trying not to ogle. She was glad she'd put forth the effort to curl and pin her half-damp hair the night before for her Veronica Lake curls. She'd also taken inspiration from Lake for her outfit, a black-and-gray paneled short-sleeved dress that fell to just below her knees and had a tiny belt. Her three-inch T-strap pumps made her a few inches shorter than Beckett, since his gorgeous, black-and-burgundy monk strap leather shoes gave him an extra inch.

"I can drive us wherever you want to go," he said.

"And ruin the surprise?"

He opened the lobby door for her. "That would be perfect, because I don't care for surprises."

Sara bit her lip, glad she'd used a tenacious lip stain. "Then you better start preparing yourself."

"Why?"

She extracted the ebony blindfold from her gold clutch. "You have to wear this."

He didn't seem shocked, which was disappointing. "Is our date taking place at a secret government facility?"

The Uber, a white Toyota, pulled up to the curb.

"Don't kill the fun, Professor. This is us." Sara opened the door for Beckett. "I'm trusting you to put this on."

He got into the back seat, but did not take the blindfold. "I have not agreed to that."

Sara fisted a hand on her hip. "You did agree I could plan our first outing, and this is the plan." She bent down and said to the driver, "Give us a sec, okay?"

The driver, a man in his thirties with too much scruff, sat in a cloud of cheap, noxious body spray. He blinked at her with his mouth open. She left him to his gaping and returned her attention to Beckett.

"I really want this to be a surprise. Can you unwedge the stick up your ass for a few hours? Please?" She almost giggled at her own joke. He'd get it later.

"Fine, but when it's my turn to plan our date, I don't want to hear any grumbling."

"I'll paste on my biggest smile while we go to some lecture on Mesopotamian literature."

Beckett huffed out a breath, but then snatched the blindfold and tied it over his eyes. Sara opened the passenger door and showed the driver her phone. "Just confirming the address for you," she said. "It's a top-secret government facility."

"Okay. Sure." He swallowed so hard his Adam's apple slid up and down like something out of a horror movie. "Are you, uh, going to sit up front with me?"

"No, sugar, I'm going to sit in back with my boyfriend." She gave him a wink to soften the blow. "Thanks."

Then she glided in next to Beckett.

"How long must I wear this? I feel ridiculous," Beckett grumbled.

"Yeah, but you look hot," she replied. And he did. Part of her wanted to straddle his lap and nip his earlobe, enjoy the brief power she had over him. "We aren't going far. Maybe fifteen minutes." It would be at least twenty, possibly thirty, but fifteen sounded reasonable.

She didn't giggle, and the suppression made her body fizzy with anticipation. The driver, luckily, didn't talk. Sara slipped her hand into Beckett's, and his grip was tighter than she'd expected. Was he afraid of the dark?

He didn't pant or sweat, and his hands were dry and almost as soft as hers. His nails were buffed and perfectly clipped. Probably a professional job. Oh! She could have arranged a his-and-her mani-pedi. That would have been so fun. Next time.

"No hints?" he prompted.

"The adventure tonight is in three parts."

"Please tell me I won't be blindfolded for the entire evening."

"You wish." She did giggle then. "Just this first part. Relax."

They rode in silence, holding hands, and he didn't try to access her mind once.

When they arrived at the Lakeview neighborhood address, Sara somehow managed to persuade Beckett to keep the blindfold on all the way out of the car, onto the sidewalk, and up to the second floor of the nondescript, redbrick building. Standing in the hall outside the business, she knocked as she removed his blindfold.

Beckett blinked at the name on the door. Curative Colonics. "What the he—" His hiss broke off as the door swung open.

"Welcome!" The woman was petite with long, red hair in a sleek ponytail. She had flawless skin and over-darkened eyebrows. "Sara and Beckett?"

"That's us," Sara said, clasping Beckett's hand and drawing him inside.

It was even more hilarious than she'd imagined. Beckett's jaw flapped, but he didn't jerk away. He followed her into the waiting room and stared, dumbfounded, at the redhead.

"I'm Jennifer, so you'll be with me, Sara," Jennifer said, her smile revealing a lot of gum and straight teeth. "Sam will be with you in a moment, Beckett."

"What?" Beckett said, sounding so confused Sara bent over laughing.

"I'll meet you back here in an hour," Sara said, guffawing all the way to the little treatment room, though she wasn't especially keen to get a colonic herself. Having water shot up her butt was not on her bucket list, but she wouldn't punk out on her own prank. Beckett would probably refuse, and if after she was finished, she discovered that he'd fled, it wouldn't surprise her.

Though he did tend to take his commitments seriously.

Whatever happened would be fine. She'd pay Sam whether Beckett rose to the challenge or not. Short of the coin she paid to dye her eyelashes and eyebrows, this was the best money she'd ever spent.

The first part took forever and consisted of questions about her diet and lifestyle, which Sara answered in a yoga-girl persona, who she decided was a vegan harboring an obsession with chia seeds. She played with the ceramic bead on her bracelet, stretching the elastic an inch and letting it snap her wrist like negative reinforcement.

Beckett wasn't the type of man who would make anyone think, *I bet he can take a joke*. But he also wasn't the type to appear rattled. She imagined Beckett in one of the sunny pleather chairs in the waiting room, reading *Digestive World* or *Colon Comrades*—or some other uber-health-sounding magazine.

The actual irrigation wasn't the most comfortable thirty minutes she'd ever spent, but the process was fascinating, and though the sensation was definitely weird, it didn't hurt.

When Sara stepped outside, Beckett was sitting on a chair, one elegant leg crossed over the other. He was talking to Sam about fencing and someone named Fabio. Sara assumed he was not the same Fabio as the I Can't Believe It's Not Butter guy.

"How was it?" she asked in a voice so bright it could have sterilized the room.

"I decided to pass on this occasion," Beckett replied. "How was it for you?"

Her mood sank a bit, regardless of her expectation that he wouldn't partake. How fun would it have been if he had? They could have talked about how warm the water was.

"Well, the runway is cleared for landing," she said with an exaggerated wink.

His mouth dropped open as if he'd been hit by a taser.

Sara took mercy on him and turned her head from one side to the other. "I'm already glowing. Can't you tell?"

He recovered, turning his gape into a close-lipped smile. "To me, you always glow."

Okay, that she hadn't expected, and though she wasn't sure if he was paying her an actual compliment or, more likely, playing their game, her mood lifted again. Energy thrummed through her body. "You are the sweetest." Even if it was all pretense, he hadn't left, and that meant everything. "I've got something a little less exciting planned for dinner."

Jennifer and Sam had drifted to the small kitchen, though they were still within earshot.

"Pleased to hear that," Beckett replied.

Sara paid for the sessions and slipped Sam and Jennifer each twenty dollars. Jennifer had actually done work, but Sam had been stuck talking to Beckett, so a tip was only fair.

Beckett waited until they were out of the building before revealing his true feelings. "Sara, I have other things I could be doing with my time. If this is some big joke to you—"

"It isn't!"

He glared at her.

"All right," she said, "this part of the date was a little bit of a laugh, but I promise the rest will be stuff I think you'll actually like."

Beckett didn't move. "If it isn't, then this will be our last date, and I'll be going home immediately. Seriously, Sara, when we're together, please try to act like an adult."

"What's more adult than a colonic?"

He started to walk away then realized he had no idea where they were going. This was the best date ever.

"News flash, Beckett, you can be a grownup *and* have a sense of humor." She pointed in the direction they needed to head. "Well, most people can."

"My sense of humor is intact. I simply don't appreciate juvenile antics." He straightened his vest, though it didn't need it. "Where are we going now? If it's edible Play-Doh, I'm out."

"Fair enough." She brushed her cheek over his. "Come on. It's not far from here, so we can walk."

They traveled down Sheffield. When they slowed near Trader Todd's and their advertisement for karaoke, Beckett went rigid and gave her serious side-eye.

"Relax," she said with a chuckle. "No karaoke. This is it." She gestured to the restaurant next-door, Barangaroos Aussie Pies. "I read on the internet that in Shakespearean times, they used to eat mincemeat hand pies. Ta-da."

Beckett blinked at her, almost as shocked as he'd been at the colonic place. "That's . . . thoughtful."

Sara shrugged. "I have my moments." As Beckett opened the door, she said, "They have mincemeat, but you can get whatever kind you want. My treat."

She examined the case of small pies, and her stomach pinched in hunger. Probably, she should eat a salad of some variety right after a colonic rather than a heavy meat pie, but she hadn't thought through her plan. Not that she would have changed her mind about coming here, because Beckett was almost animated as he studied the offerings.

"Have you eaten here before?" asked the man behind the counter who looked as if he could bench press a tanker truck.

"Nope, first time," Sara replied.

"These are meant to be eaten by hand, like a sandwich."

"That's awesome," Sara said, nudging Beckett. "Just like in Shakespearean times." She hoped he wouldn't balk at the idea of being unable to use the correct knife and fork.

"Just so." Beckett said with . . . Oh. My. God.

A smile. A beautiful smile that made him appear young and roguish.

"Have you already chosen a pie?" he asked.

"Huh? No. I didn't know what I'd feel like." There weren't any "light" pies or veggie pies, but there was a vegetarian shepherd's pie. She wanted the steak and Guinness, so she decided the chicken and mushroom would be a compromise. Not a salad, but not steak and Guinness either.

Beckett chose the mincemeat. "For authenticity," he said, "though the pie shop is Australian. The English did send their criminals to Australia after Shakespeare's time, so it might be close to what they ate then."

"Since there's nobody here to tell us otherwise, let's assume that," Sara agreed.

The little storefront had only three small black tables with yellow chairs, all metal, and a thin, fake-wood counter along the storefront window with matching bar chairs. Luckily, a couple had just finished their meal and left, so Sara and Beckett took over the table while waiting for their pies to heat.

"Now I'm even more curious as to what we're doing next," Beckett said. "You're a very inconsistent person."

"I think what you meant to say was whimsical."

"Pretty sure I said what I meant. I'm an English professor, Ms. Strausser.

I choose my words with precision." His haughtiness was a parody of his usual personality, and he delivered it so dryly, a bark of laughter overtook her.

She'd cultivated several kinds of laughs, but that had been a real one and not her most attractive. Her laugh somehow tripped Beckett into laughing, the most unexpected sound.

His laugh was deep yet full of air, almost wheezing, and made her laugh more. What he'd said hadn't been that funny, which turned the laughing all the more contagious.

Sara wiped away tears, and her stomach ached. More functional exercise.

The food came quickly, and Sara bit into her chicken and mushroom pie. The crust was buttery and flaky, the sauce of the pie nicely herbed—was *herbed* a word?—hot and delicious and just enough to keep the ingredients moist but not ooze. "Mm. Kudos to me on picking this place," she said, covering her mouth so she could talk and chew at the same time.

Beckett dabbed his mouth with a paper napkin as if it were linen. "This is delightful."

She beamed at him, as happy to please him with dinner as she'd been to shock him with the colonic. The next event would split the difference between these two.

"We have tickets to something at nine," Sara said. "It'll take about five to ten minutes to walk there."

Beckett shook his wrist to reveal his watch under his sleeve so he could check the time. Why was such a posh gesture so sexy? Why did she want to lick his wrist?

"We still have a half hour." He took another bite of his mincemeat pie.

She watched him chew, surprised at how attractive she found him. He wasn't striking. Yet, that dip in his lower lip had always fascinated her, and he had strong eyebrows and an angular jaw. But his eyes were a medium brown, his shoulders average, his manner fussy. Still, the dress shirt/vest combo was alluring. She wanted to unbutton him.

"Do you want a taste?" he asked.

"What?" Had he finally read her mind after all this time?

He held out his half-eaten pie. "You were staring."

She grinned. "Not very subtle, was I? But I'm good."

Maybe she was growing as a person, because she made no jokes about eating someone else's pie.

The wall behind Beckett held small pictures from Australia. She most liked the one with two kangaroos in mid-jump. "Have you ever been to Australia?"

"I've been to the Australian Open twice, so I've spent several weeks there. What about you?"

Sara thought of all the cities and towns she'd visited. Dark, ugly places— not on the surface and not for most people—but deep in the cancerous pockets all places held, the locations and situations she'd been assigned to work, embody, live. "I've never been out of the US." She kept her focus on the photographs. "I'd love to pet a kangaroo."

"They can be aggressive if they're feeling threatened. Did you know that a group of kangaroos is called a mob?"

"If they dance, are they called a flash mob?"

Beckett smiled. "Certainly. Though I wasn't lucky enough to witness one." He took a deep breath that Sara could not only hear but see. His struggling with this small social interaction made her want to hold his hand. "Prior to your hostess job, what did you do?"

Of course he had to go there. She frowned. "I thought you already knew. The Agency is the only employment I've had before the hostess gig and . . . this."

"The Agency is a pretty big corporate conglomerate. What did you do for them?"

"They didn't tell you?"

"No. All Ahmad said was they had a connection to you and could coordinate our meeting. Did you have an embarrassing profession? Perhaps something along the lines of colonics?"

Sara laughed despite the dread deep in her sinuses. The idea of telling him she'd slept with criminals to manipulate them into giving her important information wouldn't garner her more respect, that was for sure. And she'd gotten him to not only smile tonight but laugh. "I . . . uh . . . sort of entertained."

"Ah, corporate events."

Hardly. "What about you? Have you always wanted to be a teacher?"

"Yes. Education is so important, and I want to share what I know. I want to see the spark in young students' eyes when they first fall in love with Shakespeare. It's a great responsibility and honor."

Sara saw the bright-eyed youth he must have been when he'd been a student himself. Idealism was charming, and she wished she could have grown up with a positive worldview.

Instead, she'd experienced the worst of society—abusers, pushers, rapists, murderers, and selfish people who didn't see her as anything more than a pretty possession.

CHAPTER SIXTEEN

Beckett

Beckett and Sara walked down Sedgewick, traffic moving slowly enough that one car exhausted more than its fair share of burned oil, but Beckett barely noticed. They turned on Belmont, Beckett still talking about his love of fencing. She didn't appear bored and kept asking questions about the training, class routines, and the history.

"Fencing was a sport in the original Greek Olympic Games," Beckett said, "and has been in the modern Olympics since 1896."

"If someone tries to mug us, is it going to help?" Sara asked.

"I don't take fencing for self-defense but for exercise. It works the mind and body. You need to anticipate where your opponent will move, which trains you to spot slight muscle movements. It's a full-body workout, too."

"Do you own a cache of swords? Are any of them sharp?"

Beckett sighed. Apparently, fencing wasn't cool without the threat of injury or death. "I own several sabers, a few foils and épées, but none are sharp. Not to say there's no danger, though. Famously, Vladimir Smirnov was killed at the 1982 World Championship when his opponent's weapon broke during the bout and the broken tip pierced his mask and went through his eye."

"Brutal."

He nodded. Had he said too much? Past dates had complained about his frequent "lectures" on fencing. "That's me—tennis, fencing, and reading. What are your hobbies?"

"Makeup and hair, yoga, podcasts, and I love to dance."

Beckett didn't consider hair and makeup legitimate hobbies, but he decided it unwise to voice that aloud. On second thought, her hair, with its soft wave and bottom curls, could be considered art, so perhaps hair could be a sanctioned interest. "What kind of dance? Ballet?"

"God no. I boogie around freestyle."

Surely there was more to her life than planning social events and dancing. There was something darker, he could sense it, but he didn't want to pry. Especially since this was technically their first date. First *fake* date. Likely, fake boyfriends pried less than real ones.

* * *

"We're going to the Annoyance?" Beckett asked as the neon red Annoyance Theatre sign blazed across Belmont.

"Yes," she replied, squeezing his arm. "They have a special guest act."

"What is it?"

She sighed. "Don't you want to be surprised?"

He really didn't. "All right."

The smile she gave him made him glad he didn't press her. Also, the delay wasn't long.

"You got us tickets to see *Julius Caesar* with sock puppets?" Beckett couldn't wrap his mind around the concept. The play contained more than thirty characters. Who would endeavor to make such a production, and who was the intended audience?

"Brilliant, right?" Sara asked, bouncing on her toes as if she'd gifted him a Maserati.

"I guess we'll find out."

Beckett was unsurprised that more than half the tables in the diminutive theater were unoccupied.

"Let's sit near the front," she said, tugging his hand to the middle and second "row."

On the stage was a wide box about ten feet high with the top three feet cut open, covered by a crushed gold curtain. The puppet stage. This was ridiculous, and yet the more he thought about it, the more a laugh threatened to bubble out.

"I've seen over a hundred Shakespeare productions, in many iterations," he said. "But I've never attended one of the bard's plays in sock puppet form. Or any puppet form."

Sara giggled. "I'm so glad. I would have been so disappointed if you'd seen a bunch of these."

No woman had ever planned a date for him before. He'd always done all of the arranging—or overseen the arrangements—and paid for everything. No date he'd ever been on had been half so bewitching as this one. Should he worry that the energy between him and Sara was starting to feel decidedly less fake?

She dug a small flask out of her clutch purse. "I packed this for us." She shook it enticingly. "Made just for you."

"What is it?"

"Drink and see," she said with a wink.

He reached for the silver flask, scanning the room for anyone paying attention to them. With a bar on the premises, he was unsure about the punishment for bringing their own alcohol. Exile? He unscrewed the cap and took a surreptitious sip. Port. Tawny port. Not a great one but not bad.

Sara wiggled in her seat. "You like?"

He nodded, his stomach tumbling around like toddlers in a bouncy house. "A fine vintage."

"Glad that Binny's clerk didn't steer me wrong."

The toddlers in his gut jumped and spun as if sugar had been injected directly into their veins. "This was very generous."

He handed her the flask and cap, and she took her own sip, giggling as she capped the flask. "That's tasty. I like it."

138

Sara was quite like port—unexpectedly sweet with only a bit of burn.

His body flooded with hormones and adrenaline, the combination so potent he began to sweat and question his entire existence. Beckett felt like both a stranger and more himself than he'd ever been before—who he'd be in the absence of boundaries to keep him in the correct lane. Sara had introduced him to the kind of freedom he hadn't realized he'd been missing.

The theater ended up almost full, with people straggling in at the last minute, including a large group that might have been celebrating a retirement. The patrons were all adults, except one family included a kid who couldn't have been older than twelve.

The production was as ridiculous as Beckett could have imagined, but the incongruity of the rudimentary sock puppets and the significant talent of the actors had him laughing so hard his stomach ached, heedless of the fact that *Julius Caesar* was a tragedy.

The show was a wonderful example of how powerful Shakespeare still was today. His stories were so universal, so woven within the fabric of society, that even the twelve-year-old could become engrossed, despite the foreignness of Shakespearean language.

At the end, Beckett stood for a standing ovation with the rest of the audience. Sara's eyes glittered with tears of humor.

In their Uber afterward, Beckett found himself energized and speaking entirely too fast. "I thought they managed to cut the text in the exact right places to keep the spirit of the play intact, yet still hold it to an hour and a half. The casting was brilliant, too. I didn't realize until the curtain call that so few actors played all those parts."

"You know they're talented when they make Shakespeare understandable."

"The trick is to understand figurative language. Shakespeare is full of metaphor, similes, and imagery, not to mention themes, and—" Beckett broke off his lecture. "Sorry."

"For what? Go on. This is interesting."

Beckett wondered for a moment if she was teasing him, but she seemed eager to hear what he had to say, as she had when he'd discussed fencing.

"Okay. Say, for example, you're hungry."

She grinned. "In fact, I am a little peckish."

"Saying you're hungry means something, of course, but if you were to call your stomach a yawning chasm, that figurative language would engage more of your senses. You could say your appetite rages like a sandstorm desperate for a drop of rain. In that case, you'd be using a simile to compare one thing to another, and the intersection of those two things is not only more pleasing to the ear, it can evoke feeling in the one who hears it."

"She doth teach the torches to burn bright," Sara replied, quoting *Romeo and Juliet*.

"Close," Beckett said, brushing away the wave of hair that covered her left eye, impatient to feel the silk of the strands. Since he wasn't in the habit of quoting Shakespeare to woo women, particularly in the presence of a stranger, he lowered his voice and brought his mouth next to her ear, sure the Uber driver wouldn't hear him over the radio. "The correct line is 'O, *she doth teach the torches to burn bright.*' Every word of Shakespeare is essential, even the *O.*"

She shook her head. "You've got to learn to stop correcting me."

"I do."

The car fell silent except for the song on B96, a current hit that didn't appeal to Beckett. Sara, however, tapped her foot to the beat.

He didn't want the night to end. "The next excursion is mine to plan, yes? What about tomorrow night?"

"That's the first movie night social event." Sara frowned. "You're not going?"

"Yes, yes, of course. I simply forgot tomorrow is Saturday." He tugged on his bottom lip, mortified he'd completely blocked out the movie screening. *Scanners.* "On Sunday, I have our group meeting, fencing, and I should prepare for next week's classes, and I have fencing again on Thursday. What about Wednesday for our date? Or do you want to do Friday again?"

She shrugged. "I'm open, but let's do Friday so you have the maximum number of days to plan something amazing. I'm so excited to see what you come up with!" She didn't seem the least bit concerned he might execute a trick equivalent to the colonic farce. In fact, she bounced on the seat as if wanting him to invent some torturous event to push her buttons.

"Friday it is."

The Uber arrived at Arden, and Beckett got out with Sara. "Do you live close by, or do you want the driver to wait?" Sara asked as she opened her Uber app and paid.

Beckett grinned. "I live there." He pointed to the church-turned-home next-door set back from the sidewalk.

"Shut. Up. We've been neighbors this whole time? And you live in a freaking *church*?" Sara walked in a circle, hands clasping her head. "That is so cool. How did I not know this? Beckett, this is the kind of secret you absolutely cannot keep from me."

"On our date next Friday, I'll let you see inside," he said, enjoying her flabbergasted reaction. "But it's late, so please allow me to walk you to your door."

She gestured to the entrance. "This is the door."

"That's not proper. I need to ensure you make it to your apartment door." He wanted a few more minutes with her, particularly as she continued to animatedly mumble about churches and stained-glass windows.

Even if this wasn't a true date, it felt real to Beckett. Actually, it was far better than any other date he'd had. He admitted to himself he liked Sara, enjoyed her company, and he'd misjudged her terribly.

Sara dug into her clutch, presumably searching for her keycard. "Okay. That's fine." She unzipped an interior pocket. "Of course, I'll need to find my keycard first."

"At the risk of drawing your ire, might I suggest you keep your card in the same spot every time? That way, you'll always know precisely where it is."

Sara stopped rooting around and pointed a finger at him. "Brilliant suggestion. The problem is I can't remember which place I decided to always use." She tapped her forehead with the heel of her hand. "A zippered compartment, right? So it couldn't ever accidentally fall out?"

"Sound reasoning."

"Oh!" She yanked out her wallet and found the card in a back slot. "I change purses, so I was thinking if I kept it in my wallet, I'd never forget to bring it."

"Also sound reasoning."

"All righty, commence with the gentlemanliness," Sara drawled.

He'd never felt less like a gentleman.

CHAPTER SEVENTEEN

Sara

HE WALKED HER ALL THE WAY UPSTAIRS, FOLLOWING her on the stairs, not suggesting the elevator. She stopped at her door and turned to him. Her professional marks hadn't been the walk-you-to-the-door types, and she'd never found herself in this position before. If they had been on a real date, he would kiss her—if TV and movies were accurate.

But they weren't truly dating.

"You want to come in for a minute, see what I've done with the joint?" She didn't want him judging her lack of organizational skills, but she wanted even less to stand awkwardly outside her door.

"Maybe next time."

Her stomach twinged, and she pressed her wrist into it. It's not as if she were disappointed. She wasn't. The gesture was just a habit now. "Okay. Well, goodnight then." She gave him a dorky half-wave.

"Sara."

He licked his lips, and Sara imagined the feel of that little dip in the center of his bottom lip against her own, then tried to scrub it from her mind. "Yes?"

"Do we need to practice . . . That is, in your experience, would it be beneficial for . . . Excuse me, I'm not normally so . . . flustered."

Beckett Convery had never been so adorable in his entire life, Sara was sure of it. "What is it you want to practice?"

Kissing. Please say kissing.

"Uh . . ." He rubbed his jaw with his index finger. "I'm not well versed in public displays of affection, and I worry it might lead to a stiffness between us."

The joke was *right there*, but she refrained, not because she wanted to be more mature, but because she wanted to hear what he was going to say. "And?"

"I already think we are so different as individuals that people who have a modicum of familiarity with us will not understand the pairing. Since you intimated people will assume our relationship resides mostly in the physical plane, I wonder if, for the sake of our ruse, we might be a touch demonstrative in public." His eyes flitted everywhere before finally landing on her. "But you are the expert, so I will abide by what you think."

Sara was indeed an expert. In truth, the more aloof he acted with her, the more people would believe they were real. Trying too hard always looked forced and unnatural. But the temptation was irresistible.

She had no idea what he would do or how far he would go, and that was so rare for her. "It's important we're comfortable with each other."

He nodded. "Should we . . . you know . . . kiss? For practice?"

"I don't need the practice, but if you feel—"

"You twist my meaning deliberately," he said, tugging down his vest as if it had somehow gone rogue. His shirt was as pristine as when they'd started the date.

"Sorry, but you make it too easy." She smiled. He didn't return the gesture but stared hard at her, which made her stomach flutter. "Okay, let's do it."

She waited. In this little scenario of theirs, she was the master, so maybe she should initiate, but she wanted to know what he'd do. He was the most intriguing man she'd ever met, a ridiculous mixture of gentleman and rude.

He tapped his lip with his thumb, and if he had been anyone else, she would have assumed he meant the gesture to call attention to that perfect bottom lip, but he had no guile in his eyes. The man had zero game.

His movements were jerky, almost awkward, nothing like the confidence he'd shown at the party when he'd been angry. He moved so close she could see the fine lines bracketing his eyes, then backed up so far, they'd have to stretch to shake hands.

Sara didn't move at all, transfixed by the workings of his mind as he tried to pinpoint the exact right distance.

"Sorry," he muttered, though she had no idea why he'd apologized.

"Beckett." She lowered her voice, tossed a growl into the back of her throat. "Just kiss me like you would kiss anyone."

He frowned. "But you aren't *anyone*."

Men complimented her all the time, but Beckett's words were so honest and genuine. She allowed a blush to flush her cheeks, licking her lips.

"You're sure?" He stepped just-right close and snared her with his brown eyes. Their shade was lighter than his hair, almost like whiskey, made more gorgeous by the stark white around his irises.

Beckett placed gentle fingers along her jaw, his thumb resting on her chin. God, he smelled amazing, like money, class, and luxury all set in a meadow. She wanted to bury her nose in his neck and huff, but she held herself still.

"It's okay," she said.

His blink made him look a little drunk. His fingers slid from her jaw to her throat, reviving the goose bumps from the party a week ago. The almost-not-there touch made her body tilt like an out-of-control pinball machine. Her breath hitched.

He bent to her lips achingly slow, as if he feared she might stop him at any moment. She wouldn't, because she wanted this. Even though he wasn't her type—nobody was—and she certainly wasn't his type, which would be uptight and respectable. But he'd formed this bubble around them, and damn if she didn't feel safe, which was stupid because danger *always* lurked just out of sight.

The kiss was soft and tentative but not awkward. He seemed to kiss her like that on purpose, as if he knew how much she hated men who took and grabbed, which was most of them. His lips were gentle and quiet, and her stomach capsized. Twice.

Shivers took over her body, sprouting goose bumps everywhere, not only along her neck. She didn't jump into the kiss, but to hold herself back, she had to suck in a quick breath as she tugged his bottom lip between hers. His hand came up, his thumb resting under her chin, his other fingers still fanning out over her cheek and jaw. The way he so gently held her face gave her the impression he was spotting her, ready to catch her if she should fall.

They leaned closer, but the pressure of their lips remained light. He didn't plunge his tongue into her mouth or lick her lips to ask for an invitation. All he did was slide his lips over hers, allowing them both to explore the topography of each other's mouths. Although it was late at night, no whiskers scraped over her skin.

Her back hit the door, and she tensed, waiting for him to smash his body into hers, preparing for the end of his tender sensuality. Instead, he pulled back. Beckett's chest almost brushed hers when it rose, his breath panting, much like her own.

"That was useful, I think," he said.

Her lips quirked. "Quite instructive. Do you think it was enough?"

His thumb moved back and forth under her chin, the slightest caress. It had to have been intentional, and yet he seemed distracted. "We want to be thorough, as the stakes are impossibly high. Perhaps we might practice again another night?"

Sara blinked. He wasn't going to push her to let him inside her apartment?

Beckett wasn't like any man she'd ever met before, and though her insides bounded around at his presence, a deeper part of herself screamed at her to run away. The more he didn't disappoint her, the greater the disappointment would be in the end.

CHAPTER EIGHTEEN

Beckett

BECKETT WALKED ACROSS THE LAWN FROM THE apartment building to his church-turned-home. It was set back from the property, giving the illusion of privacy and a bit more separation from him and the students in his program. And Sara.

What had he been thinking?

Physical contact was foolish. They weren't a true couple, and it wasn't as if people were going to call out for them to kiss in public. He'd wanted to feel what it was like, and that imprudent impulse to curb his curiosity had only fanned his... What? Fascination with her?

Beckett walked inside, his body primed and a feeling of incompleteness washing over him. His thoughts were too wrapped up in Sara, which was a waste of his intellect. She might have intrigued him, but there was no future for them. He had his plans set, and she would not fit into them. She might make a sufficient partner for an associate professor, but not a college professor who was also a member of the Philotimo and a leader of memory magicians. He needed someone more serious . . . someday.

He moved to the alarm to disarm it, but it was completely unresponsive. "What now?" he said through gritted teeth. Just last month, the alarm had gone out due to faulty wiring. When he called the security company's customer relations tonight, he was informed the service had been canceled.

"Clearly, I haven't," he replied, and it took twenty more minutes and a supervisor to get it straightened out.

He blamed technology. In the past few years, he'd had problems with almost every service, from cable to pest control.

Once the alarm came back to life, Beckett contemplated his home. It had been locked, yes, but unprotected by the alarm. Room-to-room he searched, finding nothing amiss, and yet a growing sense of being watched or not alone made the back of his neck itch. He was spooked enough that he actually peered under his bed like a child might. Nothing there. Nothing out of place. Still, a frisson of violation wouldn't go away.

At last, Beckett disrobed, putting his clothing in the corresponding hampers before showering and dressing in his most comfortable pajama bottoms and a plain, white T-shirt. For ten minutes, he tried to read a Grace Paley short story, but he couldn't focus. His agitation made sleep impossible.

Barefoot, he padded into his studio. It was mostly for fencing, a fencing strip in the center; masks, lames, and uniforms hanging on pegs; shoes in dedicated cubbies; and a collection of sabers, épées and foils, both electric and dry, on the wall, though he hadn't used anything other than a saber for a few years.

The room was mostly white—walls, curtains, uniforms. Even the wood floors had been bleached. The only spots of color were the mat, the wood-colored fencing strip, and the wrought-iron lamp overhead. No stained glass in this portion of the church.

He walked to a small, blue mat in the back corner. On a low shelf was a six-inch ivory column candle. He used the lighter lying next to it to light it. He didn't like to time his meditations, as that made the activity seem more like a chore. Instead, he would stay with his thoughts until the wax melted down to the width of the candle.

Beckett closed his eyes. He concentrated on the burning candle, the acridness of the smoke and the satisfying char of the wick. It smelled like magic. Inhaling, making sure his entire rib cage moved as well as his diaphragm, he imagined the magic in the world, a bright, white light, channeling into his body and deep into his lungs. When he exhaled, he let go of any tension—both the negative kind, like frustration, and the positive kind, like his churning libido.

Beckett spent a few breath cycles concentrating on breathing, then opened the door inside himself, priming his gift. There was only his mind, and though he could sense splotches of color indicating long-term memories, what grabbed his focus were his short-term memories forming in real time.

He found that sitting with his own consciousness like this helped him to grow his gift and connect better with other magicians. He taught all the students this technique in private lessons. Some of them took to it, some found it boring, and others only feigned interest. Beckett believed finding comfort in your own presence, in your own power, was the key to expanding magic.

He should try this with Sara. The woman could use some settling, though she did yoga, and that could be a sort of physical meditation.

Focus.

His back itched. A trickle of sweat tickled the back of his knee. Why would he sweat behind only one of his knees?

The radiator ticked and clicked as if it spoke its own language. The colors behind his lids changed with his thoughts and moods, and he tried to watch the colors without attaching to the thoughts. Meditation wasn't about achieving, only about trying. That was the path to understanding. And what he most wanted to understand was Sara. More than he'd desired anything in a long time. Decoding her was something beyond ambition and a sense of duty. Something exclusively for himself.

He would try. And if he failed, he would begin again.

* * *

BECKETT PACKED HIS BAG, ONLY FIVE MINUTES OF OFFICE HOURS LEFT. He should never have opened his office for two hours on a Saturday every month. He hadn't had more than three students utilize the time all year.

Andrew came in then and locked the door, a thick yellow folder in his hand. He sat in the chair opposite Beckett and ran a hand through his hair.

"This feels shitty but also the right thing to do," Andrew said.

"O-kay," Beckett said, eyeing his friend across the desk. "How can I help you?"

"Oh man, now you're making me feel worse." Andrew grinned at him, though it was a pale imitation of his usual smile. "I . . . well, I . . . this was left in my intra-Wells mailbox this morning. I shouldn't have . . . but I read it."

"Read what, Andrew?" Beckett asked. He wanted to go home, but ever since Sara had come into his life, he'd been neglecting his friend. "What's wrong?"

"The employee file on Sara, from when she worked for the Agency."

"What? Why would someone send you her personnel records?" Beckett frowned. If Andrew hadn't been so upset, Beckett would have berated him for infringing on her privacy like that.

"I don't know. Maybe because there's fewer people in the philosophy department, less traffic to notice who slipped it in my mailbox. And it's common knowledge that we're best friends. At any rate, there's no note. I don't know who it's from. But, Beckett . . . there are things you should probably know about . . . her background. They might change how you feel about her." He winced. "You know I wouldn't bring this to you unless I thought you needed to read it."

Sara had said she'd done *entertaining*, but Andrew's distress spoke of more than simple party planning. And she had alluded to the Agency as an unsavory organization.

Andrew set the folder on Beckett's desk. His impulse was to grab the dossier and scour the contents, but that would be yet another trespass against Sara's privacy.

150

"Thank you," he said, taking the records and locking them in a drawer.

"Aren't you going to read it?" Andrew asked.

Had Andrew intended to sit and watch Beckett peruse the documents? "I'll consider it."

Andrew nodded. "Read the first few pages, minimum. You don't want to be blindsided later."

He shouldn't. The man he wanted to be wouldn't. The pressure in his chest, however, told him he might do it anyway.

CHAPTER NINETEEN

Sara

SARA BURNED ONLY ONE OF THE THREE BAGS OF microwave popcorn, but the acrid stench was overpowering. At least it covered the funk of pot, which she thought might short-circuit Beckett. There was a decent turnout for movie night. She'd commandeered Wilson's place since he had the biggest TV and a subscription to Max, though he didn't have enough furniture to seat everyone who'd come—Sara, Andrew, Wilson, Kenji, Erik, Brayton, and Beckett.

Everyone except Beckett acted happy to be there. Sara presented an empty Kind bar box with various movie treats inside: Milk Duds, Junior Mints, Red Vines, and Hot Tamales. Wilson passed around mismatched bowls, and the kids poured snacks into their containers, not one caring about mixing the candy and popcorn.

Beckett took a token amount of popcorn, eyeing her as if he expected her to do something scandalous like flash her tits. With her scar, that wasn't an option, but he didn't know that. She caught herself pressing a hand into her scar over her yellow T-shirt, which she'd paired with Pikachu sleep shorts and smiley face socks. She'd wanted to be quirky, to signal it was time for fun.

"Has anybody seen this already?" she asked. *Scanners* had come out in 1981, so she was hopeful nobody had.

Everyone shook their heads.

Beckett popped a kernel of popcorn into his mouth and chewed with dignity. He had taken a spot on the only couch, and Sara sat next to him, curling close. The boys watched, fascinated, and it made Sara want to laugh. After a tense few seconds, Beckett, acting as if he were being actively electrocuted, eased an arm around her. Sara snuggled into him, which was a chore with his rigid posture.

"Relax," she hissed into his ear before nipping his earlobe.

He jerked, squeezing her hard in reflex. Although he wasn't what anyone would call chill, he did manage a not-scowling expression. Progress.

Andrew took the bean bag chair. Wilson took the other couch space, and the other three boys sprawled out on the floor. Brayton wedged his broad back against the couch between Sara's and Wilson's legs, while the other two boys leaned back on their hands.

The movie was perfect. The acting was wooden, the special effects mostly consisting of weird facial expressions, except for a few gross scenes. The terms the characters used for the telepaths were insulting, and the crowd loved that, calling one another "telepathic curiosities."

While they watched, Beckett held her hand but didn't draw any interesting circles in her palm with his fingertips. It wasn't remotely romantic, but then, they were in a room full of other people. Still, he could have made an effort.

Afterward, Erik asked why they didn't have a psychic gymnasium, to which Beckett replied they did—they called it Studio B. The students booed, and Erik threw a piece of popcorn at him, which Sara thought was awfully brave, considering how fastidious Beckett was about his clothing, even if he had lost his blazer and rolled up his cuffs. Beckett slapped the popcorn away as if it were a pesky fly. It fell into Sara's lap, and she tossed it in her mouth with a grin.

"I'd love to mind meld with my computer," Brayton said, staring wistfully at the others. "Make it write all my papers for me."

Wilson threw popcorn at Brayton, and Kenji and Andrew followed.

"For research!" Brayton said, a clear lie.

"I'm just glad we don't look like those characters when we use our gift." Kenji winced dramatically. "Can you imagine?"

"Oh!" Sara leaped to her feet. "Bonus contest. Who can make the best scanner face? Winner gets to pick the next movie, though it has to be psychic related." She danced around, loving the idea. It would be brilliant if Beckett played the game, but she already knew he'd never do anything so undignified. "Who wants to go first?"

"You go first," Andrew said.

"Okay!" She flipped the end of her eighties-inspired herringbone braid she'd created especially for the movie. Shaking out her hands, she tried to calm her mind. It didn't work. The urge to smile was too great. "Hold on! Wait!" She held up her palms, not that anyone was rushing her.

She finally found that competitive nugget inside her and squeezed tight. "All right," she said on an exhale.

"Professor Convery, you do the countdown," Wilson suggested in his dude voice.

Sara thought he would refuse, but he dusted off his pants and gave Sara a stern expression. "Ready?"

She nodded.

He *almost* smiled. "On your mark . . . get set . . ." He shook his head and sighed. "Go."

Sara stiffened up enough that her body trembled a bit, then contorted her face, jerking it this way and that, making little growling noises since there was no soundtrack. The boys jumped up and down, cheering her name. After a minute or so, she stopped. Her body shook with energy, and her face felt hot. "How'd I do?"

Everyone looked to Beckett. "Spectacularly," he said in his driest tone.

Sara beamed, her face flushing, even if the compliment had been halfhearted and unavoidable.

"Seriously, we need someone impartial," Brayton said.

"Are you questioning my ability to make these decisions honestly and ethically?" Beckett sounded genuinely affronted.

"No, sir," Brayton replied with grudging respect.

"We should have a panel of judges and score cards," Sara said.

"That seems excessive," Beckett said as everybody else cheered.

"More is more," Sara countered, wanting to kick him for not playing along with her. He was the worst fake boyfriend ever. "Who's next?"

Everyone took a turn except Beckett and Andrew. Andrew not participating surprised her, but maybe he was more vain than cool. A lot of people were. When they had all finished, Beckett tugged down his vest as if he were very important, and everybody laughed, including Sara. He was finally loosening up.

"The winner is Sara," he said, and her belly dropped as if she'd raced over a dip in a smooth road. "*However,* as she is a facilitator and not a student, I believe she is ineligible for the prize."

"So much for my efforts to sleep my way to the top," Sara said as a silly giddiness spread over her.

The boys all snickered and hooted. Beckett almost appeared amused. "Therefore, the best scanner imitation award clearly goes to Kenji."

Everyone clapped, including Sara, because Kenji had been able to perfectly mimic the people in the movie, and then he'd somehow twisted his lips in opposite directions. The effect had been quite gruesome when paired with widened eyes and strained neck muscles. Sara would have awarded Kenji the prize too.

As they broke for the evening, the kids jostled and ribbed one another and grinned at Sara and Beckett. She hoped Beckett recognized how much progress he'd made with the students just by showing up.

God, she loved being right.

CHAPTER TWENTY

Beckett

BECKETT LEFT THE MOVIE PARTY BEFORE SARA, SO there had been no goodnight to maneuver in front of their young audience. He had to admit she'd had great insight into what the students needed, to see them as kids and not tools to be honed. Community.

After the Sunday morning meeting, he'd asked Sara if they could meet for another one-on-one session at twelve-thirty. Her smirk had sidetracked him for a moment, but he'd been back on the path in moments.

His favorite fencing class didn't start until three, so they could take their time. He should move them in a more professional direction. Beckett set up the camera on a tripod in Studio B.

If he cross-referenced what Sara could do with all the other memory magician talents they knew about, maybe he could find ways to expand everyone's skills. He thought of the remaining mentees, searching for signs that any of them were dissatisfied. If he lost one more student to Dominion, the Philotimo might shut Beckett's program down. If they couldn't keep the participants, there was no point in having a program. Ahmad hadn't said anything, but Beckett couldn't stop worrying that the Philotimo would decide he couldn't handle his project and end it.

Still, it wasn't as if he could do anything to stop the students from defecting. He certainly wouldn't beg or bribe them, as Andrew had suggested.

Sara poked her head in the door. Her hair was styled with a braid in the front like a headband, the rest cascading down to her shoulder blades. "Hi," she said with an awkward wave.

Beckett adjusted the settings on the camera, focusing on business. "Good afternoon. For today, I want to take video of you as I try to access your memories. To forestall a headache, I'll simply attempt to connect, not actually penetrate."

Sara snickered.

She was worse than his students. "What I want to see if there's any sort of facial response when your power engages. I also want to monitor your heart rhythm and brain waves."

Sara bent over the machine on the table. "With a lie detector?"

"How do you know that's a lie detector?"

"Not my first rodeo, cowpoke. Are you, by chance, going to also ask me questions?" The inquiry seemed genuine.

"No, Ms. Strausser, this is not an interrogation. My skills don't reside in that arena. A polygraph exam is an inexpensive yet accurate way to note changes in physiological arousal factors—blood pressure, heart rate, perspiration, and respiration."

Sara sat in the chair facing the camera, a quirk to her lips. "I can beat a lie detector test, just so you know."

The kids were always saying that, but he wouldn't allow her to distract him with an inane discussion. "After we do that, I want to switch places, and film myself and log my own statistics as we repeat the process."

"Why not get double the equipment and knock it out all at once?"

He hadn't considered that. "I only have the one polygraph and camera."

"You do this with everyone?"

"Ms. Strausser, I'd like to get started and not discuss students."

Sara stood, snatched the motion sensor pad off the small table, and plopped it onto her seat. Then she reached for the thoracic pneumograph tube and held it out to Beckett. "I thought I was brought in to be part of the group."

He circled it around her chest. The blouse was silk and might wrinkle, but Sara didn't appear concerned. "We simply want to duplicate your gift, not . . ."

"Help me? Got it, Professor Convery."

"You're different, Sara, and you know it."

Sara grumbled as Beckett put the abdominal pneumography tube around her waist, inhaling the spicy sweetness of her perfume. Once her arm was in place on the raised armrest, he clipped the heart monitor onto her finger, a few electrodes to her hands to measure perspiration, and a blood pressure cuff to her upper arm. The polygraph wasn't the latest technology, but it did hook up to Beckett's computer so he could see results on screen rather than on paper.

"I'm going to start recording, okay?"

"Go for it."

"You should act natural for the best results."

She inclined her head but said nothing.

Beckett started the camera then sat across from Sara at an angle so he could sit close enough to take her hand but not block the camera.

"Are you ready?"

She nodded. He reached out and gingerly took hold of her right hand, trying not to jostle the blood pressure cuff. Her hands were dry and warm, with no signs that she was distressed. A tingle shot up his arm and landed in his gut. He was glad he wasn't hooked up to the machine.

"What are you thinking about?" he asked, though he was unsure why it mattered.

"Your eyelashes," she replied. "They're so long and dark."

"Are they?"

"I'm imagining a little girl who has inherited your lash color and length and my thickness. She has the most spectacular eyelashes in the world."

"You're picturing our children?"

She scoffed. "Don't go wetting yourself quite yet. I was fantasizing for eyelash generation, not a personal aspiration."

He smiled, wondering why he didn't feel the least bit panicked by her thoughts. "If at all, women pursue me for my fortune and position in society. I don't think anyone's ever desired me for my eyelashes."

"Well, it certainly wouldn't be for your personality, would it, Professor?"

Beckett winced, hating the truth of her words and how powerless he was to change his nature, even if he wanted to. Which he didn't. There was nothing wrong with prioritizing ethics and standards.

"I'm a bit dry, I get that."

She squeezed his hand and leaned forward. "No, you're not. I'm sorry. I was being unfairly snarky. You're kind and smart and caring, and you always try to do the right thing, especially when it's hard. I don't think women are after you for your cash quite as much as you think."

His throat tightened as if he'd swallowed a polo ball.

"You don't believe me?" she asked. "Check the tape or screen or whatever. You'll see I'm telling you the truth."

Beckett laughed, though it came out tight. "Didn't you just tell me you could beat a lie detector?"

"Yeah, but I actually have to try. This was me all extemporaneous."

They stared at each other, and Beckett wanted to kiss her more than anything. He wanted to run his fingers over her cheekbones, lightly pinch her ears. There were a lot of reflexology points in the ears, and he'd bet nobody had taken the time to explore hers.

"What are you thinking about?" she asked, eyes playfully narrowed.

"Kissing you."

She smirked. "Where?"

He wasn't going there. Slowly, giving her time to stop him, he leaned forward and brushed his lips over hers.

She inhaled a tiny gasp, and he deepened the kiss. When they broke apart, a blush appeared from her throat to her cheeks. "Do you always kiss like that?"

"Like how?" He arched his eyebrows.

"Like, PG-rated, just lips."

It wasn't a complaint. Her flushed face and heavy breathing made Beckett want to stick out his chest and beat on it. He refrained.

"Sara, I can give you an X-rated kiss with only my lips, but I kiss that way because that's what I want." For all her bluster, Sara had a wistful, delicate quality to her that inspired Beckett to take his time.

She grinned. "What does a girl have to do to get one of these X-rated kisses?"

"She has to be attentive, complete the exercise, and stop interrupting."

"Hm. It'll be a challenge, but I'm very motivated right now." She blew out a breath and sat back in her chair. When had she scooted so far forward? "Get to the exercising, Professor."

He also wanted her to earn that X-rated kiss. His body tingled with energy and a vitality he hadn't experienced since he'd first discovered his gift. So many possibilities. "Close your eyes, Sara."

She did.

His focus slowly returned, and Beckett closed his own eyes. "Sense my breathing?"

"How? You don't breathe that loud."

He smiled. "Sense. Don't question."

"Okay." She sounded dubious. After a few seconds, she said, "I think I've got it."

"You do." It wasn't actually essential that they breathe in rhythm. Her attuning to him was all he needed, and Beckett had found tandem breathing, even if only imagined, almost always worked to get students focused. "Let's stay here for a bit."

"Mm-hmm."

They breathed together, and Beckett let his mind light up, like he did when he meditated. He let the bright flashes of thoughts explode like fireworks, observing them without touching. They swirled like the infinity sign in a never-ending loop.

Beckett didn't reach for Sara's mind, but he discerned her breathing body and swirling mind next to him. Their hands were connected. He breathed in the subtle notes of her perfume.

After they'd found a steady rhythm and before either of them could overthink anything, he said, "Now I want you to reach for me with your mind."

"Like I'm a memory surgeon?"

"However that manifests for you. I want you to try and connect to me, try to see my mind inside your own."

Behind his eyes, her mind sharpened, the barrier still present, but the colors more vibrant. Streaks of red and pink probably represented distrust or fear. A few sweeps of blue were likely the grounding thoughts of being in the moment, and a wisp or two of yellow possibly indicated anxiety or distrust over him penetrating her barriers.

Having her come to him opened something. Beckett surmised if she grew comfortable enough, he might be able to read her—if she allowed it. What a gift that would be.

Her mind bumped against his, the opaque wall thin between them, but nonetheless present.

"Do you see anything?" he asked. "Any colors?"

She squeezed his hand. "No. I don't—I'm sorry. I can't."

"Shh." He gentled his voice more. "It's just an experimental experience. We aren't expecting any particular outcome."

Their minds moved close again, but she didn't reach him, which was unfortunate, because he wanted to try breaching her wall when she was close and open. "I want to touch minds," he said. "Is that okay?"

"You mean read my thoughts?"

Of course she'd caught his meaning. "Yes."

"Give me a minute. I feel like I'm already tensing up."

He brushed his thumb over the back of her hand. "Take your time."

Their bodies hummed. He held the connection but didn't push. Beckett almost fell into a trance as faint lights swirled across her barricade, glowing like moonstone, mostly white but with other colors shot through, as if the barrier consisted of every kind of memory and emotion.

It was the most beautiful thing he'd ever seen, like the cosmos come to life.

The swirls in her mind mimicked his own, moving in a different pattern but at the same pace and general trajectory. If he took another step back, trying to see both their minds at once, he thought they might find a way to merge. That would likely result in true telepathy, a two-way communication he hadn't uncovered before.

Beckett reached without pressing, opening and opening himself until he had no borders. Sara's mind remained next to him, almost as if their thoughts brushed shoulders, but he never managed to get any closer, never garnering so much as a flicker of her consciousness. He let them stay close for another minute, then decided they'd done all they could.

"That's great," he said. "You can open your eyes."

She did, her deep blue eyes finding his and holding. "Did you see anything?"

"No thoughts, but that wasn't unexpected." Mostly because everything about Sara was possible, so nothing came as a surprise.

"Did I pass?"

He laughed. "It wasn't a test, so there's no pass-fail."

She frowned. "Then how do you know if I earned my X-rated kiss?"

Beckett's cock jumped in anticipation. Strangely, he wasn't nervous about disappointing her. All the time they'd spent connected had made him only more confident that he understood what she needed. "Do you think you've earned it?"

"That seems like a trick question, but I'll say yes."

"Let me unhook you first." Beckett turned his body and adjusted himself a bit to keep his arousal hidden. He wasn't a schoolboy.

"Does this work with all kinds of memory magic?" she asked.

"Of course. It's simply a tool for concentration and focus." He released the blood pressure cuff, heart rate monitor, and sensors.

"How many different types of memory magic are there?"

Beckett shrugged, unhooking the last part of the lie detector, the waist pneumography, his form too attuned to her proximity. "I believe there's a kind of memory magic for all functions of memory in the brain. This is completely theoretical, understand. I have no documented proof, but I think it makes a logical sense. There are a few people we've discovered with gifts involving the subconscious parts of memory."

"How is memory subconscious?" she asked, wrinkling her nose.

"Do you think about what you're doing every time you brush your hair or walk across the room?" he countered.

"Thankfully, no." She tapped her nails on the desk. "So how does that manifest as magic?"

"Could be a multitude of ways." Beckett leaned into the subject, talking with his hands. "In theory, a person with procedural memory magic would be able to learn new skills at an exponential rate and retain those skills."

"Like learning Kenpo?"

He laughed. "Exactly. They still have to train, but while it takes regular human beings three thousand repetitions to ingrain something as muscle memory, a mechanic memory magician—that's just the name I use— would only need to do something a minimal number of times to set it."

"Dude, I totally want that gift." Sara rubbed her elegant hands together like a cartoon fiend declaring her greed. "What else?"

"You can't shop for powers, you know." Beckett smiled, as he'd often considered what it would be like to have other talents. "The few we know about are primers—people who can pick up on body language so well they are almost precognitive. They can anticipate what a person will do next, even a stranger."

"Any of those in the program?"

Beckett straightened. "It's not up to me to share what the others can do. You'll have to ask everyone individually. Some of the kids are open about their gifts, but some are not. Though I will say that anything other than the traditional memory magician is extremely rare." Only Kenji had a *special*

special gift, and Kenji hadn't told any of the others, as far as Beckett could tell. As a sensor, Kenji possessed an eidetic memory that extended to more than just his visual sense. It certainly had aided his *Scanners* impersonation.

Sara sat back in her chair, slouching a bit. "Whoa."

"And then, of course, there's you. I've been calling you a shield, and I suppose that name will stick. Who knows how many other types of memory magic are out there, waiting for our discovery? While some magicians are fully aware of their power, some have no idea they're different and special."

"How are you going to find them?" she asked.

Beckett smiled. "We've populated our program primarily with referrals from members of our organization. To reach beyond, I go to college fairs and the like. I usually bring up memory magicians in conversation and gauge each potential student's reactions. If they behave as if they're hungry for information, I drop hints and eventually come out myself to see if they'll follow suit."

"That's brave."

Beckett shrugged. "Not especially. If they're horrified, they're not going to come to Wells, which is the ideal outcome in those cases."

"Are you distracting me from my prize?"

"You're the one asking all the questions."

She harumphed. "Well, I'm done now."

He stood. "Come here."

She stepped up to him, her respiration already fast and shallow.

Beckett reached up and cupped her face with both hands. She stilled, her breath stopping for a moment. He pinched the top of her left ear and stroked, then moved down, squeezing and stroking.

"What are you—?"

He shushed her and continued to caress her ear while he kissed the opposite jaw, his lips skating over her skin. She shivered and gasped, her torso leaning into him. He nipped the edge of her jaw near her right ear, letting his teeth scrape before turning it into a kiss.

Sara gripped his arms as if steadying herself. She didn't urge him to rush, but held still for him—as still as she could with her trembling body.

Beckett wasn't the most experienced lover, but he understood seduction because he'd researched it and because he comprehended every woman was different. Somehow, though she was constantly unbalancing him, he intuited what Sara needed was patience. She always rushed, jumping and running without looking. She needed to be forced to enjoy the moment.

Beckett worked his lips to the corner of her mouth. She turned her head, trying to capture his lips. He edged back and tsked her. Sara growled and pouted, but calmed and waited for him. His lips returned to one corner, then the other. Teeth over her top lip. She gasped in surprise, then hummed in pleasure.

He gave her the tiniest kisses he could manage until she fell into learned helplessness and relaxed into submission. Then he pressed his mouth to hers, both lips moistened by his tongue, capturing her bottom lip, tugging enough to get a better lock.

Beckett was so hard he began to leak, which would likely leave an embarrassing stain on his pants he couldn't give a damn about.

Sara mewled, pressing her body into his, her lips almost frantic for more contact. He let her set the pace, moving from top lip to bottom lip, only their lips together. Finally, she fell back, breathless, glassy-eyed, and flushed over not just her face but her hands too.

"Holy shit. That has to be classified as a magical gift," she gasped.

Beckett laughed and buttoned his blazer to cover his erection. "X-rated?"

"Triple X. You're the eighth deadly sin, Beckett Convery, and you'll be the death of me."

CHAPTER TWENTY-ONE

Sara

By Monday morning, Sara still hadn't recovered from Beckett's XXX kiss. Her blowtorched brain crackled with a giddy horror that was almost manic. The more she liked Beckett, the worse she felt about her actions. He'd given her butterflies, and she was about to give him a knife in the back.

Why couldn't she have a life filled with kisses that made her lock her knees to keep from passing out? But no, she had to spy on the one person who'd ever taken the time to get to know her instead of just jumping into her bed, and he hadn't even tried that yet.

Beckett would understand.

If he'd come into her apartment Saturday night after their date, he'd have seen the hamburger meat from her fridge on the counter in a slab, the middle indented as if it had been punched, and he'd have understood. Well, once she'd explained Dickhead.

The beef had turned brown, red liquid dripping onto the hardwood floor, the odor of rot and iron and palpable threat hitting her the minute she'd come through the door.

Sara just wanted to live her life in peace.

She hadn't sent in a report yet, so the meat had been a not-so-subtle reminder that Dickhead could get to her whenever he pleased.

Beckett would understand that she had to protect herself. Wouldn't he choose her safety over his program's secrets?

Probably not.

It didn't matter, because her fate was in her own hands.

Sara opened up her laptop, then closed it. She couldn't file this report in the home Beckett was providing for her.

Sara took the 'L' downtown then walked to the Chicago French Market located beneath the Ogilvie train station. At 9:30 in the morning, there were a few tables open, so she bought a banana and sat outside, the warm sun a condemnation of what she was about to do. People hustled by, and no one paid her any attention.

She opened the stupid email app on her phone and glanced around, ensuring nobody would be able to hear her. She dictated the report she'd been building in her head—the lie detector technique, Beckett's type of magic, his schedule (unsurprisingly consistent), the names of all the kids and that they were all likely typical memory surgeons, since any other was so rare.

Sara had considered lying in her report. She hadn't wanted to mention the students at all, but Beckett had said Dominion was poaching his mentees. She feared that if she left out anything Dickhead might already know, there would be consequences.

She described the different types of magic Beckett thought were out there, sharing everything she remembered. Her voice turned scratchy, and she had to stop and start several times.

All those confidences, and she treated them like garbage. But getting herself hurt or killed by keeping quiet wouldn't save Beckett, not if the Agency had it out for him.

If she confessed to Beckett, then he'd go to his Phi-people and demand they do something. Which would get back to the Agency, and they would do something all right . . . about her.

No.

Beckett had a general attractiveness, class, gender, and entire life of privilege to protect and insulate him. He'd be fine. Sara had nobody but herself.

She finished the report and cried for ten minutes. Exactly six more weeks before she could leave. This wasn't sustainable.

After wiping her face and applying a far too cheerful shade of lip stain, Sara went back inside for what she'd presumably canceled her session with Beckett for: Brayton's favorite dessert to celebrate his birthday. As if it would make up for what she'd done.

* * *

THE GIRL SAT WITH HER BACK AGAINST THE WALL ON THE FLOOR TO THE right of the stairs to the Ogilvie train station. She had multiple piercings and spiked hair that had once likely been a vibrant, neon pink but now the color reminded Sara of a gray shirt washed in hot water with a pink sock. The girl's layered clothing was bulky, oversized enough for her to appear chunky, though her gaunt cheekbones belied that illusion.

A black garbage bag propped against the wall looked as if it held a few more clothes. Surrounding her were several white plastic sacks containing who knew what. A dingy sleeping bag was propped behind her back, and a Styrofoam cup sat in front of it all to collect change from sympathetic passersby.

Sara noted the cup was too far away from the girl. An enterprising thief could scoop it up and sprint to the door before the young woman could do anything. She probably hadn't been homeless long, then. That was a mistake you only made once. The tradeoff of protecting the cash was that men could get awfully close without raising suspicion.

Sara dropped a twenty in the cup and said, "You might want to put that in your sock." Pockets were the first places muggers looked. Socks weren't too far down the list, but if someone had enough control over you to get your shoes off, you were screwed anyway.

"Thanks," the young woman said, her head down as she snatched the bill like an ambush predator. Maybe she'd be fine.

As Sara turned toward the market, her back prickled, followed by a swoop of energy and the taste of blackberries at the back of her throat. She took a deep breath. She'd helped someone in need today, and she was about to do something nice for the kids in Beckett's program. If she continued like that all day and all week, then she could possibly make up for . . .

But when she passed the little French grocery store, the heavy weight returned. *What's done cannot be undone.* A line she remembered from *MacBeth.*

Well, Sara, I guess as long as you continue to listen to Shakespeare podcasts and memorize famous Shakespeare lines, then it's okay you just gave the enemy all of Beckett's secrets. Go, you.

At Vanille, the French patisserie, she ordered several individual pastries, along with an eight-inch Royal for Brayton—a chocolate mousse, hazelnut praline cake covered in a dark chocolate glaze. Since this was the first birthday since she'd become the social coordinator, she needed to make the celebration special. On impulse, she bought an extra passion tarte for Beckett. God, she hated herself.

No, she hated the Agency.

On her way out, she passed the girl again. As she got close, the tang of blackberries returned, as well as an almost meditative peace. Sara stopped walking, and a businessman behind her yelped and gave her a frown that quickly smoothed into a smile.

She didn't apologize but stared at the young woman. Sara had no idea how what she was feeling could be caused by a memory surgeon, but she'd bet everything she'd just bought that the kid had some flavor of memory magic.

Watching other people passing by, Sara detected frowns easing, people slowing a bit, shoulders relaxing.

Sara wasn't authorized to recruit anyone for Beckett's program, and she wasn't sure she wanted to expose someone innocent to whatever plan the Agency had going on. But the kid had a gift, she was living on the streets, and goddamn it, she reminded Sara so much of herself, it made her body hollow. This was a chance to do something truly helpful. Something right. She needed a win.

"Hey," Sara said, digging out a raspberry tarte. "You want some pastry?"

"I don't swing that way," the girl said, her eyes narrowed.

Sara snorted. "If you think this is a bribe for sexual favors, your street smarts suck."

The girl grinned, a baring of her teeth. "I'm not interested in whatever kind of religious conversion scheme you've got going on."

Sara burst into laughter. "Come on. My cult is the coolest." She held up her two Vanille bags loaded with goodies. "You think other cults have French delicacies? All they can offer you is sprouted nuts on a garbanzo bean bun."

The girl studied her for several more seconds. Sara was about to shrug and pretend like she'd walk away when the young woman said, "What else you got in there?"

"I'm happy to show you! All I need is a blood sample first," Sara said as she extended the non-cake bag.

"You'd be surprised at the wackos walking by."

She wouldn't, actually, but she didn't tell her that. If she came at the kid with "hey I lived on the streets for a while too," she'd lose her. Sara would have considered that a line if someone had said it to her. People who'd tried too hard had always had an agenda that had never benefited Sara, so she doubted the girl would feel differently.

As the girl rummaged through the pastries, Sara wasn't sure how to pitch the program. She also couldn't bear to leave her there, vulnerable to creeps who loved to find girls alone, especially at night.

Beckett had said he'd start hinting about himself to draw others out, but Sara didn't think that would work here. She opted for a more direct approach. "Can I ask you a question about your gift?"

The girl jerked back, the passion tart in her hand—damn it—and looking as if she might bolt.

"Sorry, sorry," Sara said, stepping back and raising her hands in a placating gesture. "That was tactless. I forget how much people hate to talk about their abilities. I wondered if it helps you stay safe."

"What do you want?" the girl asked. "Because you want something."

"Your name, for a start?" Sara edged back an inch.

"Ren."

"Is that short for something?"

"Yeah, it's short for none of your business."

"I can see why you'd want to shorten that." Sara shrugged. "I'm going to come out with this, and you can do with it what you want." She brushed a hand across her middle. "There's a group of people who are focusing on training college students on the use of their . . . magic." She felt like an idiot saying *magic* out loud but whatever. "I think they could get you off the streets and give you an education. As far as I can tell, they aren't asking the kids for anything in return, but if you're interested, I'd ask them about that."

"Sure. I'd be happy to run on down to the lab. Just because nobody would miss me doesn't mean you aren't perfectly on the level." The girl grabbed the brownie next and leaned back against the wall. "Fuck off, lady."

"It's not a lab, but I get your skepticism." She opened her purse and, of course, had to rummage around before finding her wallet. She removed another twenty—damn it, that was too like a bribe, but now she'd shown it, she'd be a tool if she didn't give it to the girl. Then she scrambled for a scrap of paper and a pen. After finally locating a pen, she decided to use her Vanille receipt and found it in her jacket pocket. It wasn't as if she were going to expense the stuff. If she didn't pay for it herself, she couldn't knock off as much on her guilt bill. She wrote her name and cell number. "In case you change your mind."

Ren took the twenty but not the receipt. Sara dropped the paper into her Styrofoam cup. "You have no reason to trust me, and I wouldn't in your situation, but think about it. If there's a way to set up a safe situation for you, I'll try to work it out."

"What would you get out of it? Some kind of commission? Because you're clearly feeling ashamed about something. Your aura is like baby-puke yellow."

Sara winced. What would she get out of it? Restitution? She retrieved the pastry bag. "I wish I got a bonus. The group is legit, seriously, but I've got problems of my own." Big problems. "Later, Ren."

She hated leaving the girl behind, but she couldn't help her if she didn't want to be helped.

* * *

THE BIRTHDAY CELEBRATION FOR BRAYTON WASN'T MUCH. THEY SANG "Happy Birthday" and cheered before Sara brought out the pastries, minus the brownie and passion tart. Then she made everyone take turns saying one nice thing about Brayton before they could have dessert.

Brayton seemed moved by everyone's comments. Sara told him she was particularly impressed by how he always held the door open for people and how it showed his kind heart and care for others. He gave her one of those rich-guy nods and thanked her in a hushed voice.

Wilson went last. "Man, you never fuck up the rotation." A clear reference to the movie *Friday*. Brayton blushed and didn't meet Wilson's gaze. Sara clocked that as a crush reaction. Young, fumbling love was so cute!

Beckett eyed her across the table, a small smile on his face. Sara basked in his approval before remembering what else she'd done that day. Her email draft was gone, presumably read by Dickhead before he'd deleted it. Dickhead had been put off for another week.

* * *

WHEN SARA RETURNED TO THE FRENCH MARKET THE NEXT DAY, SHE found that Ren had vacated her spot. Sara wasn't about to go scouring the streets of Chicago to try to find her, but the weight of the missing girl was heavy.

Two days later, Ren called. "Is this some bullshit ploy?"

"No." Sara gripped her phone too tight, words bouncing around her brain too fast for her to catch them.

"So, what do we do?"

Having memorized Beckett's schedule, Sara arranged the meeting between Ren and Beckett without once consulting the good professor. He'd love that. She wondered how he'd react to a man doing the same thing. Men were largely complimented for taking the initiative, for acting decisively. Women, however, needed to learn their place, needed to respect the hierarchy of authority, had to be team players. Beckett wasn't a blatant misogynist, but nobody growing up in America was immune to gender roles and expectations. Not even her.

Really, though, how mad would he get?

CHAPTER TWENTY-TWO

Beckett

ECKETT AND SARA SAT AT THE TABLE SARA HAD picked in the Corner Bakery at the Ogilvie Transportation Center, waiting for an eighteen-year-old named Ren. Sara had said she was "pretty sure" Ren had some mystery magician magic and that Sara had "possibly" mentioned Ren could join his "memory magician training program."

The shock of Sara's unsanctioned recruiting still stung, clinging to Beckett's throat and gut. She had no authority to offer anyone, let alone a homeless youth, a position in his program. But Sara cared nothing for policies and procedures. Could he even trust that this Ren was a memory magician? Sara was a natural shield, so how could she have been affected from across a room? On the other hand, he was insanely curious.

Sara wore ripped jeans, her hair in a messy topknot and almost no makeup. She sat next to Beckett instead of across from him, believing Ren would feel more comfortable with an open path to several egresses. The girl likely feared abduction even while in a public train station during the peak travel time of eight in the morning.

Beckett checked the time. 8:07 a.m. What if this was some sort of practical joke? "If she's not here by quarter after, I'm not waiting." His car was in the shop due to a strange shimmy and a slight pull to the left, so they'd had to take an Uber since a suitable rental vehicle wouldn't be available until later in the afternoon. He needed extra time to procure a ride back to make his 10:45 a.m. class.

"She's homeless, Beckett. She doesn't have a watch or cell phone or clock radio to keep her to a schedule. Believe me, she needs this. She'll be here," Sara said, tapping her fingers on the table and toying with her elastic bracelet with the gold bead and metal clasp.

Around him, singles dined at tables with laptops or newspapers open. Some couples, both romantic and merely friendly, chatted and ate. A bigger group sat with a few tables pressed together to form a bigger surface for what appeared to be a business meeting. The café bustled with chatter and energy.

They sat under what appeared to be an indoor pergola of dark wood, the tables faux wood and bar height, their chairs comfortable enough. Sara had "allowed" them to buy drinks, but insisted they hold off on food until Ren showed up, so she would feel relaxed eating.

"Oh my God, she's here," Sara said, breathless, as if the queen had arrived and not a homeless girl. "Wait here."

"But I have my escape route planned," he countered.

With a scowl, she pointed a finger at him. "You, be nice." Then she scampered off to meet her program prospective.

Sara waved her arms like an airplane marshaller, scurrying over to a slight young woman with short, choppy hair that had likely once been pink. She carried a gigantic duffel and two oversized garbage bags.

Sara didn't bring the young lady immediately to him, but waited with her at the bakery counter, gesturing in a way that made it clear she was offering to buy Ren whatever she wanted. Beckett could see the indecision on the girl's face, as well as a nose stud and eyebrow ring. She also sported several piercings around her ears.

In forming a community, especially one as small as the one at Wells, one bad apple could spoil everything. And if anyone would want to bring in a disruptor, it would be Sara. This girl would not fit in at Arden.

175

Sara practically dragged Ren to their table, carrying a number in one hand, holding the girl's sleeve in the other. And she'd admonished him to be nice. Beckett stood, though he didn't extend his hand. If Ren were truly were a memory magician, she shouldn't find offense. None of them liked to open themselves up to strangers.

"Beckett, this is Ren. Ren, this is Beckett. He's in charge of the whole thing."

"It's a pleasure to make your acquaintance, Ren," Beckett said. Then he remembered to smile.

"Sure, it is," Ren replied with an eye roll. "Sara says you have a training program, and it isn't experimentation, but you'll pay for me to go to college without applying or anything. Is that true?"

Beckett flicked a glance to Sara, who was nodding in an exaggerated manner, as if he would suddenly misrepresent his life's work to appease a homeless girl. She'd gotten no details correct because she wasn't privy to the particulars. In Sara's world, if you didn't know something, it was perfectly acceptable to make it up. "It isn't quite as simple as that. We're . . . the program . . ." He shook his head briefly and gestured to the table. "Please sit, and we can discuss this."

"All the kids live in the same building," Sara said. "I live there, too. I'm the social secretary. I plan events like parties and movie screenings and fun stuff. When we met, I was out picking up some treats for one of the student's birthdays. It's the real college experience, too. They go to classes like everyone else, and—"

"Sara," Beckett said, wrangling control of the conversation from her runaway mouth. "Perhaps I should explain the program."

"Sure." She bounced a little in her seat as if excited about the conversation. For the first time since he'd known her, the energy appeared forced as if the girl's approval of her mattered.

Beckett wondered what it was about the girl that had hooked Sara so entirely.

"And I can study whatever I want?" Ren asked. "I don't have to take business or accounting or some other bullshit major?"

"He teaches Shakespeare, so what you study doesn't have to be something practical," Sara replied.

Beckett shot her a condemning glare and in his driest voice said, "Thank you, Sara." He fixed his gaze on Ren. Despite her disenfranchised status and her oversized sweatshirt and jeans, she was edgy and effortlessly cool. But attitude wasn't what he curated in recruits.

Sara hopped to her feet. "I'm going to the bathroom." She called back over her shoulder, "Be nice."

"Do you think she means me or you?" Ren asked when they were alone.

"Me," Beckett replied.

Ren laughed. Her laugh was younger and lighter than he'd expected, and it gave him pause. He was judging on appearances again, as he had with Sara.

"Man, I can tell you're not feeling this." Ren gestured between them. "Which is fine. You know what they say about things that sound too good to be true. But I'd appreciate it if you didn't jerk me around."

"I haven't decided anything yet."

Ren slowly shook her head. "Dude, you're dripping with disapproval."

"No," he replied. "I'm assessing, of course, but we haven't spoken long enough for me to come to any conclusions."

"People don't work that way." Ren stopped talking as an employee plunked a tray of pancakes, a breakfast wrap, and oatmeal in front of Ren.

"I'll be back with the rest."

There was more?

"You made up your mind about me the minute you saw me," Ren said, continuing as if they hadn't been interrupted. She picked up the thinly stuffed sandwich and took a giant bite. As she chewed, she said, "Your aura screams rejection. Now you're going to spend your time backing up what you already believe. There's no such thing as an open mind."

"Did no one ever teach you not to talk with your mouth full?" His stomach turned sour as he watched her cheeks bulge with food. "You'll give yourself indigestion by taking such huge bites."

She continued masticating and shrugged, but at least she didn't say anything else.

Sara returned as the employee brought a pink lemonade, egg bowl, a yogurt parfait, and something in a to-go box. Sara scooted the lemonade over to the girl and winked at her. Ren hunched her shoulders but grinned.

Beckett decided to ignore Ren's comment about nobody having an open mind and prove her wrong by demonstrating he didn't hold tightly to his assumptions. "Our young memory magician psychic enrichment program is designed to help student memory magicians to not only hone their talents, but to become leaders, ambassadors, and examples of our positive potential."

"Do I seem like any of those?" Ren asked. "What's the catch? You educate countless kids for free, and then afterward we owe you what?"

"Yeah, what is the goal after graduation?" Sara asked, chin on her hand.

"We hope you'll leave the program as a vital part of our growing community. There's no quid pro quo involved."

"You're doing all this out of the kindness of your heart?" Ren wiped her hands on her napkin and then stared at Beckett.

He glanced around and lowered his voice, bending over the table so Ren would hear him. "This is the best way I know of to ensure our safety and to contribute meaningfully to society. It isn't intended as a self-congratulatory indolence or as a way to avoid work or other responsibilities."

Ren rolled her eyes as if the idea of pondering great questions was an uncool waste of her time. She apparently wasn't remotely interested in becoming a better person or considering the implications of whatever magic she possessed. All she wanted was the free meal and possibly free housing and a free education. She intended to take but not give back.

"It's certainly not a halfway house or a charity," he said.

Sara dropped her hand and sat up straighter, her focus on Ren. She tapped Beckett on the thigh twice, an indication that Ren was using or preparing to use her magic. An absurd fear washed over him. His heart jolted in his chest, then thrashed around as his mouth desiccated and sweat wiggled down his sides.

"Knock that off," Sara said, kicking Ren under the table hard enough for the girl to yelp.

Beckett gaped at Ren, who scowled and bent to rub her leg. "That hurt."

"You're lucky I'm not wearing pointier shoes," Sara said with a scowl. She ran a hand down Beckett's thigh in a soothing motion. "That wasn't very nice—both of you. Beckett, she's not looking for a handout. I think what Ren wants to know is how she'll be beholden to you if she joins your program."

"Who do you think is interviewing whom?" Beckett asked, his body still shaky, but beginning to calm. His eyes narrowed on Ren. "What did you just do?" Whatever it was, she'd done it without making any skin-on-skin contact.

Ren shrugged. "I can see and tweak people's emotions."

Beckett gaped for several seconds before he realized what he was doing. "I've never heard of such a talent." He ran through the list of all the functions of memory he could remember, trying to find a fit. Somatic memory, perhaps, though that was almost exclusively thought to be part of trauma. He considered Ren's homeless state and wondered if it was trauma-related.

"Hm," Sara said, tapping a finger to her chin. "A female student with a rare type of magic on one side and a struggling sausage-fest program on the other. Weren't you just telling me you think memory magic gifts are beginning to expand and grow? And your group needs more diversity."

Beckett didn't reply, mostly because she was right, but also because he still hadn't recovered from his earlier terror.

"And you," Sara addressed Ren. "Dick move with the scary vibes. I don't need that kind of aerobic workout." She plopped an extra napkin on the girl's tray and mimed dabbing the corner of her mouth. Ren wiped her mouth, eyes downcast.

"You felt it too?" Beckett asked. He would have expected her shielding to work for every sort of magic. Was her affinity for the girl a weakness for her power, or was her vulnerability because emotions could be primal, utilizing more of the limbic system? Beckett wanted to clear his calendar for the day and dive into all his questions. Except that wasn't the recruiting procedure.

Sara slid a hand over the table top as if wanting to touch Ren but stopped short. "This is your chance to get an education and have a free, safe place to live while you decide what you want to do. And you should care about what's going to happen in the future of memory magicians, because you never know when some nutjob politician is going to want to put us all in camps. Wouldn't it be nice to have a community at your back when that happens? You'd be an idiot to refuse, and I don't think you're remotely stupid."

"I'm doing fine," Ren said with so much vehemence it likely wasn't true.

"Today. You and I know the longer you're out there on your own, the riskier it gets. You two stop measuring your dicks and skip to what you both need from the other to get this baby rolling."

"Sara, can you please be professional for five seconds together?" Beckett dropped his head into his hands. Her sales pitch was highly unconventional but he'd let her continue out of curiosity and because he could see Ren's interest through her gruff responses.

"It's too suss," Ren said.

"I get it," Sara said. "But they're taking care of their own. You just so happen to fall into that category now. Take advantage. The program is new, so you can be one of the people who help shape it. Keep it from being . . ." She paused, and Beckett suspected she was rewording what she'd planned to say so that it'd sound more professional. "Too stuffy, let's say. And they need an estrogen boost in the worst way."

"Isn't that what you're there for?" Ren asked.

"I'm not a participant, just, like, the cruise director." Sara tapped her fingers on the tabletop. "Come on. At least try it."

"He doesn't want me," Ren said. "He was practically drowning in doubt."

"Well, you did goose him with your maniac mojo."

Beckett broke into the conversation, hoping to resume control. As much as he hated the circumstances, he would have been a fool not to pounce on the opportunity that Ren represented. "Sara's correct in that your unique gift would make you a valuable addition to the program. I'm curious how it compares to other memory magic, and I'm willing to offer you a slot now. We can work out housing immediately, but we're mid-semester, so enrollment will have to wait for the summer session. Because we have time, I can have the paperwork dropped off at your apartment after you're settled." He didn't want to lose her—not to street life and certainly not to another faction. Ren was unique, savvy, and with an edge, not unlike Sara. She would be a formidable asset to the program.

"You have a place for me to live right now? Like, today?" Ren asked, suddenly seeming younger and less tough.

"In my building. We'll be neighbors!" Sara clapped her hands together, making her also seem childlike. "I'm dying to try a wing eyeliner on you. I think it'll look amazing."

Ren pulled her bottom lip. "Is that part of the deal? I have to be subjected to a makeover?"

"Yes!" Sara said as Beckett said, "No."

With a small smile, Ren said, "Okay. But don't think you're going to get me to wear anything glittery."

CHAPTER TWENTY-THREE

Sara

REN MOVED IN NOISILY, AS IF SHE'D TRANSFORMED into a person who was no longer attempting to disappear. She had no belongings other than her duffel bag and garbage sacks, but her combat boots made her tread heavy, and she walked up and down the hall, jiggling knobs, checking out the security. Beckett had put her in the apartment across from Sara.

Once Ren settled and stopped pacing like a wolf marking her territory, Sara hoped they'd be friendly neighbors. Marlena had yet to warm up to Sara, and likely never would. Ren, however, was like a piece of Sara's younger self.

Sara had overcome some nasty shit, but she wanted more for Ren than mere survival. She could be the savior she'd first thought Stadler had been. It was second best, but saving someone else rather than yourself wasn't nothing.

"Hey," Sara said, leaning on the doorframe of Ren's open door. "I want new furniture, so if there's anything of mine you want, feel free to take it."

Ren cocked her head. "I don't need charity," she said, as if reading from a script.

"Yes, you do." Sara crossed her arms. She didn't know Ren well enough to know what tactic would work in this situation, so she went with honesty. "Besides, all the furniture I have has not-great memories attached to them anyway. I'd rather you take it so I can buy myself new shit than find some plausible way to slip you money to at least pay for essentials."

"I already have all the essentials I need."

Sara nodded. Ren was an artist, which explained the contents of those white plastic bags: odd bits of metal like washers, nuts, and pop-tops; scraps of different colored paper, and a collection of thin and thick markers now sat in strange piles on the counter next to several stacks of paper. Sara had learned that Ren liked making collages with found objects.

Art components, however, would not make her living more comfortable. "Yeah, you've got heating, food, and a secure place to live, but life is infinitely better with a bed, at least one decent chair, and a couple of dishes. A storage system for your art supplies would be nice too."

"I have a knife, a fork, and a spoon already." Ren peered past Sara to the door of Sara's apartment. "Show me."

Sara opened her door, the code finally lodged in her brain, and stepped back to let Ren enter. She was Sara's first invited guest, and Sara found the realization comforting. "I really want to get rid of the bed," Sara said.

Ren narrowed her eyes. "Why? Did you have a bad lay there?"

Sara shrugged. "It was fine, but the guy . . . let's just say he didn't treat me very well in the end."

"Like how?" Ren asked.

"You know, for someone who doesn't like to talk about herself, you ask a lot of personal questions." Sara contemplated her unmade bed. "I was hurt, like physically, and he dumped me off at the hospital, then ran away with my money, and I haven't heard from him since."

Ren flinched. "Holy shit. Sorry." She took two large steps backward. "I-I shouldn't have asked. It's just—you're so happy, and I—I thought it was going to be something stupid."

"Oh, it was stupid all right." Sara barked a laugh. "Man, I did *not* see that coming. We were friends long before anything happened."

Ren blinked and stared at Sara as if she'd grown a tail. "How do you do that?"

"Do stupid shit? It's easy."

"No, your mood. It's . . . I've never seen anyone straighten themselves out of a downward spiral like that. Not without help."

"Is that what you do? Help people with their moods?" Sara asked in a quiet tone so as not to spook the girl. When she'd first met Ren, she'd felt her worries lift for a short while.

Ren nodded. "I can't always control it. Sometimes, everyone around me feels how I feel, like when I get angry. And sometimes I can project, like with Professor Convery at the restaurant. But you . . . you're different. It's like it only partway works."

"Sit down for a sec," Sara said, plopping down on the couch.

Ren considered the recliner, but chose to sit next to Sara on the couch.

Sara rested her head on the back cushion. "I'm immune to memory reading, and, apparently, I'm at least a little resistant to your mood changing gift too. I don't know why. Nobody here has run into anyone else like me. You and I are alike in that way. Except, as far as superpowers go, mine's pretty lame."

"Would you rather be a memory surgeon?" Ren asked.

"God, no. I have no desire to know what other people are thinking or feeling about me."

"I sense your mood, you know," Ren said. "It was harder that first day, but now . . . It's nice. You don't pity me or want to . . . get something from me. It's like . . . we resonate. Right?"

Sara's eyes prickled, but now wasn't the time for too much sentimentality—neither of them was ready for that. "If you feel that too, why are you busting my balls with every little thing?" Sara said with mock outrage. "Take the goddamn bed, kid."

* * *

SARA SPENT A LONG HOUR FIXING HER HAIR IN PREPARATION FOR HER second date with Beckett. She tried a selection of styles before settling on a high, half-ponytail curled out into beach waves with a few face-framing pieces. Beckett had been frosty on their ride back to campus after meeting Ren, and she hadn't seen him since. She'd been checking her phone, waiting for him to bail, but he hadn't.

Probably because that would have been impolite.

Her go-to response for smoothing things over with the male of her species was to look as gorgeous as possible. He'd indicated a business casual dress code for their date, which to her meant khakis and a polo, neither of which she owned.

She decided to go with a staple—the little black dress. Time to break in her new one, which was rayon with a touch of nylon and spandex. It had a full right sleeve, but the left arm was sleeveless. The fabric fit tight to her curves down to her knees. She wore three-and-a-half-inch Jimmy Choo pumps with a Swarovski Crystal encrusted heel. They weren't her most comfortable shoes, but they wouldn't lame her if Beckett surprised her with tango dancing.

As she stood at the door, wondering if she should simply meet him downstairs, she reminded herself the relationship wasn't real and it didn't matter if he was upset with her. She'd gotten Ren into the program, and it would be great for everyone. His disappointment had no effect on her.

But she'd betrayed him in ways he didn't know. She was determined to make it up to him, and charming men was her thing. Beckett was about to have the best date of his life, and then everything would be okay.

CHAPTER TWENTY-FOUR

Beckett

"**T**HE PHILOTIMO HAS BEEN CONTENT TO monitor via reports on my progress, but now they want some kind of inspection," Beckett said as they approached the Yum Dum food truck parked near Grant Park. He hadn't intended on sharing the stress of that information, but he had yet to recover from Sara's outfit. Sophisticated. Stunning. Sexy. Incredibly sexy.

"The students aren't slabs of meat." Sara's eyes widened. "A food truck?"

"But they are an investment—even if a charitable one. The Philotimo proposed a luncheon." Beckett glowed from her delighted surprise. Yum Dum had gotten a lot of press a few years back, and they still had a brisk business. "And yes, a food truck." She'd dressed for something better, but seemed pleased enough.

"Very nice," she replied. "You should counter with a dinner party."

"Why? That's more work."

They scrutinized the menu.

She shuffled closer to him. "Have you eaten here before? Anything you recommend? Dinner is the superior choice because there's more room for distraction, and you can liquor people up."

Beckett liked the idea of the Philotimo being more relaxed since they had seemed quite uptight when he'd seen them all together. "I've never eaten here, but my internet research suggests the Kimcheesy rice balls and the Pork Belly Baowich are excellent choices." He planned to order the crispy chicken. "Wouldn't dinner raise the stakes considerably?"

"Let's share the Kimcheesy balls, yeah? What do you think about the classic veggie dumplings? It'd kind of be like a salad."

Beckett scoffed. "It's nothing like a salad."

"If you ranked the dishes from most to least salady, what would be number one?"

"Order the salad dumplings, if you like. And I'm happy to share the Kimcheesy balls."

"Thanks." Sara grinned. "Dinner does raise the stakes, which would show the people in charge how seriously you take their visit, and it would project confidence. You also forget you have me to do the arranging."

"I never forget that."

Beckett wanted to refuse. Allowing her to arrange a dinner would be ceding too much control, and he needed the inspection to go well. What if she brought in a dunk tank? If the inspection failed, he'd never get chosen as heir—not just now but ever. But he had to admit she had a gift when it came to planning things. "All right."

Sara threw her arms around his neck and smashed her body into his with an embrace so heartfelt, it tightened his throat. Too soon, the hug became too intimate for public, but Beckett didn't release her until she relaxed her hold. "You won't be sorry. I know I'm sometimes a fuckup, but when I'm serious, I get the job done. And if it's one section of the population I understand, it's men in power. I'll give them what they want. And you won't have to do a thing except show up."

Beckett ordered for them, and Sara volunteered to grab the drinks and find a place for them to sit. She settled on an empty bench and set their Japanese sarsaparillas next to her to save his spot. Passersby all gawked at the overdressed supermodel in Grant Park.

The food was delicious, making Beckett reassess his derision of food trucks. Sara loved everything and had no issues with the level of spiciness, even as Beckett's forehead broke out in a light sweat.

When they finished eating, Beckett disposed of their trash and led her back to the car. After opening her door, he brandished a blindfold he'd bought especially for her.

She saw the black fabric and laughed, and Beckett was reminded yet again how different they were. Sara thought the blindfold was fun. She'd even joked about him taking her to a city council meeting or an accounting conference.

He slipped into the driver's seat, his confidence evaporating as he started the vehicle and seriously contemplated their destination. When he'd conceived of the next portion of the date, an art exhibit, he'd thought himself clever to plan something interesting instead of boring. He'd planned to discompose her expectations, but was an art show entertaining or trite and unimaginative?

In the spirit of their game, he should have found the most tedious event possible, something that would make his own eyelids droop. A classic one-upmanship. But all he'd done was arrange something lackluster with no playful component. Dull.

It took a while to get to the Goose Island neighborhood, but Sara never grew tired of her lack of vision. She chattered a practical monologue, trying to guess where they were headed, each speculation more far-fetched than the last.

A tax code debate?

Live reading of the terms and conditions on the latest iPhone?

An autopsy?

Sara possessed such creativity, and he intended to present her with the food equivalent of an unadorned rice cake.

She wiggled in her seat, her anticipation making Beckett's right eye begin to twitch. "Tell me why you wanted to be a Shakespeare professor."

Beckett's hands remained at nine and three on the steering wheel, but he relaxed his shoulders. "The first Shakespeare play I ever saw was *Twelfth Night*. My parents took me. I must have been nine at the time."

"Child abuse."

"I thought so too, at first. The first ten minutes or so of the play were quite incomprehensible. I mean, I understood the storm and the brother and sister forcibly separated, but I had no idea what people were saying to one another." He smiled at the memory, letting his comfort in the subject ease his nerves. "After those first minutes, though, my ear tuned to the language, like driving into a radio signal."

"Is that your favorite play, then?"

"*Midsummer Night's Dream* was always my favorite, but then the Chicago Shakespeare Company did a production of *The Tempest*. It was adapted and co-directed by Aaron Posner and Teller—from Penn and Teller. And it was the most amazing bit of theater I've ever attended. The use of magic and music was sublime. I went back again and again, watching eleven performances." He'd been transported. How he wished he could take her to see that production. "After every performance, I thought about how wonderful it would have been if Shakespeare himself could have been there. I'll bet he'd be rendered speechless."

"He probably would have thought it was witchcraft and died of a heart attack."

Beckett nodded, though she couldn't see him while blindfolded. On impulse, he reached over and took one of her hands. She jumped then clamped onto him. At least he'd given her that little bit of excitement.

The art gallery had parking right out front, so he didn't need to guide Sara far to reach the space. She'd talked about Ren's artistic aspirations with such enthusiasm, he thought she would love to see a professional art exhibit. If Beckett's mother approved of the artist, then he had true talent. But he should have pushed himself to unearth something truly unexpected.

The gallery manager from opening night saw them approach and ran to open the door for them. Beckett much preferred the gallery when it was uncrowded, like now. He liked it even more when the manager showed none of the nervous sales pitchiness of their first encounter. The man wasn't fazed by Sara being blindfolded, though he appreciated her dress for three seconds longer than was polite.

"Let me know if you have any questions," he said, then disappeared into the back kitchen area and picked up a Murakami book. The man had discerning taste.

Beckett removed the blindfold carefully so as not to pull Sara's hair, dreading the moment when she had to fake enthusiasm.

She squealed when she saw the art. Maybe he hadn't failed. "This is so—"

When her gaze fell on the scorched wall, she gasped, and all the blood drained from her face. Her head whipped from side-to-side, then up and down, and she spun in a full circle, staring out the glass door.

"Sara—?"

She wrapped her arms around herself, bending over and mumbling something that sounded like, *I can't be here.* Then she gulped in air over and over as if she were having difficulty breathing.

"Sara, what's wrong?" Beckett squatted next to her, his hand hovering over her back. He was afraid to touch her when she appeared so fragile.

"I'm fine. Just—just—panic attack, I think." She swallowed in tiny gasps, and her hands were icy as he grasped them.

Beckett wasn't sure what to do for her, but standing there and doing nothing was unacceptable. "Can we get some water, please?"

The manager, who'd creeped over to them, said, "Of course," and scurried away.

Beckett scooped Sara into his arms, not feeling her weight. There was a single chair at the far back wall, and he carried her there, easing her into the seat.

"Here." The manager held out a Chicago skyline coffee mug filled with water.

Sara took it, but her hands shook enough Beckett put his own hands over hers to keep her from spilling.

"Little sips," Beckett said. "Take your time. There's no rush."

Her face was blotchy and wet with tears, but her makeup hadn't run. Beckett withdrew the pocket square from his jacket and offered it to her.

"I'm so glad I never teased you about the uselessness of a hanky," Sara said, taking the square and dabbing her face. She took another sip of water, but the cup wobbled afterward, as if it were too heavy. "This is the second time I've seen you use one."

Beckett took the cup. "Let me know when you want more." He smiled at her. "It isn't a hanky but a pocket square. When else did I use one?"

"When your mother lost her bracelet in the bathroom, and you were too scared of germs to touch it."

That had been so long ago. "Well, there you go."

Her eyes burned red, but the blue irises shone brighter than ever. "Why did you bring me here?"

He frowned. "To see the art."

She stared and stared, as if searching his eyes and his face for the truth. "That's the only reason?"

"What other reason could there be?" Beckett was missing something, but he had no idea what.

The gallery door opened, and the artist stepped inside. Beckett had already forgotten his name. It started with a—

"Cass?" Sara's voice was barely above a whisper, but the artist's head swiveled toward her.

"Sara? What are you doing here? Are you okay?" Cass jogged over, completely disregarding Beckett. He put his hand on her shoulder. "Why would you come here?"

"Why are *you* here?" she replied.

Cass held out one arm. "This is my show."

Sara's composure broke. "But why would you want to have a show *here*?"

Beckett fisted his hands. Apparently, the artist had easily comprehended the reason for her strange reaction. They had some kind of shared past, and though Beckett remembered Cass had a fiancée, she wasn't here, and she wasn't nearly as beautiful as Sara. Beckett resisted the impulse to shove the other man away from his girlfriend.

"I'd already had a show scheduled here, and they asked me again, once they rebuilt, and I thought . . ." Cass ran a hand through his hair. "We thought it might be empowering or something to reclaim the space."

"People died. Stadler died."

"Stadler deserved to die," Cass countered.

Die?

Sara pressed a hand into her abdomen. "You think everyone got what they deserved, then?"

"Oh, fuck." Cass squatted down as easily as Beckett had. "Sara, I'm sorry. No, I absolutely don't think you deserved what happened to you. That wasn't what I meant at all."

"What happened to you?" Beckett asked, the mystery unbearable.

"You don't know? Honestly?" Sara asked.

Beckett blinked, trying to decode what she was saying. He should have read the file Andrew had given him. "Of course not. How would I?"

"The Agency didn't say anything?"

"The Agency?" Cass interjected. "You're still working for those bastards?"

"Not in the same capacity," Sara said. "But they've got their thumb on me."

"Excuse me," Beckett said in a voice so calm it made Sara flinch. "One of you needs to tell me what in the hell happened here."

People died.

Cass and Sara regarded each other, as if colluding. A sharp pain started in Beckett's chest and scratched its way up his throat. He was seconds away from grabbing Cass and discovering exactly what he was thinking. His mind charged up, his power roaring to the surface. Even from a few feet away, he saw the fuchsia streaks of Cass's thoughts. Traumatic thoughts. And a smidge of amber. Guilt maybe.

Guilt. Disrepute. Shame.

Beckett heaved back his gift, holding to his principles.

"I was shot here," Sara said. "Five months ago."

Beckett swung his gaze back to her, raking her body as if he could see signs of such a grievous injury. She sat with an arm clutched across her stomach, and he recognized the action as something he'd seen her do a few times.

"It was a combination of a job gone wrong, an ex-lover, and the implosion of my work team."

"A total clusterfuck," Cass added.

Beckett heard everything, but absorbed little. "Someone *shot* you?" He couldn't imagine anyone having the coldness to try to harm someone so warm.

"Right in the gut," she said, petting her abdomen as if it were a frightened pet. Tears streamed down her face again. She looked at Cass. "How's Jolene?"

The name tickled a memory.

"She's thriving," Cass said. "I did a painting of her. It's on display here, but . . ." Cass bit his lip. "If you want to see her in person, I can call her and see if she'll come over."

"Do you think she would? She's not, like, totally pissed at me?"

Cass smiled at Sara. He was altogether too striking, more handsome than Andrew, and considering Sara with too much concern.

"I'd love to see her," Sara said. Then she clapped both hands onto her thighs and stood. Her face had color again, but she swayed on her high heels. "But first, I want to see this painting."

Cass took her elbow, but dropped it when Beckett glared at him. Beckett was Sara's escort for the evening, and he didn't appreciate the other man usurping his role, even for a few minutes. Beckett gently slipped the pocket square from her hand to his trouser pocket then wrapped his arm around Sara. She leaned into him, snaking her arm around his waist. He had never walked with a partner in such a manner, but he found it worked for them.

When they reached the sole portrait painting in the show, Sara moved close to study it. She flashed Cass a bright smile. "This is gorgeous, Cass! It looks just like her."

"We'll see if you still think so after she gets here," Cass said with his own dazzling grin, before going off to speak with the manager.

"Jolene and I worked together for almost five years," Sara said, swiping a finger under each eye. "She's one of the only friends I've ever had."

Beckett brushed a stray lash from her cheek. "How is that possible? Everyone loves you."

Sara laughed, the sound a combination of genuine amusement and bitterness. "People are attracted to me. That doesn't make them my buddies." She moved to the second row of paintings. "I've never had many opportunities to make real friends. My home life was difficult, and my mom and stepdad isolated me. I ran away when I was fifteen and lived in temporary place after temporary place for almost two years. Nobody is your friend when you need them to survive."

Luckily, she didn't seem to need a response, because Beckett's throat had tightened enough that he wouldn't have been able to speak in his regular voice. Sara had been a homeless, runaway teen? That explained why she'd been so fierce in her insistence he take Ren into their program.

"I finally was rescued by someone with the Agency. That's when I began the covert work, and you can't make real connections when you're always pretending to be somebody else. All I had were my teammates, and I thought we were as close as family."

Covert work? She'd been a spy for the Agency? Corporate espionage?

She patted her face, and Beckett realized she was crying again. "We *were* family. But our leader . . . he was a closeted memory surgeon. I'm pretty sure I was the only one who knew. He brought in Jolene, who was a known memory surgeon—like, she was known in the scientific community. She was one of the first memory surgeons to be studied, a close friend of Kiera Brayleigh's."

"Kiera Brayleigh?" Beckett's voice croaked. Kiera was the most famous and infamous memory magician. Years ago, she'd been kidnapped by a serial killer, and Beckett had always wondered if her gift had helped her escape.

They fell silent as they surveyed the paintings. Beckett's thoughts came into focus, then distorted, like funhouse mirrors until he wasn't sure which was the true vision. He'd never considered himself sheltered or naive, but he'd overestimated his grasp of the world. Someone had tried to kill effervescent Sara.

Beckett made two tours of the space with Sara without perceiving anything.

Suddenly, the blond woman he'd met at the opening burst into the gallery and stopped short when she saw Sara. "No fucking way!"

"Jolene!" Sara sounded elated.

Beckett couldn't see Sara's face, but Jolene grinned and held her arms open. Sara ran into her, almost knocking the other woman over with her hug.

"You're okay?" Jolene asked Sara.

"I'm always okay," Sara said, her manner shifting to something a little more brazen than he was used to seeing from her.

"You scared the shit out of me. We were told you'd lived but nothing else." Jolene stepped back and looked Sara up and down, her gaze pausing on her stomach, as if trying to see for herself that Sara was healed.

The idea that Sara could have been killed pressed on Beckett like damned guilty deeds to sinners' minds. There could have been a version of the world where he'd never met her.

CHAPTER TWENTY-FIVE

Sara

THEY STOOD NEAR THE GLASS DOOR, SARA wrapping her hand around Jolene's, afraid the other woman might disappear if she didn't hold on to her hard enough. Jolene was as fit as Sara remembered, more relaxed, though. She wore black yoga pants with a long-sleeved T-shirt.

Sara grabbed her into another hug. "I've missed you."

Jolene hugged her back. "What are you doing now?"

She couldn't tell Jolene the whole truth, but she wouldn't lie. "Beckett's got a program to help teach young memory magicians to be upstanding people, and I'm sort of helping him with it."

Jolene scratched along the inside of her arm. "I have too many questions. A program?"

"It's actually pretty cool. They examine the ethical ramifications of their gifts, making conscious choices about the kind of memory magicians they want to be."

"Memory magicians? You mean memory surgeons?"

Sara shrugged. "Turns out memory magic comes in more than one form. For example, I, apparently, have some type of this, uh, magic. I can't be read."

Jolene slapped her on the back. "I knew it! Your mind was always so weird."

Sara burst out laughing. "How do you know that? You never tried to read me."

Jolene's ears flushed. "No, but when we were at that bar looking for Stefano organization intel, I was all psychically juiced, and when we touched, your mind was behind a kind of wall, except for this wacko gold memory, which I swear to God was your cover story. It was perfectly spherical. I bet you can manufacture fake memories. That's how fucking awesome you are."

"Huh." That talent would be useful. "Too bad nobody can access them."

For several minutes, they updated each other on the minutiae of their lives. Jolene was working for Kiera Brayleigh's charity, which helped victims of predatory memory surgeons.

Sara jumped up and down once. Her strapless bra wasn't heavy duty enough to handle more than one jump. "You guys have *got* to come and talk to the students."

"And tell them what? Don't steal or try to alter memories without permission? That's kind of a low bar, ethically. I hope they're beyond that."

"Yeah, you'd think so, but they're *kids*. I mean, how often did you think about other people's feelings when you were that young?" Sara asked. She herself had thought of others' moods all the time, but that had been necessary for her personal safety.

Jolene and Sara talked over each other with ideas of how they could show the impact—both positive and negative—their actions could have on others, how they could translate the lessons from the theoretical to the real world.

Not wanting to get ahead of herself this time, Sara called Beckett over, introduced him, and looped him into the discussion. Beckett agreed after only three questions, not even giving her the stink eye for making offers without consulting him.

His easy compliance made Sara think she'd ruptured him with all the revelations about her past, or maybe her meltdown had done it. She wondered how Beckett might react later, once he'd digested what he'd learned, now that he knew she was so damaged.

* * *

"THAT WAS THE MEMORY MAGICIAN FRIEND YOU MENTIONED BEFORE, then?" Beckett asked when they were back in the car. "She seemed . . . nice."

Sara laughed. "Jolene isn't an un-nice person, but if I were going to pick out one word for her, it wouldn't be *nice*."

"What would it be?"

She didn't have to think long. "Fierce."

"And what word would you use to describe me?" He didn't smile, but the corner of his mouth ticked up.

Uptight was her first impulse, but that was before she'd gotten to know him. "Proper," she finally decided.

"Proper?" He frowned.

"Yeah, you always try to do the right thing. It's admirable," she replied. "What about me? What word would you choose."

"Mercurial."

Mercurial was another word for *unreliable*. She'd rather be *tantalizing* or *irresistible*. "I suppose that's fair."

"It's a compliment," he said, as if sensing her disappointment. "Nothing fazes you. You adapt to every situation without losing a moment of poise. I admire that."

"Poise? I just had a panic attack in an art gallery." Nobody had ever called her poised. She rested her head against the back of the seat. "You admire me?"

"You have many positive qualities."

Sara rolled her head to the side to study his profile. "Expound. I want to hear this list."

He did smile then. "Humbleness did not make the cut, I'm afraid."

"I didn't ask what *wasn't* on the list."

"If I give you this list, will you promise not to instruct me to repeat it ad nauseum?"

"I promise not to ask you to repeat it more than . . . five times. That's not very many. Short of half a dozen."

Beckett laughed. It was a scratchy, wheezy sound that made Sara's stomach twerk in a most unseemly way. She wondered why he didn't laugh all the time, because it was infectious. Maybe because being taken seriously was such a deep necessity for him.

"Fine." He held out his hand for her to shake.

His palm was smooth, the grip firm, and Sara thought she might cry at how reassuring it felt to be touched by Beckett. When the handshake was over, they continued to hold hands, and that was when she thought about his memory magic. She didn't detect a whiff of his gift.

"Go on, then," she prompted. She bounced her legs in anticipation.

"You're warm, charming, considerate, Puckish, clever, and fun."

Sara's heart beat hard enough it made her entire body pulse. It wasn't a comfortable feeling but also not unpleasant. "You didn't mention beautiful," she said.

"Do you need me to state the obvious?"

"Beauty is subjective." Her stomach flipped, and her face grew hot and tingly.

His eyes cut to her, but he kept his focus mainly on the road. "Well, then. You are the most stunning woman I've ever met. You could have been a vestal virgin, and they had to be without blemish."

"Are you calling me flawless?" She squeezed his hand but couldn't work up a wink.

"On the contrary, I think you are deeply flawed. But you are certainly beautiful and, like I said, warm, considerate, charming, clever, and quite Puckish."

"Puckish? Is that from *A Midsummer Night's Dream*?"

"Yes. Quite the troublemaker, that Puck." He grinned at her.

She should definitely sleep with him. She'd sworn off sex before she'd known men like Beckett existed. Probably, she'd never meet anyone like him again. This might be her only chance.

* * *

"Come inside," Sara said, refusing to pause at the threshold, not dwelling on the idea that her place might not be as she'd left it. Or empty.

"Are you sure?" he replied.

It wasn't late, and Sara's nerves were popping and sizzling. She didn't want to be alone, and she really wanted to be close to Beckett. He made her feel safe, and though safety was an illusion, she had no trouble embracing that fiction. At least for a while.

He closed the door behind him but didn't lock it.

Her chest squeezed and squeezed. Every other man she'd known would have locked the door, would have turned back to her with a leer or a comment or a gesture of what he expected.

"Can you lock the door?" Sara asked, because she didn't like the idea of Dickhead barging in unannounced and uninvited. Not that the lock had stopped him before. Maybe she should have invited herself to Beckett's.

"Sure." Beckett flipped the deadbolt, and Sara's insides fluttered.

They felt real, the two of them, and she wasn't pretending to find him attractive, to want to get close to him. Sara stood in the living room, waiting for Beckett to come to her. He took his time, as if giving her space to change her mind.

It made her want to do shocking things. Drop to her knees. Downward Dog over the sofa. Dance.

He stopped a full foot from her, his shoulders slightly forward as if he intended to wrap his arms around her. "Sara."

When had she become so enamored of her name in his fancy, oak-barrel-aged voice? "Beckett."

He traced the edge of her jaw with the light touch she'd come to associate with him. She wanted to curl within him, embed herself into his skin, then burrow deeper and deeper until she was fully encased. The imagined warmth made her shiver.

His fingers halted. He noticed everything.

"Don't stop," she said.

Beckett moved closer, exchanging his fingertips for his lips, skimming over her jaw, the underside of her chin, then around to the other side. He paused where her jaw and ear met, breathing into her flesh. Her body rippled inside like one of those giant dancing tubes in front of used car lots. He provided the wind, each exhale swirling up and out of her, until she floated, crested, billowed, and flew higher and higher.

His hand on her waist grounded her, kept her from leaving her body entirely. His lips returned to her skin, inching tiny kisses down the side of her neck. Sara made an embarrassing mewling noise, and he lingered on the spot for precious seconds. She wanted him to stay there and to be everywhere, all at once. If only Beckett could clone his lips and spread them over her like a coat of many colors, painted in every shade of desire.

He could ask her for anything, and she'd give it to him, but all he did was kiss her. His touch wasn't tentative or self-conscious. If she hadn't known she couldn't be read, she might have suspected something supernatural. How could he know how slowly she required him to go to feel safe?

His lips reached the base of her throat. He lingered there, one hand still gripping her waist. The other hand fluttered down the opposite side of her neck. Her knees buckled as if he'd somehow hit her restart button.

Beckett caught her—of course he did—and gently set her on the couch. "Are you well?"

With a static charge of clarity, she realized Beckett Convery could be an arrogant prick, but nobody could call him inattentive.

"I'm fine," she replied, sounding as if she'd jogged up the stairs.

"Would you rather . . . take a break? Can I get you something to drink?"

His words turned on the burner behind her eyes to eleven. Maybe he treated everyone so considerately, his manners as inbred as his class, but it felt, in that moment, so personal. He saw her, all the way inside, all the way to the shriveled abomination of her soul. And like in a horror movie, that burned husk took in a shallow breath, signifying to the audience that it wasn't truly dead. At least, not yet.

"Sara?" His strong eyebrows dipped.

"Sorry." She smiled at him. "I believe you've kissed me stupid, Professor."

His cheeks pinked. "Glass of water?"

In truth, she could use a few minutes away from the magnetic draw of him, but she'd never been what anyone would call practical. "I'm good."

He sat with his perfect posture, both relaxed and alert, rumpled only near his collar. Everything about him seemed opposite to her. He had an internal peace and calm she could achieve only after an entire night of dancing or a two-hour hot yoga session. Energy pinged inside her like a package of Mentos dropped into a two-liter bottle of Coke.

She angled her body toward him, kicking off her pumps and tucking her feet under her. When she looked at him, she forgot to peer from beneath her lashes or to turn her head to showcase her long neck. She forgot about herself altogether, too bespelled by the smoothness of his jaw, even so late at night, and the dip in his lower lip.

Beckett's stillness broke as he reached out and traced the line of her collarbone, focusing on the bared patch of skin in a slash of her dress, using the same gentle touch. "This is a stunning dress. Is it designer?"

She tried to smile but was too dazzled by him. "I don't know designer names on anything except shoes. For dresses and everything else, I just . . ."

His touch didn't move down, but hesitated, and Sara felt his intention moving toward her breasts.

Her nipples ached in anticipation as she girded herself for the inevitable. Once a man got his hands on her tits, it tripped some switch inside his testosterone-filled brain, and he turned frantic for sex. She'd never understood the rush, but it happened every time.

"You just what?"

"Huh?"

"Your clothes?"

Her clothes? They were in the way. She blinked and backtracked her brain. They'd been talking about designer clothing.

Beckett's hand stroked down her arm rather than her chest. She groaned, her nipples throbbing in time to her heartbeat. The denial made her almost insane with need, despite the want tinged with dread she'd experienced only the moment before. Sara loved surprises.

"Someone else used to buy my clothes, so I don't follow designers. Want to check my tag?" Not her best seduction line but also not her worst.

"It doesn't matter."

She scooted closer to Beckett, and the lingering scent of his cologne ramped her libido up higher. For a moment, it occurred to her that sex might have a standard process for him, like table manners. It was entirely possible posh people had sex differently than the working class.

Moving slowly, she slipped her hand around his neck and tugged his face nearer to hers. "Is there, like, something I should be doing?"

Beckett's eyes flicked between her eyes and lips. "I have no idea how to answer that."

"Just, do you have any specific expectations?" She could have waited for his answer, of course, but she didn't. Instead, she licked her lips and pressed them against his. Press and slide, minutely to the left then right, then back to the center. She adjusted her lips to capture his top lip, then the bottom.

His lips parted, and he increased the pressure. She scratched her nails over his scalp, her fingers sliding into his soft hair. Their kisses gained intensity, like a rockslide. Finally, *finally*, he licked her lips.

The proximity of his tongue to her mouth turned her body into the shimmery sort of heat that flowed up from hot asphalt, more gas than liquid or solid.

Beckett made a noise somewhere between a growl and a groan, the sound vibrating against her lips. Their tongues met, the kiss deep and satisfying, and she expected to careen out of control.

She broke the kiss to trail her lips to his ear. Scraping her teeth along his earlobe, she fought to catch her breath, panting softly into his ear. His body locked up, and out of the corner of her eye, she found his hand white-knuckling the back of the couch.

His restrained passion did more for her than any touch could have accomplished. "Beckett." She didn't recognize the husky whine in her voice.

"I'm trying," he replied, as if she'd asked him for something specific.

Had she? Did he understand her better than she understood herself?

"What are you trying?" She kissed his lips again instead of allowing him to answer.

"To go slow enough for you."

The words he'd spoken stuck in her chest with a burning ache. "What?"

"It's as if you can read my mind, and every time I think I'm going to press into you, you tense."

She did? "I do?"

"Have men pushed you in the past?" His eyes were glassy and his pupils large, as if he were drugged. "I don't want to scare you or hurt you."

Sara's consciousness blinked out for a moment, and when it returned, she found herself straddling Beckett, her dress rucked up to the tops of her thighs as she ground against his erection like a nymphomaniac on X. "I need you." She didn't care how desperate she sounded, how her voice rasped as if someone had tied it behind a truck and dragged it over a mile of gravel road.

"Anything you want," he replied, his hips providing the perfect counterpressure.

His fingers cupped her face with a gentleness made more intense by the lewdness of their mashing pelvises. Already, the sparks of an impending orgasm flickered up from her core, to her chest, and out her mouth in an explosion of humming and dirty words like *fuck* and embarrassing words like *please* and *thank you*.

"Sara. Sara." He chanted her name like a warm warning. "Sara, I'm going—You're going to—"

"Yes." God, yes, that was exactly what she wanted, for him to come apart like a teenager. "Yes." She rubbed against him like a hussy goddess, the rush of power she usually felt during sex all the more potent because Beckett wasn't some douchebag she wanted to trick, but a man of integrity she wanted to please. Which was why she shocked herself by blurting, "Hold me."

One of the hands cupping her face slid behind her neck and cradled her head, while the other pulled her chest to his chest, his arm a protective band of warmth and safety. She came, the orgasm a sandstorm, whiting out her vision, pricks of sensation whipping everywhere, higher and higher into the sky, all her insides shifting, and as she came down, everything had settled into a different space and configuration. Sara breathed into her disorientation as Beckett cried out, a grunting growl against the oversensitive skin of her neck, making her body buck into him, her fingers digging into his shoulders.

As he relaxed, he kissed her, his lips so soft and pliant her stomach flipped, and her desire for him spiked again. Could they have sex after they'd just dry humped each other—one another?—damn that Beckett, she couldn't remember exact grammar after coming so hard.

She wriggled in his hold enough to look into his eyes without going cross-eyed. He gazed at her, his skin glowing with perspiration, and a questioning expression like a dog expecting a scolding. "I wish you'd been my first time," she said.

With a single finger, he moved a lock of hair that had fallen over one of her eyes. "Because that was so juvenile?"

Sara huffed a laugh. "That was very, very adult." She smiled at him, wanting to gift him with honesty, if only a slice. "Because you . . ." What was she trying to say? "You make me feel important."

"You are," he replied, as if that was something simple and obvious and not an arrow into her heart. "Was your first time not enjoyable?"

The memory's sharpness had dulled considerably in her afterglow. "Worst sex of my life. Think of every way sex should be, turn it inside out, and that was my first time. But I don't want to talk about that."

His hands ran up and down her spine in a soothing caress. "What would you like to discuss, then?"

She waggled her fingers. "Cleaning you up?"

"Definitely not. That's bound to be awkward."

"Okay, we'll save that for later."

Sara traced a finger across his lips, lingering in the appetizing divot on his bottom lip. Beckett groaned, his head falling to the back of the couch. Sara wanted to lick up the column of his neck but refrained.

He scanned the carnage that had once been his pristine shirt and winced. "Well, this is certainly going to help us look more like a real couple."

It wasn't that she'd forgotten they weren't truly together, but his words reminded her that he hadn't chosen her. He'd enjoyed the sex stuff, she had no doubt, but she knew better than anyone how little sex could mean—or how disparate the meanings could be.

CHAPTER TWENTY-SIX

Beckett

BECKETT MASTURBATED TWICE—ONCE IN THE shower and again lying in bed when sleep wouldn't come. It barely took the edge off. He couldn't stop imagining Sara on top of him, rubbing against his erection, her soft lips on his. If they'd had actual intercourse, would he have buzzed and burned even after he'd ejaculated?

More likely, he suspected, Sara was simply addictive.

After it became clear slumber was nowhere in the vicinity, Beckett got up and put milk in a double boiler and scraped in half a vanilla bean and a dollop of maple syrup. He docked his phone to play some oldie classics. While Sam Cooke sang "Wonderful World," Beckett removed a leatherbound notebook from its place in the kitchen drawer and opened to the first blank page.

Now what?

He needed a Sara distraction.

Beckett wrote *Ren*. Below that, he listed everything he'd learned about her and her gift.

His music cut out because of a text notification.

Sara. *What are you doing still awake*

He should ignore it, as talking to her was hardly likely to remove her from his thoughts.

How do you know I'm not deeply asleep?

Her reply came quickly. *Because I'm your stalker girlfriend and I can see your lights on from my bedroom window you are not the type of person to waste electricity by keeping on lights when you're sleeping*

The compulsion to correct her punctuation was almost overwhelming, but that hadn't gone so well in the past. She also did talk-to-text, so the errors were possibly phone-related and not Sara-born. One day, he'd discover the correct approach to addressing her probable dyslexia and the manner in which she compensated. He wanted to ease her mind.

I do like to conserve when I can. Why are you awake?

I'm a short sleeper I don't sleep much

Beckett did a quick Google search on "short sleeper" and found it referred to someone who slept less than six hours a night. *How much do you sleep? Are you fatigued?*

If I sleep more than four or five hours a night I feel awful the next day why are you up

He contemplated how honest he wanted to be. Because of the late hour, he was more forthcoming. *A lot happened tonight, and I've been thinking about you. When will I see you again?*

Tomorrow movie screening Kenji picked what women want UGG

He'd forgotten about movie night. *Would you be amenable to coming to my place afterward?*

Very amenable

Goodnight, Sara.

Goodnight professor

* * *

ALL THE KIDS SHOWED UP TO THE SECOND SCREENING, EVEN MARLENA, who rarely participated in group activities. They piled into Wilson's room again. Sara had asked everyone to bring their own seats. Some of the kids brought kitchen chairs, but Brayton had dragged his purple club chair, and

Jason toted a green camp chair complete with a sun umbrella, which he opened.

Sara professed her love for everyone's seating. She'd convinced Brayton to bring her an ottoman, which she set directly next to the end of the sofa to make it a chaise longue. "We're going to sit here together," she said to Beckett with a waggle of her brows.

"That sounds highly inappropriate," Beckett replied, though he didn't inject much energy into the statement.

"Please. PG-13 at best. Oh. Unless we throw a blanket into the mix, then we can bump up to an R, possibly an NC-17. What do you think?" She arched her eyebrows. She wore black lounge pants low on her hips with an oversized T-shirt and bunny slippers.

"I think we should keep it strictly PG until we are back at my place," Beckett replied. This would be a suitable locale for strict PG-foreplay: holding hands and stroking arms, necks, the shell of her ear.

"Yes, sir," she said with a wink, then she shuffled Ren into the group with her spindle kitchen chair, wedging her between Kenji and Wilson, the friendliest of the bunch.

When everyone had crowded around the seventy-two-inch screen, Sara announced, "We're about to watch *What Women Want*, Kenji's choice of psychic movie. Afterward, we will have a heated discussion. Don't forget to share snacks, and if anyone's seen it before, no giving away the plot. I hate that."

Wilson gave Sara control of the remote, which was, apparently, a great honor.

"Let the screening begin!" She hit play and then nudged Beckett's knees apart so she could wedge herself between them, sitting with her back to his chest.

She harbored no self-consciousness. As she lay against him, the students whooping and bickering around them, Beckett had the oddest sense of family, though this was nothing like his own. A comfort threaded through the room, a connection he hadn't known to want.

Unfortunately, having Sara so close opened up not only a world of emotions, but physical responses. Awkward physical responses.

Beckett closed his eyes for several seconds, trying to gain control of his traitorous body. Sara's hair tickled the side of his face, her perfume toyed with his senses, and her warm figure fit perfectly into his. It was a bliss that couldn't last. Luckily, the movie's intro was long enough that he didn't miss any of the feature.

The premise of *What Women Want* was well known, though Beckett hadn't seen the film. They all loved that it took place in Chicago. Mel Gibson's character, Nick, was an exaggerated example of toxic masculinity. The men found the film far more humorous than the women did.

At the end of the sex scene between Nick and Marisa Tomei's character, Lola, Sara stopped the video.

"Okay, who here has done this?" she asked, referring to Nick reading Lola's mind and adjusting his technique.

No one responded.

"Oh, come on," Sara said, sitting forward. "You guys are telling me none of you have memory read while you were making out with someone?"

Silence.

Beckett comprehended why nobody talked. After watching the scene, it was especially clear what a trespass it was, even if the intentions were strictly to please a lover. "I have," Beckett said, hoping if he admitted it, others might follow. "When I was younger."

"Dude," Wilson said, raising his can of Mello Yello in a toast. "Me too. It was wild."

"It's not quite like it was in the movie—at least for me. I wasn't interested in having someone see me as a sex god, but the connection enabled me to know precisely what my partner wanted," Beckett said. "I truly believe I was unselfishly motivated."

"Okay, but in the movie, the guy couldn't stop hearing other people's thoughts. You guys did that shit on purpose," Ren said, one combat boot resting on the bottom rail of Erik's chair.

"And you've never done that?" Brian countered, scowling.

Ren scoffed. "My gift isn't thought related. I suppose I've used my talent to tweak situations to my advantage, but I've never used it to get laid."

"Because girls don't need to," Brian replied.

"Nobody needs to," Marlena interjected. "You're pigs."

"No name calling," Beckett said, using his professor voice. This debate hit too many hot buttons for a casual gathering, but it was too late now. "Why don't we finish watching the film and then have a further discussion?"

"Why would we want to watch more of this shit?" Marlena said.

Beckett nodded. "I see your point. Nick's character is quite reprehensible right now, but that's part of his narrative arc. The inciting incident is when Nick can hear women's thoughts. He can't escape the plot after that. This is at the bottom of the arc, where he's using his gift for selfish purposes. As the movie continues, I imagine—"

"Eh, eh, eh." Sara clapped a hand over his mouth. "Don't give away the story."

He arched his eyebrows, and she removed her hand. He continued, "I haven't seen this before, so I'm only speculating. Is that not allowed?"

She frowned. "Not by you. You're too smart. We get your point. He's going to improve his choices as we go through the movie."

Ren chuckled. "It's not like he could make worse choices."

"Hey, he's being nice to the suicidal chick," Erik said. "And he's getting nothing out of that."

"I guess he's a great guy, then," Marlena grumbled. She huffed and stood. "I'm out of here. This is bullshit. A shit-pile of misogyny wrapped up to pass for feminism. So fucking condescending."

"Although I don't disagree," Beckett said, "why not stay until the end, and then we can debate the movie as a whole? I know I would welcome your perspective, which you can't share if you leave now."

"Fine." Marlena crumbled into her chair, arms crossed aggressively. "But for the record, this movie sucks."

Sara hit play, then snuggled into Beckett's chest before shifting to kiss his jaw. He looked down at her, and they gazed at each other for several long seconds, ignoring the movie entirely.

Bringing her into the fold had been one of his best decisions. He hoped.

The importance of the dinner party niggled at his mind, though. It felt as if it would be a turning point, a moment in time that would decide everything. And he had no idea which way it would go.

The movie ended pretty much as Beckett had predicted, and a lively discourse followed. Heavy input upfront from the women:

Sara: "I think men's efforts would be better spent paying attention *before* sex."

Ren: "Uh, just ask if you want to know if a girl is into something."

Marlena: "You all make me sick."

"I've never attempted memory magic during sex," Kenji said. "Mostly because I never thought about it. I'm too into myself, I guess." He turned pink and wouldn't look at any of the girls. "But I've used it a few times to see if a girl liked me. That's different, right? Because it was so helpful."

They had a spirited debate about that too.

* * *

It took Beckett two tries to get the correct six-digit code into his home, though that might have been because Sara had wrapped her arms around his waist, her breasts pressing into his back. When he flipped on the lights, she gasped, stepping inside with her mouth open.

"It's gorgeous," she whispered, kicking off her bunny slippers at the door. "I think this is the most amazing house I've ever seen. Can I snoop?"

"Let me give you the grand tour."

The church had been one floor, but Beckett's architects had made it two stories. He loved the way the stained-glass windows were bisected and how all the arches and columns had been retained, adding hallways and bedrooms and special areas, like the laundry room and his study. He'd had everything painted white, and it always had a beautiful glow, whether from sunlight, sconce lighting, or candlelight.

He showed Sara all of it. She laughed at the size of his laundry room and all his ironing accoutrements. At his bedroom, she touched the velvet curtains on his four-poster bed. "Wow."

"It's . . . I bought the bed to suit the space and not my own personal tastes." He didn't want to confess he felt like a king sleeping in the large bed with the curtains drawn to keep it as dark as possible.

"Who cares? It's a killer bed. Can I sleep here tonight? Please?" She jumped onto the bed, bouncing on her knees. "This is going to be so fun."

Beckett was unsure if he could provide *fun* sex, but perhaps she was referring to slumbering. "You are cordially invited."

She giggled. "I'm dying to find out if you're a cuddler."

The temptation to take her in his arms and kiss her almost overwhelmed him. They'd been building to this for weeks... Except she was holding a hand over her abdomen, reminding him they needed to have a proper conversation about the past first.

"Sara," he said, sitting on the edge of the bed, angled toward her. "Can I ask you about five months ago?"

She dropped her hand from her stomach. "I was on a job." Her eyes drilled into him. "I've sort of downplayed the details when we've talked before, but I think I need to be explicit. I slept with men to get information. That was my role on Agency jobs." She stared at him, obviously bracing for his response.

"That must have been hard," he said. "But that's all in your past, right?" She'd have no cause to seduce him for intel. He didn't know anything useful to an organization like the Agency that would be worth that level of effort. Plus, he and Sara wouldn't have had such a rocky start if her goal had been to deceive and seduce him.

"I'll always carry that with me."

His chest ached and burned, and Beckett struggled with violent impulses that were at odds with how he saw himself. "Something happened with one of your . . ."

"Hm. Yeah." She scooted off the bed to stand near the foot, keeping the wood post between them. "This last one . . . he was . . . scary. Aggressive, possessive, and . . . abusive. I pushed to finish the job faster, and mistakes were made."

He wanted to ask more questions, but her skittishness was approaching that of a cornered animal, so he did his best to stay perfectly still.

"He blamed me and Jolene for his brother getting killed, and he found us at that art gallery. He executed our team leader and shot me in the stomach before Cass saved the rest of us with a grenade." Sara tossed up her arms. "That's it."

A grenade? *That's it?*

She petted the drapes, playing with the nap of the velvet. "I was taken to the hospital. My boyfriend at the time dropped me off and then disappeared with most of my money. I haven't heard from him since. And the Agency said I could go . . . they said . . ." Her face pinched, her voice growing tight. "But then they forced me to work in your program. I'm never getting away."

Beckett moved then, unable to witness her pain for another second without doing anything. He guided her around the post and bunched up drapes and into his arms quickly but carefully, his hold loose until she gripped him hard, then he squeezed her close.

"Is working with me that bad?" He would have done almost anything to ease her pain, even lose her as a resource. She was so much more than a test subject. "Should I try to have you released?"

He held her, and though she didn't cry, her body vibrated. His gift roared to life, part of him wanting to delve into her mind to find out what she needed from him. But he realized he didn't need his power to be there for her.

"That's okay." She sighed and rolled her forehead into his collarbone. "You're not so bad."

He kissed the top of her head. "So flattering. You know you don't have to sleep with me, right?" he asked—not that he thought she felt obligated, but because he hoped she would laugh at the idea of sex with him for information.

"Oh, yes, I do." She giggled, her breath warming his neck. "I've been looking forward to this since last night—since—for a long time now." She gazed at him, her eyes so blue, the whites of her eyes a little red. "Unless my story changes things for you. It would be okay if it did. I know it's not what a man wants to learn about a woman he's fake dating."

He didn't laugh. "Are we, though? Fake dating? Because what I feel is real."

"What do you feel?" she asked in a small voice.

Beckett kissed her—not a playful kiss or teasing kiss, but a firm kiss, a bold kiss he hoped told her how special and incredible she was to him. But then he thought she might also need the words. "I'm quite proud to call you my girlfriend."

"Really?"

"Yes. You're still warm, charming, considerate, Puckish, clever, and fun." He kissed her again. "But I want you to be comfortable, so if you feel the need to delay physical intimacy, I'm—"

"No!" She grinned. "To be honest, I didn't expect to want anyone ever again, but you make me feel like anything is possible. But, Beckett, I'm truly damaged—like, physically." She closed her eyes for a moment. "Nobody's seen the scar." Opening her eyes, she rolled them and added, "Other than, you know, doctors, nurses, and the plastic surgeon who's going to fix it."

Beckett wondered how extensive the injury had been if she required reconstructive surgery. "Does it hurt?"

"No," she replied. "It itches some, but it's mostly hideously ugly."

"If you'd rather not—"

"No, it's time." She pushed down her yoga pants, her hands trembling. Her long shirt covered her to the tops of her thighs.

Beckett wanted to scoop her into his arms, but he understood she needed to do this her way, as painful as it clearly was for her.

"Okay," she said then yanked off the shirt quick and fast as if it were a Band-Aid.

Beckett tried to see everything at once but could take in no details other than her black lace panties and matching bra. Her breasts were amazing, full and round. Eventually, his eyes found the jagged red scar, longer than he'd anticipated, shaped roughly in a J with a little tail, traveling from just under her ribs to her panty line. The diameter was as wide as a straw, the color of half-ripe raspberries, the texture looking as rough as stucco.

She shifted her weight, and her fingers scratched against her thighs.

Beckett reached for her, but paused before making contact. "May I?"

Sara nodded, watching him with only flicks of her gaze, as if afraid he would reject her. He brushed a finger over the top of the scar, tracing the raised tissue, then he bent to kiss her stomach above and below the scar. "It makes you no less lovely, you know."

She made a noise as if trying to snort, but it wouldn't catch. A tear slipped down her face, which she quickly wiped away. "I know I'm supposed to be grateful I don't have a colostomy bag, or that he didn't blow half my face off, or I didn't, like, die, and I *am* thankful to be alive, but . . . I can't let it go. No matter what I do or how hard I try. He vandalized me."

He held her and kissed her neck, whispering to her all the comforting words he could find, about how she would be all right, how strong she was, how beautiful, how much he respected and admired her. He told her he was there for her, whatever she needed, that she wasn't alone. Almost, almost, he confessed he loved her, because how could he not? But it was too soon for a declaration like that.

"Will you hold me?" she whispered.

Since he was already holding her, it took him a moment to comprehend that she wanted to lie in his arms. She'd made the same request the night before. She needed comforting touch, not just sex.

Intertwining their fingers, he turned down the comforter, crawling in fully clothed and lifting the duvet for her to follow. She scampered into the bed and clung to him, all curves and lace and vulnerability.

CHAPTER TWENTY-SEVEN

Sara

THE MONDAY AFTER REN MOVED IN, SHE KNOCKED on Sara's door, her makeup from the day before Alice-Coopering her eyes. In her hand was a printout of some kind, creased so severely she must have crumpled then smoothed it. "I—I can't," was all she said, holding out the paper.

"Come in," Sara said, taking the document and gesturing Ren to the sofa. "Can I get you something to drink? Eat? I've got a few energy bars."

Ren hurled herself onto the couch and started bouncing her knees, jostling the elbows she rested on them. Her eyes darted around the room. "I knew it was too good to be true, that there had to be a catch."

Sara squinted at the paper, but the creases, and her dyslexia, made it hard to read. She set it on the coffee table. "Just tell me what this is about."

"They need ID and transcripts for my enrollment."

"And . . ."

Ren flapped her arms. "I wasn't living rough for fun. I can't contact my old school, and I can't go by my old name. It isn't safe."

Sara's face prickled, then went numb. No transcripts. No ID. Their backgrounds couldn't possibly be so similar. Nothing lately seemed random.

"What did you think would happen?" Sara asked as gently as possible.

The girl dropped her head into her hands. "I just thought they'd enter my name into a database or whatever."

"My guess is they can smooth away some obstacles, but you'll need an ID and transcripts, even if your grades weren't great."

Ren started crying, her entire body rising and falling with her sobs. "I shouldn't have come. I shouldn't have let myself hope. The apartment is so nice. I slept . . . I slept like a normal person." She resembled a kid now, not a tough young woman. "How long do you think I can stay?"

Ren's tears shredded Sara. She wondered how many decent people could have helped Ren by making a little effort instead of leaving her on her own.

Sara tapped her foot. She couldn't imagine Beckett kicking the girl out, but she also couldn't picture her being allowed to be part of the program without also being an enrolled student. Would he permit her to stay if Ren agreed to extensive evaluation of her gift?

Already, he'd been skeptical, grouching about Ren bypassing the usual vetting process. He'd never empathize. Beckett lived in a world where if someone threatened you, you went to the police, and they took care of everything.

If Sara told Beckett what was going on and he didn't agree to allow concessions, she couldn't take it back. She couldn't say, *ha, just kidding; she's all good.*

There was a way to help Ren with what she needed. The cost, however, would be significant. If Ryan had been her handler, she would already be helping Ren decide on the details of her new identity. But she didn't have Ryan. She had Dickhead.

"What's the situation?" Sara held up a hand before Ren could say anything. "Just between you and me. You have to be honest, and I swear I won't judge."

Ren bowed her head. "My dad owes some people a lot of money, and he used me as collateral. My aunt is in on it too."

"How, exactly, are you collateral?" She hated to make the girl spell it out, but there were too many possibilities. Most likely, he'd promised her virginity or the use of her body, but sick fucks could get awfully creative.

"My gift, I think. They wanted to pimp me out to some mob guy like an indentured servant, but they didn't give me details, so it could be anything. I didn't stick around to hear the whole plan." She kicked Sara's coffee table.

Sara put a hand on Ren's arm. Ren finally raised her head, her eyes bloodshot, her skin sallow, radiating defeat.

Last night, Beckett had held Sara until she'd fallen asleep, making no move to seduce her when she'd been vulnerable, like so many other men would have done. She couldn't repay that generosity with more betrayal. He needed Ren, and Ren needed the program. Surely there was a way to help Ren without relying on the Agency, which would, no doubt, exact a terrible price.

"Let's brainstorm ways to get those transcripts safely," Sara said.

"My aunt is the headmistress of the school, and she's connected to those guys my dad owes. She'd never forward my transcripts, even if I went to see her and begged. That bitch is the most spiteful person I've ever met."

Fucking family. They could be the worst. "Is there someone else who works in the office we can appeal to or even bribe?" Sara suggested, warming to the idea.

"She surrounds herself with toadies." Ren said. "It's a prestigious school, and enrollment is a bit of a racket."

"Could we break in and get your transcripts ourselves?"

Ren cocked her head, no longer sniffling. "Do you have the skills for that?"

"Locks, yes. Electronic security, no."

"She's got everything." Ren collapsed back on the couch, her body shrinking into itself. She was too small. "Thanks for trying, but it's useless. Will you tell Professor Convery?"

And admit the candidate she'd pushed him to accept had no ID or transcripts? Maybe it wouldn't hurt to find out what Dickhead's terms would be. "Let's hold off for a day or two and see if I can't work out a solution."

"Whatever." Ren shifted onto her back on the sofa, staring up at the ceiling. "Got any Coke?"

"I hope you're talking about the beverage."

Ren rubbed her sleeve over her nose. "No drugs for me, but caffeine and sugar are manna from the heavens."

"I don't have any drugs or caffeine, but I think the common kitchen stocks quite a bit of food and drinks."

"Are we allowed to help ourselves?"

Sara shrugged. "Until someone tells us otherwise, I say yes."

Ren grinned for a few seconds before her mood pinned her down again. "Might as well eat while I can."

* * *

SARA CONTEMPLATED HER PHONE, THE ANGEL AND DEVIL ON HER shoulders duking it out. The deciding factor was envisioning the most likely repercussion of each choice. In the end, she couldn't abandon Ren to the cruelties of the world and watch Beckett lose another student, not if she could avoid it.

She debated texting or calling. Texting provided her the greatest distance—and she wanted as much distance as possible—but it would also enable Dickhead to take time to form a reply, rather than dealing with her on the spot.

With a deep-cleansing mask on her face that smelled of lavender, she called Dickhead. He answered on the second ring. "What can Daddy do for you, Princess?" he drawled in his oiliest voice.

"I need an ID and transcripts for a student so she can be part of Beckett's program." Her tone was as professional and neutral as she could make it. He'd know this was important to her. She never would have contacted him otherwise.

"For little Ren?"

Fuck. Of course he already knew about her.

"Easy enough," he continued. "And what do I get in return?"

This was the response she'd expected, but it still tightened her throat like a garrote. She opted not to ask him what he wanted. "This student is my protégé, so I'll be able to share greater details about the training they're doing."

"You gonna recruit her for the Agency?" he asked.

"No." She'd decided that would be a dealbreaker. Serving Ren up to that life wouldn't do her any favors in the long run. "She's free and clear."

Dickhead laughed, a raspy guffaw more theater than genuine. "Sunshine, I only got that one report from you telling me shit I already knew, and you think I'm gonna do you favors?"

She said nothing, always the best choice when a specific tack wasn't obvious.

"All right," he said with a magnanimous sigh. "I can get you your ID and transcripts. Draft an email with the specifics. In return, I want details on this visit by the Philotimo."

Their focus was the leadership of the Moralists. Sara's alarm system blared—sirens, flashing lights, the whole package. She did not want to get involved in the Agency blatantly fucking over Beckett's group. And how did they know about the dinner? The Agency probably had spies everywhere, metastasizing like cancer, possibly even into the Phi.

"Why?"

"You don't get to ask me that, Princess. And you're gonna do it anyway, so you should take the shit for the kid. Besides, all we want is info."

Was he lying? His saying those words, as if to assure her the Agency was no danger, made her automatically think he was. What would the Agency do with the intel? She was sure the Agency meant Beckett's program, and possibly its participants, harm. And Dickhead would make her a party to it.

Yet if she refused, he'd apply another, more painful type of pressure to get what he wanted from her. And she wouldn't get what she needed for Ren. "All right."

What if Dickhead planned to kidnap one or all of the Philotimo? What if he wanted to arrange a hit on them? Fuck, fuck, fuck.

The memory of Ren in her layers of dirty clothing haunted her. Abandoning Ren would be so much like abandoning part of herself, and she couldn't do it. Maybe the only cost really would be something as benign as simple information. Though this first deal with Dickhead would undoubtedly be leveraged into a bigger betrayal.

Later, she'd figure out how to deal with this situation.

"Deal," she said before he jacked up the price. "I'll text you the details once they're decided."

"No. Email draft, Princess. We want this nice and secure."

As soon as she disconnected, her hands shook so hard she dropped the phone. Dark motes floated behind her eyes, and a shrill note reverberated in her ears.

She had to take several deep breaths to clear her vision and stop the ringing. "Well, that was intense," she muttered.

* * *

"You what?" Ren said when Sara gave her the news. Her eyes filled with tears, and the girl launched herself at Sara, her thin arms gripping her like she was a spider monkey.

Sara held up her phone. "We just need to email this guy the particulars— name, date of birth, and a rough idea of the transcript you want. I'm going to tell you right now, giving yourself a 4.0 will red-flag the records, so I recommend sending general instructions, like a 3.4 GPA with strength in math and science, and let the forger, who has experience with this stuff, choose the details. Make it as close to your real GPA and strengths as possible, but I wouldn't go lower than 3.2."

"And I can study art?" Ren asked.

"Sure." Sara had no idea if Wells College's art program was great, though.

Ren laughed and danced around her apartment. Her dance moves were more stomping than bumping and grinding, but they made Sara glad she'd taken a chance on the girl. This. This was what she wanted for Ren.

When Ren had exhausted herself, Sara opened up a new email and handed the phone to Ren. "Make your choices."

"Daddy?" Ren asked with both eyebrows raised.

Sara's face flushed. She couldn't explain the sick dynamic between her and Dickhead, not to mention all the danger. If Ren discovered how much Sara was risking for her, Ren would feel indebted, and Sara didn't want that.

"Stupid joke," she replied. "Quit busting my balls and tell him what you want." She winked to show she wasn't mad.

Ren's mouth quirked down, but she obeyed.

Once Dickhead retrieved the details, there would be no going back. Sara had saved Ren. Now she had to figure out a way to save Beckett too—from her.

* * *

Two days later, Sara came home to an apartment rife with negative energy, vibrating as if an 'L' train were passing directly outside her place. Run. Hide. Call out hello. No choice would change the outcome, only delay it.

"In here, Princess," Dickhead called from her bedroom.

She needed him for Ren. He wielded all the power. Puking was not an option.

Deciding against a peek-and-see approach, Sara strode into her bedroom. Dickhead lay on her bed, hands behind his head, ankles crossed. His dirty shoes had marked up her white bedding. His greasy hair was staining her pillowcase. At least he was fully clothed. Tactical black again.

"Transcripts are done. I've had them emailed to you, and the official documents will be sent directly to the college. Little Ren has an appointment to get her ID on Tuesday." He reached into a front pocket of his cargo pants and fished out a folded piece of paper. "I've written all the particulars here."

He held out the square, about the size of a matchbook. She'd have to move close to take it, definitely within grabbing range. Not allowing herself to hesitate, she stretched to grab it.

Dickhead jerked it away. "I'm going to require something in return."

Sara needed to swallow but didn't want to attract his attention further.

He set the paper on his stomach and dug into the opposite front pocket of his pants. If he pulled out a condom, she wasn't sure what she'd do. Instead, he removed a flash drive.

"Get this into the teacher's computer."

She stepped back. "Is it a virus?"

"Keystroke recorder."

Used for capturing passwords and weaseling into accounts, like, say, a trust fund. Her scar itched. The memory of how her stomach had flipped when she'd found her bank balance decimated skated through her mind.

"I thought we were playing nice," Dickhead said, snatching up the paper with the ID details in the same hand as the drive, sitting up, and extending his arm.

Sara took them both and nodded.

He brushed against her shoulder on his way out. Sara didn't move to lock the door, only stared at the items in her hand—Ren's gain and Beckett's loss. How could she do to him what Jorge had done to her?

The sting of that treachery hadn't eased, and yeah, Beckett would never be destitute or without resources, but he also had a lot more to lose. And that was if the only target was Beckett's money. The Agency could be after any kind of information.

With Stadler's group, Sara had had only tangential dealings with cyber stuff, but Stadler had liked to cleave minuscule bits of data from their targets that they didn't necessarily need to get the job done, always in service of something bigger. But Dickhead didn't ping her as the surgical strike kind of dude. Who was directing this operation? What were their ultimate goals?

What the hell was she going to do?

She wished she could reach out to Jorge. He was the only tech-oriented person she knew who could have told her how to run the flash drive and protect Beckett at the same time. She would gladly let him keep all the money he'd stolen, even thank him. But like everyone else, he'd deserted her when she'd needed him. All she had was herself.

CHAPTER TWENTY-EIGHT

Beckett

BECKETT SUSPECTED SARA WAS AVOIDING HIM. She'd canceled their standing Monday appointment, again, this time claiming she needed to accompany Ren to buy some furniture. A kitchen table was not an emergency. However, Sara had been so exposed and defenseless when she'd bared her scar and told her tale that Beckett could understand if she felt the need for some distance.

But then he'd had to push back their next date and skip movie night because his father had called him about an important celebration during the coming weekend for some commercial real estate bid he'd won. He'd insisted Beckett attend, even making the call himself instead of having Folger, the family secretary, invite him.

His mother had phoned him the very next day to propose he join her that weekend at their Michigan lake house. She must have heard about his father's party and wanted to assess Beckett's loyalty. After he'd told her he'd already committed to his father's event, his mother had let him know with a sniff and a quick, cold ending to their conversation that he had failed the test.

Now, on Wednesday, he was waiting for Ren to meet him. He'd chosen his office as the location for her first evaluation because other students in the program might linger around Studio B to try to snoop. Beckett never talked to the students about one another, and each decided who to share the specifics of their gift with and how much they wanted to reveal.

Ren arrived five minutes early to their 4:00 p.m. appointment, wearing those awful, unlaced combat boots that made her sound as if she weighed three times more than she did when she walked. The ensemble wasn't helped by the ripped jean shorts, faded Rob Zombie T-shirt, and a leather jacket skewered with dozens, if not a hundred, large safety pins. Her hair was shaved on one side, the color now a vibrant blue that reminded Beckett of Sara's eyes. Apparently, a trip to the salon had been included with the furniture shopping.

"Hey," she said, stomping into his office, her eyes darting everywhere and then lingering on the bookcase.

"You're welcome to browse, if you'd like. We're in no rush."

"Yeah, okay." She walked close enough to the books Beckett suspected she needed glasses. Her body moved back and forth like a typewriter as she scoured the titles.

He sat at his desk and checked his email to give her space to observe without being observed herself.

After she'd examined every title, she flopped into the chair in front of his desk. "So, like, what do we do now?"

Beckett secured his laptop and pushed it to the side. The office was decently sized, and he wanted to shut the door for privacy, but he remembered Sara saying Ren needed a clear exit to ensure her safety.

"What are you worried about?" Ren asked.

"Pardon?"

"Your emotions went swirly, which means you're concerned about something. Are you kicking me out of the program? Is that why we're meeting here and not at Arden?" She bent over and growled into her hands. "Damn it."

"No. Nothing like that." Beckett half stood then thought that might come off as overbearing and sat again. "I usually close the door for privacy, but I don't want you to feel trapped."

Ren laughed, a cackle almost like a coughing fit. She slapped a hand over her heart. "Dude, you scared me." She spun off her chair, closed the door and returned, still snickering like a witch. "But *you* don't scare me."

For a moment, Beckett was offended, but then the ridiculousness of that reaction had him chuckling. "I suppose I'm hardly menacing."

"Oh no, you're intimidating," Ren replied with a grin. "Just not in a physical way."

"Overly stern?"

She shrugged. "You're fine."

He smiled at her and started the assessment by asking what she already knew about memory magic, which wasn't more than the general populace. So, he explained everything. In the interest of gaining her confidence, he spoke plainly about his talents, both the positive and negative aspects.

"But you can't tell what I'm thinking from there, right?" she asked.

"Correct. As far as reading memories goes, I know of no memory surgeon who can use their gift without physical contact. In fact, it takes training to read someone who isn't actively open to it. Beginners need an alternate state like exhaustion or controlled substances to access another's memories without the person allowing it. With practice, we can slip inside someone's consciousness with distraction, and then, at last, with simple touch."

"That's why the general public thinks a memory read has to be consensual? But you could read my mind with a handshake?" Ren seemed more intrigued than nervous.

"Possibly, but your generalized mistrust likely shields you a bit. It's akin to hypnosis, people have varying degrees of susceptibility."

"The students in the program have been here a while. Could all of them—"

"We don't use our gifts on one another—it's grounds for expulsion from the group if done without explicit consent—and not all the students are necessarily memory surgeons, but might possess other types of memory magic."

"Hm," Ren tucked one foot underneath her and swung the other. "I don't know if I can stop myself. Sometimes it just pops out."

"I'll give you a special dispensation until you gain control."

She nodded and started chewing a hangnail on her thumb. "Will you tell the others in the program about me?"

"No," Beckett said. "Only Sara, Andrew, and I know the particulars of your talent. I suggest you control your power as much as possible and share the details judiciously. The rarer the gift, the more others might take an unhealthy interest."

"Rather than your healthy one?" She squinted and picked out whatever she'd bitten off her thumb and wiped it on her shorts. "I can't read minds, but I see and feel moods. It's not foolproof, but I have a decent idea of who's lying, who wants to hurt me, and who's helping me. You . . ."

"Yes?" he prompted, swallowing down a sudden self-consciousness that she might read too much into his revulsion at the hangnail remnants on her clothing.

Ren chuckled. "Relax, Professor Convery, we're cool. I know your motives are not . . . completely selfless, let's say. But that's people for you—everyone's got an agenda. Sara, though, *she* is looking out for me, and she has complete faith in you. It transfers."

"She does?"

"Oh, yeah, but that's all I'm saying about her feelings, so don't ask. I don't like to be anyone's personal lie detector or love note passer."

Beckett almost smiled at the image of the little punk girl passing impassioned messages between him and Sara.

He moved on to telling Ren about all the types of memory magic he imagined were out there, until he got to his most likely supposition for Ren.

"There's a type of memory called somatic memory. It's a sensory form of memory, meaning when certain senses are triggered in specific ways, it can manifest the traumatic response in the body as if the event is taking place in real time. PTSD can have a component of this."

"I'm like a walking PTSD bomb?" she asked, bending to tug on the tongues of her unlaced boots.

"Not at all." He waited for her to restore eye contact before continuing. "This is simply a sign the mind and body are intricately joined. If the brain can store trauma responses, it makes sense it can store *any* response. I believe your gift somehow accesses that connection. Your magic provides a kind of decoder for the physical reactions of those around you, and conversely, your magic interconnects and manipulates the somatic memories of others to affect a distinct change that elicits a particular response."

"Say what?"

"Our brains do so much automatically, it's astounding. What I'm suggesting is that via your gift, your brain is able to read emotional states and direct them as you command." He held out his hands. "At least, that's my best theory."

She twisted one of the threads at the hem of her cutoff jeans around her index finger until the tip turned dark red. "That sounds about right. But .. . what do I do with that? Is there a way to shut it off? I get tired of feeling other people's feelings."

He smiled. "That's one of many things we can work on. The first, if you like."

"What else would we do?"

This he'd given a lot of thought. "You'll learn as much control as possible, starting with blocking it out, then we can train you to affect others at greater and greater ranges. With something as nebulous as emotions, we could try to either condense and pinpoint a specific emotion, like clearing out everything but fear. When we first met, the fear you produced in me was palpable, but not overwhelming, which was perhaps because that was your intention, but I suspect it's hard to harness a pure emotion, since I believe we rarely experience a single emotion exclusively."

"Huh."

"We might explore the reverse and see how many emotions you can manifest at once. Or what combinations of emotions you might evoke in people. And the results might vary widely from person to person. The idea is to coach you so the gift does what you need it to, then continue until it responds how you want. Personal safety first, then the safety of those around you, and then, though I wouldn't put it in a brochure, what you find fun."

She laughed, as he'd hoped. "You make it sound so cool."

He smiled. "It can be, but it can also be dangerous—for yourself and for others. There are other groups of memory magicians. I don't know if Sara's told you."

"A little." She didn't elaborate, and Beckett didn't push. He wasn't altogether sure he wanted to know how Sara had described the other factions.

"I want you to graduate and live a full, happy life where you utilize your gift to help people and, like a doctor, do no harm. To the extent you can, and with the caveat that these gifts are also, I believe, meant to protect you. So, you wouldn't, say, deploy it to make a rude sales clerk curl up in a ball in terror, but you might do that to a person attempting to mug you."

"So, don't be a dick, is what you're saying."

"Eloquently put."

"When can we start?"

*   *   *

As Beckett drove the hour to his father's estate in Naperville, he thought about Ren's descriptions of the colors she saw in certain emotions, how fear manifested as anywhere from yellow to black, and the range of feelings encapsulated in all the shades of red—anger and betrayal all the way to love and courage. Those all correlated with what Beckett experienced when he read minds.

It made sense that emotions, like thoughts and memories, had colors associated with them. He contemplated primers, someone who could anticipate the future based on past experiences, and if they might view colors either in actions or people.

Rather than having to spend the weekend with Thomas and Katherine Convery, Beckett wished he could be in his study writing down these revelations and devising experiments for when he found other kinds of magicians or, even better, getting ready for a date with Sara.

He arrived at the manor just before six, in time for dinner. No other cars were parked in the small lot at the side of the circular drive. Beckett's stomach sank. The other guests were likely not arriving until tomorrow. He could have had his date with Sara and then come in the morning with the rest of the guests.

Quale, his father's butler, greeted Beckett at the door, took his bags and coat, and led him through the marble entry to his father's study. Already, he could feel his body tensing, his aura probably a nasty shade of yellow for the disquiet of the selfish judgments Beckett had made regarding his dad and his choice of new wife.

"Father," Beckett said after Quale had knocked and opened the door for him. His father sat at his desk, poring over paperwork, glasses perched on the end of his nose.

"Beckett, son, so glad you're here." His father rose, extending his hand as he rounded the desk.

Their handshake lasted only a moment before his dad pulled him in for a hug. It had been quite a while since they'd embraced. His final graduation? Was his father dying? "Dad?"

"Sit, sit." His father indicated the two club chairs by the fireplace. "It's been too long."

His father looked well, not the least bit ill. He'd lost a few pounds, looking more fit and trim than the last time Beckett had seen him. He seemed closer to age fifty than sixty. Likely, Katherine had him on a diet and exercise routine.

"How are you?" Beckett asked, wondering how many minutes it would take for them to run out of conversation, and Beckett could leave to hide in his room.

"Excellent. Never better. And you, how's the teaching?"

Beckett surveyed the study. Nothing had changed. Still dark, heavy wood and leather. The drink trolley in the corner still held several types of bourbon, his father's alcohol of choice. He wondered what Sara would think of the room. "Everything is going very well."

He should have invited her, but showing up with someone as stunning as she was might have come off as him trying to compete with his father. *Yes, you have a young, pretty new wife, but look what I've got.* Katherine might have felt threatened. And Sara bumbling through the delicate and strained relationship between him and his father might expose wounds Beckett wasn't equipped to examine, certainly not in the midst of a celebration honoring his father. Her Loki nature was more than he was willing to risk. All the same, he missed her sunshine and sardonic humor.

His father got up and poured himself a few fingers of bourbon. "I've got some tawny port, if you're interested."

"Sure," Beckett said. Alcohol certainly couldn't make the atmosphere more awkward.

"How's your mother?" his father asked in a subdued manner.

Beckett was unsure how to answer. His mother wasn't coping well, but his father had lost his right to know the state of her suffering. "She's been focusing quite a bit on art lately," he said with a finality he hoped his father would respect.

"Good, good. Always had a great eye for talent, your mother." He handed Beckett a cordial glass overfilled with port and sat across from him with his tumbler of dark brown bourbon.

His father was still dressed for work—Italian leather loafers, navy suit with a white dress shirt and silk tie. Always put together, like his mother and like Beckett too. They all enjoyed dressing well. It was about the only thing they had in common.

"Son, I asked you to come earlier than the other guests because Katherine and I plan to announce something tomorrow, and I want you to hear it from me first so you have some time to process it."

Oh, God, his father *was* dying. He had cancer or congestive heart failure. Was illness forcing him to retire? Surely, he didn't intend to pick up the old argument about Beckett leaving academia to take over his father's commercial real estate firm. Beckett downed his port. "Okay."

His father laughed. "Don't look so somber. This is exciting news."

So, not dying.

"Katie's pregnant."

Beckett stopped breathing for a moment. When his father had told him he was marrying Katie, Beckett had asked about children, and his father had sworn Katie had no interest, that they'd already discussed it. She'd obviously changed her mind.

"Congratulations," Beckett said after a too-long pause.

"Yeah, it took me a minute to process too." His father sighed. "It was unexpected, and I'm old as hell, but the more I think about it, the happier I am. But, son, it's perfectly understandable if you're not pleased, especially not right away."

"No, it's fine. I'm happy for you and Katie—Katherine."

His father chuckled. "She gave up on having everyone call her Katherine. I told her she was a Katie and that's fine, and she's finally come around."

Beckett nodded.

"There's a lot I want to say to you." His dad drained his glass and set it on the side table. "I wasn't a devoted father, Beckett. I worked all the time, and when I was home, I was distracted and far too wrapped up in myself to give you the attention you deserved." He rubbed his forehead and grimaced. "The *love* and attention you deserved."

Beckett sat still, in shock. His father didn't admit mistakes, and he never talked about feelings, certainly not love.

"I do love you, son, more than anyone or anything in this world. But I can't fix the past. I want to raise this child differently. I want to be a better man and father, but I don't want you to think I'm trying harder because I care more about the new kid. I want us to all be a family, you included. The last thing I want you to think is that I've moved on. There's no moving on from you, son, ever, even if you hate me. I'll always be your father, and . . ."

"I don't hate you, Dad." Beckett reached out and touched his dad's knee. It was awkward yet right. "It's weird because Katie is younger than me, but I was serious when I said if you're pleased, I'm pleased. You were—I always knew you cared in your way. I'm glad you've got a chance to do things more deliberately, and I'll be thrilled to have a little brother or sister—do you know which? When is Katie due?"

"Early days. She's only three months along, so we don't know the sex yet. I'd like a girl, but this is it for me. I've already taken steps to ensure there are no more."

Beckett didn't want to envision anyone's vasectomy, least of all his father's. "That's good, I guess." He stared into his empty glass, letting the news sink into him.

His father poured them both another drink. Beckett took the time to breathe in the aroma. He hadn't recognized how exceptional the port was until now.

"You're going to have a baby," Beckett said, taking a sip. "Holy shit, Dad."

CHAPTER TWENTY-NINE

Sara

REN HADN'T STOPPED TALKING ALL WEEKEND about Beckett and their first session together.

"Did I tell you he's having me keep a mood journal?" Ren asked, pushing the grocery cart then putting her feet on the bottom bar and coasting with the momentum. She almost crashed into a display of yellow onions.

"That's weird."

"No, it's genius."

Beckett's intellectual superiority had been already thoroughly discussed, but, apparently, Ren wasn't finished with the topic.

"See, emotions aren't only one thing. Like, fear, for example. There's, like, concern. Did I forget to turn off the oven? Stuff like that. Then there's oh-shit-we're-gonna-crash, adrenaline-type stuff. Is there a guy in my house? Is my boyfriend cheating on me? Will I die alone? I mean, the possibilities are endless, and they're all a little different." Ren plonked a cantaloupe into the cart without thumping it. "They all have a slightly different hue."

Sara picked up the cantaloupe and thumped it, a little disappointed it sounded fine. No lesson to teach yet.

"And most moods aren't a single emotion, but a combination." Ren stuck four varieties of apples, one each, into the cart. "Like right now, you're irritated, but also proud and a little worried . . . oh, and now there's a bit of panic."

"Knock that off."

"I can't help it!" Ren shuffled away, her combat boots making loud squeaks on the tile floor. She stopped near the pre-packaged salads. "Okay, I can't feel anything from here."

Sara laughed at the absurdity. One session with Beckett and Ren had not only drunk the Kool-Aid, but had opened up a lemonade stand. Witnessing Ren without the gloom hanging over her made every sacrifice worth it.

Sara's life at Wells College had come together in ways she hadn't anticipated, the people around her growing into more than the dysfunctional family she'd formed while at the Agency. This family was richer and more honest—in feelings at least. Maybe Sara didn't have to leave. She wasn't that fifteen-year-old girl any longer. She could have nice things.

Except for the dinner party. And the flash drive.

If she could find a way to, say, steer the Agency away from Beckett and his program, maybe she could stay. Maybe she could keep it all.

"Get back over here, nut."

Ren returned, carrying a bag of shaved brussels sprouts. "He thinks it's possible for me to learn to shut it on and off and totally control it."

She'd mentioned that before, but Sara only smiled. "So, it was productive, is what you're saying."

"Yeah, and I helped him too, testing out his moat."

"He's building a moat? There isn't enough room."

Ren bent over laughing. "Psychic moat, not a real one. He said it was your idea."

She recalled their conversation about how she had a moat around the walls of her mind. He'd told her that he hoped assessing her would help him learn how to shield himself, but she'd never truly thought that could happen. "Did it work?"

"Kind of. It only lasts as long as he can hold his breath, but it snuffs out his aura. It's cool when it comes back. It's almost like a psychic fog machine." Ren laughed and juggled three lemons for about five seconds before dropping two to the ground. She glanced around, and although nobody was paying attention, she guiltily set all three in the cart. "Stupid morals," she muttered.

*   *   *

ON MONDAY, SARA SHOWED UP AT STUDIO B EARLY, READY TO PUT forth an effort to preemptively atone for what Dickhead was forcing her to do. She'd not let the future darken the now. Beckett was about to get the Complete Sara Experience.

She'd styled her hair in braids then into a twist. Her outfit included jeans, three-inch booties, and a magenta, silk blouse. Casual and light, an ensemble that didn't try too hard. Her belly swooped and circled.

Beckett was already there, as if he'd missed her too. His face lit up with a smile when she entered the room, and she tossed herself into his arms. He held her close, inhaling her hair then her neck, groaning in pleasure as she squelched a moan of her own from his fresh fields and violets cologne.

"Hey, stranger," she murmured into the side of his neck.

"I'm never going away without you again. The weekend after the Philotimo dinner will be the end of term. Let's go away to my family's lake house in Michigan, just the two of us," he said.

A weekend together? Not for show, but because he wanted her. That would be the weekend before her surgery. "Okay."

Beckett wore dark jeans and a leather belt with his brown vest, and a white button-down rolled to mid-forearm. His hair had been cut, maybe for his dad's party, but it lay as it always did, in a loose wave that begged to be touched.

She kissed the underside of his chin then quickly worked her way to his soft lips, letting her thumb reach his bottom lip first to play with the little divot there. He nipped at her finger. She pushed her thumb into his mouth, as a joke at first, but he sucked on it as he nipped the pad with his teeth, and the sensation zinged straight to her pussy. Maybe they could skip the session and use the time a better way upstairs in her bedroom.

His phone chirped, and he drew back, breathing hard and staring at her as if she were a two-hour sale at the bottom of the second hour. It took him another moment before he completely released his hold around her waist.

"How was your weekend?" she asked as she staggered her way to her chair.

"Fine. Weird." He didn't check his cell but sat across from her. "But hopeful, I think. I'll tell you about it later. Right now, this is about you and your gift. How's it been going?"

Since she had a non-power talent, Sara didn't practice. The idea of sitting in the Lotus position trying to see her own brain didn't appeal.

"Nobody tried to read me, so I guess it's going adequately."

"Sara, we have a building full of memory magicians. Why aren't you asking them to test your boundaries?" He said it in such a caring tone Sara squirmed in her chair.

"But that's so awkward," she said. "*Hey, hold my hand and try to read my thoughts. Psych! Sorry, gotta go lay in the dark with an ice pack now. See you tomorrow.*"

He didn't laugh but pursed his lips. "How might you phrase the request in a way that isn't so . . . dramatic?"

She blew air out of her mouth like a horse before remembering how much time she'd spent painting her lips. Her lipstick was probably already marred from their kissing session but motorboating wouldn't do it any favors. "It just . . . feels icky to ask the kids for help. I'm supposed to be helping them."

Beckett nodded. How had she ever resisted him? He had a beautiful nose, soulful eyes, and that sinful bottom lip. "Sara."

"Yeah?"

"I can understand it might be difficult for you to request assistance, but perhaps you might frame it as mutually beneficial. Trying to perceive your boundaries would be instructive for the students, more so because they don't have to be as afraid of accidentally breaching your confidence."

"Oh." That was doable. He was so smart and helpful.

"Also, it's easier for you to find your own edges and guard when there's another mind in opposition—not as in something antagonistic, but a touchstone."

Definitely true, since she couldn't sense her mind at all by herself. "Okay."

"Can we try now? The two of us?"

"Wouldn't you rather make out?"

He smiled then, and Sara thought her ribcage might crack down the center and flop open like a display case, offering up her heart. "It isn't about what I'd rather do, but the right thing to do."

She loved his properness, so she supposed she had to take the annoying side of that quality too. "Fine."

Once they started, her mind shifted into hard focus, and she managed to enjoy the process and make progress. She could feel a sort of cushion between his intrusion and herself. It was thick and spongy like a bouncy house, and Sara had an inkling of why nobody could penetrate her mind, not because her wall was titanium but because it was adaptable, bulging somewhere else when the invader poked into the wall. She described it in detail.

"Brilliant!" Beckett hugged her, his enthusiasm contagious. "Sara, that's a *huge* breakthrough! All this time, I've been imagining my own guard as something hard and impenetrable, almost the exact opposite of your natural inclination. The solution to holding strong might be the ability to bend. We should have considered that. I can't wait to tell Andrew and test the theory."

He was so excited, he didn't kiss her again, but ran off to test the theory and then teach his last class of the day.

Sara regretted the loss of his him, but maybe they had time.

* * *

THE NEXT MORNING, SARA AND REN WENT TO THE RAVENSWOOD neighborhood to get Ren the ID Dickhead had promised would pass any inspection, including E-Verify to work and the DMV for a driver's license. Though the ID cost the Agency twenty thousand dollars, a price tag she didn't share with Ren, Sara expected a seedy setup—a basement with a single bulb and a man in a trench coat with a nicotine-stained mustache and a crooked overbite.

Instead, they found a redbrick warehouse with wood floors and metal railings and varying businesses. Their contact was on the second floor, the smell of lemon cleaner subtle and bright in the hallway. Inside, floor-to-ceiling windows filled the space with light. A huge green screen was set up almost to the ceiling, stretching out into ten feet of floor space. To the side were wooden shelves stuffed with photography equipment, from lights to colored gels to rolled up backdrops to boxes of who knew what.

At the other end was a smaller setup with a chair in front of a white backdrop. In between was a small kitchenette and two sofas and a recliner, all in like-new condition. The furniture was definitely better than what Sara and Ren owned. Of course, at twenty thousand a pop, the forger could afford fresh furniture. She wondered if Dickhead intended to steal the money from Beckett's accounts to cover the cost.

The man in question was probably in his forties and had thinning sandy hair with brown eyes so dark they were almost black. He wore a T-shirt ripped at the collar, faded jeans, and no shoes. "Come in, come in," he said. He had glasses perched on top of his head and ink-stained hands. "I'm Corbett, but you can call me Cor."

"Hi," Ren said, beaming at the guy. She gave Sara a thumbs-up, signaling that she had perceived Cor was a decent sort. Selling fake IDs for Twenty. Thousand. Dollars.

Sara decided to hold out on making a too-quick decision to trust him.

"Sit down," Cor said gesturing to the cozy setup. "Can I get you some tea? I've got hot chocolate, too."

"We're fine," Sara said.

Ren snuggled into the microfiber black couch, and Sara sat next to her so Cor couldn't take that spot.

Cor plopped into the recliner. "I've got a few questions before we start."

For what he was charging, he shouldn't have any questions. "Like what?" Sara asked.

"How did you find me?"

Did he think they were cops? "Through a . . ." God, it was such a lie. ". . . friend. He said there wouldn't be a problem. He's taking care of the payment."

"Yeah, that's a red flag," Cor said.

"For what?" Sara asked. What was this guy getting at?

Ren stared at Sara, clearly feeling her rising concerns.

"Okay," he said. "I'm going to tell you an abbreviated story as to why I became a part of this network that helps people like Ren, and I'm going to be honest. I'd like the same in return."

"You got it," Ren jumped in. "We're listening."

We certainly are.

"I had a sister who was married to an abusive man. The family tried to help her, but we couldn't do anything until she was ready."

This was not going to be a feel-good tale.

"Eventually, she left him, and she did everything she was supposed to do—found a safe place to stay, filed a restraining order, made sure to never be alone. He fought her every step of the way, but she finally had a court date to divorce him. Night before, she stayed at a hotel and paid cash. Only . . . they said they needed a credit card in case of damages. She explained the situation and told them they could keep the number on file but couldn't run it." Cor sighed. "You can see where this is going. Someone must have entered her card anyway. He tracked her down, and shot her in the hallway when she came back from the pool. Six times. Then he shot himself."

Ren was wiping tears, probably experiencing the man's pain.

"I'm sorry," Sara said, though it wouldn't help him.

He nodded. "All she wanted was her freedom, and he took it. He could have just killed himself, but for whatever reason, he had to control her all the way to the end. That's why I do what I do, so in-peril women can start over fresh."

"That's so nice of you," Ren said, her voice nasally and wet.

"I'm a man looking out for women, so I know we exist, but when a man wants a clean ID for an eighteen-year-old-girl, I have to ask questions, because this ID is high-quality enough you can disappear, or you could *be* disappeared. And I won't be a party to that. So, what's this ID for?"

Ren told the man more than she'd previously shared even with Sara. She explained about her father's gambling debts, her aunt's involvement with petty organized crime ("family, not corporate"), her memory magic gift, her aspirations to be an artist and maybe a vet (a vet?), how the only thing standing in her way was a valid ID.

"And what about Kyle Ludwig? Who is he in all this?" Cor asked.

Dickhead's name was *Kyle*? How perfect. "Big guy? Scruffy in a serial-killer way? Head like a block of cheese—well, blocky, anyway?"

Cor huffed a laugh. "Squinty eyes that mean trouble. That's the one."

Sara decided to be as honest as possible. "You're right to be wary of him, but not for the reason you think. He's arranging this as a favor to me, so I owe him, not Ren. He's also getting transcripts created for her, so it's not like we can hide the changed name from him. I know it's risky, but she can't get into the program she mentioned without this."

Cor covered his face with his hands. "I suppose a new ID can't make the situation worse."

"Hey, can I look around at your photos?" Ren asked out of nowhere.

"Sure," Cor said.

"I'll be way over there," Ren said, nudging her head in Cor's direction.

Ren was many things, but subtle was not one of them.

"You need assistance too?" Cor asked Sara gently. "From Kyle?"

Sara's face heated with humiliation at being so transparent and for getting herself into a mess she couldn't find a way out of. "I'll figure something out."

"I can help you."

She shook her head and lowered her voice so Ren wouldn't overhear. "I can't afford it."

Cor frowned. "I wouldn't charge you anything."

"Kyle told me you're charging twenty thousand for Ren's new ID," Sara said. What would he want in lieu of cash?

"That bastard," Cor said, his face red. "I would never charge that. He's paying me a thousand, and only because I use fresh hardware for every job, scrubbing and trashing the hard drives when I'm done." He rubbed the spot between his eyes vigorously as if trying to remove a stain. "I've already said too much."

Dickhead had totally lied, all part of his mind fuck. Sara wanted to say yes to Cor's offer of a new ID. Though she might never need it, the safety net would be life-changing. However, the cost wasn't her sole concern. She also wanted to be a better person, and that required not putting someone like Cor in the Agency's cross hairs. "They might send someone here to ask you about me." With guns.

Cor bent forward to catch her eyes, straightening as she looked up. "It's about time for me to move on anyway. You could be my last job, and since you guys already know about the memory surgeon thing, I can tell you that there's a woman in this network of ours who scrubs my mind after every ID. They can question me all they want, but I literally won't be able to betray you because I won't remember the tiniest detail."

"Could you have it ready by the fifteenth of next month?" Sara asked. If the heat became unbearable, she'd have the option of running. But surely she would find a way to stay.

"I can have both IDs finished by next week."

Sara grabbed him in a hug before recognizing he hadn't given her permission to do that. "Sorry," she said, backing away. "I'm not used to people being so altruistic."

He shrugged. "It's not selflessness. All of us, everyone involved in this network, met through grief support groups. Every time we help someone, we get to feel—just a little bit—like we saved the person we lost."

It hit Sara hard, the truth of it, because that was exactly how she felt about Ren, though the person she had lost was herself.

CHAPTER THIRTY

Beckett

AFTER HIS WEEKEND WITH HIS FATHER, BECKETT was obligated to have dinner with his mother on either Friday or Saturday. Sara had given him permission to push their date night yet another week.

Sara unhelpfully invited herself to Beckett's to help him dress for dinner with his mother, which involved her making him disrobe to his underwear so she could outfit him like a Ken doll. He was embarrassingly hard, and she stroked him once through his boxer briefs before dropping to her knees. Beckett lifted her to her feet before he could succumb. He wanted to pleasure her first, and they didn't have time for him to do that properly.

She frowned at him, but picked out his outfit, the exact ensemble from the first day they'd met. Beckett owned several pairs of tan pants, but she selected the exact trousers. It shouldn't have astonished him, since he also recalled exactly what she had worn and how she'd styled her hair.

"Hey, do you have an old computer I can borrow?" she asked as he dressed.

"Certainly. Do you want me to grab it now?" Beckett had two old laptops that he kept to lend to students in an emergency.

"That would be great," she said, her smile incandescent. "Be sure it doesn't have anything sensitive on it. I'm a terrible snoop." She winked.

Beckett leaned against the center island in his closet, almost comfortable being only half-dressed, not wanting to leave her. "The hard drive has been wiped, so don't waste your time."

"Perfect." She spun in a circle, causing her skirt to flare, though it didn't reveal her panties. "Can I still access the internet?"

"Of course." He dragged her close and kissed her lightly on the mouth. "And if you want information about me, just ask."

"Okay."

Sara shook out his shirt and slipped it over his shoulders, her hands gentle and sure as she buttoned it for him. She took her time with his tie, executing a fancy cape knot without fumbling. He regretted not being able to cancel with his mother, but he needed to let her know, in person, about his father's impending fatherhood before she heard it from someone else.

Having Sara there to excite him and make him laugh didn't make it easy to stick to his plans, though. They'd spent too much time apart, and he wanted to soak in her positivity.

She walked him all the way to the garage and his car, the spare laptop held against her chest. He paused as he backed out to watch her bound back to Arden to torture Ren with something she called *fox eyes*.

Dinner with his mother went exactly as he'd expected. She blanched and spoke little, every word out of her mouth pinched and tight. For Beckett, he recognized he'd unfairly judged his father's relationship with Katie, assuming the age difference meant they couldn't have anything real. His censure toward his father hadn't benefited anyone, hadn't made anyone's lives better. He'd also embraced an unhealthy loyalty to his mother. She would have been happier if she let go of the past, stopped obsessing about what her ex-husband did, and made a new life of her own.

It served no one to live in response to others.

* * *

FOR SATURDAY MOVIE NIGHT, SARA ASSIGNED A DRESS CODE SHE CALLED Party Like It's 1999, since *Strange Days* took place during the lead-up to the year 2000. She showed up in a gold crocheted dress with a matching skimpy slip underneath. Beckett strongly suggested she cover up.

"Hey, this is much tamer than what Juliette Lewis wears in the movie," Sara complained, but she put on Wilson's terry bathrobe, grinning at Beckett's conservativeness or jealousy—he was both.

Everyone except Brayton and Beckett came dressed in a costume, although Jason's only cosplay items were fifty Mardi Gras beads around his neck. Marlena and Andrew missed the screening.

This broadcast was livelier than *What Women Want*, because of the intensity and the addictiveness of the "wire tripping." It was something memory surgeons could technically do, take someone's memory and let another person live it. That was called memory preserving and some magicians did that for a living.

The group agreed there was likely a black market for bootleg memories, that enterprising magicians might steal, say, great sex memories and sell them to others. Beckett hadn't considered that before, but the consensus was that would be egregious. He was far more comfortable with the intellectual discussion than the frivolity, and yet, a part of him ... He didn't want to party and act silly, but sometimes, he wished he could be someone who embraced easy enjoyment.

Sara leaned back against Beckett as if sensing his unease. He wrapped his arms around her, wondering how he had gotten there, watching a movie with a group of teenagers, his girlfriend between his knees, kissing him on his neck and mouth whenever she thought she could do so without the kids catching them. Neither professional nor unprofessional. Not himself but not *not* himself.

* * *

FOR THE SUNDAY MEETING, BECKETT SUPERVISED THE SETUP OF THE food, slightly adjusting the dishes for a more balanced presentation. They had fifteen minutes until the surprise guests arrived, but nobody had made it to the conference room yet. Where was Sara?

As if his anxiety had conjured her, she bounced into the room, wearing jeans and an off-the-shoulder blouse. She careened straight into his arms, pressing her body close. "Quick, before the children arrive, kiss me."

Public displays of affection from the program director were inappropriate, but he still found himself brushing his lips to hers. He didn't stop there. Why wasn't he stopping? He kissed her softly, licking her lips in that teasing manner that made her tense in the desirable way.

They broke apart just before the door opened, and Ren stomped through in that way she had, as if she had to compensate for her small stature.

"Morning, sunshine," Sara said in a syrupy sweet voice. "Don't you look cute today."

Ren gave her the finger and slumped into the chair in the back corner, jerked up her hood and scowled. The rest of the students filled the space little by little. Beckett struggled to keep from stalking Sara's every move.

Her phone buzzed. She squealed and bustled out of the room to fetch their guests. Andrew slipped into the seat at the end of the table, fist bumping a few of the guys and winking at Marlena.

Beckett hadn't seen his friend much in the last week or so. He'd have to arrange something. They hadn't had a serious discussion in quite a while, and Beckett wanted Andrew's take on Sara's positive impact on the program. Beckett also desired Andrew's opinion on whether he should suggest that Sara move in with him. The thought of spending every night with her . . .

Sara popped back into the conference room. "Okay, guys," she said, her hands clasped. "We've got something different for you today. We've brought in a couple of memory magicians who can talk about the real-life consequences of using your gifts."

Andrew frowned and gave Beckett a questioning eyebrow. He should have at least clued in Andrew, but Sara had insisted on what she'd termed a *media blackout*. Andrew would understand once Beckett explained.

Sara paused, drawing out the occasion. "I'd like to introduce you to Jolene St. John and Kiera Brayleigh."

Her pure enjoyment of the reveal made Beckett grin. Everyone in the room straightened. Jaws dropped. More than one student gasped. Kiera Brayleigh was both famous and infamous in the magician community. Sara beamed at Beckett as she opened the door, sharing the moment with him.

Having already met Jolene, Beckett focused most of his attention on Kiera. She had an angular face with a pointy chin and black hair that seemed to showcase her blue eyes. Although there was a hardness to her, she came off less rigid than he'd expected.

Beckett dragged two chairs to the center, stroked his hand down Sara's back, and returned to his seat.

Sara grinned at the students. "What you probably don't know about Jolene and Kiera is they work with people, mostly women, who've been victimized by memory magicians. That's the focus of what they're going to be talking about today." She winked at Jolene. "Oh, and don't be assholes."

After plopping into her chair, Sara gave Beckett a thumbs-up. He sighed over her profanity.

Kiera started. "You're young, so you think having this special ability is cool and fun and you can do fuck-all with it."

Jolene picked up the thread. "But you need to understand the damage you can do to others simply by using your gifts."

Everyone fidgeted except for Sara and Ren. Even Beckett found himself smoothing the thighs of his slacks. They'd debated this often, the drive to hone skills in contrast to the violation that could require. If they wanted to improve and strengthen their talents, they had to practice, and finding a willing participant was not easy or practical.

Kiera leaned forward. "I have a client that attended couple's therapy with her husband. Eventually, she discovered the therapist was actually a memory surgeon, and he'd been systematically removing any memory that didn't put her husband in a favorable light. Things like cheating, stealing from her trust fund, and smacking her around a few times."

"How did she find out?" Marlena asked.

Kiera eyed her for at least ten seconds before answering. "I'm not here to give a tutorial on how to get away with it, but let's just say we can only remove the memories of those we touch. We can't affect anyone else who witnessed, was told, or who was also involved. So, when ER bills, or jilted side-pieces, or bank statements come in, it can cause a disconnect. It can lead to people thinking they're having a psychotic break or experiencing dementia or some other medical condition, because those motherfuckers gaslight like nobody's business."

Jolene picked up the narrative as if they'd practiced. "The victims frequently show signs of PTSD, trichotillomania—"

"What's that?" Sara asked.

"Pulling out hair from the head, eyebrows, eyelashes—fun stuff."

"The moral of the story is that your actions have consequences," Kiera said. "I'm not saying don't use your . . ." She turned to Jolene. "I'm not calling it a gift."

Jolene held up her hands. "Whatever. Call it what you want."

"You can use your power, but make damn sure you think about the repercussions to *others* before you do. Because you can seriously fuck up some shit if you're not careful." Kiera tossed her arms. "That's about all we got."

That was their presentation? Beckett looked at Sara, who shrugged. He gave her a half smile. "Thank you, ladies," he said. At least what they'd shared could be a launching pad for further discussion. "You are open to questions, yes?"

Sara raised her hand like an eager student.

Jolene pointed to her. "Ms. Strausser."

"This program is supposed to help the students figure out how to use their talents ethically. I'd be curious to know your thoughts on how to do that."

Beckett had intended to ask them that very question if it didn't come up within the discourse. He watched Sara's thoughtful face. She really cared about the youths. With everything she did, she put her entire self into the endeavor. Would she want to live with him? Perhaps she didn't crave his company as much as he did hers.

"You go first," Jolene said to Kiera.

Kiera smirked. "Fine." She stood, pacing by the table and eyeing everyone individually before she spoke again. "I think each person has to determine for themselves where to draw their lines. For myself, I have looked into someone's memories without their permission only twice. The first was when I discovered my gift, because I didn't know I was doing it. It was with my brother, and luckily, he thought it was cool." She shook her head with a rueful grin. "But he's a dipshit like that."

She stopped pacing and poured herself a glass of orange juice. "The other time was with a coma victim, but her parents approved, and the detective involved . . ." Kiera smiled, and it made her interesting face lovely. "Well, he was pretty persuasive."

"Sit down, already." Jolene stood and waved Kiera into a chair. "I haven't been quite as . . . ethical as my friend here," she said, also beginning to pace.

"Nobody needs to know the details," Sara said, seeming to know where Jolene was going.

Beckett hoped Sara would share more of her past with him, including the parts involving Jolene.

"S'okay," Jolene said. "I used to get information from people—criminals—and I practiced on regular people in small ways. Mostly, I hooked into people's minds quickly without actually jumping in. You guys know what I mean?"

Everyone nodded.

"Every once in a while, I'd meet someone who was kind of a tool, and I didn't feel so bad about practicing on them."

"What about friends and family?" Ren asked. "Did you ever, you know, want to be sure what they were saying was true?"

Jolene shrugged. "Sometimes it'd cross my mind, but do you really want to know the fleeting, petty thoughts people have? When I'm mad, I think all kinds of crazy shit that I don't mean. When you take a small sample from someone, you find the truth of the moment, but not necessarily the *truth* truth. And that's an awful big violation of a person you supposedly care about."

"Okay, yeah," Wilson said, his typical sleepy demeanor suddenly more watchful. "But what if you do something stupid, and you, like, want a do-over?"

"There's something else you should consider," Jolene said. "I've had my memories messed with, and . . . there's no coming back from that. If that person finds out, the relationship is ruined forever."

The kids listened and engaged. It was the best discussion they'd ever had, which meant it created far more questions than answers. The session was everything Beckett and Andrew had envisioned when they'd dreamed up the program two years ago. All thanks to Sara.

CHAPTER THIRTY-ONE

Sara

HOW THOSE PAPERS WORKING OUT FOR YOU? *Feeling like a party?*

Sara stared at the text for the third time. Why was Dickhead suddenly texting her?

She fidgeted in her seat, unable to get comfortable, her focus split between Kiera and Jolene and the dread twisting her guts like spaghetti on a fork. She calculated how long she could realistically ignore the message before she had to respond. Scrambled eggs sat in her stomach like hot coal.

She'd downloaded the spyware from Dickhead's flash drive onto Beckett's old laptop to buy herself some time, and her mood afterward had been downright delighted. But how long before her ruse was discovered? How long could she put him off about the dinner party?

Beckett had given her two dates that worked for the Phi, and she'd chosen the latest possible, May 12, the Friday before her surgery. Just under three weeks away.

She squeezed her eyes shut for a moment and then shoved the phone back into her purse, her attention locking on to Kiera as she talked about ethics.

* * *

Eventually, Sara couldn't stand the suspense. She responded. *Thanks dinner date should be set soon*

Dickhead's reply was immediate, as if he'd already typed out the message. *You're going to ruin the party. When you're done, the program will be destroyed. Anything short of that and the police will be picking up little Ren for identity fraud and you'll remain permanently disfigured.*

Sara's hand ached from how tightly she clutched her cell. Her lungs froze, making breathing impossible. Her scope of vision narrowed.

His demands could be worse.

She repeated those words over and over, but they failed to penetrate her cyclone of panic. Nobody would die, the outcome she'd been half-expecting when Dickhead had demanded to know details about the Philotimo's meeting. Beckett could revamp and relaunch the program after the scandal had turned from fire to ash.

Tears pricked her eyes. He'd recover, but he'd never forgive her for obliterating his brainchild right in his face.

With a new ID in the works, she could run instead of demolishing the program, maybe even take Ren with her. But she'd have to give up Beckett forever.

She never should have allowed herself to believe the situation could be resolved in a way that let her keep him.

"Everyone," Beckett said, standing and smiling. Smiling. In public. "Let's thank our guest speakers for an illuminating discussion."

The kids all clapped.

"And thank you to Sara for bringing in Kiera and Jolene and for making the program a little more . . . extra." Beckett grinned at her, his admiration so genuine and heartfelt that Sara thought she might drop dead.

Instead, she smiled in return.

The students were awake and chattering. Even Marlena had participated, talking to Kiera with enough animation that gestures had been involved. The energy in the room had a charge, the kids' hopes inflated as if they could accomplish anything.

Sara was the needle, primed to pop that balloon.

Her gaze snagged on Ren, jolting her. If Ren caught sight of her aura, she'd ask questions.

Sara stuffed, crammed, and jammed all her fluttering worries down deep into her gut where they would hopefully ferment out of view. She pushed on the buffer between her and the world, begging it to protect her. Insulate her. Isolate.

"Let me walk you guys out," she said to Jolene and Kiera, edging toward the door.

Jolene slung an arm over Sara's shoulders. "You got some time? Kier and I have a surprise for you."

Sara stopped walking. "For me?"

Kiera laughed. "Not expressly for you. Jolene's making me do something, and she went on and on about how much you'd appreciate it, and wouldn't it be fun if we all did it together, and blah, blah, blah. I thought we should tell you ahead of time, but she insisted it be a surprise."

"Color me intrigued," Sara said, her limbs tingling in anticipation, as if she'd just come out of a sauna. This was exactly what she needed—a perfect distraction. She gestured to her ripped jeans. "Can I wear this?"

Jolene nodded. "Except the shoes; you need sneakers."

"Back in a flash." She bolted up the stairs, unlocked the door, and flew into her closet, tossing pumps and boots to the side to find her Skechers, as if the women might leave without her if she wasn't fast enough.

Once she'd changed shoes, she tore down the stairs and stumbled into the lobby. Andrew and Beckett were there talking to Kiera and Jolene. Everyone's attention swung to her as her momentum carried her too quickly toward them. "We're going on a surprise outing," she announced, wishing she could keep running right out the door.

"When do you think you'll return?" Beckett asked, clearly amused.

Jolene shrugged. "We'll have her home by midnight."

Since it was only 10:00 a.m., that left a lot of time for diversions. Beckett had his fencing class at three, anyway. She could possibly avoid him all night.

With a flash of a hug for Beckett, she was out the door. Jolene pointed her to a silver RAV4. Sara scrambled into the back.

By the time they finally arrived at their destination, Sara thought she might vibrate out of her skin. The diversion had been an epic fail. Then she comprehended the white sign on the blue building. iFly.

"We're going in one of those air tube things like skydivers?" Sara's voice came out too high-pitched and too loud. "Oh my God!"

Going to iFly was cool, but it became cooler when Kiera explained she'd booked the entire place for an hour for just the three of them. This was a once-in-a-lifetime kind of outing, and goddamn it, Sara was going to have fun.

The orientation video made Sara more excited, though she had to push and squeeze her energy into enthusiasm, the burden of her predicament weighing her down. She loved the jumpsuits. She braided Jolene's long hair in a Dutch pattern and put her own in a French braid. Kiera refused to let Sara do anything with her shoulder-length hair, happy to just secure it with a simple elastic. As they got dressed and prepped, Jolene peppered Sara with questions about Beckett's program, not realizing she was picking at an open wound.

"Why do you want to be part of a program like that? It's such a structured environment."

Sara shrugged. "I get to party plan, and that's fun."

"How do things stand with you and the Agency?"

She'd already explained the situation to Jolene at the gallery, and she didn't want to think about the fingers of the Agency tracing up her spine, burrowing holes into her vertebrae every damn day. How they were making her turn traitor. Forcing her to exterminate the only life she'd ever wanted.

Sara bounced on her toes, ready to end the conversation and start flying. "Fine."

"I was at Starbucks in December," Jolene said, suddenly deadly serious. "Some skinny tattooed dude in front of me turned around and said, 'As long as you continue to keep your mouth shut, we're prepared to leave you alone.' Then he ordered a blond vanilla latte." Jolene put a hand on Sara's wrist, her grip tight enough to hurt. "Right out in public, Sara. I want nothing to do with the Agency, and I'm happy to live and let live, but you were in it a lot longer than me."

Sara rolled her wrist out of the hold. "What's your point?"

"You're not saying everything." Jolene's posture was loose, knees bent, hands up near her face as if she thought Sara might jump her. Stadler's preferred fighting stance. "What did they ask you to do?"

"Nothing." Nothing she wanted to share.

"Don't. Fucking. Lie. To. Me." Jolene shoved Sara's shoulders. "What do they want with me?"

Sara stumbled back and plonked down on one of the wooden benches in front of the lockers. She'd forgotten the depths of Jolene's paranoia. "Nothing—as far as I know, at least."

Jolene bullied closer. "You showed up at Cass's art show. At first, I was thinking about the world being small and all that shit, but . . . I don't like coincidences, Sara. Are you spying on me?" Her eyes had hardened, and Sara didn't care if she had no right to feel offended or hurt.

She had been so thrilled to see Jolene again, but Jolene had been filled with suspicion at seeing her. And though Sara wasn't surveilling Jolene, she was spying on someone else she loved—cared about—maybe loved. The pressure inside her head grew until she thought she would explode, splattering guilt and shame everywhere. "I would never do that to *you*. What the hell, Jolene?"

"Forgive me, but I have no idea what's true and what's bullshit," Jolene said.

Kiera crowded next to Jolene, forming a united front, leaving Sara alone to defend herself against everyone and everything.

She huffed. "I don't know how I'm supposed to prove to you that I'm not spying on you."

"I want you to let Kiera take a look," Jolene said.

Sara pressed her hand into her stomach. "I have a natural shield. No one can—"

"Then you won't care if she tries," Jolene said.

It hurt that Jolene didn't trust her, and it chafed that she was justified. Sara wasn't trustworthy. She held a trembling hand out to Kiera, whose hands were cold but dry.

Kiera softened her eyes, and Sara felt a tingling in the back of her head. She gritted her teeth against the sensation, careful not to slam her mind closed, though the instinct was almost overwhelming.

Kiera dropped Sara's hand. "She's right. I got nothing but a white wall. I can see a whole bunch of ocher memory strands, which ain't encouraging but aren't threatening."

Jolene wasn't her friend. She hadn't invited Sara to this place because she was fun, but to interrogate her. Sara should have known Jolene hadn't forgiven her. Nobody ever did. No matter how hard she tried, she couldn't be free, couldn't just be herself. She was destined to live a life at the bottom of Maslow's stupid pyramid, where all that existed was survival.

"It's not *you* the Agency is interested in," Sara said. She pressed her fingertips into her eyebrows, trying to make the brimming tears recede, tamping down her disgrace. "It's Beckett." Her voice broke.

"What?" Jolene and Kiera said in unison.

Sara jumped to her feet. She'd leave Chicago now. Fuck everyone, even herself.

Jolene put a hand on her arm, gentle this time. "Wait."

"I don't think so," Sara replied, shrugging her off. "I've got places to be."

"Damn it." Jolene kicked the bench, and Kiera moved to the door, maybe to give Jolene space. "I'm so stupid." Jolene pressed the heels of her hands into her temples.

"No." Sara unzipped her flight suit. "I'm the stupid one, always have been."

"You aren't remotely dumb." Jolene grabbed both her shoulders, fast as a snake strike, but this time, she didn't push Sara, only held tight. "You're in trouble. I should have known. Just when I think I've got a hold on my paranoia, the fucking Agency shows up everywhere. But that's no excuse. Sorry, Sara. Tell me everything."

The instructor peeked her head into the locker room. Kiera slipped out to talk to the woman.

Trapped in Jolene's grip and her own misery, Sara spilled the entire story, from how much she'd hated Beckett at first to the fake dating that wasn't fake lately, to Dickhead Kyle replacing Ryan, to helping Ren and owing Dickhead a favor, the Agency's demand for her to download spyware on Beckett's computer and blow up the dinner party that she desperately wanted to go well because it was so important to him. How time was running out. She did giggle a little when she talked about how she'd been playing solitaire and watching cat videos on Beckett's borrowed laptop, but mostly she struggled not to cry.

"I'm completely screwed," Sara finished.

Jolene scowled at her, which, okay, she deserved. "Wait. Dickhead took your phone?"

"Yep. Totally cut me off from Ryan, that prick."

"Sara." Jolene sat on the bench she'd kicked earlier. "I still have my Agency cell."

"So?"

"My future brother-in-law works for the fucking *Feds*, and the Agency let me keep my cell. Why would they replace your phone just because you got a new handler?"

"I went off book." As she said it, Sara comprehended the weakness of that answer.

Jolene snorted. "You live off book." She jumped to her feet and began pacing the dressing room. "Ryan wouldn't screw *you* over, right? Not with Stadler gone."

Ryan hadn't had Jolene's back when Stadler had turned psycho-stalker, and Sara could see Jolene hadn't gotten over that—not that Sara blamed her. The shit that had gone down those last few days when they'd been a team had been messed up.

"He was really upset about that," Sara said, wanting to mend that bridge for both of them. They were all the "family" she had left, especially if things with Beckett went pear-shaped. And how could they not?

Jolene waved her hand. "We're not talking about that right now. My point is, Ryan wouldn't ghost you, would he?"

Sara had entertained similar doubts, but having someone else voice them aloud opened her mind. "Oh, man. I am an *idiot*." It hadn't occurred to her that Dickhead might be manipulating her, even after she'd found out about the ID price tag inflation.

"Actually, you aren't." Jolene took Sara's hand. "You're used to the people you trust fucking you over—I get it—and that made it easy to believe Ryan would just drop you."

Sara nodded.

Jolene plopped back down on the bench, bumping her shoulder against Sara's. "You came back for me. I haven't forgotten that. You wouldn't have gotten shot if you hadn't come to warn me about Stadler. Now it's my turn to come back for you. We'll fix this. I promise."

We.

Sara was so tired of being alone, of trusting only herself. It was time to take a chance on those she loved—Jolene, Ren, and, of course, Beckett.

CHAPTER THIRTY-TWO

Beckett

"**C**OME INSIDE," BECKETT SAID WHEN HE MET Sara at the door of Studio B for their regular Monday session. His thoughts overlapped and crowded one another, the energy carrying over from the great meeting he'd had earlier with Brayton.

Beckett was talented at bringing out gifts, and Sara's moat trick was succeeding to some degree with everyone, but Brayton had mastered it. They'd both gotten excited over it, and then Brayton had opened up to him about his interest in Wilson as a possible romantic partner and his concern that two memory magicians together would be doomed. He'd asked for Beckett's advice.

Beckett was more worried about how it would affect the program should the relationship not work out, but he hadn't voiced that selfish concern. Instead, he'd channeled Sara's optimism. Though Brayton was as polished as Beckett, and Wilson was . . . not, regard and respect mattered more, and their magic shouldn't be an issue at all. He'd advised Brayton that while love was always a risk, it was one worth taking.

He couldn't divulge the conversation to Sara, but he could share the boost of enthusiasm for the program the exchange had given him. "I've been thinking about how we can possibly help you get some control," he said.

"Okay," she said, her smile bright but reserved. "What's your grand scheme?"

"Color," he replied, scolding himself for reading too much into why she wasn't smiling like usual. "When I see thoughts, I see them as colors. When Ren sees emotions, she also views them as shades and hues."

"So, you think I should try to see colors?"

"No, I—well, perhaps." He frowned. "Imagine a specific shade first, I think. We can search for a hue that's naturally blocking, enabling you to exert less effort, if any, to prevent a memory invasion. Your gift shouldn't hurt. Wouldn't it be wonderful if we discovered focusing on a certain color could provide protection? Want to try?"

She laughed, seeming like herself again. "Absolutely. I love how juiced you get just from the idea of trying something new. You should approach all of life like that, Professor. You'd be a lot happier."

He kissed her, though he'd told himself earlier that he wouldn't. Not during work time. But he was excited, his body buzzing with all the possibilities.

Sara broke away, fiddling with her bracelet, biting her lip. "What color do you suggest I take for a spin first?"

"I think you're better off thinking of a tone that feels right to you. Close your eyes."

She did, her face pinched in concentration or perhaps nerves.

"Imagine a light surrounding you, holding you, protecting you. What color is it?"

"White. It's a spotlight."

"Only you would find a spotlight protective," he said with a laugh. "But let's go with it and see what happens."

He took her hand in his, as he had so many times. Her skin was as soft as always, the nails French tipped with a thin, gold line between the white tips and the clear polish on the rest of the nail. Elegant hands, a little cool, and they fit perfectly within his own.

Closing his eyes, he let the lights in his mind grow and glow. The opalescence of her consciousness was there, as always, and Beckett thought white could be the right shade for her.

Sara exhaled and her fingers tightened.

"Talk to me," he said.

"Doesn't feel like anything. I can sense you there, but thinking of a white spotlight doesn't affect anything. I'm sorry."

"Don't be sorry. We're just playing around. Why not try a black light next? In many cultures, black is a protective color."

Black didn't work; neither did blue nor red. At last, she found marginal success with a shiny and shimmering gold. Beckett saw it, looming behind her like a sun dipped in glitter and slipped inside a shell.

She mesmerized him, and he basked in her radiance, marveling that she was his. He forgot completely to try and move closer to her thoughts. When he came to his senses, he still couldn't move closer, the brightness too sharp.

Eventually, he dropped her hand and cleared the scratchiness from his throat. "I think that could work. It feels different from your typical shield, more like a typical mind."

"Jolene said she saw a gold memory in my mind once that she thought was the cover story I was running through my brain."

"Fascinating." Beckett wanted to pick her up and spin her, so he did. She wrapped her arms around his neck and laughed.

He set her down but hugged her close. "If this translates to other people, this could change everything. Your mind is so dazzling, it's an engrossing distraction. If the students can replicate the effect, then any casual contact would be over before the offending magician could even try to push through."

Time would tell, but perhaps he'd found a way to protect her from the pain of a memory magic attack, and the means to find a way to defend them all.

CHAPTER THIRTY-THREE

Sara

SARA GOT OFF THE BUS AND WALKED ACROSS ARCHER Avenue to the Archer Heights branch of the Chicago Public Library or, more specifically, to its narrow parking lot. Sitting there was an obnoxious yellow Ford Focus. Ryan opened the driver's door and leaned onto the car's roof.

Then the driver's side back door opened, and Jolene got out. Sara felt a moment of shaky satisfaction that they'd resolved their issues enough to work together again. That had become part of Sara's plan when she'd discovered that Jolene still had Ryan's number in the contacts of her Agency phone. Unsure how tightly Kyle was monitoring her, Sara had asked Jolene to reach out to Ryan, hoping the request would help repair their rift. They could be simply playing nice for her sake, but she hoped not.

At the same time, the deep-seated belief that she was alone and couldn't count on anyone to help her gripped her tighter for a moment, as if urging her not to believe her eyes, which were swimming.

"Guys," she said, half the word caught in her throat. She couldn't stop herself from running to them.

Ryan grabbed her first. "I can't believe you thought I ditched you," he said, but his affectionate squeeze made his reprimand painless.

Jolene didn't wait for Ryan to release Sara to join in the hug. "The band's back together . . . sort of."

Yes. Yes, they were.

"Okay, get in the car," Ryan said, giving Sara a little push.

She ran around to the passenger seat. "Where are we going?" she asked.

"Nowhere. Shit's going down right here."

"This library?" Sara arched one eyebrow. "Well, he won't expect that."

Jolene, who'd gotten into the back seat, stuck her head between them. "I kind of miss the action, I have to say. But don't tell Cass that."

"What's the plan?" Sara asked, bouncing. She'd missed this excitement, too, though mostly the teamwork.

"Before we start, I want to be clear that what Kyle made you do didn't come from the Agency," Ryan said. Then he winced. "Not the part of the Agency I'm working for, anyway. You were truly supposed to be there only to support the training program. No spying."

Jolene harumphed. "Yeah, the Agency is totally on the level. Being upfront is their thing."

Sara's gut twisted at the remembrance of how she'd once defended the Agency, too. But the demolition of their group and a gunshot wound had clarified her view of them. "She's got a point, Ry. They have no scruples at all."

"They're changing. I'm employed by the legit side of the Agency. Leadership wants to shed the criminality altogether. Not everyone is going quietly into that good night, though."

"They're *changing*? Bullshit," Sara said, rubbing her thumb over the contours of her scar through her shirt.

Ryan frowned. "I'm serious. I listen to entrepreneurs pitch projects, and I help decide if the Agency is going to invest or not. It's actually the cushiest job on the planet. I get taken out to dinner all the time, and people are always trying to bribe me with shit. It's sweet."

"Why didn't you tell me that before?" Sara asked.

"You never want to talk about the Agency, so I didn't bring it up."

It was true. She'd been so hurt by Jorge's and Stadler's behaviors that whenever Ryan had brought up anything Agency-related, she'd always cut him off.

Jolene shoved the back of Ryan's seat. "And you believe all that crap about being legit? The Agency is really forgoing the lucrative drug business because it's, what, the right thing to do? They're like the boyfriend who swears he'll never, ever hit his girlfriend again."

"He's changed," Sara said in gushing mock agreement.

Ryan ignored their teasing. "It's unclear how Kyle got into the position he did, or how I got assigned an out-of-town gig. The electronic records on both transfers have been wiped. Someone with clout is manipulating things, but it isn't coming from the big bosses."

"Sure it's not," Jolene said.

Sara had to agree. It would take a high-level executive to make shit in the system disappear.

"I'm the one working there, but you guys know better." He held out his hand to Sara. "Let me check your cell for spyware and trackers."

She gave him her cell as he withdrew a tablet and plugged her phone into it.

Sara looked back at Jolene while Ryan did technical stuff. "Too bad Jorge turned out to be such an asshole. He would be handy about now."

"What do you mean?" Ryan asked, looking up. "Jorge's good people."

Sara scratched the back of her neck. "Yeah, if good people drain their lover's bank account."

"Jorge would never do that," Ryan said, his voice a whip crack.

"Then where'd all my money go? Jorge dumped me, not even staying to see if I lived after I got shot, then took my savings and fucked off." Sara's voice didn't quaver, as she'd mostly come to terms with his deceit.

"He offered to stay and watch over you," Ryan said, "but we thought it'd be smarter if I did that. We didn't know what was going to happen, and he's the only one of us who could totally disappear, so I told him to go. I sent him word via a code that you were fine. I explained all this when you got out of surgery."

Jolene laughed. "You expect her to remember shit right out of surgery? I guess someone's never had anesthesia."

"He checked up on me?" Sara squeezed her head between her hands to keep her brain focused. "Who took my money if it wasn't Jorge?"

"Had to be the Agency," Jolene said. "If you had enough saved that you didn't need them, then that loosens their hold. Had to ensure you wouldn't testify to anything." Then she added dryly, "Like any legitimate business would."

Ryan reached back and tugged on Jolene's ponytail. "Baby steps. You can't expect a complete turnaround overnight."

"If that's the case, why haven't they given me my cash back?" Sara asked. At least Jorge hadn't totally deserted her or stolen from her. She hadn't misjudged him after all. The Agency, on the other hand . . . "Bastards. I want my money."

Ryan nodded. "You sure the hell earned it. I'll see what I can do when we straighten all this out." His tablet beeped. "Interesting. Your cell is clean."

Sara had expected at least a tracker.

"Fuck the Agency. Tell her *our* plan to get rid of the dickhead," Jolene said, pushing again on Ryan's seat. "It's brilliant."

Ryan grinned. "You call Kyle, keep him on the phone for two and a half minutes, and my guy traces him. The Agency has a team ready to run him down. That's it. All you have to do."

"What about whoever put him in the position to monitor me? This is such a power move, right? I bet that Agency person is working for Dominion," Sara said. "That faction has pretty deep pockets, and they're ruthless. They've already stolen a bunch of Beckett's recruits."

Jolene practically hurtled herself into the front seat. "That's where I come in. After they pick up Kyle—that's a douchebag name if I ever heard one—I'm going into his greasy little brain to find all his connections. If you're going to pull a weed, you've got to get the root, or it just grows back."

Sara gaped at Jolene. "Why would you do that? I thought you were totally out."

Jolene shrugged. "I'm doing it for you, so you'll be safe."

"But you'll be putting yourself back in their crosshairs. They've left you alone so far. Believe me, if you can make a clean break from them, do it," Sara said. That had certainly been her plan before Beckett and Ren had entered her life.

"Whoever these assholes are," Jolene said, "they're targeting the Moralists. I have no intention of joining any kind of magic club, but if I do nothing, then those Dominion pricks could take over the Agency, and then they might decide to come after me. Nope. I'm culling them now while the task is manageable."

"And I'll make sure the executives, the highest higher-ups, take them out," Ryan added.

Sara thought she might burst into song like she was starring in the world's most bizarre musical. "You're the best big brother ever." She tackled him in a hug. "And you're the best sister." Hugging Jolene was a lot more awkward through the gap in the seats.

"Let's nail this motherfucker so you can be free," Jolene said.

Sara clapped her hands. "Child's play." She turned on her phone and selected Kyle's number. Studying her friends, she narrowed her eyes. "You guys better not try to make me laugh while I'm doing this."

"You're the only one of us who would do something like that," Jolene said.

Sara had to agree. "Okay. Watch and learn, kids." Without hesitation, she called Dickhead one last time.

"Whatcha got for me, Princess?"

"The dinner for the Phi has been scheduled. May 12, starting with cocktails at 6:30 p.m. I've got the whole thing planned. There'll be nothing left of the professor's program and his reputation when it's over." She ended the call.

Ryan and Jolene gaped at her.

"What are you doing?" Ryan hissed. "That was not two-and-a-half minutes."

Sara held up a finger. Her phone rang. She smiled. Kyle wouldn't suspect a thing if she drew out the conversation now. "What?"

"Not good enough. I want to know the specifics of your plan."

"Don't you trust me?"

Huh. He didn't.

She went into detail about how she would wear a dress scooped low in front, secured with two-sided tape. She'd remove that tape mid-party to ensure a wardrobe malfunction during her drunken speech about how she and Beckett were getting married, and everyone there was invited. That would just be the start. Kyle stayed on the call for a full seven minutes as she elaborated on every embarrassment she could concoct.

"That'll work," he said, sounding very smug, and disconnected.

Ryan and Jolene both wore expressions somehow combining horror and admiration. "Remind me to never piss you off," Jolene said.

"I wouldn't do it, you know," Sara said. "I'd never do that to Beckett." She'd take Ren and run before she'd hurt Beckett that way. She loved him too much to destroy what he'd worked so hard to create.

Ryan's phone buzzed, and he answered. "Yeah? Okay, tell me when it's done." He grinned at Sara. "They've got a lock on him. Just a bit more time, and you're home free."

"Let's get ice cream," Sara said. Now that they'd set the trap in motion, her insides began to burn as if she'd swallowed drain cleaner. If they didn't catch him, if he figured out Sara had betrayed him, then he would strike at her. He was the spiteful sort, and Sara wondered what he might do in his death throes.

She could totally see him shooting her in the stomach or face or both.

* * *

AFTER DOUBLE SCOOPS, RYAN AND JOLENE TOOK SARA UP TO COR'S PLACE in Ravenswood. The IDs he handed over were perfect. Lauren Ankrom would now be Ren Reeves, which allowed her to keep her nickname. Since Ren hated her family, she'd been eager to relinquish her surname, just as Sara had all those years ago when she'd been Sarah Strauss. Never again.

She hugged Cor, and he patted her on the back as if she were four rather than twenty-four.

Ryan dropped her at home and insisted she promise not to leave her apartment until Kyle was in custody. The Agency had people watching Arden's front and back entrances, so if Kyle figured out her deceit, he wouldn't be able to get to her.

Assuming the Agency really did have good guys who would do what they said they would.

CHAPTER THIRTY-FOUR

Beckett

SARA BARRAGED HIM WITH TEXTS, ALL IN HER horrible run-on sentence style. He'd missed her, longed for her, and he'd found himself saving up stories she might find amusing and talking to her in his head throughout the day. In his mind, he used to practice lectures or what he might say to Ahmad, the other Philotimo, or his mother, but now his thoughts were full of Sara.

She invited him to her place, where she would make him a wine and cheese plate, as she'd heard fancy people liked that sort of thing. He'd planned to read student essays, and they already had a date scheduled for Friday, which she'd promised would not involve colonics.

He should wait.

Finally, he conceded to what they both wanted. *I'll stop by for a bit.*

* * *

SARA WORE HER HAIR DOWN. IT FELL IN WAVES AND KINKS, COMPLETELY un-put together, and it almost undid him. She wore only blue sleep shorts with black sheep on them and a tank top that reached just past the waistband of the shorts. Her scars might show if she moved just right, and he knew that meant she trusted him.

"Where's the cheese board?" he asked, mostly to stop himself from grabbing her and ruining all the progress they'd made with his patience and care.

She gestured to the coffee table, where there was a brie wedge and chunk of cheddar and several Ritz crackers.

"And the wine?"

Sara strode to the kitchen and returned with two bottles, a chardonnay and a cabernet. "The Binny's guy said this one"—she held up the chardonnay—"pairs well with the brie, and the red one pairs well with an older cheddar. This cheddar, I'll have you know, is fifteen and ready for a learner's permit."

She set both bottles on the coffee table, then twisted her fingers into the hem of her tank top. He walked to her and took her hands in his, stilling their fussing. "What's wrong?"

"I'm nervous," she said.

"Why? It's just me."

Her face pinked, and her eyes watered. She turned away, putting her back to him, but didn't leave the room. "Sorry," she said. "I don't know what's the matter with me. Just . . . please stay with me tonight, even if we only, you know, sleep."

He scooted closer to her, until his chest almost brushed her back. With deliberate slowness, he pressed a kiss to her shoulder.

"Tell me about your weekend at your dad's," she said abruptly.

She seemed nervous, so he obliged as he rubbed his hands up and down her arms. "I think last weekend was the first time my father and I ever had what could be termed a heart-to-heart. He's never been a demonstrative father—neither of my parents have never been all that affectionate. I hadn't realized I'd felt the lack, but then he told me he loved me. I think the reason I went into English—although I didn't know it at the time— was because of words." He hadn't even realized that revelation until he'd spoken. Sara hadn't simply opened him, but also shone a light on what lay inside. "Words matter, particularly the ones we say to one another and the ones we say to ourselves."

She tilted her head to catch his eyes. "Have you been saying mean things to yourself?"

Beckett laughed and eased his hands around her waist. He held her close, and she layered her arms over his as he enveloped her, pleased she allowed him to touch her stomach. He hoped if he touched her there enough, she might grow comfortable.

He didn't think she needed surgery to make her more appealing, but it was her body, and he would never give her his unasked-for opinion.

"I think you're amazing," he whispered into her ear.

She spun in his arms, nimble and graceful, her eyes so big and blue and piercing straight through him as she finally faced him again. "So, you'll stay? *Stay*, stay?"

What else could he say? "Yes."

*　*　*

THEY NEVER DID OPEN A BOTTLE OF WINE OR CUT A SLICE OF CHEESE. Sara took his hand and led him to her bedroom. He expected a boudoir aesthetic, but her bedroom consisted only of a mattress on a frame—no headboard or footboard—a tall dresser and mirror, and a white velvet chair that likely came from a dining set. Her duvet was stark white, the sheets white, the walls a heavy cream color. It was a sad room with no personality, so unlike Sara. She needed colorful scarves over lamps and a mirrored side table or cushions on the floor with a coffee table.

As she tugged him toward her bed, she wasn't brazen or confident but almost shy, her eyes downcast. He drew her to a stop and tilted her head up with gentle pressure from his fingers and kept them there as he kissed her until she relaxed. He luxuriated in the kiss, each lock of their lips slow and sensual.

Then something changed, as if the kiss woke something primal in her. She bit his bottom lip, not enough to hurt but with an urgency Beckett felt low in his belly and in his balls, his cock already hard and eager. She ran her palms up his chest and into his hair. She hauled him closer to her, pressing her body into him at the same time.

"More. I need more," she said, struggling to unbutton him without breaking their contact.

Beckett stilled her hands and took one step back. Sara watched as he unbuttoned his vest. He didn't draw it out like a striptease, which would have been ridiculous, but he didn't rush. She stared as if she found him utterly fascinating.

When he shed his vest, he searched for a place to put it. Sara took it from him and inhaled the fabric, which made Beckett even harder. There was something visceral about her craving the scent of him. She folded the vest carefully and set it on the chair, returning her gaze to his chest as he unbuttoned his shirt. He removed it and handed that to her, as well.

She folded it, dropped it on the chair and then lowered to her knees.

His belly flipped and then flipped again. He should please her first, but . . .

Sara glared up at him, her eyes almost snarling at the idea he might refuse her. As if he could deny her anything, especially this. The reticence he typically sensed in her was gone. A fierce hunger shimmered through her, and Beckett comprehended this was their moment. No stopping.

She reached for his belt, unbuckling him and sliding it from around his waist in seconds. She unbuttoned and unzipped him without hesitation or fumbling. He considered how often she must have done that in her role with the Agency and about all the men she might be comparing him to, but the doubts glowed, flickered, and then were blown away by the pink flush that sprang over her chest and neck and into her face. She might have been able to fake the expression on her face, but not that physiological response.

"You don't need to do this for me," he said.

"I'm doing this for me." She winked at him and fished his hard cock out of his underwear, his pants dropping to the floor.

He should undress entirely, but he was held in place by her siren spell. And her hand.

She stroked him twice, lightly, watching his face, testing his reaction. He'd never been so hard in his life. She licked the tip of his cock and then drew him into her mouth, her lips sliding and sliding and sliding, swallowing him whole.

Beckett had heard of deep-throating, of course, but he hadn't imagined it was something he'd ever encounter. He sucked in air as she dragged her suction upward. Watching her watching him with his dick in her mouth was the most erotic experience of his life, and he focused on holding back his orgasm as she worked him, making fine adjustments until she found a pressure and rhythm that would have him spilling too fast if he didn't do something to prevent it.

He cupped her cheek. "Slow—no, stop. I'm—I don't want to come yet."

She let his cock slide out of her mouth with an obscene pop. "Please? For me?"

Beckett had the most gorgeous woman on the planet begging him to allow her to fellate him. He blinked and nodded, and she took him back in her mouth, maneuvering herself slightly on her knees. She had to be uncomf—

Her rhythm increased, and with her other hand, she tugged gently on his balls, which were high and tight to his body. Her nails scratched lightly, and the orgasm tore through him, building so hard and fast it was deeply uncomfortable, almost painful, and then came the sweet moment when everything turned, and he was releasing, pleasure rushing from him. Black spots dotted his vision as he continued to spurt and spurt.

Beckett reached out blindly for something to hold on to, to support himself, and found the edge of the dresser. He panted, though he was fit enough that standing there and doing nothing but ejaculating shouldn't have exhausted him.

Sara rose to her feet as his eyesight returned, wincing and rubbing her knees.

He kissed her, cupping her jaw with both hands, plunging his tongue into her mouth too quickly, completely forgetting his manners. She tasted of him, and that had his cock stirring, his refractory period nonexistent with her. Her arms twined around his neck. He wanted to pick her up and carry her to the bed, but his underwear constricted his thighs, and his pants were still around his ankles.

She laughed at his minute flailing, squatted to unlace his shoes and pulled them off, soon rendering him naked and free. Her eyes glittered with satisfaction as if she'd been the one bewitched with ecstasy. A few women had given him oral ministrations, but none had beamed with delight afterward.

He kissed her again, this time with as much tenderness as he could muster. Staring into her eyes, he said, "Get on the bed, because I'm about to do unspeakably wicked things to you."

Sara yielded to him, following him like a curious lamb, allowing him to remove her clothing without flinching or tensing. He kissed up her ankles and thighs and over her hips. She held still as he peeled the silicone coverings from her scar and brushed his lips over every centimeter of red, raised skin.

"I don't feel much there," she said, though she didn't ask him to stop. More like sharing a curiosity.

"You said the person who did this to you is dead?" he asked. When she nodded, he kissed the top of the wound, a few inches below her breasts in the center of her body. "Good."

"How bloodthirsty," she purred as he moved to the underside of one breast, kissing and licking the skin there.

"Do you feel much here?" he teased as her body arched into him.

She groaned and writhed and twisted until his mouth was at her left nipple. He breathed onto the tight bud, and she pushed into his lips. For several seconds, he let her squirm before he scraped his teeth over her nipple and sucked gently.

Sara gasped and grabbed his head, her reaction so over-the-top he considered she might be faking, but the desperation told him her reactions were genuine. He thought of the sensitivity of her neck and hypothesized that she was responsive to a light touch everywhere. As a man of letters, he tested his hypothesis thoroughly, eliciting a moan as he ghosted his breath over her.

When he reached between her thighs, she was jerking, her heels dragging back and forth over the bed, her fingers gripping the covers so tightly her knuckles glowed white.

Her body tensed and tensed—in exactly the way he wanted—as he stopped each time her breathing changed.

"Beckett," she finally growled. "Stop fucking around."

He laughed, the burst of air brushing her clit making her groan again. "As my lady commands," he said, licking and flicking his tongue light and fast and relentlessly until she screamed his name, her body locking up before releasing as tears streamed down her cheeks.

Beckett might have worried about the crying if she weren't also smiling and laughing and sprawling like an indolent cat.

"I hope you drew that out so you had enough time to recover, because I need you inside me, Beckett Convery."

He'd done it only for her, though his erection had returned long ago. "I don't have protection with me," he said.

"I have condoms, but . . ." She propped herself on her elbows, making her glorious breasts rise. "I'm clean and on birth control. I can show you the paperwork if—"

"Are you not concerned I might have something?" he asked, because, clearly, she hadn't considered the possibility.

"No."

"It's been . . . a while since I . . . and we always used protection during intercourse, but not . . . oral sex. I've not been tested. I'll remedy that, of course, but in the meantime, I think we should use a condom for your safety." How ironic that his paltry sex life was the problematic one.

"I don't mind," she said.

He scooted up her body and kissed her. Not all women were amenable to kisses after oral sex, but Sara did not hold back her reciprocation. "You should mind. Always," he replied. "Now, where are those condoms?"

They started missionary, but Sara flipped and turned at regular intervals, mewling about needing to feel him from every position. When she repositioned herself on her hands and knees, Beckett guided her hips to him and found themselves reflected in the mirror over her dresser. Her heavy breasts dangled tantalizingly, and he dominated over her, his bare chest glistening with sweat. He slid inside her, feeling her slick tightness around him as he watched their bodies moving in tandem.

Sara dropped her head to the bed, then lifted her face to the ceiling, arching her back. The long length of her neck held him captive, her blond hair messy and falling everywhere. She finally caught his gaze in their reflection, and they stared into each other's eyes.

Beckett saw her muted thoughts blooming behind his eyes, close to his mind, their barriers brushing. He might have pushed, might have tested if this intimacy might be enough to allow him to breach her natural shield, but he didn't try.

She tightened, which made him moan, which spurred a whimper from her, and then his balls tingled with a warning.

"Sara, please, you need to come. I can't—"

She reached underneath and touched herself, losing their eye contact, but the tightening inside her almost immobilized his cock. He waited, pushing into her as she started cursing and mumbling and then fluttering around him.

"Come," she begged. "Please, please, oh God, please."

And he did, his body unloading in a never-ending bliss. He bent to rest his forehead between her shoulder blades, kissing the salt off her skin. It was a moment of perfect peace, and Beckett had the rare certainty that all would work out.

CHAPTER THIRTY-FIVE

Sara

For their next date, Sara added a fencing component to the Shakespeare theme—a production of *Henry V* by Babes with Blades. If Kyle wasn't apprehended before then, though, she'd have to make it an in-house date.

Ryan called, and Sara's esophagus spasmed. "Hey," she said.

"I've got some, well, good but disturbing news."

"About Kyle? Did they get him? Is he talking?"

"He died trying to escape custody before he could be interrogated. So we still have no idea who within the Agency he was working for."

"Oh." All she felt was relief. He couldn't hurt her now. Did it make her a bad person that she was so relieved he was dead? She hoped not. "Thanks for letting me know. I'm glad at least Jolene didn't have to muck around in that asshole's mind."

"Me too," Ryan said. "It's possible they'll uncover a few connections once they start combing through his stuff. I'll keep you apprised."

Sara didn't care for the somber way he was talking. "What's wrong?"

"We don't know who's trying to manipulate you. They might send someone else to try to finish what Kyle started. Be careful, okay?" Ryan said.

It was as if the Universe refused to give her even one fucking break.

* * *

LATER THAT DAY, ANDREW CALLED SARA TO COME TO STUDIO A AT eight. The Phi would be paying a visit. She assured herself that they had no idea about what had happened with Kyle, and if they did, they wouldn't be calling a meeting for it. But she couldn't shake her unease.

Everyone else had already assembled when Sara entered the room. The three Phi dudes were there. Only one of them was white, which surprised her, although the white guy, Gerald, was totally white—hair, beard, and skin. Even his glasses were white.

Luis was Latinx, light-skinned, clean shaven, and somewhere in his forties—the youngest of the three. He wore a pale orange suit he totally rocked, the cut and fabric luxurious.

"Thank you all for being here." The final Phi-guy was a dark-skinned Middle Eastern man in his fifties with facial hair that was more than stubble but less than a full beard. His brown eyes matched his skin color, which was striking. "For those of you who don't know me, I am Ahmad Sofer of the Philotimo."

The famous Ahmad. He hadn't proclaimed himself the head of the Phi. Not needing to mention it was evidence of his confidence in his power.

All the Philotimo were obviously moneyed.

Beckett had kept the seat next to him open, and she scurried into it, hoping the smile he gave her wouldn't be his last. His hand snaked under the table to take hers, and he brushed his thumb across the back of her hand.

Tingles shot through her body, and she squelched the urge to push his chair back and straddle him right there in Studio A in front of everyone.

"I wanted you all to gather here tonight to witness the honor we are about to bestow," Ahmad continued.

Beckett inhaled and held his breath. He must have an inkling of what Ahmad was about to announce.

"At last, I am sure of my decision. When we formed the Philotimo, it was our intention for leadership to only serve only temporarily. No re-elections, no dynasties. We've already held our positions far longer than we intended."

Gerald, the white dude, didn't look as if he wanted to relinquish his position. His beard twitched in displeasure. Luis had on an enigmatic game face that showed nothing of what he thought.

Ahmad focused on Beckett, a small smile on his face. "My heir will be Beckett Convery."

The room broke into applause, nobody clapping as enthusiastically as Sara did. Beckett was going to be a leader. He'd be marvelous at it, and she could tell from the flush of his cheeks that he'd wanted the position badly.

"Please join with me in congratulating Professor Convery on his hard work and dedication. I believe he will help us move with conviction and purpose into the future. He will shadow me for the next year, then take over at the Ides of March."

What the hell were the eyes of March? Nobody else seemed confused, so she kept her mouth shut. She'd ask Beckett about it later.

Everyone got to their feet, shaking his hand, clapping him on the back. Beckett grinned her favorite smile of his, with teeth and squinting eyes. After a few minutes, Ahmad pulled Beckett away, wanting to go over whatever Phi-people needed to go over. Sara kissed him chastely on the cheek before he left. He'd earned this, and seeing him so pleased made her effervescent.

Andrew sidled up next to her. "Well, this changes things."

"What do you mean?" she asked.

He shrugged, a tense jerking of his shoulders. "He'll have added responsibilities and expectations. This is going to change everything, and he'll need to approach all his decisions based on the duties of his new office, not just his own happiness. He'll be under a lot of scrutiny, and he'll deny himself in order to do what's right. I wonder what room he'll have left for us in his new life."

Sara's stomach twisted in opposite directions, tightening to the point of pain. Andrew was right. How would she fit into Beckett's life now? A pointed investigation into her background would not turn out pretty. But the Phi already knew about her history, didn't they? Through the Agency? Unless they hadn't considered that important enough to check—yet.

Andrew patted her on the shoulder. "Maybe I'm wrong."

Maybe he wasn't.

* * *

SARA DECIDED TO CHANGE INTO MORE CASUAL CLOTHES BEFORE MEETING Beckett in the dining room for banana splits. He'd decided to forgo his fencing class to celebrate his ascension with her.

When she entered her apartment, she found a dead man on her couch. At least a should-have-been-dead man.

"Princess. Did you miss me?" Kyle's scruff had crossed into unkempt. His green-gray eyes were mighty unfriendly.

The Agency was no longer watching Arden to protect her, because Kyle was supposedly no longer a threat. Once again, she was on her own. And when she didn't meet Beckett downstairs in the next fifteen minutes or so, he would come to her apartment looking for her. Would he discover her dead body? Maybe Kyle wouldn't be finished with her, and then he'd kill Beckett just for spite.

She pressed her back against the door, putting as much space between them as possible. Instinct told her to open the door and run, but experience stopped her cold. If he had a gun, he'd shoot her in the back. And he mostly likely did. Otherwise, he would have been waiting just inside the door to grab her. He allowed the distance because he didn't need close proximity. Not yet.

"I heard the most fucked-up story about you," she said.

"Rumors of my death have been greatly exaggerated." He sniffed and pushed his lips around, or maybe his lips moved like that because he was grinding his teeth. "Were you heartbroken?"

She shrugged, using her peripheral vision to search for anything within reach to use as a weapon. "I figured you'd want me to move on."

Nothing. Even the floor lamp was closer to him than her.

Kyle stood, and Sara forced herself to manage her breathing so she wouldn't hyperventilate and lose focus and motor control. Her heart and brain chemistry didn't follow the program and urged her to flee.

Once again, she thought of her mentor, Stadler, and how shoddy he'd been with her physical training. Shoddy wasn't the same as nonexistent, but she still couldn't out-power Kyle or out-class him. Out-thinking him was her only move.

"I was pissed at first, when I had to abandon my oat milk in the cracker aisle at Whole Foods," Kyle said, stalking closer to her. "But the afterlife gives a man some perspective."

He moved inexorably, a foregone conclusion of menace meant to frighten her.

It worked.

He was cornered with nothing to lose. He was fueled by vengeance. He reminded her far too much of Walther, who'd tried to kill her by shooting her in the stomach. She hoped Kyle ended up as disappointed and dead as that asshole.

His monologue continued. "Better to have fun with it. At first, I thought I'd shoot you in the gut. Try to hit the same spot. Double bullseye."

Her head prickled as if ice coated her scalp. She clamped down on the impulse to wipe the sweat off her top lip.

"Then I thought about carving up your pretty face."

She tucked her hands behind her back to hide the shaking, then remembered she should have them up near her face to block a punch. Already, she was losing.

He was close enough now for her to see the fern-like patterns of blood vessels around his nose. She leaned back and the ceramic bead on her elastic survival bracelet dug into her wrist. The ceramic bead. The bracelet's primary purpose was using the elastic like a slingshot. You pulled back and releasing the bead, proving enough force to break car glass in case you ever needed to escape a vehicle. Or a psychotic asshole bent on revenge?

Kyle's breath wafted over her face, the reek of cigarettes unmistakable. "What am I going to do, I wonder."

The little bead wouldn't do much unless she could nail the hollow of his throat or, better, his eye. But he would see that coming and easily block her.

He grabbed her neck, fingers digging deep, cutting off her air. The last self-defense Stadler had taught her was getting out of a neck hold. She pressed rolled the ceramic ball into the palm of her hand and clasped her fists together down low, out of his view.

"Stupid cunt. Couldn't just do what you're told."

Sara blasted her double-fists up between Kyle's arms, breaking his grip. She stomped on his foot with her three-inch boot heel, raised her hand, stretched the elastic back, and shot the bead into his left eye, ignoring the sickening squish.

Kyle screamed, clamping a hand over the eye, and Sara kneed him in the balls with all the force she could muster. He wheezed and collapsed to the ground. She stomped again, this time on the hand covering his groin.

He gurgled.

Sara ransacked through her purse for her small atomizer of perfume. She sprayed that in his unprotected eye.

Dickhead squealed and thrashed around while she tried to see where he'd stashed his gun. He had one, she was sure, so she had to incapacitate him so she could find it. She grabbed the floor lamp and jerked the cord out of the socket. It took three blows to his head before Sara felt comfortable enough to search his still body for the gun.

He'd tucked it into his back, a Glock 9mm. Bullet in the chamber. She ejected the magazine, then popped it back in, ready in case Kyle revived enough to come after her again.

Her first call was to Ryan, a frantic rambling that he eventually understood. He was sending people. Hopefully, Kyle would stay in custody this time.

She'd wonder about how he had escaped and faked his death later. Now she had to text Beckett to cancel their banana splits and stop him from coming upstairs to find her armed and a bludgeoned man on her living room floor. She didn't want to explain that.

Something came up but I'll see you for dinner tomorrow

He responded quickly. *Is everything all right?*

Sara laughed, sounding only slightly hysterical. *Fine*

If I can't see you, then I might as well make my fencing class. Date tomorrow at seven, yes? I'm exultantly anticipating celebrating with you.

Celebrating. Right. She felt sick. Beckett was moving into the ultimate leadership position with the Phi, and his girlfriend was watching blood pool on her hardwood floor. Okay, it was more of a spattering of blood, but still . . .

Her hands shook as she kept the gun trained on Kyle's still form. Sara had to be prepared to shoot him, because hesitating might mean her own death if he attacked her again before Ryan's people got here. What if it wasn't Ryan's people who arrived?

Ten minutes into the wait, Kyle laughed, a wet chuckle that made Sara grip the 9mm tight, careful to keep her finger away from the trigger. If she killed him, she wanted it to be intentional.

He rolled over to stare at her with swollen, bleeding eyes. "You have no idea who you're dealing with. This goes deep, Princess. There are some powerful people who are not going to be happy with you."

Sara focused only on his movements, watching for tensed muscles that could signal a lunge at her, but he did no more than try to infect her with his horrible face, slippery words, and toxic energy. She tried to ignore his warnings of conspiracies and power and greed. He'd lost, and this was his way of flipping over the game board.

But even after three beefy men who moved with an economy of motion that belied their bulk toted him away, she didn't feel safe.

She called Ryan when she was sure her voice wouldn't shake. Probably she was imagining it, but the earthy tang of blood coated her nose and throat. "What the fuck, Ry?"

"I know, I know. I'm sorry . . . I don't know how we got that intel."

Sara opened her freezer and let the frosty air cool her blazing face. "How is everyone coming and going from Arden without anyone seeing them?"

"The basement door has a regular deadbolt, and it's easy to time the stairs with how much the stairway echoes."

"Well, fuck me."

Ryan exhaled loud enough for her to hear it. "This should be the end, babe."

CHAPTER THIRTY-SIX

Beckett

BECKETT SAT AT HIS DESK, PICKING AT A CROISSANT as he read through the student essays he'd put off, hoping to finish grading them before class so he'd have them done before his date with Sara.

Someone knocked on his door, then immediately opened it.

Andrew stood panting in his doorway, his face red and sweaty.

Beckett stood. "What's wrong? Are you all right?"

Andrew shook his head. "It's bad. It's really, really bad."

"What's bad? What are you talking about?" Beckett helped Andrew into one of his guest chairs.

Andrew bent over as if attempting to not pass out, gulping in air. "I don't want to tell you."

Then why are you here? "That's fine. Just breathe."

"There's a video," Andrew gasped.

"Of a student?" Beckett wondered who had been caught doing something unethical with their powers. What could a video capture that would make Andrew so distressed?

"You and Sara."

Beckett frowned. "Our relationship isn't a secret, and we're two consenting adults, so I don't see—"

"A sex tape, Beckett. There's a sex video on naughtyprofessors.com."

It hit him like a half-frozen water balloon to the face. "There must be a mistake or some sort of body double or CGI. Don't worry, Andrew." Though Beckett's heart thudded in his ears and his throat went scratchy. He coughed. "It's not possible. We only . . . we were only together in private places."

Andrew swiped a hand down his face, his eyes wide and bloodshot. "It looks like it was filmed at her place. There's no mistaking it's the two of you."

"Show me." *It can't be real. It can't be real. It can't—*

"Here." Andrew thrust his phone at Beckett.

The video had been paused, and though the lighting was dim, Beckett instantly recognized the scene. Sara was on her hands and knees on the bed, facing the camera, her head thrown back, and behind her, gripping her hips . . .

"H-How is . . . How did you even find this?" Oh God, who else had seen this? The frozen water balloon fell down his throat to his gut. "How do I get the video taken down? Maybe nobody else has seen it yet."

"It went out in an email to all Wells students and faculty," Andrew said.

Beckett scrambled to his computer, his mind whipping into circles like a whirlpool, moving faster and faster, drowning anything swept into the current. From a Hotmail account, the sender Anonymous. The subject line read: *HOT FOR TEACHER.* In the body: *Who knew Wells's most boring teacher, Beckett Convery, had it in him?*

"Th-This isn't possible." Beckett thudded onto his Corinthian leather chair and listened to the rushing in his ears, the sound of his dreams and ambitions conflagrating.

"You're right, though," Andrew said, standing next to him now, squeezing his shoulder. "You are consenting adults, and it's not like you're to blame, though allowing Sara to film you might be considered poor judgment."

"She didn't film us," Beckett retorted.

"Who else would have recorded you having sex?"

Beckett felt as if he'd been slashed with a rapier. "She wouldn't do that."

Andrew ran his hands through his hair. "I don't know, Beckett, in the video she keeps looking in the direction of the camera, and you know she's done it before."

"Done what before?"

"You didn't read her file? She made sex videos and had pictures taken of her with men a few times for the purposes of blackmail."

She had confessed to terrible transgressions in her past. But blackmail? With sex tapes and photos? "She's not blackmailing me, though. She—She wouldn't want this either. Oh, shit, I'm going to have to tell her."

"I'm sure she already knows," Andrew said, a bitter note suffusing his words. "Beckett, what if she plans to use that video to force you into a commitment?"

"How?"

"By making you defend her!" Andrew started pacing the office, messing up his hair. "Your mother would never approve of your relationship. This could be Sara's way of pricking your honor, making you declare something serious as a way to protect her reputation. I mean, where was your relationship even going? It's not like you could marry her."

Beckett couldn't imagine Sara wanting anyone to see her like that, particularly if her scar could be seen. What they'd shared had been more than sex, and she wouldn't jeopardize that.

His phone rang. His mother. She no longer had a Wells email account, so there was no reason to think she'd received the video, and yet his gut churned as he answered.

"Hello, Mom," he said.

"What are you going to do about that recording?" she demanded with all the sympathy of a shark.

CHAPTER THIRTY-SEVEN

Sara

SARA WAS APPLYING EYELINER AROUND THE LOWER lash line of her Egyptian cat eye when someone pounded on her door. The authority of the knock made her momentarily lightheaded. Had the Agency come back?

"Who is it?" she called out.

"It's Ren. Open up!"

Sara's body locked up at the idea of opening the door, especially to Ren and her rare gift. She thought she could still smell the tang of blood under the perfume she'd sprayed to cover it. Not that any blood remained. The Agency were fuckers, but they cleaned like bosses. "I've only got half my eye done."

"Nobody gives a crap. Let me in. It's serious!"

She'd never heard Ren sound so frantic, not even when she'd been convinced her lack of ID and transcripts would doom her entry into the program.

Ren burst inside the moment Sara turned the lock.

"Stay calm," Ren practically shouted, clearly not taking her own advice. She huffed, staring at Sara with too much eye contact. Ren tended to look away most of the time. "Damn it!"

"What is it?"

"Sit down."

Sara complied, tucking her hands under her knees. "Tell me."

"There's a sex tape of you and Professor Convery, and it was sent to, like, the whole school. All the pig-dudes keep watching it over and over again, like . . ." Ren growled.

"What?" Sara disappeared, her mind floating away, putting a nice, numb buffer between her feelings and her thoughts. This was *sooo* not what she'd been expecting.

Nobody had died. Nobody she cared about had been injured. This wasn't the worst news. She repeated that to herself a few times.

"Are you okay?" Ren asked, biting into a hangnail.

"Do I look hot in the video?" she asked with a smirk, death-gripping a go-with-the-flow attitude.

"That's all you care about?" Ren said, then sucked in a huge breath. "Oh, shit. Oh, Sara, I'm sorry. Don't . . . Don't do that. You're freaking me out."

Sara dealt with every shitty thing that happened to her with humor, and she wasn't about to change to make Ren more comfortable. Hey, that was the one advantage to being a victim—you got to act however the hell you wanted afterward. Only, of course, that was a lie. If you didn't behave the way you were supposed to, then nobody believed you. And it was already hard enough, especially if you were as attractive as Sara.

"It'll be fine. Eventually, everything works itself out," Sara said.

"Stop that." Ren pushed the heels of her hands into her eyes. She was going to smudge her mascara. "Your aura is the ugliest shade of yellow I've ever seen, like thrown-up mustard. You . . . you didn't do anything wrong."

"I'm not sure what you're talking about." Sara sat back down in front of her makeup light on the kitchen table and started on her other eye, her hand steady as she drew the liner pen over her lid and just past the corner, curving the slightest bit up at the end.

"You're doing something weird with your emotions, and it's making me dizzy and kind of sick."

"So, turn it off." Sara yanked out her purple eyeshadow palette. "My emotions are going to do what they're going to do."

Ren squawked and flapped her arms before going still, dropping her chin to her chest. A warm sweep of power washed over Sara. It wasn't a comforting warmth but a prickle like freezing water on a sunburn. Her mouth filled with the taste of blackberries gone too ripe. Sara likely could have stopped it, but it would mean shutting out Ren, and she didn't want to do that.

Ren's gift flowed over Sara but muted, like the remembrance of a hug. Ren's desperation to soothe cracked part of the buffer between Sara and her emotional pain. It had been a while since she'd felt anyone other than Beckett caring that much.

Beckett.

Sara swallowed. He was going to absolutely hate her when he found out about Kyle and what he'd made her do. She hadn't gotten away with anything.

CHAPTER THIRTY-EIGHT

Beckett

WHEN BECKETT GOT HOME AFTER A DAY plagued by titters and snide glances at every lecture, he discovered Sara sitting in his living room, all the lights off. It wasn't the moment he'd anticipated when he'd given her the security code to his home, back when life had made sense. Perhaps she hadn't called or texted him for the same reason he hadn't reached out to her—the magnitude of what had happened demanded a processing period before they discussed the situation in person.

"I take it you've heard about the video?" he asked, deciding to start with the present before working to her past.

Sara nodded and spoke with a tight voice. "Yeah. I watched it all the way through once."

Part of him wanted to ask her how it was, since he hadn't viewed any of it, needing only to see that one, frozen frame. But that question invited a levity he didn't feel. "Any idea how that was captured?"

"The Agency."

Beckett dropped his satchel on the floor. "They sent you to us to aid the program. Why would they want to . . . expose us in that manner? For what gain?" He unlaced his Oxfords.

"Someone in the Agency replaced my previous handler with some asshole. Whoever assigned him didn't want to help you, but demanded I sabotage your program." She spoke with none of her usual energy but like a hollowed-out version of herself.

Andrew had been right. She'd lied to him from the start. He'd let her inside, and she'd carved him apart.

Sara continued as if she hadn't split him in half. "He knew what buttons to push to get me to do whatever he said. But I rarely do exactly what I'm told—it's so boring to live life that way." At this point, she usually would have laughed or at least smiled, but she did neither. "I tried to shield the program as much as I could, but I did give him information I figured he already knew. He was particularly interested in you."

She looked at him then, her eyes overdone, thick eyeliner on her top and bottom eyelids, like Cleopatra, but her lips remained bare. "When you and I started getting along, I realized you weren't the arrogant prick I thought you were. I didn't want to fuck you over to begin with, but once I got to know you, I *really* didn't want to fuck you over."

Beckett said nothing. Couldn't say anything.

"I won't get into his tactics or demands. But when I found Ren, I reached out for his help."

"Ren's involved?" How many people had betrayed him?

"God, no. She's just a kid with a shitty family who needed saving, and, for whatever reason, the person to rescue her was me." She slammed her thighs with her fists. "The point is, once he knew I cared about her, he had serious leverage and demanded I obliterate the dinner party in a way that ensured you'd be completely humiliated and discredited."

Beckett slumped into his armchair, elbows on his knees, head in his hands, squeezing, trying to make sense of the world. "The dinner with the Philotimo in two weeks?"

"I fixed it," she replied, still without her usual verve. "Kyle's out of the picture now."

"Who?"

She shook her head. "The guy who took over as my handler. Some

Agency employee working for Dominion. At least we think so. Who else would benefit from the program failing? His objectives were not the Agency's official orders." She sighed. "I don't know if he always had this video thing planned or if it was a fail-safe, in case he wanted to blackmail me or just fuck me over in general, but there's no doubt in my mind that this was his doing."

"How did he do it?"

"I found the camera on the edge of my mirror and destroyed it. Thoroughly. He'd broken into my apartment numerous times and had the resources to set up the camera, doctor the recording, and send it wide."

"Doctored?"

She lowered her face into her hands, her voice muffled. "He added fake audio with grunts and moans and you saying some pretty non-Beckett things." She lifted her head, palms skating over her face, her eyes red. "It doesn't even sound like you."

"What, precisely, do I presumably say?" He needed to slow his breathing but couldn't. A gray flurry of snow crossed his vision.

Sara squared her shoulders. "The worst was . . . *yeah, your shithole feels so good.*"

Beckett's brain went not white but fuzzy, like static come to life. They hadn't had anal sex, and even if they had, he would never, ever say something so vile.

"From the position we're in," Sara said, "it's possible we were doing butt stuff, which, whatever, it's not like there's anything wrong with that, or the dirty talking—if it had been real."

"Nothing wrong with that?" he parroted, his mind still cloudy, as if he were outside his body.

"What two consensual people do is nobody else's business. You know that, right?"

"Tell me you weren't involved," he said. The moment he said it, his conscience popped back into place. *Of course* she wasn't involved. He might have trusted her more than he should have, but he knew to his bones that she would never do something like this to him. "I didn't mean that. I didn't—not what it sounds like. I know you had nothing to do with the video."

She stared at him in shock, as if he were dangerous. Him! He hadn't been the liar in their relationship. He had never deceived her.

Earlier today, Andrew had cornered Beckett with another copy of Sara's file and had insisted on showing him photographs of her dancing on a table, men surrounding her in a smoke-filled room, hands all over her, pleasure on her face. And then there'd been the police report.

"Do you still have a drug problem?" he asked.

Sara squinted at him. "What?"

"Meth. Do you still have a meth addiction?"

Her fingers dug into the tops of her thighs. "Why would you think I was an addict?"

Beckett sighed. He wasn't a game player, and he needed her to stop. "I saw the missing-persons report your parents filed in Utah when you were fifteen. They brought in your . . . stash, and there's an entire accounting of erratic behavior, how you stole money, how you sold yourself for drugs, how—"

"Shut up." Sara stood, hands balled into fists. "Shut the fuck up, Beckett. You don't—" She shook her head like a rabid dog. "I've *never* done meth in my life. I never prostituted myself. I—" Sara swallowed and then swallowed again. "When I left home, I didn't have shoes."

"Why—"

"I. Said. Shut. Up." Rage filled the room like a dark cloud, making her vibrate.

Beckett's own body flooded him with neurochemicals, and he had no idea what to do with the rush.

"My stepfather raped me when I was fifteen," she said.

The moment Beckett heard the word *raped*, the oxygen in his windpipe turned to ice, and he struggled to breathe. His vision wavered as if peering into a series of warped mirrors. He couldn't grasp on to what was real. His Sara. His Puckish, vibrant Sara.

She continued, "My mother came home and found him on top of me, and even though I was crying, she accused me of seducing her husband. She hit me, tried to cut off my hair, and I was pretty sure she was going to kill me. I ran to Salt Lake and then to Denver. I never heard about the missing-persons report, but they no doubt filed it, stuffed full of lies, so that if I ever went to the cops, they could discredit me."

She threw up her arms then fisted her hands. "Smart move on their part. If my grown-ass boyfriend who supposedly cares about me believes I sold my body for drugs, or maybe thinks I'm just that much of a slut, the police would have thought the same."

Beckett jerked. "I never called you a slut."

"No, you asked me why I never told you I was a meth-head whore."

He had, hadn't he? "After the video and then the file, of course I had questions." Beckett remembered her telling him how her first time had been *every bad thing,* and yet he'd never considered assault because the idea was so alien to him. He was giving her his worst self, right when she needed him at his best. "Sorry. I'm—"

"I lived on the streets or couch-surfed for almost two years. Not once did I exchange sex for cash, but if you're in the mood to judge, I did pay for every sofa, bed, or floor I slept on with my body."

Beckett pressed on his chest, trying to stop the ripping sensation.

She stared over his shoulder. "Nobody comes out and says *hey, I've got a place to stay, but you have to fuck me,* but everyone knows that's the deal. Some of the guys put me up for weeks or a month, and some suddenly remembered they had a girlfriend the minute they finished and kicked me out in the middle of the night."

He couldn't process the cruelty she'd lived, the complete devastation. And he couldn't believe he hadn't allowed her a chance to explain, just lunged into her. "I'm—"

"So, when the Agency came along, offering me a new life, I jumped at the opportunity to finally take control. I didn't care if it was illegal. We weren't hurting innocent people, just shuffling the deck of criminal people.

I'm not going to apologize for surviving."

"Sara, I'm sorry."

Her face was sheened with sweat, almost waxen. "Whatever. It's fine."

"It isn't. None of this is fine. I'm so sorry that happened to you." Silence smothered the space between them. "I'm not thinking straight, and I shouldn't have lashed out at you."

She shrugged. "That shit's easy to believe. I get it."

"No, it's—"

"Do you have lawyers who can take the video down?" Sara tugged at the hem of her T-shirt.

"They're on it, but the damage is already done. Everyone with a Wells College email account received that recording."

"Yeah, Ren said the guys were all in the common room watching it on repeat."

Beckett's mouth dropped open. The idea that the members of his program would watch at all, let alone multiple times, hadn't occurred to him. Had they learned nothing of ethics? That they would use his and Sara's victimization for entertainment caused him to question what he was doing at the school, with his life. "I have a meeting with the dean tomorrow at eight to strategize damage control. Once I clarified you are not a student, she was kind enough to reassure me my job is in no way jeopardized."

"That's good, right?"

Nothing about the situation was *good*. He pressed his fingertips into his brow, trying to stave off the headache that had been dogging him all day. Since he was scheduled to meet both the dean and his mother in the morning, he doubted the headache was leaving any time soon.

* * *

BECKETT'S MOTHER STOOD IN FRONT OF THE DOMINATING SEURAT painting *A Sunday Afternoon on the Island of La Grande Jatte*. The Chicago

Art Institute had opened only twenty minutes before, and the buses of kids had yet to arrive, so only a few other people occupied the room.

"Perhaps we could grab some lunch afterward," Beckett said as he moved to his mother's right side, conscious as always of the hearing loss in her left ear.

She wore a Tia Dorraine red power suit, complete with matching stiletto heels and a pinched expression. "I'm fasting today, which is why I suggested we meet here."

His mother had gained ten pounds in the last ten years and had managed to lose only five, which she considered a personal fault. She looked fantastic, but Beckett had learned long ago that his opinions about her appearance were never welcome, even if they were supportive or complimentary.

Beckett cupped the back of his neck, readying for the world's most embarrassing conversation with his mother. She didn't make him wait.

"What are your plans to recover your reputation?"

Beckett sighed. "I met with the dean this morning. The college intends to focus on the violation and misuse of the school email system, doubling down on our anti-bullying policy and not addressing the salacious aspects of the scandal at all."

"Sensible," his mother replied. "And the girl?"

"Sara's put on a brave face, but she's very upset by the whole thing."

"I mean, what are you going to do about her? She's worn out her usefulness and dragged you into something distasteful. Pivot, Beckett, and find someone eminently respectable. I talked to Sonja Steele—you remember her, right? Her daughter, Paris, is an estate lawyer, representing almost everyone in our social circle. Make an appointment to see her and test the chemistry."

Her brusque tone scraped Beckett's already tender sensibilities. It was time to come clean. "Mom, I want you to listen to me, really listen. Sara and I . . . we haven't been faking it for a long time. I know she isn't exactly what you envisioned for me, but her spontaneity and openness complement my more somber nature. She's a great listener, and the students respond to her."

His mother nodded, as if she understood, but the glint in her eye troubled him. "I'm not saying Sara isn't a lovely girl, and I'm sure she's exciting and original-seeming, but, Beckett, when you see yourself in five years, do you see *that person* with you? Of course the kids like her—she's a child herself, maybe not in age but certainly in temperament. You need a more sophisticated woman, one who can discuss art, literature, current events, who can entertain with dignity and class. She doesn't understand our sphere, dear."

What his mother said rang true, and yet, Sara was more than what his mother saw. "Sara is the kind of person who doesn't let the world drag her down. If you'd spend some time with her, I'm—"

"I think you need to sit for five minutes with the comments on that deplorable site." His mother shuddered. "Read what a few of those people have to say, and then tell me I'm wrong. Tell me she's right for you."

"I'm not interested in the commentary of trolls."

"It isn't only trolls, son. Five minutes."

* * *

THEY DIDN'T WALK THE MUSEUM TOGETHER, AND BECKETT LEFT FEELING abandoned rather than supported or bolstered. He sat on a bench in Millennium Park and withdrew his cell. Reading comments wouldn't change his mind about Sara, but he set a timer on his phone and pulled up the page with the recording so he could tell his mother later he had.

His throat tightened when he saw the video had gotten over ten thousand views. The comments were abhorrent and almost exclusively targeted Sara. They called her a slut and a whore, some speculating she was an escort of some sort. Even those that were "positive" simply wished their own girlfriends would "give up their asses" or moan like her, or any number of derogatory sentiments. Many comments consisted of what they'd like to do to her or have her do to them. Great appreciation was shown for Sara's enthusiasm.

The way they talked about her, as if she were a porn star, sickened Beckett, mostly because Sara had told him a lot of people assumed the worst about her. He didn't want to be the man who terminated a relationship because of the false speculations of others, but he could see his mother's point. People would view Sara as a trophy wife should they ever marry, though she was only six years younger than him. Being with her might close certain doors, or at least make people pause.

She'd lied to him. Spied on him. Didn't trust him enough to tell him when she and Ren had been threatened. She brought too much of the unknown, and Beckett needed stability and not the exciting but unpredictable nature of life with Sara. Not long term.

This incident made it a reasonable time to make a change.

But when he thought about life without her in it, he couldn't. He couldn't go back to how he'd lived before Sara.

However, putting some distance between them would be judicious. Only for a short while, maybe until after the end of the semester. Give the family secretary, Folger, time to run a PR campaign highlighting Beckett's career and heritage, charity work, and anything else that might scrub his image.

Smaller doses of Sara might be all the better for him. She'd somehow come to dominate his life.

Still, the idea of stepping away from her, even for a limited time, tightened his chest. He'd miss the way her chatter bolstered him, the casual way she kissed him, how she listened to not just what he said, but what he didn't say.

His head and his heart battled, rendering no clarity, only more confusion. If he could catch his breath—think—not just about today but his future. He might know the right thing to do.

CHAPTER THIRTY-NINE

Sara

SARA WOULD GET THROUGH THIS ROUGH PATCH. The humiliation was temporary, even if it felt interminable. Together. She and Beckett would weather the storm. She'd prove herself an asset to him.

Beckett had believed her when she'd told him about her past. After her extensive experience with powerful men, she'd been sure Beckett would desert her, abandoning her to save himself and his reputation. She wouldn't have blamed him, since he'd been targeted because of her. Men of his social stature were used to causing collateral damage rather than becoming a victim to it. Although they'd both proclaimed the dating was no longer fake, a part of her hadn't dared to believe it, that someone so sophisticated and smart and caring and encouraging would want fucked-up Sara. She'd ensure he never regretted choosing her.

Maybe her luck was finally turning for the better.

She was glam-gluing a trio of gold stars on the outer corner of her left eye when someone softly rapped on her door. The boys might have repeatedly watched the video, but they were also being supportive. Earlier tonight, most of them stopped by her apartment to check on her, offer assistance, and express outrage on her behalf. None had leered or laughed or asked inappropriate questions. It gave her hope—not just for the program but for humanity in general.

Her impulse had been to downplay her pain and embarrassment, but after some thought, she decided to allow the students to see how much damage something like that could do to a person, particularly women. After all, she and Beckett had done nothing wrong and had been exploited in such a horrible, personal way. All of them had told her, unprompted, that they'd known immediately that it wasn't Beckett's voice on the audio. Maybe that was why they'd watched it multiple times, to try to ferret out the identity of the voiceover person?

When she opened the door, Beckett was standing there. He'd never simply stopped by her place. He was far more likely to invite her to his house or meet her downstairs. She'd assumed it was his way of respecting her personal space.

"Hey," she said, grabbing him by the blazer and yanking him into her apartment. She needed to reconnect with him after the terrible day before.

She closed the door and wrapped her arms around him. His familiar grass and violet smell made her feel safe and at home.

"How are you holding up?" she asked, easing back and smoothing the part of his tie between his neck and the V of his vest. It was green with little checks of baby blue. No matter the struggle, he remained poised and put together. She wished she had his confidence and presence. Nobody would ever call him a whore (or man-whore) to his face. They wouldn't even think it.

"I'm well enough." He gripped her elbows and gave her a short squeeze. "Let's sit down and discuss."

Sara smiled, but she had to shove some effort into it. His words sounded too much like *we need to talk*.

"Sure. Would you like some tea? I bought some Darjeeling for you."

"No, thank you."

She'd been honest with the students about how upset she was over the video, and she would do the same with Beckett. School officials might have offered support, but people tended to cling to their preconceived notions. Maybe she should show him the texts she'd gotten from unknown callers. How they'd found her number, she couldn't guess. Most of the messages had consisted of lewd offers, with only one vaguely threatening message about the worth of a whore's life. Spoiler: not all that valuable.

"This situation has given me time to think more long term," Beckett said from his spot on her sofa. He sat with his body angled toward her, both feet on the floor, spine rigid. Overly formal.

Sara's hands were freezing, so she smashed them together and tucked them between her knees. "Okay."

His chest expanded and contracted twice in a slow, measured rhythm. "When I picture my five-year plan, Sara, I don't see how our relationship fits."

No. Not her Beckett. She had to be misunderstanding. He couldn't be dumping her. She wanted to shout that she saw clearly how they fit.

We work to grow the program. You continue to teach while I run the social activities and help you train the kids. You ground me, and I loosen you up. We make love and hold each other.

Beckett took another breath and continued as if he weren't destroying the most loving connection she'd ever had. "We've been exceptional together, haven't we?" He half-chuckled. "It surprised me, in the best way. So, who knows what will happen in five years?"

Five years? Was he asking her to reapply for the girlfriend position in half a decade? Heat pricked her eyes.

"But this scandal has made me assess what I'm doing and where I want to go. Teaching and education are in my blood, but my passion never came alive until we started the psychic enrichment program. I feel like my actions are making a difference, and I have to protect that."

"And I'm jeopardizing everything," she said flatly.

"Not at all. It's not you, but the situation. We need to take a step back, do some image revamping, and then we can revisit our relationship."

His gaze was focused on the stupid gold stars she'd glued to her eye to cheer herself. And it was a silly way to deal, but it wasn't as if she could take down the video or stop people from watching it, downloading it, or sharing it.

"If you don't want to . . . be with me . . . then you don't. You don't owe me an explanation." Mostly, she didn't want to hear it.

"That's not what I'm saying at all. This would just be a break, a few weeks at the most, while my people do damage control with my reputation."

"I thought you needed five years, and—wait—being with me tarnishes your reputation?"

"In my world, image means more than it ought—I realize that—but appearances—not physical but character—they matter. Without propriety and respectability, doors I need open will close."

"That video wasn't my fault." Which wasn't exactly true. She'd been the one to provide Dickhead with motive, means, and opportunity.

He pinched the bridge of his nose. "Unfortunately, people always judge women more harshly in these situations than men. I simply need distance from the . . . scandal."

"Scandal? We did nothing wrong, but you don't want to face it together. You want to extricate yourself from me." He was ashamed to be seen with her. She was disreputable, a stain on his pristine existence.

"We are dealing with it together, just in different ways. With your past, how can you face a bank of microphones and imperturbably answer questions about that video with grace?"

Imperturbably? Bank of microphones? He certainly had an inflated sense of himself. As if anyone gave a shit beyond the ten minutes it took to watch the recording and laugh at his terrible, fake dirty talking and ogle her perfect tits. This was him wanting out of their relationship and not having the balls to break it off.

A few weeks would turn to a month, which would become—well, it didn't matter. Her surgery was soon, and she didn't have to stay. She didn't have to stick around and endure this torture.

Except Ren. But Ren would be fine, better off without Sara to taint her too.

But Sara still wanted Beckett. More than she'd ever longed for anything or anyone. She liked who she was with him and who he was with her. Even if he didn't agree.

Why she would want someone who valued her so little boggled her, but the ache inside her was undeniable. Hating herself, she said, "I can be poised and proper for you, Beckett. Whatever you need. Give me a chance, you'll see. I'll reinvent myself."

His eyes softened—not in a loving way but pitying—and he put a hand on her knee. She wanted to smack it away, but the sucker part of her hadn't given up yet. The part of her that still held out hope that maybe she was completely misunderstanding him, that he wasn't like all the people in her life who'd hurt her—for whom she'd always been disposable— her stepfather, who'd tried to make her believe she'd been asking for his attention; her mother, who'd blamed Sara's rape on Sara, choosing her despicable husband over her kid; Stadler, who'd saved her from the streets but never acknowledged the physical and psychological damage the job had inflicted; all the marks who'd forced her to her knees, who'd slapped her ass, who'd thought of her as nothing more than a status symbol.

And now Beckett, who'd treated her as if she mattered.

Until she didn't.

"Sara," he said, squeezing her knee. "You're perfect as you are."

"Then why don't you want me?"

He winced. "I do. You're incredibly clever, the most exceptional woman I've ever known, but this situation . . . it requires a delicate touch."

The words pierced her all the way through like a butterfly pinned to a specimen box.

"When do I need to move out?" Her voice was wooden but at least it wasn't wispy or, worse, weepy.

"What? No. No, I still—You're a part of the program now. I can't imagine it without you. And this break is only until the controversy dies down. I honestly don't think it will take longer than a month at the most. Besides, Andrew and I have come to rely on you, and your perspective is so valuable. The students adore you." He grimaced, which was maybe his attempt at an awkward smile. "*I* adore you. You know that."

"You have a tendency to tell people what they think and feel," she replied, yanking her hands from under her knees and abruptly standing. Already he'd backed away, moving the timeline from a few weeks to a month. Did he assume she was too stupid to notice?

Her original plan, she decided right then, still worked. She'd get her surgery in two weeks and then disappear, not just from the Agency but from Beckett.

She would reinvent herself one last time. The real her. 100 percent. She was as serious inside as anyone else, and in her next iteration, she'd make sure she was not only admired but also respected.

Two more weeks, and then she could escape this hell.

She crossed to the door. "Thank you for telling me in person," Sara said over her shoulder.

"Of course. This is something we had to do face-to-face so there'd be no misunderstandings." Beckett stopped at the door. "Can I have a hug, so I know we're conciliated?"

She should have said no. Why would she hunger for someone who used the word *conciliated* non-ironically? Instead, she wrapped her arms around his neck and took one last deep breath of his cologne and the slightly salty scent of his skin.

Beckett

ECKETT HAD BEEN HOME FROM SARA'S FOR FIVE minutes. He'd intended to wash and iron shirts to keep his mind occupied, but a cold nausea sat in his gut. Taking a break from Sara already felt all kinds of wrong.

He'd made the reasons her fault when nobody was to blame. Clearly, he'd left her feeling as if she were deficient, when that was as far from the truth as possible.

In many ways—most ways—he was the one who didn't fit with her, not the other way around. She had the ability to connect with people quickly and genuinely. People admired and remembered her. Beyond gorgeous, she was also down-to-earth, helpful, and caring. Funny. Innovative. Always surprising.

She might be too colorful for his world, but he was undoubtedly too drab for hers. Too starched. Too set on a path established long ago. His family had history and traditions, and reputation was everything. Sara wasn't obsessed with appearances, but he was.

Should he text that to her? Likely, that would make the situation worse.

Beckett snatched his phone, unsure if he wanted to contact his mother to bolster his resolve, Andrew to distract him, or Sara to hear her voice. Fate decided for him as Andrew called.

"Andrew," Beckett said, trying to force cheer. "Fortunate timing."

"Oh yeah? What's up?"

Beckett picked up his distilled water spritzer then placed it back on the ironing board. He didn't want to iron. "Upon reflection, after all the tumult, I thought it best I hiatus my relationship with Sara. But now I'm having second thoughts."

"I know you're fond of her, Beckett, but I think that's the right decision. The video aside, she's got a tarnished history, and who knows what a reporter might dig up because of the video?"

Beckett hadn't considered that. "It's not that—"

Andrew continued. "If you've broken up, then anything salacious uncovered won't reflect on you. In fact, it might showcase your sound judgment. I mean, anyone could get suckered into an affair with a woman as hot as Sara."

"She's more than beautiful, Andrew," Beckett retorted, hating that everyone said that about her, as if her appearance were her most important aspect instead of merely the most obvious.

"I know. She's fun, too, and we all like Sara. That doesn't mean she's a good fit," Andrew replied. "Nothing wrong with taking a break, especially now your heir status is in jeopardy."

He winced at Andrew's words. "Do you think Ahmad will change his mind?"

"Did he call to tell you he's in your corner?"

"Not yet." Beckett walked into the parlor, intent on a few fingers of whiskey.

"He will when he's less busy. Want to go grab a drink or something? We could catch the Uptown Poetry Slam tomorrow afternoon at Green Mill."

Sara would love a poetry slam. He could picture her participating. Writing gave her trouble, but her spoken word skills would likely excel. "I think I'll just hang out at home."

"Let me guess, you're going to do laundry."

Beckett blew out a chuckle. "That was my plan. Am I seriously that predictable?"

"I'd say reliable; predictable makes you sound boring." Andrew made the clicking sound that indicated he was thinking. "With the video and everything, I think we should do something special for the meeting tomorrow. Want to brainstorm? I could come over, bring some sushi."

"That would be great. Much better than ironing."

* * *

ANDREW'S UPBEAT CHATTER HELPED BECKETT RESIST THE YEARNING, bordering on compulsion, to check in with Sara. His skin literally itched and his blood ran fast, as if he'd drunk a pot of coffee and consumed half a bottle of NoDoz.

Beckett and Andrew worked well together, as always. Their only point of contention was Andrew's suggestion that Sara not attend the meeting.

"The kids will be more honest if she's not there," Andrew said.

"By that supposition, they'd be more forthcoming without me there too."

For a while, they debated if both Beckett and Sara should abstain, but Beckett didn't want the mentees to assume he and Sara were too ashamed to show up. In the end, they decided Andrew would talk to Sara and let her decide if she'd rather be there or not.

Beckett wanted her to go, to demonstrate to the students her inner strength and fortitude. And, if he were honest, he longed to soak in her presence, find a way to smooth over his botched words. Show her his affection and respect through his actions. This separation was only temporary.

He picked out an outfit to wear, almost as if he were a kid readying for the first day of school. It was a bit formal for a Sunday morning meeting, but his clothing would project professionalism. His choices had nothing to do with Sara's admiration for his vests. He'd eschew the jacket and tie, striking a balance between casual and formal. Less to iron, too.

As the evening deepened into night, Beckett sprawled on his back in bed, sleep nowhere in the vicinity. With how little Sara slept, she might have still been awake. He couldn't reach out to her, though, not when they were laying low.

He missed her soft breaths against his neck, which was ridiculous considering how few times they'd been that close. Somehow, Sara had changed him on a cellular level, and he couldn't return to the man he'd been before. Surprisingly, he didn't want to revert.

He remembered Sara's face as she'd told him she would change for him to fit the mold she thought he wanted. He imagined her in neutral-colored business suits, discussing Faulkner with terms she'd learned from some podcast, toning down her over-the-top cheer to something merely pleasant.

She'd continue to make him a better man, and he would leach all the joy out of her. Ultimately, she'd leave, worse off for having known him.

Should he make the break permanent?

No. Even if she eventually fled, he'd take every moment he could.

At two in the morning, he drank a glass of water and thought about societal roles and the pressures of legacy and asked himself what life might be like if he relinquished those. If he wasn't an heir, wasn't ensconced in power, if he lived an ordinary life. With Sara.

Could life with Sara ever be ordinary?

It wouldn't work. His brain knew it wouldn't work, but his smitten heart wouldn't come to heel.

What the hell had he been thinking? He didn't want a break from Sara, not for one minute.

* * *

BECKETT WENT DOWN TO THE SUNDAY MEETING A HALF HOUR EARLY TO await Sara, who, according to Andrew, had said she wanted to attend and put on a brave face for the kids.

Sara arrived at the last moment with Andrew, the two of them laughing. *Laughing*, as if nothing had changed.

She smiled at Beckett with a friendly aloofness that cut through him worse than if she'd glared or ignored him. Beckett couldn't stop staring at her like a five-year-old eyes a puppy.

He'd grown up with privilege, he comprehended that, but what he hadn't realized was how little he longed for things. His money and position easily bought comforts and extravagances. If he wanted something, he acquired it. Interpersonally, he'd never invested in a relationship enough to bemoan a breakup. He'd simply moved on, always more concerned with his professional life anyway.

Watching Sara poke Ren until the tired girl slapped her hand, a chasm cracked open in his chest, and yearning spewed over and through him, weighing him down so thoroughly, he worried he might fall to the ground, never to rise again.

Andrew started the meeting, but Ren took over.

"This bullshit needs to be addressed now," she said, slamming a fist on the table. "Nobody fucks with our people without repercussions."

A line from Shakespeare's *A Midsummer Night's Dream* whispered in Beckett's ear: *Though she be but little, she is fierce.*

Anyone who raised questions about integrity or reputation met with her swift wrath. Andrew tried to rein in her tirade after she'd cut off Erik, who'd been saying he didn't think the video was too bad since Sara looked so perfect. They didn't normally allow interruptions at these meetings, but Ren would not be restrained.

Beckett heard each sharp word and impassioned grumble Ren made, and yet, a numbing cloud fogged his mind and pinned down his body. Ren squashed all the conversation like a child stomping on an anthill. It wasn't a debate but a lecture.

She rallied all the students to text, tweet, and advocate for privacy and respect with peers, the college administration, and society in general. If she used her gift, and Beckett supposed she had, it was done with enough subtlety he hadn't detected it—not that he'd been all that astute in the moment.

Just when the meeting was drawing to a close, Ahmad Sofer stepped into the room.

Ren peered at the head of the Philotimo for a tense breath before giving him a sharp nod and sitting down. When had she stood?

"Excuse me," Ahmad said, holding up his hands in a *mea culpa* gesture. "I wanted to come by as a gesture of support." He grinned, his teeth stark white against his dark skin. "Nothing has changed. Beckett is the man I want to succeed me. We all need to rally around him in these difficult times."

Beckett rose as Ahmad crossed to him, palm extended to shake his hand, an overt endorsement of trust. His temple throbbed like a fist had slammed into his skull. In the silence of the room, the chuff of Ahmad's shoes on the industrial carpet was loud.

"Sometimes, we can't avoid bad times and scandal, and it's how we deal with adversity that reveals true character," Ahmad continued. "I'm impressed by Mr. Convery's level-headedness with the personal nastiness that occurred."

Had he been level-headed? In retrospect, hadn't his response with Sara been rash and, perhaps, cowardly?

Beckett cleared his throat and pinched his brain to rise to the moment. "Thank you, sir."

This was all he'd been working toward, and the satisfaction would hit him soon. Right?

Sara

"**C**ONGRATULATIONS," SHE SAID TO BECKETT, giving him her socialite smile—not to win him over but to prove to him she could still smile. She patted him twice on the arm, then sought out Ren, who was stuffing bagels and cream cheese into her messenger bag.

Sara wondered how much longer Ren would hoard food. She had hoarded for a solid six months after getting off the streets. Nothing wrong with being prepared, and if it made Ren feel safer, then why shouldn't she? The leftovers went to waste otherwise.

Ren's lips were pressed tight, like when she experienced someone else's bad emotions.

"What's up, grasshopper?" Sara asked, leaning against the conference table in a casual way that kept her back to Beckett.

"Nothing." She lowered her voice. "All that dude talked about was Beckett, as if you weren't even there."

"Beckett's his boy, and I'm nobody." Sara shrugged. "At least to men like that."

Ren huffed and wrapped her arms around her body as if trying to hold in her words. She'd been on a serious roll. "Total bullshit."

In two weeks, it wouldn't be Sara's problem, so she refused to concern herself. "Want to go with me to Sephora?"

"Oh my God, what could you possibly not have? You own, like, every makeup in existence." Ren stood and lifted her bag strap over her head. "Let me put this away."

Sara laughed. "If you're going to sleep in mascara, you need a different brand."

"Mind your own business," Ren replied, though it lacked her usual snap. She wiped a fingertip under her eye, giving Beckett a scowl as she escaped out the door.

* * *

SARA LOITERED IN FRONT OF THE URBAN DECAY SECTION AT SEPHORA, looking without seeing, her empty basket sitting in the crook of her arm. Ren had disappeared into the fragrances. Sara didn't want to be alone, didn't want to leave behind the people she loved (beyond Beckett). Ryan, Ren, Jolene, all the boys in the program. Even Marlena had lent support, though all she'd done was give Sara a head nod.

Ren tugged on Sara's basket, peering inside at the emptiness. "Now I know something is horribly wrong."

What if she took Ren with her? Just one person. Yet even as she thought it, she dismissed the possibility. Sara could never take this new-found security away from her. Jolene and Kiera would watch over Ren going forward, likely far better than Sara ever could, so she should take solace in that. But she didn't. All she felt was sorry for herself.

That was unacceptable.

"Bare shoulder season is almost upon us," Sara announced, clamping down hard to shield her emotions from Ren. "What do you think about some gold body glitter?"

Ren scrunched her nose. "I think that's way more your thing."

"You could get some black or smoky gray body dust." Sara snapped her fingers twice in rapid succession. "Silver and black glitter would be so rock 'n' roll."

"Sounds awfully eighties to me."

"Makes it retro."

"Aren't you supposed to be budgeting?"

Ren made a valid point.

"You're too young to know this, but there's a heartbreak clause in every budget. When the man you're madly in love with leaves you because you're not good enough, you have pretty much carte blanche to soothe yourself with retail therapy."

Ren shook her head. "Uh, no way he said that. And how does that explain you wanting to buy *me* body glitter? Which I don't want, by the way."

Sara waved her hand in a magnanimous way. "Sharing is caring, misery loves company, just shut up and accept my offer—all the usual sayings."

As Sara moved to ask a store clerk about body glitter, Ren tugged on her arm. Her expression was almost pained.

"What's wrong?" Sara asked.

"I'm having a moral crisis," Ren replied.

"Sephora is the perfect place for a moral crisis. Hit me." She motioned off the store clerk heading their way, wondering if all Sephora clerks were memory magicians, because they always seemed to have a sixth sense about when she wanted assistance.

"You know how everyone is always going on about us not reading people's thoughts and memories without their permission?"

Sara frowned. "Are you worried because you're picking up some of my not-so-awesome emotions? That's okay. You can't help it."

"Yeah, I know. It's not you, but . . . other people. Sharing with you what other people may or may not be feeling . . . that's kind of not cool, right?"

Beckett. She had to be talking about Beckett. Did Sara want to know what he was feeling?

It depended on *what* he was feeling. She had no interest in torturing herself, though Ren wouldn't say anything to purposely hurt her. But she might warn her about something she needed to know.

Oh, who was she trying to kid? "Tell me."

"Are you sure it's okay?"

"Ethically, no. Personally, absolutely." Sara wiggled her fingers in a *gimme* gesture.

"I don't think you guys are going to stay broken up." Ren's shoulders rose. "He really cares about you."

Ren's slow delivery and careful tone told Sara she had more to say, but the hope scraped Sara's nerves. She moved over to the Beautyblender display.

Ren followed. "Maybe he's being influenced by other people."

Sara picked up a Dream Big makeup sponge she didn't need. "Undoubtedly. His mother hates me."

Ren's head dipped. "It's not just her. People are upset, and they want to blame someone. Nobody knows who sent the video, so they blame you."

"I can see why they'd think I'd post it. The attention has been positively awesome." Sara replaced the sponge and moseyed to the hair product section and started smelling various extra shine shampoos. Ren trailed her like a duckling.

"He wants to get back together with you, so you wouldn't have to make much of an effort."

Sara inhaled Paul Mitchell's Everyday Shampoo, undeterred by the phosphates. Pleasant but nothing to make her all that excited. Beckett having second thoughts about his second thoughts. Maybe he missed her as much as she missed him. Still, she'd practically begged him not to abandon her, and he had anyway.

"I don't think so." As she said it, Sara finally accepted the situation. "I don't want to be with someone I have to talk into being with me." She shelved the shampoo and faced Ren. "I love him, but that's not enough. The next guy I let close to me isn't going to be conflicted or need to be convinced he wants to be with me. That's pretty fucked up. Aren't *I* worth a little effort?"

"Of course, but the situation is complicated."

Sara nodded. "Probably too complicated." The idea of never resting in his arms again made her eyes burn and her stomach tremble, but it didn't affect the truth of her words. "Maybe I'm supposed to be on my own for a while, get my shit together."

"I think you're doing better than you think." Ren scrunched her face. "You're leaving, aren't you?"

She wouldn't lie to Ren, even if she could. "In two weeks, after my surgery."

"Like, gone forever?" Ren read the answer in her aura, or whatever, and grumbled, "Harsh."

"I don't know what I'm going to do, only that I'm done letting other people determine my worth."

* * *

SARA ARRIVED HOME EMPTY-HANDED FROM SEPHORA. A FIRST. THE store hadn't had body glitter, and no amount of new makeup was going to patch up her broken heart. What would cure her was space and purpose. It was time to move on. Embrace her honest self.

She checked her bank balance. The Agency hadn't returned her money. Shocker. But she'd saved enough to make her escape comfortable for three months. Then she'd need a job. She'd have to pick a career carefully, because she wanted to do this only once. She would put down roots and craft a life instead of following the path of least resistance. She would thrive.

With an industriousness she didn't usually possess, she sorted her belongings and started packing her suitcases. She would be ready to leave in an instant.

Her phone buzzed with a text from Ryan. *Hey, girl. Can you meet me? It's about Kyle.*

Sara replied, *Always when and where*

He sent an address and asked her to come right now.

Sara frowned. Ryan wasn't the cloak and dagger type. He liked to meet in large, public places, claiming they were safer because it was easier to get lost in a crowd.

Where is this

Safe house.

Are you okay

I will be. When can you get here?

Shit. He must have uncovered something substantial. Sara had to research how to get to the address using public transportation, because Uber could be traced. The address was in Canaryville, the neighborhood just south of Bridgeport. She could walk there. *About twenty minutes okay*

Yes.

Sara's body hummed with a nervous energy. *Light your candle for me*

I will.

She frowned. The situation was dire if Ryan didn't tease her about the Taurus candle she'd made him buy. She'd never known him to be so discombobulated that he wasn't up for some banter. That was what they did.

White knight to the rescue, she texted Ryan, then left to go save his ass.

Beckett

BECKETT READ THE TEXT AGAIN.
I need a thousand dollars. You'll help me right. How soon can you meet me? And then an address.

He wanted to say it wasn't like Sara to be so cryptic or to use proper punctuation, except she was so unpredictable he wasn't sure he could say what was or wasn't like her. She'd offered to change, to try harder, and now she was backing up her words. He kept reading her message, though all it did was heighten his anxiety. She was in trouble, and after everything, of course he would do whatever necessary to assist her. And then they could seriously talk and straighten out this ridiculous misunderstanding of how he felt about her.

Why did she need a thousand dollars? Why did she need to meet at some random location? She wasn't replying to any of his follow-up texts. He was on the north side, luckily near a bank branch, but far from campus. A Google street search had shown the address as a single-family home in Canaryville. What was she doing there?

Sara was stalwart, he reminded himself, and she loved surprises and keeping him on his toes. She was fine.

Still, he drove well over the speed limit, changing lanes repeatedly on I-94 until he reached the 43rd Street exit. He couldn't tolerate the radio—

not music or talk—so the only sound in the car was the tapping of his fingers on the steering wheel and the dull rumble of the highway.

She was fine.

He brought an extra thousand, just in case.

What if she owed dangerous people money? Maybe the Agency was threatening her again. Beckett decided he would do whatever it took to protect her from them, and then he would do everything in his power to make her happy.

Her lovely face kept blossoming behind his eyes. Her pain. Her smile. Her laugh. Her mischievously twinkling eyes. Her wink.

He hadn't been sleeping, his body anxious without her next to him, which made no sense since it wasn't as if sleeping in the same bed had become a habit. They'd slept together only a few times, and she'd been in constant motion then, even in slumber, slipping her leg between his, rolling into his back or side, stretching her arm across his stomach, her foot tapping his. How could someone else's restlessness become so calming?

She was always awake when he woke—night, morning, or in the small hours. In person. In texts. In tune. They'd tuned into each other.

Sara was in trouble.

He didn't care about the money, though it disturbed him that she'd asked for it, since it implied desperation. She always avoided asking him to pay for anything. Perhaps she'd spent all her savings on clothes and makeup. It didn't matter. He would save her, any way he could.

When he directed his Audi into the working-class neighborhood, he questioned why she would be here. The house at the address she'd given him matched every other home on the block. He strode to the door, glad to finally get some answers.

He was jittery enough he accidentally rang the bell twice, like a stutter. The door opened, but Sara must have been standing behind it.

"Are you well?" he asked, stepping inside.

The door shut, revealing not Sara but Andrew.

"Andrew?" Beckett asked, trying to comprehend why Andrew had also been called to assist Sara.

His friend wore skinny jeans, a thin, army-green sweater, and an expression Beckett had never before seen on his face—a hard coldness. Beckett's gut tightened as if he'd been stabbed with a rapier.

"Thanks for joining us," Andrew said, raising a gun.

Beckett swallowed and blinked to make sense return. "What are you doing?"

Andrew smiled, cruel and brittle. "You'll see."

Beckett followed Andrew's orders to walk down the narrow hallway to the room at the end. When he opened the door, he saw Sara sitting on a stool, her hands behind her back. She didn't appear surprised to see Beckett. She showed no emotion at all.

"What's going on?" Beckett asked. He didn't care who replied—all he wanted was answers.

The room was the home's main bedroom. A mattress stained with what could have been blood lay on the floor. Half of the fireplace mantel had broken away, its pieces strewn across the floor with broken baseboards, quarter rounds, crown molding chunks, and other debris, like fast food wrappers and cups and nails, dust, and chips from the pockmarked ceiling. A slum.

"Phone, please." Andrew held out his free hand.

Beckett fished his cell out of his pocket and handed it over. "Could you please stop pointing that at me? It's making me nervous."

"Sure thing." Andrew motioned to the stained blue and white striped mattress in the corner of the room. "Sit."

Beckett sat on the end closest to Sara's stool. His mind churned, but nothing made sense. Had Andrew had some kind of psychotic break? What did he even want?

"Before I reveal my master plan in pure evil antagonist fashion, I'm going to need you to secure yourself," Andrew said, tossing a pair of padded handcuffs to Beckett. Where had they come from?

Beckett let them thud to the scuffed oak floor. "Why?"

"I'm not going to hurt you or Sara. Scout's honor." Andrew held up two fingers.

"Scout's honor is three fingers," Beckett said. "I'm not sure what that is."

"Really?" Sara said. "It's like you want him to shoot you."

Beckett grimaced and picked up the handcuffs. He latched one around his wrist, but when he started to secure the other wrist, Andrew made a tsking sound. "Behind your back."

"Why does he get padded cuffs, and I get these nasty metal ones?" Sara asked. "I'm not the one you're mad at."

She sounded alarmingly calm, and Beckett wondered for a moment if she and Andrew were playing an elaborate prank on him. When he studied her face, however, he saw the tightness of her mouth.

"Shut up, Sara," Andrew said, though with little venom.

Sara's words caught up to Beckett's racing brain. "Why would you be angry with me?" Beckett asked.

"Cuffs first, answers second." Andrew spoke as if Beckett were a kindergartener.

Beckett put his hands behind his back and clasped the second cuff around his right wrist.

Andrew sniggered in approval, then strode behind Beckett and tightened the cuffs, though he didn't make them dig into his skin. "Perfect."

"Now what?" Beckett asked.

"I'm glad you asked," Andrew replied. He fished Beckett's phone out of his pocket and waggled it. "One minute."

Andrew strolled out the door, tucking the gun into the back of his pants.

"What the fuck?" Beckett said once he and Sara were alone. He lowered his voice. "Do you know—"

"Shh." Sara stared through the doorway as if following Andrew's movements.

Clearly, she knew more than Beckett did, and she'd had more time to adjust to the situation, whatever it was. How had he misunderstood his relationship with Andrew for so long? They'd been friends for fifteen years. Or Beckett had *thought* they were friends.

He considered the spate of recent misfortunes: his security alarm service canceled, missing mail, odd anonymous complaints to the English department. Even in retrospect, he couldn't manage to convince himself that Andrew had anything to do with any of—

The video.

He and Sara had assumed the Agency operative had been behind the recording. But Andrew could easily gain access to Sara's place, as he had an Arden security override code in case of emergencies.

The video had nothing to do with Sara or her past. She'd simply been a victim of circumstances.

Andrew returned, holding Beckett's cell in one hand and his own red iPhone in the other. Humming, he started texting.

Sara narrowed her eyes, studying Andrew. Beckett's phone buzzed.

"What are you doing, Andrew?" Beckett asked.

"Probably covering his tracks," Sara replied.

"You don't know shit, bitch," Andrew said in a low hiss.

"First, don't talk to her that way. Second, please tell me what's going on." Beckett tried to keep his voice calm and even.

"You think you're so smart." Andrew wiped down Beckett's cell with the hem of his sweater, then pitched the phone into the wall, where it thumped and crashed to the floor. Then he smashed his heel onto the display repeatedly until it was in pieces. "I've hated you from the day we met. Everything comes so easy to Beckett Convery. Always has. What happens next is going to come easy too. It's the least you deserve."

Beckett flinched at the venom. Andrew had been not just a friend but his best friend for years. And all that time, Andrew had resented him—enough to hold him and Sara at gunpoint—and he'd never known. "Let's talk about this. What can I do to make amends for—"

Andrew stormed out, slamming the bedroom door in his wake. "Get fucked, Beckett!" He pounded the closed door three times.

In the silence that followed, the click of the lock was unnaturally loud. Beckett stared at Sara in shock.

"He's going to kill us," she said.

CHAPTER FORTY-THREE

Sara

"**I**F HE WANTED TO KILL US, HE COULD HAVE already done it," Beckett said, managing to look dignified despite sitting handcuffed on a soiled mattress.

"Sure, if he doesn't mind going to jail. Whatever he's doing now, it's to cover his ass. Once he's finished with that, we're toast." She eased off the stool and crept to the door, resting her ear against it to listen.

Andrew was devolving fast. He'd mumble-ranted about Beckett as he'd handcuffed her, which in her experience was a disheartening sign. He'd told her how he had gotten his gifts almost a decade before Beckett had and resented how his extra ten years of experience as a memory magician had never made a difference. His jealousy of Beckett's repeated and continued success had been palpable.

Satisfied Andrew wasn't on the other side of the door eavesdropping, she shook her hands, and her opened handcuffs fell into her palms. Her survival bracelet had really come in handy. First, with the ceramic bead to break glass (and eyeballs) and then with the handcuff key snapped onto the elastic that looked like a clasp or charm.

She sprinted to Beckett, avoiding the detritus littering the floor. In seconds, his wrists were free. He stood and moved to the room's single window—as if she hadn't already checked that out.

She put a hand on his arm and shook her head. She bent close to whisper in his ear, "Opening that window will make too much noise. I tried it when I first got here, and it's seriously stuck."

"So, what do we do?" he mouthed.

Sara had an excellent instinct for danger, and though Andrew wasn't physically intimidating, his manic fury screamed of impending violence. He wanted Beckett to suffer, not just die, which she was sure was the real reason they weren't dead yet. Not only did Andrew want Beckett's pain, but he intended to turn their deaths into a statement of some sort.

She squeezed his forearm. "Get a grip. If we panic him, he'll shoot us."

"You're sure? We're friends. Steadfast partners. We . . ." Beckett's lungs started to heave as if he'd suddenly swallowed a helium balloon. If he kept that up, he'd pass out, and then he'd be a liability rather than potentially helpful.

"Sit down. Breathe through your nose." She eased him onto the stool. "I can't speak for the past, but that dude is not your friend now. He's got a buttload of resentment."

Andrew hadn't unrolled his plan for her, but he had muttered about Beckett "getting everything." He wasn't wrong, but it wasn't as if Beckett had cheated or screwed people over to move ahead. Maybe Andrew begrudged him his money and social connections.

Regardless, in the hour she'd had to discern what Andrew was up to and what she might do about it, she'd come to a few conclusions. After observing how Andrew had interacted with Beckett just now, though, she'd made adjustments.

Andrew hated Beckett, and she wished Beckett would get past his shock and start using his huge brain.

"You know Andrew—sort of," she said. "You need to think like he thinks and circumvent what he plans to do. He's waiting for someone—I'm guessing a Dominion dude, or dudes—to come help him do the dirty work."

Beckett blinked at her. "Maybe he doesn't intend to kill us at all. Maybe he plans to give you to Dominion for them to study. If he does that, you should convince them you're willing—it wouldn't be hard with our breakup. They might lower their guard then."

"Why would he need you here for that?"

"Perhaps to implicate me in your disappearance."

"He brought you here to plant evidence? Make it look like you were killed when I was taken?" Why the padded cuffs, then? That detail didn't fit any of her theories. And why was Andrew okay with Sara having cuff marks but not Beckett? "How did he get you here?"

Beckett tugged on his hair. "A text from you saying you were in trouble and to meet you here with a thousand dollars."

"You thought I'd come to *you* for cash?"

"Why not? I have money, and you know I'd assist you, no questions asked."

Sara snorted. "After you dumped me? Is that how pathetic you think I am?"

"I never dumped you. That was never my intention. Besides, who else would you go to if you needed help?"

"Jolene, Ryan, probably even Kiera."

"Damn it." Beckett rubbed his temples. "Maybe I wanted you to need me."

"I don't need you, Beckett. I learned a long time ago that the only person I can count on is myself, and that's fine. Don't worry, I'm sure you'll have no trouble finding a damsel in distress . . . you know, if you live." She tried to smile, but it only half worked.

"So, what do we do?" Beckett's voice was soft, as if he'd already given up.

"You move from denial to anger. Anger is far more productive. There's only one way we get out of this: We need to flip the script on Andrew, make those Dominion assholes a better offer than whatever Andrew has planned." Without ever having met any Dominion folks other than that Rider douchebag, brainstorming solutions was difficult, but Beckett likely had intel they could use. If she could get him to focus, they had a chance.

She possibly could have escaped before he got there by tossing the stool through the window. But she couldn't count on the glass breaking in a way that would allow her to scramble through unscathed. And she hadn't known where Andrew was at the time. He might not have gone far. She would have had five to ten seconds at most. Not enough time. She could have screamed, but in the afternoon on a Monday, maybe nobody would have heard her, and the idea of being shot again, probably in the back, had frozen her.

That backstabber. What a shitty friend. Hm.

"What if he's pulling an Iago?" she asked. "Didn't Othello strangle Desdemona because he thought she was cheating on him?"

Beckett stood in one, fluid motion. "Pretty much. That does have an irony that would appeal to him, the Shakespeare professor engaged in the worst Shakespearean behavior." He put his hands on her upper arms. "You have to get out of here."

"Murder-suicide?" Everything about that scenario fit. Her wrists would show obvious signs of restraint, as if Beckett had tortured her before killing her, while his would have none. The text message would make it appear as if Sara had tried to shake him down, and when Beckett had "discovered" he was being played, he had snapped and killed her in the heat of passion.

"Oh my God, he's fridging the girlfriend."

"What?"

"It's when dudes kill a woman to motivate a man. Really patriarchal bullshit stuff. It means he doesn't give a shit about me, I'm just a tool to use against you." She should have risked running when she'd had the chance. "But he doesn't want to get his own hands dirty, so he's going to make the Dominion people do it. Or threaten to do it. Maybe they're planning to blackmail you?"

Beckett watched her with only half his attention, the other half clearly drawn inward, possibly grappling with his new reality. Figuring how to get out of this was all on her for now.

Because the unmistakable tromp of multiple footsteps echoed on the hardwood floor leading straight to the room.

Beckett

NDREW HADN'T CONTACTED DOMINION. Beckett comprehended that the moment he saw the three men. Two were dressed in jeans and T-shirts with jackets that likely covered firearms. The other wore a rugby shirt, jeans, and a Cubs baseball hat. The way they entered the room, each taking a corner, searching and evaluating, made it obvious who they were. Survivalists.

This changed everything.

The Survivalists would definitely feel threatened that Sara could identify when memory magicians were using their gifts, particularly if they knew she was also immune to their powers. But how would Andrew convince them to kill Beckett? He wasn't a threat to them, and since he'd just been named Ahmad's heir, his death would garner a lot of attention from the Moralists, not to mention his family. That would be the chink in Andrew's plan.

"This is her," Andrew said, gesturing to Sara as if she weren't human. "One of a kind."

"She's not a danger to your faction." Beckett stood and stepped in front of Sara, keeping his hands behind his back as if his wrists were still secured. "You have no reason to wish her harm."

"Only if you find her ability to flag people as memory magicians disturbing. Without so much as a touch," Andrew countered. "Read my memories and see for yourself," he said, holding out his hand.

Beckett realized then that Andrew's distrust about being touched and fear of being read were clues of his betrayal.

The three men didn't confer, but the one in the Cubs hat stalked over to Beckett, pulling out handcuffs.

"He's already wearing the padded cuffs. We don't want to risk marks," Andrew said. "Remember the plan." He winked at Beckett, a mockery of their friendship.

The man grunted and pointed at Beckett. "Sit. If you move, my friend is going to pistol-whip you. I don't give a fuck what the plan is."

Beckett backed to the wall and slid down to a sit, ignoring the scritch of grit from the filthy floor. He crisscrossed his legs and waited for an opportunity.

The man jangled the cuffs at Andrew. "I guess these are for you, then."

"What? Why?" Andrew's eyes darted among the three men.

"Insurance. We survive by leaving nothing to chance. If you try anything in my head, I'll know, and you won't like what happens."

Menace oozed through the room, bitter like the scent of blood on ice. They were the coldest people Beckett had ever met. He doubted they could be reasoned with.

Andrew allowed the man to cuff him, his palms upturned as if asking for benediction. The man gripped his wrist. "Show me."

Nobody made a sound as Andrew's brows turned down, as if he were constipated or had a headache. The other man's face was a mask of indifference.

When they broke apart, Andrew took a deep breath and then seemed to remember the handcuffs. "As you can see, I was telling the truth. You can take these off now."

"In a minute," the man said, sounding distracted, his reptilian gaze focusing on Sara.

"Okay," Sara said, her entire manner changing from the fun-loving woman Beckett knew into a stranger. She held up her cuffs in one hand, and when she spoke, her voice was deeper, rougher, and she stood taller. "I can see this game has played itself out."

The two Survivalists in jackets pulled their guns on her.

She raised both hands as if they were having a pleasant conversation. "I'm unarmed and, I assure you, not a threat."

"Too late," Cubs hat said. "I've already seen."

"Oh please," she said. "This has been the easiest con I've ever pulled off. Of course he believes I can spot a memory magician." She grinned. "Did he show you how I can't be read, too? Convenient, right? No way anyone can tell if I'm the real deal or not."

She plopped on the stool. "Here's my offer. You guys let me and Beckett go, and I'll show you how to block a read. That's one trick I actually can do."

"She's lying!" Andrew shrieked, stumbling toward her, his cuffed hands outstretched as if he meant to strangle her.

A different kind of asphyxiation than Desdemona being smothered with a pillow, but just as effective.

Sara rolled her eyes, not even flinching. Cubs hat snagged the back of Andrew's sweater and hauled him backward. After Andrew had been cowed, she nodded once as if she'd resolved something in her mind. "You're obviously professionals, and this isn't personal. I can show you the con and how I did it, and you'll see it's pretty much smoke and mirrors."

The Survivalists said nothing.

She huffed out a breath. "This took me a long time to set up, and if the hardware situation was different"—she scowled at the guns—"I'd be insisting on restitution." She curled her lip at Andrew. "Little jealous weasel. You had to screw up everything, and for what? To pin my murder on Beckett? His people aren't going to sit back and let that happen, and my people will fuck your shit up. Hope you've got a nice nest egg, because you pop your head above ground in the next six-to-nine months, and you'll lose it. The people I *really* work for don't dick around."

Everyone watched her, spellbound, as she, completely unarmed, owned the room.

"Sorry, Professor Shakespeare," she said to Beckett as she gracefully sat on the lone stool. "I enjoyed our time together, but this is more drama than I bargained for."

Sara crossed one long leg over the other and extended her hand, palm down, as if she expected Cubs hat to kiss it.

He frowned at the cuffs in her left hand, then stepped up to Sara. He grabbed her throat.

Beckett started to rise, regardless of the confusion that made his mind fuzzy and slow, but then stopped himself. Professor Shakespeare. The change in personality. Who was she? And yet, even as he thought it, he wasn't nearly as disoriented as he should have been, because he was certain this was a ploy.

She hadn't been faking anything with him.

This was Sara saving their lives.

Sara

THE LEADER OF THE THREESOME, THE ONE wearing a white-and-sunshine-yellow shirt, had a firm grip, and if she hadn't been choked more times than she had fingers—recently too—she might have panicked. He wasn't like Kyle, who'd literally tried to crush her windpipe. This was normal I'm-a-man-and-bigger-and-stronger-than-you posturing. Like a kid playing dress-up.

Sara decided she'd call him Matt, the first friendly name that popped into her head.

She'd been spooling the cover story in her mind from the moment she'd pegged the guys as Survivalists.

Jolene thought Sara had the ability to create false memories. Of course she could. Sara had manufactured many lives and personalities over the span of her life, not only as a spy but as a pretty girl who didn't want to be targeted by predatory boys and men. The best lies had elements of truth.

She'd once convinced herself an overweight, balding, sweaty man in his fifties was hot. Not just faking it, though lube had certainly helped sell the lie, but she'd found something in him to admire—his tenacity, his loyalty (not to her, but to his friends and family), and his lips had had a nice shape to them, full on both top and bottom, a perfect match.

This situation wasn't any different. Her backstory was solid, and she'd heard Jolene and even Beckett describe memory readings enough to know how they felt, how they flowed. Sometimes, they were linear, but with something like this, a plan stretching over months, it wouldn't be a single memory but a cascade of scenes, of snippets blending together to form a picture. She'd collected the moments in her head, and she'd rooted real emotions in them, not only the ones she'd actually experienced, but those she always strived to feel, even if she always fell short.

Like power.

What if she were the mastermind, the all-powerful grifter? She'd craved power so badly for so long, she already knew how sweet it tasted, like Maraschino cherries.

Now was the time to live it, to make all these pricks believe whatever the hell she wanted them to.

Sunshine-shirt Matt's talent sliced into her—or tried, as she envisioned her barricaded mind as sparkle-gold.

She held her breath and smiled at him. "Ready?" she whispered, then she drew back the moat and let loose the story she'd fabricated and eased it through the barrier of her consciousness. She and Matt were connected in a strange way. She couldn't read his thoughts or memories, but she could sense him tugging on the memory she'd created.

It was far easier than she'd imagined, like putting on a play for a delighted audience. He sucked down all the intrigue and drama she'd concocted. Because he wanted it to be true, wanted to feel safe and believe she was a fake.

* * *

Sara sucked in a breath and sucked the gold further into her mind.

Beckett leaned over her hostess stand, aloof and superior, barely seeing her. His hands were on hers, his eyes tightening at the corners.

God, why did all memory surgeons do that? It was like announcing who they were. Hmm . . . what could she do with that? She held her breath, her mind full of the deep blue of the ocean. So gullible. Memory douches thought they knew everything.

336

Sara refusing Beckett's offer to work together. If she refused at first, it positioned her better for negotiations. Push away, push away. Show up at the party. Dazzle. Snare him.

Beckett's eager face, believing everything she told him, because people didn't lie to Beckett—or so he thought. Poor little rich boy, so naive.

Nice biceps. Decent ass. Sweet kisses. Gentle.

Teasing. Sex. The taste of Beckett's collarbone, the slick slide of sweaty skin over her. His soft lips over her scars. The intimacy shredding her beneath her armor. Remembering herself, laughing at his gullibility. Distance. Work. Beckett's ascension.

The video. The breakup. The boredom. Ready to move on.

The text. The trap. Fucking Andrew.

Options, options, more options . . .

* * *

MATT RELEASED HER NECK, AND THE ENERGY CONNECTING THEM snapped, luckily not slamming into her mind, but trailing away like dandelion fluff in the wind.

Sara looked at Beckett, aiming for a smile somewhere between genuine and condescending. "Sorry, Professor." She winked. A subtle tell that she was playing them all, but she couldn't risk anything more overt. He either trusted in her or he didn't.

"I should have known you were too amazing to be true," Beckett said.

"Yep." She gave him her real smile, the high from the grift nothing compared to his faith in her.

They weren't out of danger yet, but she could see Matt deliberating. He didn't bother to consult with his buddies, apparently more of a dictator than a democratic leader.

"Did you catch the shielding trick?" she asked Matt. She'd buried it inside the memories, hoping he'd need help figuring out how to delay a read.

"Yeah." He turned to Gray Jacket first, then Blue. "If you hold your breath while you try to block, it makes your mind almost impenetrable, and you embrace the color that suits you best. She can hold her breath for over two minutes."

Sara wished that last tidbit hadn't accidentally slipped into the memory. She'd been prepping herself in case she needed to hold her breath for two minutes while he tried to choke her to death. But she smiled as if proud of that skill. The real talent was not panicking.

"Why take the chance that she's faking it?" Andrew said, tugging his wrists as if he might strong-arm his way out of the cuffs. Too bad he didn't have a survival bracelet like hers, with a metal piece attached, which could be snapped off to make a handcuff key.

"We're not interested in starting any kind of feud. She's harmless," Matt said. He narrowed his eyes at her. "You're moving on, right? So we don't have to hear any more about this supposed gift of yours? Already you've drawn too much attention. If anyone in the media thought—"

"I get what you're saying." Sara winced. "Any chance we could not share this little revelation with Dominion? They're busy putting together a package for me, and I'd really—"

"No." Gray jacket's voice rose. His square jaw went even squarer, his cheeks pinking. "They're already too reckless. I wouldn't be surprised if they let her fake her way onto *Good Morning America* or some shit."

"Excellent point," Matt said, then turned to Beckett. "If we can agree that no harm was done, we're willing to let bygones be bygones and go our separate ways." He stared pointedly at Sara. "You will stay away from Dominion, and we don't hear another peep about an ability to ferret out magicians."

"Fine, fine," she said. "I'm planning to skip town anyway."

"No!" Andrew charged over to Matt, his hands still cuffed together. "We had an agreement. I deliver you the girl, and you kill her and frame Beckett for it. You agreed. I upheld my end, and you still need to uphold yours."

"We ain't your personal assassins," Matt said, chuckling as he uncuffed Andrew. "You got yourself conned. Get over it."

Andrew dashed to the side, grabbing a piece of the fireplace mantel that lay broken on the floor. He swung it toward Beckett with surprising force and speed.

Beckett twisted out of the way and lunged to his feet. Andrew's blow missed. By a lot. The Survivalists gave Andrew and Beckett room, moving Sara to the side with them. They were unconcerned with the fight or the revelation that Beckett was no longer handcuffed.

Beckett didn't run from the room, as Sara would have done, but he charged forward, shifting his body to the side with an economical movement when Andrew attempted an overhead strike. The wood hit the floor with a crash, kicking up splinters and denting the floor.

Bending and sweeping his hand, Beckett picked up a piece of trim and slashed it at Andrew's face. The contact made a loud smacking sound, and a line of red blood fell across Andrew's cheek. Beckett didn't stop moving, driving Andrew back with nothing more than a length of flimsy wood and the force of his presence. When they reached the fireplace, Andrew curled into a ball, covering his head.

Beckett squatted and clamped a hand on Andrew's neck. Andrew whimpered and twitched but didn't move to try to fight off Beckett.

Energy pulsed around Beckett as he drove into Andrew's mind.

Sara shifted her weight to her toes, ready to storm over if Andrew struck out at Beckett as he used his gift.

"You should be ashamed of yourself," Beckett said, his voice rigid with scorn. He stood, his focus turning to Sara, his face tense.

Andrew snarled and scrambled away. He reached behind him. Sara opened her mouth to scream at Beckett about the gun, but Beckett must have sensed Andrew's movement. He turned and kicked the Glock from Andrew's hand just as he pried it free from the back of his waistband. That would teach Andrew to wear tight pants. Nobody looked attractive in skinny jeans.

The gun skittered a few feet away. Beckett picked it up, but didn't raise it or take his eyes off Andrew. The good professor needed help.

"There's your liability right there," Sara said to the Survivalists, gesturing at Andrew. Forget fridging the girlfriend. It was time to fridge the villain. Andrew had the sort of sick obsession that couldn't be cured. His jealousy of Beckett would spread like cancer on crack. This elaborate scheme hadn't worked, so how long before he decided to shoot Beckett in his home or the classroom?

Andrew was a rabid dog who had to be put down. And these young gents were the conspiracy nuts to get the job done.

This time, the three Survivalists did pow-wow.

Sara kept her spine supple and casual, keeping all the tension in her toes, scrunched tight in her shoes. If they decided not to take Andrew out, then she'd have to consider asking the dark side of the Agency to do it. It would make her plans to sneak away more difficult, but she couldn't desert Beckett with a target on his back. He might have some impressive moves against a lunatic attacking him with a hunk of wood, but she didn't think he'd fare as well if Andrew returned for him and decided to use a replacement gun. Also, the good professor had zero skills for recognizing treachery.

"You've got a few choices," Matt said to Beckett, which pissed Sara off. She didn't want to negotiate with them herself, but still, always a boys' club. "We can shoot him and leave him here."

"No, that won't be necessary," Beckett said.

Uh, yes, it was. He wasn't thinking clearly.

Sara pressed her fingers into her forehead. Beckett was terrible at this game. Men like these guys respected ruthlessness and strength, not mercy and prudishness.

"We'll deal with him internally," Beckett said.

Matt and Sara shared expressions of doubt. Matt continued, "Second option. I'm gonna wipe him of us, but I could also wipe him all the way."

"Yes," she said as Beckett said, "No."

She almost choked on her shock. "I don't know if you're imagining all of us strolling out of here holding hands, but that ain't gonna happen. He's unstable."

"Our two groups have maintained a respectful distance," Beckett said to Matt, "and I'd like to keep it that way." He held Andrew's gun loosely in his hand. "If you need to take some of Andrew's memories, that's fine. Do what you think is best, but you don't touch mine or Sara's. As a professional courtesy."

That would never work. No way would they just take Beckett's word for—

"Agreed," Matt said.

Huh. Fucking boys' club. No wonder women couldn't catch up.

Beckett

BECKETT NEEDED TO GET SARA OUT OF THERE before the Survivalists changed their minds about letting them go. Andrew's thoughts spun in Beckett's mind, the details of his sick deal, not laid out in crime show fashion, but a patchwork of snippets and glimpses.

* * *

Andrew couldn't wait to see the look on Beckett's face when he figured out exactly what Andrew had planned for him.

* * *

FLASHES OF MYRIAD VICIOUS ACTS AND INTENTIONS HAD FOLLOWED— seducing Beckett's past girlfriends; canceling his security service, cable packages, pest control; writing student complaint letters; stealing mementos from his home; working with someone named Kyle from the Agency to undermine the program; loosening the lug nuts on his tires; planting the camera in Sara's bedroom; inviting Ren to lunch intending to drug her and give her to Dominion to try to recruit her; how they wiped student's memories if they refused the pitch to join Dominion; snickering at the sex video and dubbing the soundtrack; his sick, deep-seated hatred of Beckett. His resentment that he'd been gifted first, and yet still played a supporting role to Beckett's hero, how Beckett had to develop a talent too, almost a decade later, when it should have been too late; and now Andrew could never achieve the greatness that was his destiny, not Beckett's shadow. How he wanted to burn Beckett to ashes.

And then Beckett had found his plan, running like an underground stream below all his thoughts.

* * *

He couldn't wait for the Survivalists to smother Sara like Desdemona in Othello. *Her threat eliminated and Beckett's potential to find more like her or hone skills to dangerous levels neutralized. Sara's dead body discarded on the disgusting mattress. Beckett shaking his head and bumbling around, the last few hours stripped from his mind.*

Death was too good for Beckett Convery. Let him spend his life in prison, drowning in guilt over that bitch's death. He had to pay for everything he'd stolen from Andrew.

* * *

ANDREW'S POISONOUS JEALOUSY CIRCULATED THROUGH BECKETT'S bloodstream. Beckett had never experienced such hatred in his life, the complete bitterness, and he couldn't take the time now to process Andrew's anger and his own conflicting emotions. He had to protect Sara first.

"I'll contact Ahmad in the car to make arrangements for Andrew." He grabbed her hand. "Sara, let's go."

"Hold on." Sara shook off Beckett's grasp, then kicked Andrew in the thigh with the heel of her sneaker. "Misogynist, girlfriend-fridging bastard." She prepared to kick him again.

"Remind me not to get on your bad side," the head Survivalist said with a chuckle.

"With pleasure." Sara kicked Andrew once more, in the exact same spot, not holding back. He had almost gotten her killed and Beckett framed. "That a sufficient reminder, or do you need more?"

The leader smirked. "I think I got it."

Andrew screeched and scurried into a corner to get away from her. Sara followed, but instead of more violence, she jammed her hand into his front pocket and extracted his keys, ensuring the handcuff key was on the chain.

"You," she said to Beckett, stripping the gun from his hand and trading it for Andrew's keys. "If you plan on lecturing me in the car, then I'm going to fucking walk."

"No sermons planned."

She saluted the Survivalists and strolled to the door. "Cuff him to something, and we'll send someone to pick him up."

Beckett hurried after her, desperate for answers to all the questions he'd held back, even from himself.

* * *

"How did you do that?" Beckett asked when they'd finally driven away.

Sara had never mentioned to him that she'd discovered a way to lower her natural shield.

"Do what? Save our asses?" She slumped into the passenger seat and expertly ejected the magazine from Andrew's gun before slamming it back in again.

Andrew had had a gun. Sara knew far more about guns than Beckett did. "How did you convince him you were faking everything?"

She smirked. "I gave him a big, fat, false memory."

He'd assumed she had managed something like that. "But how?"

Sara explained her ball of fake memory stuffed with real emotion, her attitude blasé, as if she hadn't done anything extraordinary, as if she hadn't saved both their lives.

"If you can form a hole in your barrier to send something out, do you think you could allow someone in?" He wanted to be inside her, in all the ways. He yearned to know her mind, read the rhythm of her thoughts.

He pulled in front of Arden, the ride too brief. Sara had her door open before he'd come to a complete stop. "I don't think that will ever be necessary. Thanks for the lift."

She strode away.

Beckett scrambled after her, his need for her urging him forward. There had been finality in her words. He was halfway to her when he realized he hadn't activated his hazard lights.

He didn't turn back but continued to sprint after her. For once, she instantly found her keycard and swiped open the door.

"Aren't you curious about Andrew's plan?" he called out to her as he caught the door before it closed and chased her up the stairs. "I saw it all."

"Not remotely." Sara slammed her apartment door in his face. He waited in the hallway, unable to leave, incapable of releasing her.

He slid his back down her closed door, unsure what to do. He should contact Ahmad and the other Philotimo and tell them about Andrew. Beckett comprehended the urgency, truly, but he could not free himself from the churning sickness sloshing within his stomach. In his mind, he made a list of everything required of him, but he didn't move.

Being away from Sara was unbearable. Nothing like a brush with death to clear the cobwebs.

Beckett had allowed his mother and Andrew influence him. He remembered some of Andrew's more questionable advice through the years. To date his TA, a relationship that undoubtedly would have been mysteriously discovered. To not trust Sara, to break up with her. True, she was not the obvious choice for a partner, but she'd shown today how strong and capable she was. Hell, she'd been strong and capable from the very start.

He liked the person he became around her. He craved the way she saw him, the way she found things interesting simply because he did. She might not be an academic, but she had a deep thirst for knowledge, always wanting to know everything, all the details, enjoying others' enjoyment.

"Are you sitting outside my door?" she asked through the wood.

"Of course not. That would be undignified."

She opened the door and he landed flat on his back and looking up at her. She smirked. "Quite."

He rolled and got to his feet. The state of her living space resembled a home invasion, appearing partially looted, clothing and makeup everywhere, a large suitcase propped open on the couch.

"Are you . . . you're not actually leaving, are you?"

She crossed her arms. "Yes, I'm out of here. There's no reason for me to stay and a shit-ton of reasons to go."

He watched her, the enormity and permanence of what she planned sinking into his bones. She was going to flee—not just leave but disappear—and he'd never see her again.

He'd never catch the scent or taste of her skin, never squeeze her hand or skim his fingers over her sensitive neck. She'd find someone else to do all that for her, because a woman as remarkable as Sara wouldn't be alone for long.

"I'm sorry," he said.

"For Andrew?"

He snorted, a sound he was sure he'd never made before. "Well, yes, I suppose I do feel sorry about him too, but what I'm seriously apologizing for is the way . . . the fact that I . . . I never should have . . ."

Beckett ran a hand through his hair and gritted his teeth. All that time outside her door, and he might have prepared something far more eloquent to say to her. "I shouldn't have walked away from you, should never have let other people's expectations color my perceptions."

"Yeah, well, you live in a different world from me, I get it. You have a certain kind of lifestyle you want to embrace, and I don't belong there.

346

That's fine. You can want whatever you want from life. I've had a few epiphanies myself with the fun events of today. I'm not going to pretzel my personality to fit into the mold of the perfect woman for you, so it's fortunate we broke up. It's better to leave sooner than later, right?"

"But we were only taking a pause, and . . . what if I want you just as you are?"

"If that was true, you wouldn't have broken things off in the first place. You're just having . . . shit, what's the opposite of buyer's remorse? Breakup's remorse? People want what they think they can't have. I'm sure there's a psychological term for it. And today, with all the adrenaline and excitement, it's making you not quite yourself."

"No, it's made everything clear," Beckett replied. "Please, Sara, let's talk about it. Let's find a way to make this work. The Moralists will absolutely protect you."

"Nobody has ever protected me." She threw up her arms. "Nothing is different—other than discovering your best friend has been screwing you over behind your back."

He reached out, desperate, and clasped her hands in his. "We'll figure it out together. You've breathed life into the program and into the kids. Now that I know how and why we lost our students and the likely source of almost every other issue, we can improve. Help me. We can make the program better."

Sara pulled her hands away. "What can I do other than plan an awesome movie night? I don't have the skills or personality you need, and I'm tired, Beckett. I want to be with a man I can rely on, not someone who's going to leave me when things go sideways, because my life always eventually goes off the deep end." She swayed in place for a moment as if not sure what to do, then rested her palm gently on his cheek.

Beckett closed his eyes and inhaled the moment. Her skin was soft and warm and the energy between them impossibly sweet. "But I love you."

She kissed him, a brush of her lips against his.

"*Love is not love*

Which alters when it alteration finds,
Or bends with the remover to remove.
O no! it is an ever-fixed mark
That looks on tempests and is never shaken."

His eyes widened, her recitation from Sonnet 116 jolting him.

"According to the bard," she said softly, "you don't love me."

In fencing terms, her words were a point-in-line, the move where a fencer pointed their weapon with a fully extended arm. That fencer, Sara, claimed the right-of-way, and the other could not respond until that fencer removed the blade from the line. And it was clear that would be never.

* * *

ON BECKETT'S STUMBLING WALK HOME, AHMAD CALLED. THE Survivalists had contacted him directly, though they hadn't given him much detail about what had happened. Beckett explained as best he could. Ahmad congratulated him on his cool thinking, which Beckett didn't deserve. The Moralists had a floor in a high-end rehab facility they used for aberrant memory magicians, a place where they did a sort of de-programming, and Andrew was already on his way there.

Beckett hoped Andrew got the help he needed. In small increments, he allowed himself to mourn the loss of the Andrew he'd thought had been his friend, even as he struggled to comprehend all the lies and deceit. Beckett was glad Sara had kicked him.

Her surgery was a week away. Surely, she would stay until she'd recovered, the packing preemptive, and he hoped she would allow him to assist in her convalescence. He had a week or two to win her over, to show her he wasn't inconstant, that the drama of the previous weeks had not broken his affection for her but honed it. Nobody would do for him except her, and he would prove himself worthy every day of the rest of their lives.

* * *

Beckett stood outside Sara's door the next morning, a bouquet of summer blossoms in hand, wondering if she was out or simply avoiding him. He returned that afternoon. No response.

Ren opened her door and stared at him, her face scrubbed of makeup, making her appear almost childlike. "She's gone already."

"Before her surgery?"

"She was afraid she'd lose her nerve and take you back," Ren said. "No matter what her note says."

"What note?"

"The one she left inside her apartment for you." Ren frowned at him as if he'd failed her personally, then shut her door.

* * *

Sara's apartment was in worse shape than it'd been the night before. She'd strewn clothing everywhere; hair ties and bobby pins and an unreasonable amount of makeup spilled over the bathroom vanity, and her perfume haunted the air.

On the kitchen table was the note. Beckett expected something handwritten and was disappointed to find the message computer-printed and mostly punctuated.

Dear Beckett,

Sorry about the mess. I took all I could believe me. Please remind Ren to try to sell some of this stuff. There is probably money in the designer clothes especial the shoes and she needs help. Look out for her. She doesn't have anyone else.

Look out for yourself too. You're the first and last man I'll ever beg to love me. I don't regret it.

Sara

PS Dude, Ren has a big list of movies. You need to keep movie night alive. It's my legacy.

Beckett sat on her couch long past when it had turned dark, a sweater pressed to his nose, tears falling down his face.

Sara was truly gone, and Beckett wasn't entirely sure he'd survive her loss.

CHAPTER FORTY-SEVEN

Sara

ONE MONTH LATER

BECKETT'S NAME FLASHED ON HER SCREEN. SARA'S heart slammed into her chest repeatedly, as if wanting to answer the call itself. She swiped it to voice mail before she could acquiesce. He wasn't what she needed, even if she wanted him with her entire soul.

It took her a full hour to work up the courage to listen to his voice mail.

"Hello, Sara. Please don't be angry with Ren for giving me your number. Our deal was she would allow me this one phone call, and I'd never contact you again and wouldn't continue to pester her to pass along messages to you.

"I hope you're well and happy, and life is as adventurous as you could ever want. But I miss you. Terribly. I wanted . . . But I have to respect your wishes. So, I'll leave you with this. It's Shakespeare's Sonnet 27.

"Weary with toil, I haste me to my bed,
The dear repose for limbs with travel tired;
But then begins a journey in my head,
To work my mind, when body's work's expired:

For then my thoughts, from far where I abide,
Intend a zealous pilgrimage to thee,
And keep my drooping eyelids open wide,
Looking on darkness which the blind do see:
Save that my soul's imaginary sight
Presents thy shadow to my sightless view,
Which, like a jewel hung in ghastly night,
Makes black night beauteous and her old face new.
Lo! Thus, by day my limbs, by night my mind,
For thee and for myself no quiet find.

"I do think of you every day and every night, and I wanted you to know that, what an impact you've had on me. You said I didn't love you, but I don't want you believing that, because I did and I do, and I always will. There is no one in this astonishing world for me but you."

CHAPTER FOURTY-EIGHT

Sara

EIGHT MONTHS LATER

S ARA CALLED REN BACK TO THE PRIVATE
treatment room at Indira Ink, which Ren had
researched and found Lacey, an expert in scar camouflage. Sara had been
to see her for a consultation two months prior, slipping into Chicago for
a quick weekend trip, staying with Jolene and Cass and avoiding Beckett
like a coward.

Her scar was now a thin, red line, which had finally healed enough for
a tattoo. Lacey, boxy and brash, had recommended three to four sessions
to complete it, and she'd warned Sara she would likely need touchups as
the ink settled. Sara had wanted it all finished at once, but an hour into
the process, she wanted to curl into a ball and die. It hurt worse than being
shot, especially along the sensitive skin of the new scar.

Ren bounced into the room an hour after that, and Lacey peeled
back the gauze to show her the partially done tattoo. The pain hadn't yet
dissipated, and Sara couldn't unlock her jaw, but she was thrilled with the
outcome.

She'd gone sentimental and chosen colored roses on a vine that wound
its way across her scar. Below the flowers were the words *That which we call
a rose.*

353

Although she toyed with the idea of taking a photo and sending it to Beckett, she didn't. Until she could go a day without listening to his voice mail, she wasn't ready.

"That looks amaaaaaazing," Ren said, bending over the tattoo, which was particularly awkward considering the tattoo's placement just above the band of her tiny panties.

Lacey put on some cream and gave Sara maintenance instructions, but Sara didn't pay attention. She had Ren to remember those sorts of details. Once it was covered again with gauze, Sara pushed down the hem of the cashmere dress she'd chosen because it was thin and soft, though not warm enough for February in Chicago. But that was what coats were for.

"You know," Ren said, "if this were a movie, you wouldn't get the tattoo. You would have learned to love yourself as you are, flaws and all, and embraced your scar."

"Fuck that. Besides, I think there's a difference between needing a tattoo because of low self-esteem and wanting to retake control of my body."

"Are you going to show Beckett?" Ren asked with a smirk.

"I don't think it's an ace idea to see him at all." She swallowed twice. Ren already understood because of her gift, but Sara had learned through therapy that stating the obvious could be healing and not purposeless. "Nothing's different." Including her ridiculous love for him.

He might have balked at the end there, but he'd seen deeper into her than anyone else ever had. He'd made her feel magical, and that was a feeling she wanted again, only without all the other shit.

Sara paid cash for the tattoo, tipping generously because the work had exceeded all her expectations. When it was completely healed, nobody would know she'd been shot. Nobody but the people she would tell, which would be no one. At least not for a long time. Not because she was ashamed but because her trust needed to be earned.

When the Uber arrived at Arden, Sara's heart beat soundly in her throat as if she'd swallowed a hyperventilating frog, though Ren had promised her Beckett had classes and wouldn't be around for hours. As Sara worked up her nerve, Ren jumped out and ran to open the door as if Sara were injured.

When Sara stepped into the lobby, her breath caught. All the students from the program were waiting for her, along with several new additions, including a Black girl with a bull ring in her nose and a T-shirt that read, *I Fucked Your Girlfriend.*

Sara grinned, dropped her purse, and shuffled over to the group. She'd just finished hugging Brayton when the energy in the room changed. She turned to find Beckett less than a foot from her. His sable lashes were as long as ever, his bourbon-brown eyes as deep and intelligent.

She looked over at Ren, who shrugged. Shrugged!

"We've got a few things to show you," Beckett said, holding out his elbow.

It scalded her heart to see him, to stand so close, but Sara looped her hand through his arm, startled by the familiarity, as if they'd walked like this a week ago and not several months ago. He guided her down the hallway toward the study rooms, his cologne of violets and meadows making every part of her ache. There was a miniature curtain over the signage for Studio B. Sara almost laughed. Beckett gestured for her to peel back the drapes.

The sign read: The Strausser Theatre.

Beckett opened the door to a three-tiered movie theater. It had twenty-four seats with rich gold cushions, giant cup holders, and footrests that slid out when you leaned back. He'd had to bump out the building to do it.

Beckett had expanded the building for something as frivolous as a movie theater. "Tonight, we're screening *Serenity*, which I'm told is a follow-up to the TV show *Firefly*. One of the characters has a psychic ability."

He'd built her a goddamned theater for her legacy.

"There's also an unofficial costume party. There's a tiara for the winner of the best costume." Beckett watched her as if waiting for a specific reaction.

"A tiara?" She'd wanted a crown since she was four.

"Yes," he said, his hand covering hers on his elbow. His fingers stroked over the back of her hand and short-circuited her brain.

"Would you allow me a private audience?" Beckett asked, his voice a croak. "At my place?"

She should definitely say no, but he'd built her a theater.

And, God, she missed him—his quiet formality that highlighted his gentlemanly nature and the sweetness of who he was deep in his soul. "Do you have a girlfriend or someone who might mind?"

Beckett shook his head. "No, of course not. There's only you."

Her eyes burned, her chest cramped, and she'd lost any chance to resist him. "Okay, then."

He cleared his throat and avoided eye contact with everyone as he guided her out of the Strausser Theatre.

Once they were inside his home, he turned to her, cupping her face, his lips landing on hers with desperate reservation, the way only Beckett could have kissed. Letting him kiss her like that wasn't her savviest idea, but it felt so divine, she leaned into him rather than pulling away. They kissed until she could barely catch her breath, then he dropped to his knees on the hardwood floor.

"This is me begging you to love me," he said. "To still love me. This is the first and only time I'll ever do this."

He'd quoted her words back to her. As if he'd read her note over and over, the same way she'd listened to his voice mail.

The big stained-glass window painted the side of his face in purples, reds, blues, and golds. He looked like an angel. She drove her fingers into the silk of his hair before tracing his bottom lip with a finger, lingering in her favorite little divot.

"Damn it, Beckett."

"Stay, my love." His eyes were bright like topaz, glowing with a fervor that made her belly bubble. "Please, stay with me." His hands held her hips as he gazed up at her, unconflicted. "I've kept your position open. Your apartment too, if you . . . if you don't want to live here, with me."

"The Survivalists . . ."

"We've taken care of that. The Moralists have agreed to maintain secrecy, which, frankly, was our inclination anyway. We met with Ezra—he was the leader of those three at the house—and I worked with him on his shielding, and he volunteered to keep a friendly eye out for you. He said you were in Madison. Is that true?"

Sara's mouth dropped open. "Son of a bitch. An airtight ID and those assholes still found me?"

"He said you didn't change your name."

She bit her lip. "Well, shouldn't that have been the last name they expected me to use?"

He laughed, that deep wheeze that made her stomach undulate.

"You're the heir now, and—"

"No, I turned it down." He grimaced as if ashamed and sat back on his heels. "I only wanted it because that's what I was supposed to aspire to, but you opened my eyes. This program, *you*, that's what I want. I want my life to mean something, and we had that. I had all I could wish for but was too obtuse to see. By the time I figured it out, it was too late, I'd already botched everything."

Sara's body couldn't contain the emotions bursting inside her like a glitter bomb at a Pride parade, only twice as sparkly. Stepping back, she paced, though she couldn't stray far from him. She hadn't dared hope, which wasn't exactly true since she'd listened to every Shakespeare podcast she could. She'd relived each moment they'd spent together. A continual bittersweet ache of their time together had filled her days.

Actually being near him again was like gazing into the sun on a summer day after having her eyes dilated and living in a completely darkened cave for a month beforehand. She couldn't stop blinking, her eyes watering, the intensity too much, but Beckett was the sun, and she'd missed him. She couldn't live without him.

Well, she *could*, but she didn't want to. And, even better, she didn't have to.

Beckett rose to his feet, but didn't leave his penance spot. He watched her not with the full force of his gaze but with tiny flickers, the regal bearing she remembered softened as if time had taken fine grit sandpaper to all his sharpest edges. His body oriented to wherever she moved, turning as she walked around, leaning toward her like a plant seeking light.

She was his sun, too.

In all her time away, she hadn't thought much of him missing her, wanting her. Mostly because she'd been too consumed by her own losses and longings, but also because part of her had feared he'd thought little of her. The theater, however, told her more than his words ever could.

"I think I would have missed an arm less than having you gone," Beckett said, as if she needed verbal confirmation too.

Maybe she had, because it was those words that propelled her into his body. His eyes widened, but he didn't step back or brace for the contact. Beckett simply opened his arms and enfolded her, his cheek resting on her temple, his chest expanding as he took a deep breath, as if he could snort her like cocaine.

"I missed you too," she said, squeezing him. "Even with all the shit that went down, I was happier here than anywhere else."

"You brought this place and this program to life. You brought me to life. I do not possess your green thumb, I'm afraid, but I've tried my best to keep everything in the program you created alive. Please, Sara, please stay. Stay here with me, and I'll direct all my power to make you happy, to make amends. I'm so sorry. I love you. I desperately, desperately love you."

Her heart had withered but hadn't died, and his words pushed vitality into the organ until it not only pounded in her chest but warmed her entire body. Too much. She worried a stroke was imminent. "I thought love meant never having to say you're sorry."

"What rubbish. Sounds like something people say when they're too narcissistic to admit to making a mistake. And I made several mistakes, though I hope I've learned from them." He stroked his fingers through her hair, clearing his view of her face. "Is that all you caught from my declaration? That I'm sorry? Do you need me to repeat the rest?"

She shook her head, more to keep in the building hot tears. "I often joke when I'm feeling overwhelmed. It gives me a chance for my thoughts to catch up to my mouth."

"Understandable. I'd do almost anything to catch up to that mouth."

Sara sputtered a laugh. "What are you going to do when you do have it?"

His hand encircled her throat, grip loose, his breath wisping over her lips. "This." He kissed her, softly, gently, so tenderly that if he hadn't exhaled in a rush afterward, she might have thought him barely affected.

Sara couldn't bear the sweetness. She stepped into him, though he was only inches away, her lips pressed hard into his, her teeth teasing his bottom lip before he opened for her, the kiss deepening as he drew her closer. They fit together perfectly, even clothed.

After several minutes, Sara giggled, dizzy and exhilarated. Beckett brushed his fingers through her hair, his smile breaking out. He was handsome enough to make her legs weak.

"That's a yes, correct? To staying?" Beckett's eyes crinkled, but the purple under his eyes belied the stress he'd endured.

He needed her to take care of him. She would gift him a life that was more than what was expected of him, and he would gift her a life that was more than simply surviving. "Good luck getting me to leave," she replied.

Beckett laughed, the wheeze that had haunted her dreams now making her laugh in return. He kissed her again, hoisting her against his torso. She wrapped her legs around him, ignoring the burn of her fresh tattoo. He walked them upstairs to his bedroom and gently lowered her onto the duvet which smelled of spring, with hints of lilac and clean breezes. She'd missed the softness of his bedding and the hardness of his body.

"Will you take your clothes off for me?" she asked, wanting to consume him whole with her eyes first and then her body.

"Anything you want."

Oh, she liked the sound of that.

Beckett unbuttoned with crisp, precise movements. It shouldn't have been sexy, but Sara's skin tingled and wetness pooled between her legs. She wanted him to hurry, to put an end to her waiting, but she gave him free rein. His form remained as it had been months ago, when she'd last seen him. Fit but not overly muscled, taut without sharpness. Elegant and graceful. Sexy AF.

He watched her watching him, the loop betwixt them directly connected to her core. She wondered if she could come from how much she wanted him. Simply from his presence.

Finally, he was down to his boxers, his erection leaving a wet spot near his waistband. She wasn't the only one weeping with desire. He bent down and pushed her cashmere dress up past her thighs, up to her waist, pausing at the bandage.

"Your tattoo?" he asked.

"Want to see it?"

"Most assuredly."

Sara couldn't stop her laugh. "I really missed that overly proper mouth of yours."

Gingerly, she peeled the tape around the gauze. The tattoo was vibrant but blushing, the irritation as intense as ever. It was only a quarter done, but the potential was obvious.

His fingertips hovered over the *That which we call a rose*. He blinked several times before squeezing his eyes hard enough that the faint lines at the corners of his eyes crinkled. A tear slipped down his cheek. Though the quote was because of him and partially for him, she hadn't expected such an overwhelming reaction.

"This . . . This means there's a chance . . . That you already forgave me?"

Sara reached up, grabbed a pillow, and chucked it at his head. Score.

Beckett straightened, an indignant expression at odds with the twinkle in his eyes. "Did you just strike me?"

"You can't strike someone with a pillow, Professor. That was a bonk."

He huffed a breath, his haughtiness hotter than she recalled. "Can't you go two minutes without a euphemistic term?"

She scrunched her nose until she comprehended what he was saying. Turning onto her stomach, she laughed so hard her tattoo ached. "You're thinking of boink, not bonk."

"I can assure you, I have never thought the term *boink* in my life." But the pinking of his cheeks indicated that wasn't true.

"It's so annoying when people correct you, isn't it?"

He smiled, though he looked as if he were trying to hold it back. "I don't mind it so much from you."

"Well, that's not reciprocated." She sprang to her knees, still on the bed, and tipped forward in a trust fall.

Beckett caught her easily and held her tightly. "I adore you."

She pulled her dress off in between kisses, so drunk from their potency, it took real effort to extract one of her arms. Beckett lay her onto the bed, his nose tickling her throat before moving down her body. He was careful to keep his weight off her tattoo, and that small gesture had her insides liquefying as he slipped off her panties with an efficient gentility.

He licked her center without hesitation or pause, and Sara arched her back and almost levitated from the pleasure. He took his time and varied his speed and pressure until she writhed and called him several unkind names. She wanted him inside her, but the magic he wove froze her vocal cords.

"I've dreamed of your taste for months," he said, pausing just as she was about to come.

"In that dream, did I punch you in the face? Because if you stop again, it's go-time." Already, she had his hair in a death grip.

He broke out one of his rare smiles and her heart swooned and her insides clenched. Then he licked and sucked her relentlessly until she spilled over the edge and screamed as her body flashed hot and her muscles locked into the rapture.

"Beckett Convery, you are the most amazing person I've ever known," Sara said as she came back to herself. She waggled her eyebrows. "The oral was nice, but now do me."

"As my lady commands."

She hadn't caught her breath, but she didn't want to. She was finished with waiting. But Beckett was still Beckett. He kissed her forehead and eyelids before nipping her chin as he slid into her. It hadn't been sex that had been uppermost in her mind, but having him back inside her made her think she'd not prioritized well enough what she'd missed most. Their physical connection awakened both her body and mind. His lips were soft and insistent everywhere they landed, and Sara couldn't think of anything beyond that moment, their bodies joined, her insides flipping and twisting and buzzing.

Beckett eased her on top of him, letting her set the pace, take control. His eyes roamed over her, always returning to her face—not her breasts or lower, but her eyes. He'd always seen her like that, as a whole, as a person, not some collection of female parts.

Their lovemaking slowed, and though it should have been too intimate with their eyes locked, too overwhelming, Sara couldn't look away. This was her future.

She tightened around him and leaned forward, needing a change of angle. When she found the right spot, Beckett's eyes went glassy and his mouth hung half open with his lips forming words she could have sworn were dirty, begging her to ride him, encouraging her to grip him just like that. He filled every part of her from her pussy to her heart to her brain.

"I love you," he said. "You're warm, charming, considerate, Puckish, clever, and fun."

She laughed, her love cracking wide for him.

Sara came, her ecstasy rising and rising, taking Beckett with her. When her body stopped shaking, she lay her head on his chest, their bodies still connected. With a deep breath, she closed her eyes and sank into her mind, the way Beckett had taught her, the way she'd practiced every day. She conjured a hole in her barrier and reached out to Beckett.

He twitched and lifted his head, squinting at her, obviously sensing her.

"Open for me, Professor," she said.

His gift engaged slowly like a dimmer switch, and she welcomed him into her mind.

"I love you too," she said, and then she showed him.

Beckett

T HEY CONGREGATED IN THE STRAUSSER THEATRE. Before the screening, Beckett ate half his pizza with his left hand to keep his right on Sara's knee. Not that he expected she might disappear, but he wasn't willing to take the chance.

Her cheeks were flushed but her face relaxed. The kids talked over one another to update her on their progress. The few new students stared at her, clearly astounded that the tales of her charm and beauty hadn't been exaggerated. They couldn't be.

Ren wouldn't stay in her seat. She grinned and laughed and ran around, experiencing and reflecting his joy. She'd come a long way with her gift, and he owed her a debt for her role in luring Sara back to Arden for him to win her over. Her grin turned downright maniacal as she flicked off the lights for the movie.

Sara wore the Inara costume he'd commissioned for her, red and gold, cinched tight below her breasts, highlighting the magnificence of her cleavage and the narrowness of her waist. They watched *Serenity* from the back row with her head on his shoulder, their fingers threaded together. Shakespeare, as always, had said it best, "The course of true love never did run smooth."

A sense of rightness soothed all his fraught nerves. His life had been black and white from the moment she'd left, and with her return, all the colors came back. The vibrancy had changed from standard to high definition.

She kissed his jaw and whispered into his ear, "I want to win that tiara."

"Heavy is the head that wears the crown." Beckett dropped a kiss on her forehead. He didn't add that the tiara had always been hers.

AUTHOR'S NOTE

Sara appeared in *The Color of Betrayal* and it wasn't until maybe halfway through the novel that I knew she had to be the protagonist of my next book. I fell even more in love with her as I wrote this book. Sara has a pretty serious level of dyslexia and never received any support or encouragement in dealing with her learning difficulties. I wanted her to have a struggle with shame both internally and externally.

Let me be clear: there should be no shame associated with any type of divergency. Our society, however, isn't always kind to people who are different. This can be particularly difficult in school as kids don't always understand that someone can have trouble with reading and spelling and still be wicked smart. A few careless remarks can stick with us for decades.

Like with any neurodivergence, dyslexia is on a scale and those who have it are not a monolith and everyone's experiences are unique. It's also a much smaller part of who real people are, as opposed to my fictional character.

Thanks to all the people who let me know they were also dyslexic as I talked about my character or as they beta read the story. Your sharing was appreciated.

If you would like more information on dyslexia, a good resource is the International Dyslexia Association. Website: https://dyslexiaida.org/.

ACKNOWLEDGEMENTS

You! Thank you so much for reading this novel.

Randy, of course, for being always so supportive and letting me ramble about my stories and characters. If you're not actually interested in my writing, you pull it off beautifully! You're the best man I've ever known. Love you.

My son, Quinlan, also needs some props for his encouragement. He may only be nine at the time of this writing, but he's planning a graphic novel for *The Color of Trauma* once he's old enough. You've brought so much to my life. Thanks!

Special recognitions:

Clark Rowenson for your help brainstorming factions, and helping me to realize I needed them in the first place. I'm so grateful to have you in my corner.

Elke Liewald for being beautiful, intelligent, and the sweetest person I know. Thanks for letting me look at all your shoes and clothes and giving me your feedback on the assumptions about beautiful people. And for being a kickass friend.

Tracy Koeppel - thanks for helping me understand what it's like to be dyslexic and some of the emotional wounds it can cause.

Carolyn Rahaman for telling me, "That's not how mirrors work." I didn't believe it, but you were so right!

Faith O'Neil for not just proofreading but doing it so quickly!

Joyce Lamb for taking on not just the line editing but the developmental edit as well. Thanks for helping me find the right path.

Julie Schrader for copyedit work and being a wonderful cheerleader. Remembering my launch day for the last book was above and beyond professionalism.

My fantastic critique group also needs some love thrown their way: Susan, Dani, Carolyn, Rae, and Meg. I don't know what I'd do without you guys, but my writing would certainly suffer.

I'm also so lucky to have a wonderful accountability group, though we've been more chatty than accounting lately. I can always turn to you guys for advice any time day or night: Susan, Tracy, Lyssa, and Sheri (who continues to meet with us even after moving to England). Thanks, you guys!

I also want to give a shout out to the organizations that help me with writing and help make Chicago such an awesome writing community: OCWW (Off-Campus Writers' Workshop), Just Write Chicago, Sisters in Crime (particularly our great Chicago branch), CWA (Chicago Writers' Association).

Online resources I'd like to acknowledge: The Gentleman's Gazette and Sven Raphael Schneider, for all things gentleman. I had no idea there were so many shirt collars and tie knots. You helped a lot in the formation of Beckett. Common Ego for your information about narcissists and how they operate. Some scary stuff there.

Lastly, I'd like to thank my extended family, who have loved and supported me my entire life. I'm so lucky to get to write about messed up families from fantasy and not experience. Not everybody gets that.

If you're interested in deleted scenes, a bonus short story, or keeping in touch with me, please visit my website to sign up for my newsletter: **holliesmurthwaite.com**.

Also, if you're looking for a good deed for the day, reviews help readers decide if a book is right for them. Even simply leaving a star-rating helps books gain visibility. I'd appreciate an honest review.

Thanks so much for reading this novel!

Made in the USA
Monee, IL
28 October 2023

45303165R00215